Misery Loves
Cabernet

ALSO BY KIM GRUENENFELDER

A Total Waste of Makeup

Misery Loves Cabernet

KIM GRUENENFELDER

ST. MARTIN'S GRIFFIN

NEW YORK

' MISERY LOVES CABERNET. Copyright © 2009 by Kim Gruenenfelder. All rights reserved. Printed in the United States of America. For information, address St. Martin's Press, 175 Fifth Avenue, New York, N.Y. 10010.

www.stmartins.com

The Library of Congress has cataloged the first trade paperback edition as follows:

Gruenenfelder-Smith, Kim.
  Misery loves cabernet / Kim Gruenenfelder.—1st ed.
    p. cm.
  ISBN 978-0-312-34875-5
  1. Women in the motion picture industry—Fiction. 2. Single women—Fiction. 3. Los Angeles (Calif.)—Fiction. 4. Chick lit. I. Title.
  PS3607.R72M57 2009
  813'.6—dc22

                                                              2009004798

ISBN 978-1-250-02450-3 (trade paperback)

Second St. Martin's Griffin Edition: May 2012

10 9 8 7 6 5 4 3 2 1

To Brian and Alex—who taught me that
testosterone and estrogen really can coexist

Acknowledgments

Thanks to Kim Whalen, my brilliant literary agent, for encouraging me to write this book, even during months when I would just stare at the computer and sigh. And to Rebecca Oliver for introducing us, and changing my life.

Thanks to Jennifer Weis, my wonderful editor. Thanks for believing in me, and for believing there's an audience for women's fiction not set in New York's Upper East Side. I've got another L.A. comedy for you soon!

Thanks to Jennifer Good, my awesome film agent, who is making me turn this book series into a pilot. Let's hope you're right!

Thanks to the friends who are willing not only to look at my crappy first draft but also to give honest notes about what needs to be fixed: Gaylyn Fraiche, Carolyn Townsend, Dorothy Kozak, Susan Schofield, and my wonderful husband, Brian Smith.

Thank you to Joe Keenan for letting me bounce around ideas as we trudged the WGA picket line last year. I am in awe of your talent. And I'm totally stealing your idea for my next protagonist's man problems! Someone who's willing to listen to my ten mediocre ideas to get to the one good one is worth his weight in Bollinger.

Thank you to Irishman Cormac Funge for helping me get all of the Liam nuances correct. You answered every e-mail question about your country, no matter how stupid, and for that you're worth your weight in good Irish whisky.

Thanks to my family: Carol (Mom), Ed (Dad), Janis, Jenn, Rob, Jake, Declan, and all of my wonderful aunts, uncles, and cousins. And to my in-laws, who welcomed me with open arms: Caryol, Walter, Bonnie, Toni, Sonia, Eric Sr., Eric Jr., and Kyle.

Thanks to Elizabeth Porter and her wonderful fiancé, Bryant York, for describing a perfect first date in DUMBO in such amazing detail.

And, of course, to "the winetasters" (I guess Misery really does love Cabernet)—my female pack: Jen, Dawn, Gaylyn, Christie, Marisa, Missy, Dorothy, Cecily, and Nancy. And to newer friends Susan and Jamie. I treasure all of you.

And finally, here's to the next generation of women: Haley, Maibre, Lila, Janni, Emily, Korie, Scarlett, Katie, Adeline, Karina, and Sophia. You guys are going to kick ass, and I can't wait to be your biggest fan when you do!

One

Do not read and reread a man's text message, or e-mail, or listen to his voice message, over and over again. Do not try to delve into his words for hidden meaning, or call your friends to get their opinions on "what he really means." It's a message, not the Constitution— you're not supposed to study it.

I'm sitting on my living room couch, an empty bag of Doritos to my right and an unopened pack of Marlboro Lights to my left, writing a book of advice for my future great-granddaughter.

Why am I writing a book that won't be read for almost a hundred years? A few months ago, I started thinking about all of the things I wish I had known when I was sixteen and wish I could remember now that I'm thirty.

I began my book a few months ago by telling her things like:

You should never have a job that you hate so much you think, "Thank God it's Friday" every week of your life.

Not to mention:

You won't meet your future husband at a bar.

And, my favorite:

Some days are a total waste of makeup.

In the past week, I've come up with a few other pieces of advice I like, such as:

If you are going to show up at someone's house unannounced, call at least five minutes in advance. This gives your hostess four minutes to race around the house collecting dirty dishes to throw in the sink, and another minute to plan your death.

All women think they can utter the following phrase: "If I had a dime for every sane member of my family, I'd have a dime."

Never drink wine from a box.

And just now . . .

Do not read and reread a man's text message, or e-mail, or listen to his voice message, over and over again. Do not try to delve into his words for hidden meaning, or call your friends to get their opinions on "what he really means." It's a message, not the Constitution—you're not supposed to study it.

Which is stupendous advice, if I do say so myself. So stupendous that I must immediately ignore it, walk over to my computer, and stare at the e-mail on my screen:

> Charlie, you're overthinking this. Have fun at the Halloween party. Talk to whomever you want. As you said before, we'll figure this out when I get home. No worries.
> xoxo
> J

Crap. What did Jordan mean when he wrote that? That we're a couple who trust each other, and therefore I can have fun talking to whomever I want while he's away in Paris?

That he likes me, even though I've insisted that we should be on a break while he is in Paris?

That he's already on the set sleeping with the Second A.D.?

The past six weeks have been alternately perfect and hideous, and the hideous parts may be my own damn fault. I recently wrote to my great-granddaughter:

You know what the right thing to do is, even though it's usually easier (and temporarily more fun) to do the wrong thing.

The problem is, I don't even know if I have done the right thing.

Let me back up. Six weeks ago, after a particularly brutal weekend acting as maid of honor at my little sister's wedding, I thought I had finally found my perfect guy, my reward for all of my torturous years of dating. Jordan Dumaurier. After several frustrating starts and stops in our relationship, both of us were totally free of our entanglements, and we were now dating each other.

Those next six weeks should have been bliss. I wasn't working much, since my boss was out of the country. One of the perks of being a personal assistant to a successful boss is that they sometimes take off for Belize on a moment's notice, and you get some unexpected free time. So while international movie star Drew Stanton dined on plantains and readjusted his chakras in a Yucatán villa, I got to hang out with my new man and still collect a fat check every week, made out to Charlize Edwards.

Yes, Drew Stanton. As in *the* Drew Stanton: Golden Globe winner, Academy Award nominee, "Sexiest Man Alive" . . . complete lunatic.

But I say that with love. Drew is one of those forces of nature that seem to irreparably change all who enter his sphere of influence. In chaos theory, they refer to this as the butterfly effect. But if Drew is a butterfly, I'm frankly never sure whether to stare at him in admiration or pin him to a corkboard.

But enough about him, let's talk about me. And Jordan.

Jordan's gig as set still photographer on Drew's last film ended when the shoot wrapped, so he had time off, too. We spent four delicious weeks holed up in my little house, eating lots of takeout, talking for all hours, and having sex, sex, and more sex.

Then, the unthinkable happened. He—gasp!—got a job offer. Oh, the horror.

Yes, I know, I'm being a big baby. People have to work. It's reality. And I even advised my great-granddaughter:

Don't be jealous of spoiled rich kids. If you don't work, you don't have honor.

But here's the problem: he didn't actually get one offer, he got two. One was to shoot stills for a film shooting in Los Angeles for the next three months. Taking that job would have allowed us to be in the same city during the holidays. The other job was for a movie shooting in Paris until the end of February. And he had to leave the next day.

He chose Paris. And I couldn't help but feel that he had chosen Paris over me.

I spent the next sixteen hours hanging out with him as he packed, and temporarily breaking up with him.

I didn't actually break up with him. What I did was tell him that long-distance relationships don't work, and that we'd be deluding ourselves if we thought we could weather a four-month split after a four-week courtship. I then quoted the "if it was meant to be" line, and said that when he got home, if we both wanted, we could start up exactly where we left off.

It all sounded perfectly logical at the time. I've worked in the entertainment business for years, and (with the exception of the marrieds) I've yet to see a four-month break ever lead to anything but a breakup.

Ever.

So, at the time, I felt like I had no choice.

That said, the moment he left, I backtracked like crazy. My first day alone I worked myself into a tizzy, convinced that the moment he walked off the plane, he would go to the film set and run right into a gorgeous, thin woman with a sexy French accent and her sights set on my hunky American man.

Oh, she's out there, and I hate her already. Cheeky little . . .

Anyway, I have spent the last two weeks continuing to work myself up into a psychological frenzy, and this past hour has been no different. I cannot leave my computer screen for more than two minutes. Gazing at his latest e-mail is like watching a bad car wreck, or the latest Tom Cruise Scientology video—you want to turn away, but you can't.

I walk back to my living room, grab my notepad and my unopened cigarettes, head back to my office, look at the screen again, and stew.

> Charlie, you're overthinking this. Have fun at the Halloween party. Talk to whomever you want. As you said before, we'll figure this out when I get home. No worries.
>
> XOXO
>
> J

He wrote *xoxo, J.* Not *Love, Jordan.* Not even *Love, J.* Nope—*xoxo.*

Okay, yes, it's better than *Cheers! Jordan,* or (God forbid) *Best, Jordan.* Or his initials—*JAD*—that would be obnoxious.

But, I don't know, I use *xoxo* for the friends I adore, not the man I'm sleeping with.

Was sleeping with.

Then dumped for no good reason.

Scratch that. A very good reason.

Besides, we've never said the L word to each other, and I'd rather hear it in person (preferably when he's sober and standing up) rather than in an impersonal e-mail.

My God, if I spent half as much time exercising as I do obsessing about men, I'd weigh what it says on my driver's license by now.

I glance over at the pack of cigs and sigh. I also quit smoking six weeks ago. I didn't do it for Jordan, I did it for me. Well, the first six hours I did for me. After that, my only motivation was the promise of sex whenever I wanted. Which does help with those oral cravings, I must admit.

But then the sex went to Paris, and now I'm just abstaining because I really enjoy getting road rage, eating enough in a day to sustain a small horse, and constantly wanting to slam my head through a wall.

My home phone rings. I pick up on the second ring. "Hello?"

If you ever become a rock star, whether you have one hit or twenty, you are still never entitled to have a CD entitled **The Essential Collection.**

"Huh?" I ask.

"That's my advice for your book," my best friend Dawn says. "I mean, you know, the Beatles could get away with it. But Hall and Oates? Tom Jones? Please."

"Not bad," I say, writing down her advice.

"Or *The Ultimate Collection,*" I hear my other best friend, Kate, say in the background on Dawn's end of the line.

"Who has that?" I hear Dawn ask Kate.

"Shalamar and Ace of Base," Kate says.

I hear Dawn mutter "Ugh," as I ask her, "Where are you guys?"

"The Grove. Kate dragged me here so we could do a little Christmas shopping."

Ah, yes, the last week in October. The week most stores start putting up Christmas decorations—and Kate becomes a raving Christmas lunatic. You would think one of the city's top political radio show hosts would view the holiday season with a certain sense of perspective and decorum.

You'd be wrong.

Last year, Kate's apartment included one dancing Santa, two Christmas trees, and a life-size flying reindeer.

"Tell her about the New Year's resolutions," I hear Kate say cheerfully.

"The what?" I ask.

"Don't ask," Dawn says under her breath. "Poor girl's got issues, and should not be encouraged. Now listen, I got the e-mail you forwarded from Jordan."

"Good. What do you think it means?"

"It means you are one crazy heifer," Dawn says emphatically. "You've become the girl who forwards a man's e-mail to all of her friends. You made the right decision: get rid of him for now. Men are like trains: one doesn't just come every twelve minutes, it usually doubles back eight hours later, during the afternoon rush hour."

My phone beeps. "Hang on, that's my call waiting," I click over. "Hello?"

"Don't listen to her!" Kate counters from her cell phone. She's probably all of two feet away from Dawn. "Breaking up with Jordan just because you've had previous problems with long-distance relationships is making him pay for the mistakes of his competitors. It's important that you greet every relationship with your mind completely open and emptied for the joy that is to come."

"Did you just tell Charlie to be an airhead every time she dates a new guy?" I hear Dawn ask incredulously in the background of Kate's line.

"You're paraphrasing my words in a foolish manner to defeat my position of love and openness. This is a reflection of your pain, not a condemnation of my hope. According to this book I'm reading—"

"Don't make me come over there with a shoe!" Dawn counters.

"Well, I'm not going to let you sabotage Charlie's love life just because you can't make yourself emotionally available to a man," Kate says firmly to Dawn.

"Can you hold on a sec?" I ask Kate.

"Sure."

I click back over to Dawn. "What the hell is she talking about?"

"I begged her to stay out of the self-help section," Dawn tells me, and I can almost hear her shaking her head, "but not only did she sneak in, she bought books, took notes, and is trying to drag us into her sick little world. . . ."

Kate's voice suddenly comes in loud and clear, meaning she has taken the phone away from Dawn. "Sometime next week, you're both coming to my house so we can do our New Year's resolutions."

"New Year's isn't for more than two months," I remind her. "And I haven't finished ignoring the ten pounds I planned to lose last year."

"No, no. I just read this amazing book: *Dream It, Do It, Deal with It*. It's all about figuring out what you really want in life, then forcing yourself toward your goals every day. One of the tricks is to make New Year's resolutions every month, instead of once a year."

"Tell Charlie what the *Deal with It* part means," I hear Dawn say dryly.

I hear Kate sigh. "That's the negativity talking," she insists to Dawn.

"Ya think?" Dawn asks sarcastically.

"What does the *Deal with It* mean?" I am curious to know.

"Oh, that's for when you get your dreams, but you're still not happy," Kate says quickly, trying to skirt over that part. "But I'm telling you, the rest is genius."

"Boo, can I have my phone back?" Dawn asks, "I want to text Charlie."

"Sure," Kate says. "Charlie, click back over to my phone."

I click back to Kate's phone, and hear Dawn hang up. "You really think Jordan still likes me?" I ask Kate.

"Of course he does," Kate assures me.

My iPhone gives me a little explosion to let me know I have a new text. Hoping to God it's Jordan, and not following my earlier advice to my great-granddaughter:

Don't wait by the phone.

I immediately click on my text inbox to see Dawn's number, followed by the message:

> Blow him out of the water, and leave him for dead.
> What are you wearing to the Halloween party? Be sexy, but not desperate.
> Love,
> Dawn
> P.S. (Note how I did not dare write xoxoD)

That's easy for her to say. Dawn is stunningly beautiful. The product of three interracial marriages (her grandparents are Hispanic, Jewish, Japanese, and African American), she seems to have swum through the world's largest gene pool, and come out perfect. Well, not perfect. She flunked Physics back when we were in college together. But I've yet to hear a man ask her about that.

Don't obsess about your looks, but don't ignore them, either. Potential suitors can't see your brain from across the room.

"Do you think I need eyelid surgery?" Kate asks.

The girl has rendered me speechless for a moment. "As opposed to what?" I finally ask.

"Well, a boob job, I suppose. Or maybe the collagen lips thing."

"Trout pout's over," I hear Dawn warn in the background.

"Fair enough," Kate concedes. "But I have to do something. I haven't been out in the dating world for nine years. I need something to spruce up my image."

"Hey! Size four!" I hear Dawn yell, "For the love of all that is holy . . . put the diet book down!"

I hear Dawn take the phone from Kate. "We gotta go. I have to get the girl to a hot fudge sundae before she completely loses it. Are you gonna be okay?"

I stare absentmindedly at Jordan's e-mail. "Yeah, I'll be fine."

"Good. We're meeting at your place at eight. Call me if you need to talk. Bye."

"Bye," I say, and hang up the phone.

I let my bottom lip puff out in self-pity as I read again:

Charlie, you're overthinking this. Have fun at the Halloween party. Talk to whomever you want. As you said before, we'll figure this out when I get home. No worries.

xoxo

J

I stare at my computer, and click on my inbox. An e-mail telling me I've just won twenty-five million pounds in the British lottery, and another one trying to sell me Viagra. (I am curious as to how I got on *that* spam list.)

I force myself to walk away from the computer, only to see a different pack of unopened cigarettes beckoning me from the dining room table.

I purse my lips together as I stare at them.

Cigarettes. I really should quit buying them. Although I've decided to quit, I like keeping packs of them around. It's like a little black book of old boyfriends' phone numbers: just knowing they're there in an emergency makes me feel better.

My iPhone rings. I check the caller ID. My boss, Drew Stanton. The butterfly has emerged from his cocoon.

I pick up. "Hi, Drew."

"What does a manic depressive act like?" Drew asks me, sounding like he's in a state of utter distress.

"Well," I begin, trying to come up with a succinct definition. "They act sort of like you, only they get depressed sometimes."

"Okay, then that's not it," Drew says quickly. "Then I think I'm having a panic attack."

"Did you accidentally climb into that crocodile exhibit again?" I ask sternly.

"No."

"Are you hanging three thousand feet in the air without a net?"

"No!" Drew blurts out. "And I thought we agreed you would never speak of that incident again."

"My bad," I apologize. "Are there any sharks, snakes, or hitmen within ten feet of you?"

"No."

"Then you're probably not having a panic attack," I conclude. "You only tend to have those when there's a genuine need for panic."

"Okay," Drew concedes. "So then, what does a heart attack feel like?"

"You know, this would go a lot faster if you'd just tell me what happened."

"I've been fired," Drew says, sounding like he's hyperventilating. "The head of Pinnacle called my agent to say that they don't think they should be spending two hundred million dollars to make *Men in Motion 2*. I'm out of a job!"

Oh, crap. If Drew is out of a job, that means he's going to spend the entire holiday season filling his days by trying to find the perfect religion, the perfect woman, or the perfect Pre-Colombian pottery. And he'll be dragging me along with him on that quest.

Before I can respond, Drew's voice changes completely, going from a tone of sheer terror to one of contemplation and calm. "You know, he's telling the *Hollywood Reporter* it's 'creative differences,' but, really, I think he's mad about the hippo."

The hippo. I think to myself.

Drew is silent on the other end, waiting for my response. Finally, I oblige him. "And by hippo you would mean . . . ?"

"Ida."

"Ida," I repeat, trying to figure out what clever wordplay he's used for his latest animal acquisition. Last month it was an elephant named Cindy (short for Cinderelephant—isn't he clever?).

So Ida must be . . . "Is it short for, 'Ida thought I wouldn't do something so insane as to adopt a hippo'?" I ask.

"Nah," Drew says, and I can hear by his tone of voice that he's waving me off with his hand. "I named her after my aunt Ida. They're both short and fat, and have huge legs. I rescued her from an estate in Costa Rica."

I'm dead silent. It's like joining an in-progress conversation that includes the phrase "Dirty Sanchez." You won't be able to catch up, and you won't have anything interesting to add, so just stay quiet.

"I was going to name her Hippocrates," Drew continues. "But then I thought, that's a little on the nose. Besides, she's a girl. What would people think if I gave her a boy's name? Then of course, I thought of naming her after my uncle: but it turns out the word hypocrite has a 'Y' in it."

I still stay quiet.

"Are you still there?" Drew asks.

"Barely," I say, sighing.

The next words out of my mouth are words I never thought I'd have to utter in my lifetime. "Didn't I specifically tell you that you couldn't get a hippo?"

"Yes, you did," Drew says breezily, "but then I remembered that you work for me, I don't work for you. Which means you're not the boss of me."

Well, he sure told me.

"In my defense . . . ," Drew continues.

"Can you hold on a second?" I ask Drew.

"Sure," he says.

I jot down in my notebook:

No good has ever come from a conversation that began with the words, "In my defense . . ."

"Okay, you were saying . . . ?"

"In my defense, there were a bunch of hippos that were about to be destroyed if no one took them. It was on the news. A bunch of zoos took the other hippos, and the only hippo left was Ida. So, I found this wildlife refuge that agreed to take Ida if I could get her to them, and pay for the ninety pounds of food she eats every day. And all that was supposed to happen was that I was supposed to pay to have Ida transported to the refuge. Only, the company in charge of the move I guess got confused, because they sent her to my house."

What the fuck? Who sends a two-ton hippo to the middle of Brentwood?

"Only, they didn't actually send her to my house," Drew continues. "Because I specifically told them I live at 3592 Greenlawn. But they sent her to 3952 Greenlawn. Which, the good news on that is, the owners of 3952 have a pool, and they've graciously allowed her to stay for the next hour or two while we get someone to bring her to the refuge."

I shake my head and sigh. "And the bad news?"

"The bad news is the owner of 3952 Greenlawn is also the head of Pinnacle Studios. And I've been fired due to 'creative differences.'"

"And by creative differences you mean . . ."

"He thought sending a hippopotamus to the head of a studio was not particularly creative."

"Ah."

Figures. This is just so typical of Drew. Working for a movie star is like working for an unhousebroken puppy with a Black American Express card: You spend part of your life cleaning up after him, part of your life wanting to yell, "Sit. Stay," and part of your life wondering how someone so stupid can be so successful that they have a Black American Express Card.

Drew continues, "I need you to come here with one hundred pounds of grass, and by that I don't mean pot, I mean actual grass. Plus a pastrami on rye for me, light mayo, extra tomatoes."

I roll my eyes as I jot down his demands on a notepad. I went to college so I could ask my next question, "You want fries with that?"

"Yes, the curly kind. Oh, and call whomever it is one would call to wrangle an amorous hippo."

"Wait," I say, closing my eyes to wince as I unconsciously lift up the palm of my hand in a "Stop" motion. "What do you mean 'amorous'?"

"Um . . . amorous. It means lovesick, in heat, horny as a teenage boy on Jell-O shots. . . ."

"I know what it means," I interrupt. "I meant, *why* is she amorous?"

I hear what sounds like a tuba playing on Drew's end of the line. "I don't know," Drew answers, "but if I wanted to be sexually involved with a hippo, I would date my old high-school girlfriend."

I spend the next thirty minutes making arrangements to have Ida picked up and moved to a wildlife refuge, and calling a stable and a deli so that when I get to 3952 Greenlawn, I will be armed with one hundred pounds of grass, and a pastrami on rye with curly fries.

Well, on the plus side, I haven't thought about Jordan's e-mail for two of those thirty minutes.

Man, why can't I stop thinking about Jordan? Why am I letting this relationship color every other aspect of my life? It's becoming like OCD: I'm obsessed with figuring out what I have to do to get him to want me all the time. I have entire conversations between the two of us—completely in my head. All I can think about lately is kissing him.

I once read that an alcoholic's brain is set up to always think about finding a way to get more alcohol delivered to the body. No matter how satisfying the job the alcoholic holds, she thinks about happy hour at the end of the day. No matter how fulfilling a family life the alcoholic has, or what hobbies she enjoys, all her brain does is compartmentalize those things while mentally in search of the next drink.

For me: I'm not appreciating anything great that's going on in my life because in my mind all I'm doing is killing time until the next time I get to see Jordan.

I'm a Jordanoholic.

Sigh. Maybe admitting it is the first step to recovery.

I look over at the cigarettes centerpiecing my dining-room table with a longing that should only be reserved for high-school crushes and Johnny Depp sightings.

I pick up the cigarettes from the table, and examine the little cellophane tab on the pack.

One pull and they could all be mine. . . .

Maybe some nicotine gum would make me saner.

Maybe a new relationship would make me saner.

Goddamn it. I am so tired of being a silver medalist.

Every two years, I find myself feeling sorry for the person who wins the silver medal at the Olympics. They spend their entire lives focused on one goal: to win the gold medal in an event, in anything from men's skiing to women's synchronized swimming. Years and years of training: waking up at five in the morning when your friends are sleeping in; enduring bruises, sprains, and broken bones while your friends are off at the mall. Forgoing school dances, or the prom, so that you can travel to amateur athletic events in states you never had any interest in seeing. So much sacrifice, just in the desperate hope that you will one day attain your goal, the elusive gold medal.

And that's what dating is like. You spend years and years training: You work out, (okay, I don't, but I know I should), you diet, you learn how to wear the right clothes, apply the right makeup—anything to make you look good to the opposite sex. You study; you listen to all of your friends' theories on how to find the perfect man. You read books about relationships, or how to improve yourself to get a relationship. (This includes everything from diet and exercise books to self-improvement books.)

And then you train in the methods of dating: The first few years, you order the salad on the first date and barely touch your food. Then, by your early twenties, you realize that men would prefer you to actually eat, so you order the chicken, or the second cheapest thing on the menu if you don't want to look too obvious. Then you realize they're onto you about the chicken, and you look ridiculous so, fuck it, you order the steak.

In other words, you observe your skills in this arena, you adjust your behavior, you perfect your technique. The goal is always the same: Do anything you have to do to get that gold medal!

And—finally!—you find the guy. *The one.*

Only it's not everything you want it to be, and the relationship just makes you feel like you're almost there, but not quite.

A big honkin' silver medal.

Why do relationships always have to be so hard? Why must we constantly be tested? Shouldn't it be enough to find the guy? And what is it about our genetic makeup that even when we have the guy, we still aren't sure what to do next?

I shake my head to clear the cobwebs. *Hippo,* I think as I throw down the cigarettes, grab my purse, and head out the door.

Maybe Ida can keep my mind off Jordan for a few more minutes.

Two

Oh, crap.

I knew it! Four hours, and one dead iPhone later, I *knew* I'd come home to a blinking red light on my answering machine.

I glare at the machine—not so much because I hate the machine as because I hate my boss. I press PLAY.

"Hey, it's me!" I hear Jordan yell into the phone. "It's about midnight my time, middle of the afternoon your time. I tried to call you on your cell twice, but the weirdest thing happened. The first time I heard this whooshing noise, and then the second time I called back, it went right to your voice mail."

"Well, of course you heard a whooshing noise," I say out loud to the machine. "Wasn't it obvious your call would trigger my cell to play the ringtone 'Jungle Boogie,' scaring Ida the Hippo enough to unlock her jaw, and roar so loud that I would drop the phone into the pool?"

"Anyway, so I'm calling you here, in the hopes you'll pick up . . . ," Jordan continues to yell into the phone.

"Jordan, love," I hear in a lilting (very female) French accent, "did you want a pint of Guinness or a Stella Artois?"

"Stella is fine," I hear him yell to the mystery girl. Then, I listen to the people in the background laughing and talking as Jordan waits for me to pick up. "Okay, you're not there. Which is not a big deal, I know you have a life and you're not sitting by the phone waiting for me."

Was that a joke?! He says it lightheartedly, like it was some kind of joke.

"I was just calling to wish you a happy Halloween and to tell you I miss you. They don't have any pumpkins here, so I turned an orange into a jack-o'-lantern. It's. Not. Pretty."

He pauses for a moment. Maybe hoping I'll pick up?

"Anyway, I'm going to have a quick beer with a couple of the crew guys, then head off to bed. Call me if you get this in the next hour or so. Miss you! Bye!"

And he's gone.

"Two oh seven," the automated voice on my machine tells me.

Three hours ago. Which means he's asleep by now, and I can't call him.

Or, he's having sex with that bimbo (or whatever word the French use for bimbo), in which case I could call him, but then I look like the clueless girlfriend.

Ex-girlfriend.

Good friend?

I open my purse, and look at the recently opened box of Nicorette gum I bought from Costco on my way home. One hundred pieces of heaven, each with four milligrams of nicotine.

I didn't want to resort to nicotine gum. It just seemed like trading one addiction for another. But when I dropped my iPhone into the pool, one of my many unopened packs of cigarettes went in with it. And, despite Ida's roar, I almost went in after them.

It's when I put my toe into the pool water that I learned that when hippos feel threatened, they spin their tails while pooping, thereby spraying the shit everywhere, including all over me and Drew.

I then learned that a hippo can get so freaked out if you get near it that it can throw itself on top of you and crush you to death.

Despite the poop and the threat of death, I was still tempted to go in after my cigarettes. It was at that moment I realized that I might be more addicted to the little sticks of joy than I had been willing to own up to.

After admitting I might be more addicted to cigarettes than a 1930s beat reporter, I bit the bullet, bought the gum, and bit down into my first precious piece on the way home.

The moment I felt the gum start tingling in my mouth, I was sure the experience would be better than an orgasm. I actually pulled the car over and parked for a few minutes just so that I could enjoy my gum.

The package said to chew at least nine pieces a day for the first six weeks. That was not going to be a problem.

I pop another piece of nicotine gum out of its foil prison, and into my mouth.

Then I take a deep breath, and continue to ponder the mystery of Jordan.

Okay, on the one hand, clearly Jordan misses me: he called me twice on my cell, then called me at home, then waited for me to pick up. That definitely sounds like he wanted to talk to me.

On the other hand, he didn't say "Call me whenever you get this." And he did say he was having beers with some crew "guys," but clearly that wasn't the case—there was at least one girl there, maybe more.

But maybe he just said "guys" meaning "people." And, if he were trying to hide something from me, he wouldn't be so stupid as to let me hear the girl he's interested in buy him a drink. Right? And maybe that was just the cocktail waitress who was just being friendly. . . .

I pick up the phone, ready to call Dawn and Kate, to play them the message, and to get their opinions.

It's at this moment, staring at my phone, that I see how crazy I've become. And even I'm tired of it.

I hang up the phone, take a deep breath (okay, granted, only after putting my index and middle fingers up to my lips, then inhaling an invisible Marlboro), and calm myself down.

Tonight, I'm going to focus on me. I'm going to enjoy the party, talk to whomever I want, and get on with my life.

Three

Two hours and four pieces of gum later, as I finish applying mascara to my lashes, I hear the doorbell ring.

I put on my dinosaur head, then lift my big green feet up and down, slowly making my way to the front door. As I do, I hear a dinosaur roar, and the sound of big foot stomps crashing down.

I open the door to Dawn, who is wearing a formfitting trench coat with the hem taken up enough to resemble a modest minidress. She wears dark glasses, and has unbuttoned the top button of her trench coat to make guys wonder if she's wearing anything underneath.

"Slutty secret agent?" I ask, guessing.

"First of all, it's sexy, not slutty. Slutty is when you unbutton your blouse to your navel, and your dress is short enough for men to see your garter belt."

"I stand corrected," I concede.

"And I stand here mortified," Dawn responds. She walks around me, scrutinizing my dinosaur costume. "What the hell are you wearing?"

"You like it?" I ask, so excited. "I got it for free from the costume designer on Drew's last movie. I couldn't wait to show it off. Watch, it makes dinosaur noises."

I happily stomp up and down in my costume. As I do, my feet trigger a sound like a T. rex advancing toward his prey. Then, when I stop, a thunderous dinosaur roar echoes throughout my living room.

My face beams with pride as I look at Dawn. This is the coolest costume I think I've ever owned.

Dawn puts her hands on her hips. "Put on your old cheerleader costume."

I clench my jaw, purse my lips, and narrow my eyes at her. "First of all, a cheerleader wears a *uniform,* not a costume. . . ."

"First of all, the fact that you not only have that information, but choose to put it out there, is pathetic," Dawn counters.

I ignore her and continue my point. "Second of all, I wear that every year. And every year it's the same thing: You and Kate make fun of me for having ever been a cheerleader."

"Yes, and it is the highlight of my Halloween, so for that I thank you."

"And every year I have at least two guys ask me if I'm wearing underwear, ten guys ask me to give them a cheer, four ask if I can do the splits, and at least one drunk guy ask me what naughty things I can do with my pom-poms."

"No, wait!" Dawn says, hitting me on the arm and laughing. "*That's* always the highlight of my Halloween. You never know who the dork will be who thinks he's not only come up with an original bon mot, but one that is so witty you'll go home with him."

I roll my eyes and walk away from her to get my purse. As I do, my footsteps continue to trigger the sounds of dinosaur feet pounding on the ground.

Dawn happily follows me, clearly amused. "Halloween 2006 was my favorite! I loved it when all the comic-book geeks kept whispering they wanted to . . ."—Dawn lowers her voice to a sinister whisper—"save you . . . save the world."

I glare at her. I have gotten to the point in my life where I actively *hate* that cheerleader uniform, even though becoming a cheerleader seemed like a brilliant idea at the time.

Almost half a lifetime ago, when I was fifteen, I had this huge crush on Quentin Claiborne—the quarterback of our high-school football team. Anytime I talked to him, I made a huge fool out of myself. I never had an actual conversation with him. Instead, I would hang around his locker in the desperate hope that I would accidentally/on purpose run into him (kind of inevitable, since he had to go to his locker at some point). Once I had him in my sights, I would nervously talk at him in a streaming monologue until he politely got away from me.

Then, one morning during my sophomore year, I was so busy monologuing at him, I didn't realize he was opening his locker, and I walked right into the door. That led to a bloody nose, and a very guilty Quentin whisking me off to the nurse's office, where I proceeded to get bandaged up as Quentin talked to Jane Kwikaz, the head cheerleader.

The bitch had the audacity to have a—dare I say it?—*normal* conversation with him! It was insidious. They talked about mundane stuff like history class, parents, and the upcoming dance. She talked to him like he was a normal person, not the God that I knew him to be. And he seemed to *like* her!

As I kept the ice bag over my nose, and glared at Jane for effortlessly moving in on my man, I immediately decided his fondness for Jane had nothing to do with her perfect body, her clear complexion, or perhaps the fact that she could hold a conversation like a sane person.

No, no. The boy must have an obsession with cheerleaders.

I immediately signed up for cheerleading tryouts.

Don't do anything you're not comfortable with.

The following fall, I was a cheerleader, and Quentin and Jane were going steady.

Story of my life.

Nonetheless, for two years I cheered my little heart out, wowing the crowds with creative little ditties such as, "You might be good at basketball, you might be good at track. But when it comes to football, you might as well step back. Might as well step back! Say what? You might as well step back." (After hearing that cheer, Dawn's response was to imitate my cheerleading moves exactly, only with her own ditty, "Hell no, you are not black! Say what? Hell no, you are not black!")

Overall, I kind of liked being a cheerleader, because, in high school, being a cheerleader was cool.

And then you hit college. Tell the kids in your dorm you were a cheerleader in high school, and you might as well tell them you were homecoming queen. They'll divide up by sex. The girls will tease you relentlessly, and the boys will look at you lasciviously, and ask you if you still have the outfit.

And, by the way, this still happens at thirty. If I had a dollar for every man who asked me if I still had the outfit, I would have paid for the outfit five times over.

But back to Dawn and my argument.

"I'm wearing this," I insist, reaching into my purse, and pulling out another piece of gum.

"Who is going to talk to you tonight looking like Rex from *Toy Story?*" Dawn asks.

"It doesn't matter who talks to me. I've decided I'm taking a break from men for a while."

Dawn crosses her arms. "Mm-hmm."

"Don't give me that tone," I say, popping another piece of gum into my mouth. "I don't need a man to validate my self-worth."

Dawn looks at me dubiously. "And what are you planning to use as a replacement? Your glamorous career, or your stellar fashion sense?"

I take a moment to enjoy my gum before responding. "You know what? I'm not talking about this. I'm wearing the dinosaur costume. I don't need to dress like a slut and hook up with some random guy just to boost my ego and prove I'm still of value to society."

My doorbell rings again. I open the door to Kate, who is wearing a slutty schoolgirl uniform. Her shirt is unbuttoned to her navel, showing off a brand-new red lace push-up bra. And her skirt is so short, you can see her matching red lace garter belt.

I turn to Dawn and mutter, "Like some people . . ."

"Hello, ladies!" Kate says, her face beaming as she walks in. "What d'ya think?"

Kate proceeds to strut around my living room like an anorexic model during Fashion Week, walking across the room, giving the proper turn, and coming back to me. I've never seen her look so proud of herself.

"Don't you love it?" Kate says to us. "Say hello to the new Kate. She's wicked, she's fresh, and she's not afraid to put it out there and be noticed."

"Neither's Britney Spears," Dawn says dryly. "And look at how that turned out."

Kate ignores her, and focuses on me. "Are you chewing gum?!"

I sigh. "Yes, but . . ."

Kate puts out the palm of her hand. "Spit it out."

Then Kate tells me something I need to write in my book later:

Don't chew gum. No woman has ever looked attractive or intelligent while chewing gum.

Kate has a point, so I spit the gum out in her hand.

"It's nicotine gum," Dawn warns Kate.

"Yikes! Why didn't you say so?" Kate says, immediately pushing the chewed gum back into my mouth. "Now go change into your cheerleading costume. I have a cab outside waiting for us."

"Unif . . . ," I start to blurt out. Then I decide to pick my battles. "I'm going like this."

Kate looks at me disapprovingly. "Seriously, Charlie, what could be less sexy than a dinosaur?"

"A dinosaur chewing gum," Dawn answers.

As Kate turns to Dawn to nod in agreement, I shake my head, grab my purse, and walk toward my door, causing the loud recorded foot stomps to start again.

No one follows me.

"What the hell is that?" Kate asks, alarmed.

Dawn answers. "Every time she walks, the feet make that noise."

"Can't you turn them off?" Kate asks, her jaw dropping.

"I can, but I won't," I say. "The sound effects make the outfit."

"I was wondering what made the outfit . . . ," Dawn mutters. "Come on, you're both being ridiculous. Kate, put some clothes on. Charlie, take some off. The cab's waiting."

"I can't," Kate says, her body deflating as she puts her hands on her hips and begins lecturing us. "According to *Dream It, Do It, Deal with It*, if I want to attract a man, I need to think sexy and put myself out there." She pulls the book out of her little schoolgirl backpack, and opens it to a highlighted page. "Tonight, I have to be . . ."—she reads from the book, with the greatest degree of seriousness—"flirty, fun, and I have to strut like I mean it."

"The only women who can strut like they mean it are drag queens," Dawn points out.

"Don't be afraid to be a size sixteen at a size eight party," Kate continues reading. "Just put it out there, and the men will be panting."

"This from the woman who went to the Playboy party in college dressed not as a bunny, but as Christie Hefner," Dawn retorts.

"Exactly," Kate says, as though Dawn has proven her point. "And where did that get me? Nine years with the same dull guy, only to have my life shattered when he proposed and I had to dump him."

"Wait, is your self-image so low that you think you're a size sixteen?" I ask Kate disbelievingly.

"Well, no," Kate admits. "But I shouldn't be afraid to be a size four at a size two party."

"Size zero party," Dawn and I correct her in unison.

Kate shakes her head. "Why do we live in L.A.? Seriously, I'll bet if we were going to a party in Ohio right now, people there would think we were cute."

"We're thirty. People there would think we were lesbians," Dawn counters.

"Maybe," Kate concedes. "But cute lesbians."

My dinosaur outfit roars on its own.

Dawn shakes her head. "Seriously, Boo, go change."

I sigh. "I can't. The truth is, since I quit smoking, I've gained twelve pounds. I don't fit into the uniform."

"You gained twelve pounds in six weeks?" Kate asks.

"Can you wipe that absolutely horrified look off your face?" I ask Kate harshly. "The truth is, I ate and drank a lot the weeks leading up to turning thirty. Then, I had to be the maid of honor at my younger sister's wedding, so all bets were off. And then I quit smoking. The fact that I have any clothes that fit should warrant praise, not judgment." I grab my purse. "Now, I'm going as the dinosaur."

I walk out my door, and the girls reluctantly follow me.

"And by the way, Dawn, a lot of people think my career is glamorous."

"Hippo poop," Dawn says as she closes the door behind us. "How many of them have been covered in hippo poop?"

About an hour later, I was really going to regret my choice of costume.

And really regret that I did not bring along a carton of Marlboros.

Four

A lady should never arrive at a party empty-handed.

The Halloween party at Robert Hazan's house has become legendary in Hollywood. The producer of thirty-five films, Robert has a twenty-thousand-square-foot house right off of Mulholland, overlooking the city. Every year, Hazan employs his Academy Award–winning production designer to transform his house into a haunted mansion, complete with a cemetery out front. Inside, we see the curtains have been shredded, and coffins and cadavers litter the living and dining rooms (yes, living and dining *rooms.* Because doesn't everyone need two dining rooms?)

Also decorating the house are a variety of cheerleaders, naughty schoolgirls, and slutty nurses (or doctors, if I'm not being sexist). All of them thin, most with fake boobs.

I'm the only dinosaur here.

Which is a good thing. It's nice to be at a point in my life where I have enough confidence in myself that I don't have to try so hard to get noticed.

"I feel fat," Kate says as she looks around at the girls.

"Parties like this are supposed to make you feel fat," I say as I watch two girls in French maid costumes giggle hysterically at the witticisms of two men dressed in—wait for it!—T-shirts and jeans. "That way, you'll drink to forget the feeling of self-loathing you're having right now. Which means you'll be easier to get into bed."

"Not all the men who come to this party want to get laid," Kate says to me in all kinds of seriousness.

Which makes Dawn laugh out loud. "Now that's funny. You should do stand-up."

"I mean it," Kate says, starting to pull out her book from her mini backpack. "According to *Dream It . . .*"

Before she can get the book out of her pack, Dawn grabs it.

Never let a man see you with a self-help book.

Dawn whispers to Kate, pushing the book back into the backpack, then throwing the pack behind a nearby couch.

Kate chooses not to argue, and instead follows Dawn and me as we make our way over to the inside bar, which has been built to look like a really gross laboratory. White tiled walls appear to have been stained with blood, and beakers filled with various colored potions are smoking all around us. I inhale the smoke of one of the beakers, hoping it will smell like Marlboros. No such luck.

I pop another piece of gum into my mouth.

The line to the bar is six feet deep, and people are already starting to push each other and jockey for position, so we decide to find drinks outside.

We make our way out to the backyard, and pass a Dracula serving bloodred shots, an alien serving green shots, and a Wolfman serving what looks like the brown LSD at Woodstock swimming in a sea of blue.

We've yet to find a bar serving wine, so, when Frankenstein appears carrying a silver tray with clear shots, Kate grabs one.

Dawn says to us:

Don't do shots at the beginning of a party unless you want to wake up the next morning wondering where your panties are, and the name of the guy on top of you.

"I'm not writing that in my journal of advice," I respond. "My great-granddaughter is only supposed to be sixteen when she reads it."

"It's not for your journal. I was just talking to Kate," Dawn answers.

"It's only one shot, how much can it hurt?" Kate says, lifting the shot glass to her lips.

Dawn turns to me. "Do you want to tell her about the Professor Whigman incident?"

Any woman who says she's never done anything she regrets because it made her into the woman she is today is either lying, or delusional.

Dawn's statement stops Kate cold. She lowers the shot glass from her mouth. "You slept with Professor Whigman?" she says to me, visibly shocked. "Is that how you got an A in English 101?"

Now it's my turn to be visibly shocked. "No!" I say, not meaning to raise my voice as much as I do. "I got an A in English 101 by reading *Beowulf* and the *Canterbury Tales* in the original Middle English, and with a stunning report. . . ."

"Was it oral?" Dawn jokes.

"Very funny."

Kate winces, then returns the still full shot to the tray of a passing mummy.

I suppose that's for the best.

As we make our way to the outside bar, we pass a huge pool that has been darkened to look jet black, and has shark fins zipping around ominously, an attempt to resemble the frightening opening scene from *Jaws,* a movie clearly before the time of the many drunk bikini-clad girls frolicking around amongst the fins.

"Do you see those shark fins?" Kate says. "It would completely freak me out to swim in there."

"It's only a pool," I remind her.

"Doesn't matter," Kate insists, trying to suppress a shiver. "When I was seven, I saw *Jaws* for the first time. I spent the next three summers making my older sister jump into the pool first, just in case there was a shark there, swimming about, that I hadn't seen yet."

Dawn looks at her, pondering the ridiculous notion. "How would you have explained your sister's death if there actually had been a phantom shark?"

"I was seven, I wasn't thinking clearly."

"I used to make my sister Andy go in first," I admit, watching a fin slither by a girl in a pink string bikini.

"It's October 31," Dawn points out, nodding her head toward the girls. "To me, that's the horror of it. They must be freezing."

The attached Jacuzzi looks warmer. It's about the size of a small lake, it's been dyed bloodred, and it has more drunk bikini-clad girls with perfect bodies frolicking around.

Kate juts her chin in their direction. "I think that's the scariest sight I've seen all night. All those perfect women in such a small space: makes a girl want to let out a bloodcurdling scream."

The backyard has a fabulous view of the Los Angeles lights below, which almost compensates for the not-so-fabulous view of more naughty schoolgirls, cheerleaders, and nurses.

It would appear that I'm the only woman here with a sense of creativity and confidence when it comes to fashion. Hah!

"Oh my God!" Kate exclaims. "It's Mike!"

Kate immediately starts buttoning up her blouse to cover up her bra.

"Mike who?" I ask.

"Work Mike," Kate mutters, hiding behind us as she continues buttoning up. "You know, the guy I slept with right after I broke up with Jack."

"You mean the asshole from work you hooked up with at a bar who then hid from you at the radio station for a week afterward?" Dawn asks, as we turn to see Kate flip up the hem of her skirt ever so slightly to reveal several inches of fabric folded and taped underneath.

"He did not hide from me," Kate says defensively.

I try not to roll my eyes as I say to her sympathetically, "Kate, sweetie, he hosts the show right after yours, and you still didn't see him for a week."

"He had a lot going on that week," Kate insists as she peels off the tape, and begins to carefully unfold her skirt.

"When you finally did talk to him, it was after finding him crouched under a desk, trying to avoid you when he saw you coming down the hall," Dawn reminds her.

"Fine, he's an asshole. But I still don't want him to see me like this." Kate says as she continues to peel the tape.

"But *he* was the bad guy, not you. Why are you hiding from him?" I ask her. "Wouldn't you prefer to confront him, looking like your new fabulous self?"

"Don't be absurd," Kate says, pulling off the rest of the tape, thereby lengthening her skirt by about six inches. "I tried putting it out there, and I look ridiculous. I'm a respected political analyst for God's sake. I can't pull off a thong and a smile unless all the lights are out."

Kate crumples the tape into a ball, and puts it on the silver tray of a passing Bride of Frankenstein waitress.

It's at that moment Mike sees her from across the room, smiles brightly, and waves.

Kate nervously waves back. "Okay, all those comments you made about the self-loathing causing the need to drink?"

"Bring it on, ma' bitches?" Dawn asks lightly.

"By the gallon," Kate nearly whispers, walking away from us to approach Mike.

My eyes follow Kate as she nervously walks up to a gorgeous blond man dressed as a firefighter. "I wonder what it is about that guy that gets her so flustered?"

Dawn turns to me. "I think maybe you need to get your eyes checked."

"No . . . I know he's good-looking," I clarify. "I just mean, after the way he treated her, why would she go back for more?"

"If I could answer that, I could write a self-help book for half the single women in this country," Dawn answers. "Cut the girl some slack. At least she didn't dress like a pregnant carnosaur just to prove she 'doesn't need a man to validate her self-worth.'"

"I *don't* need a man to validate my self-worth," I say, trying to get a *You go girl!* snap into my voice. "I am finally at a point in my life where how a man sees me doesn't have any bearing on how I see myself."

It's at that point God decides to emotionally bitchslap me.

Less than ten feet from me I see Liam. The exquisitely handsome, and disturbingly sexy, Liam O'Connor.

"Oh, crap!" I say out loud, then immediately turn my head, and spit my nicotine gum out in a ten-foot arc through the air and into the bushes.

"Charming," Dawn says dryly.

I throw off my dinosaur head, and try to fluff up my hair. "How do I look?" I ask as I grab my purse to pull out my lipstick.

"Like a beheaded T. rex," she answers matter-of-factly.

"Crap, crap, crap," I mutter under my breath as I quickly put on more lipstick. "Damn it all to hell! Why did I have to quit smoking, knowing I'd gain twelve pounds? Why did I have to turn thirty? Why did I have to eat that whole bag of Chips Ahoy last night?"

Dawn starts looking around the backyard. "Okay, who's the dude causing all the drama?"

"You see the guy in the tuxedo?" I say urgently.

"Damn . . . ," is all I get out of Dawn.

Which is her way of saying she's seen him, and she approves. "And why have we not seen *that* stud in your little stable over the years?" she asks me.

"Please, he's just a friend," I insist as I throw my lipstick back in my purse, then grab my powder compact, open it, and quickly powder my face. "I know him through my sister. They went to Harvard together."

"Right," Dawn says dryly. "This is exactly how I act when I run into an old friend."

"Okay," I admit, powdering my nose so quickly a cloud of dust forms between Dawn and me. "I *may* have *had* a tiny, miniscule, ever so slight infatuation with him way back when. But that was years ago."

"Charlie?" I hear in a lilting Irish accent behind me.

I stuff my compact into my purse, hand it off to Dawn, then turn around, my face blushing to the point of sunburn.

"Liam! How are you?" I say brightly.

I haven't seen Liam in six months. Naturally when I do, I am in a dinosaur outfit, making noises with my feet, and looking like I'm either two hundred pounds, or seven months pregnant. Or both. Why, oh why, didn't I wear the cheerleader outfit? Hell, at this point, why didn't I wear flannel pajamas and a bathrobe and go as a Desperate Housewife? At least that would have made me a two on a scale of one to ten.

Liam would be my favorite crush if it weren't for the fact that the man is so far out of my league, I would need an oxygen tank and a mask to approach him in an atmosphere that high.

Every woman has a guy in her life who's so totally gorgeous and perfect that she ends up becoming "just friends" with him, because she doesn't have the self-esteem to do anything else. And then at some point, she's been friends with him for so long that, even though it tortures her every time she sees him (because all she can think about is what it would be like to kiss him—just once, just to *know*) there was no way in hell she'd ever have the nerve to try and be seen as anything other than a friend. (Except on those occasions when there was a plethora of booze available, at which time she seriously considered getting him drunk, just to see what would happen.)

For me, that guy is Liam.

First of all, he's six-foot-two, which to me is the perfect height, I don't know why. And he is in perfect shape. Not the annoying *I'm at the gym every morning at six* A.M. *lifting weights* kind of perfect. More like, *Everything's perfectly proportioned, and yet he can probably be talked into staying in bed on a Saturday morning (preferably naked)* perfect. And he has this dirty blond hair that complements his clear blue eyes perfectly.

Plus, his hair doesn't have any product in it. I know, this is a silly thing to think about. But I live in Los Angeles, the West Coast capital of the metrosexual. It's refreshing to see a guy who doesn't obsess about his looks. There's a certain ruggedness to the guy that I find irresistible.

The first few months I knew Liam, I couldn't look directly at him. I feared that staring directly at him might be like staring directly at the sun during an eclipse—it might blow out my retinas, and I'd be blinded for life. Instead, I would stare at the ground, glance over his shoulder, or stare at my hands.

I know—Rico Suave, right?

Liam is a producer who I met through my sister Andy years ago, back when they were getting their MBAs from Harvard. He puts together financing for studio films that also need private investors, and that's all I know about his job. He has tried to explain his job to me several times, but I never can seem to get past staring at those gorgeous blue eyes and those perfect, chiseled cheekbones long enough to actually hear what he does for a living.

One time, as he was explaining the nuances of some deal he was working on, I absentmindedly asked him what moisturizer he used on his face, because his complexion was so flawless.

Yeah—that was one from a long list of "reasons Liam must think I'm an idiot." I think the list topped out at four hundred and ninety-six before I stopped keeping track.

Anyway, I've known him for years, and he is no longer a crush.

That said, I still feel like a skinny, flat-chested, pimply little high school sophomore every time I'm around him. Or, in this case, a really fat headless dinosaur.

And I still can never get enough of him.

"I was just thinking about you today," Liam says before kissing me hello on the lips. "How are you, darling?"

I fall backward ever so slightly (knee lock). Fortunately, Dawn is right behind me to subtly prop me back up.

"I'm good," I say nervously, my words catching in my throat. "Have you met my friend Dawn?"

He puts out his hand and they shake hands. "Of course. We met at Andy's housewarming party. Lovely as always to see you."

"Lovely as always to hear that cute little accent," Dawn flirts. "I'm going to get us some cocktails. Can I get you something from the bar?"

"Oh, that's so kind, but no," Liam says. "My date went to get me a martini about half an hour ago. She should be back by midnight," he jokes.

"Okay, martini for me," Dawn says, then turns to me. "Malbec for you, right, Charlie?"

Oh, I just hate it when people define how trendy I am by whether or not I saw the movie *Sideways*.

"Merlot," I correct her.

She jokingly rolls her eyes, then winks at me.

Dawn takes her leave, leaving Liam and me to talk about . . . nothing.

"So," I say awkwardly. "You came with a date?"

Good opener, Charlie. Very dry, very witty.

"Yes," Liam says uncomfortably. "I'm afraid this outfit was her idea. Now I look like a waiter."

"No, you don't!" I insist, nearly spitting on him by accident. "You look like a groom."

Yup, Edwards, that's perfect. Why don't you shut up now, point to something over his shoulder, and when he turns to look, run and hide.

Liam seems taken aback by the comment, but I can't tell if he's amused, or just thinks I'm the most socially awkward woman on the planet. "Ummm, thank you. Actually, I'm supposed to be James Bond. My date wanted to go as a Bond girl, since she's one of the Bond girls in the newest movie. She thought it would be funny."

He's here with a Bond girl. Nifty.

At that moment, Kate appears with a tray of purple shots. "I just talked to Mike, then I ran and got these. They're all I've been able to find. I know the rule and Professor Whigman and all, but I'm going to need at least two of something before I can talk to Mike again." She looks around. "Where's Dawn?"

"Getting us drinks," I say, grabbing a shot and downing it.

Kate looks confused by my behavior. "Didn't you just say you're not supposed to . . . ?"

"Have you met my friend Liam?" I ask, cutting her off. "He's a friend of Andy's."

"Oh, hi!" Kate says brightly, holding out the tray to him. "Can I interest you in a shot?"

"Um," he says, debating, "well, I suppose if you ladies would like to join me, I'd be hard pressed to resist."

Liam, Kate, and I all pick up a filled shot glass. We toast, then put the glasses up to our lips, and Liam and I drink. Kate however, stops short of drinking, a thought suddenly occurring to her. "Liam. Your name is Gaelic for 'strong-willed warrior.'"

I choke on my drink.

Liam appears charmed by that information. "Why, yes it is. How on earth did you know that?"

At which point Kate innocently says, "Well, I remember looking up the name one night when . . ."

It's at that moment that Kate realizes she should be ending the sentence with, "When Charlie was so infatuated with you that she was looking up your name on babynames.com."

Then, to her credit, Kate does an amazing save. ". . . when Liam was a character in one of Cecelia Ahern's books. You know . . . the Irish writer?" Before he can answer, Kate turns to me. "You know what we need, we need some club soda. And I'm going to go get some. Because God knows I wouldn't want to drink too much and say something stupid."

And, with that, she takes her silver tray of shots, and walks away without another word.

Liam just looks confused as his eyes follow her away. "You have a lot of beautiful friends."

I don't know how to take that. "Um, well, you know what they say: blind-date rule. . . ."

"I'm sorry, blind-date rule?"

"You know, beautiful women never hang out together, that's why when you get stuck with your friend's hot girlfriend's best friend on a blind date. . . ."

Am I saying this out loud? I'm still talking! Jesus, stop talking! Back up like a dump truck: Beep, beep, beep . . .

Never talk about your theories on dating with the man you have a crush on.

Liam squints his eyes, and smiles ever so slightly as he looks at me. "Why are you always so self-deprecating?"

Before he can continue, a stunningly beautiful (and spectacularly drunk) size 00 of a girl walks up to us in a sparkly purple minidress and five-inch pumps. Megan Travers: This year's Bond girl. Megan carries two martinis, both of which she nearly spills on me. "Here I am, sweetie!" she slurs, handing a martini to Liam while simultaneously practically falling into him. "Stirred, not shaken."

Liam gently takes his drink as he puts his arm around her waist and props her back up. "Thank you, dear. Megan, have you met my friend Charlie?"

Megan beams as she puts out her hand. "Hi, I'm Megan."

She's not the least bit jealous of me. I hate her. "Hi," I say, "I'm Charlie."

Megan immediately pulls me into a hug. "Oh, Charlie, I loooovvveee your outfit."

"Um . . . thank you," I say. "I love yours, too."

Then Megan turns to Liam and hugs him. "And I love you."

I can't tell if it's a real "I love you," or a drunken "I love you, man!" but I'm bitterly jealous that she can say such a thing out loud to him anyway.

Never answer "I love you" with "Thank you."

"I love you, too," Liam returns in a slightly patronizing tone that only sober people can hear.

Drunken I love you. I feel better.

"Finger Eleven is playing!" Megan says excitedly to Liam. "We should dance!"

Liam gently pulls himself away from Megan. "I'd love to, sweetie. But first I need to tell Charlie how beautiful she is, and then talk to her about the movie. Could you give us a few minutes?"

"Sure," she says happily. She downs her martini in one gulp. "I need to go find another drink anyway." She turns to me. "Can I get you a drink, Charlie?"

"No, I'm good," I answer.

"Perfect," Megan slurs, pointing to me as she stumbles away. "And you are beautiful!"

Great. I can't even hate her, and who needs that?

"She's had a bit to drink," Liam says apologetically.

"I see that."

Liam watches her as she finds a group of men to talk with. "Boyfriend broke up with her yesterday. She's a mess."

And the plot thickens.

Where's my lipstick?

"You're still working for Drew Stanton, correct?" Liam asks.

"Yes," I say, not able to think of anything else to say to him. Except, maybe, "Do you want to lie down on a couch, and wear me as a blanket?" (Which I don't say—although two more shots each of that purple glop and I'd consider it.)

"I heard his most recent project just fell through," Liam says.

Oh God, please don't make me talk about Drew . . . , I think to myself as I try to change the subject. "He's fielding other offers. So how's life at Sony these days?"

"Actually, I quit last year. Now, I put together financing for independent features. Low budget stuff—in the five million range. Did you see *Yellow Cake*?"

"I have seen it," I say, visibly impressed. "It's brilliant. You're going to get a ton of Academy Award nominations."

Liam smiles, and looks down at the ground. He scratches his ear, a bit self-conscious. "Well, let's hope so. Anyway, Ian Donovan, our director, is doing another independent film that starts shooting next week. It's a thirty-three-day shoot. Low budget, about six million. Drew and Ian are both with CAA, so we sent Drew the script today. We'd only need him to shoot for eighteen days. Rehearsal period's already over, but we could catch him up pretty quickly. We start shooting Monday here in L.A. Three weeks shooting in town . . ."

My shoulders tense up. I'm Drew's personal assistant, I don't get involved with his career decisions. So, I'm saddened to have to interrupt Liam by saying, "I'm afraid I really don't have anything to do with—"

". . . then a week off for Thanksgiving, and then we head to Paris for the rest of the shoot," Liam finishes.

And I stop dead in my tracks. "Paris," I repeat. "You're shooting the film in Paris?"

Liam nods. "From the end of November until Christmas. I'm pretty excited about it. Paris is absolutely magical at Christmastime," he says in his lilting Irish accent. "My parents live there, and they love it."

"Isn't your mother from Ireland?" I ask him, trying to get him to talk more about her. For some reason I think that if a man brings up his mother in any way, shape or form, that should always be taken as a good sign.

A good sign of what, I'm not sure. But definitely a good sign.

"Why on earth else would I have this name?" Liam answers. "Mom's from Ireland, Dad's from here. Now they're in Paris. Anyway, we'd only need Drew for a few weeks here, then a few more days in Paris. And I think with Ian directing, Drew would be a shoo-in for an Academy Award nomination for best supporting actor."

"Well, Drew does love Paris . . . ," I say quietly, quickly thinking about my built-in excuse to see Jordan again.

"Of course, he wouldn't have the regular perks of a studio shoot," Liam warns me. "We don't pay for drivers to pick him up, and things like that. And the paycheck wouldn't be what he's used to. But if you could maybe put our script on the top of his reading pile—"

"I'd love to," I interrupt.

Liam seems taken aback by my enthusiasm. "Really? Well, that's fantastic. Thank you."

As I look at that handsome face, and lose myself in those beautiful eyes, I can't help but want to kiss him.

Instead, I turn away, and pull my brand-new iPhone out of my purse.

"Cool phone," Liam observes.

"Thanks. It's new," I say as I dial Drew's number. "It's waterproof and I'm told it can withstand hippo attacks."

Drew picks up on the first ring, "Do you think Megan Travers is gay?" he asks me.

"I don't think so," I answer. "Why?"

"She's making out with a girl wearing a shark fin."

I look around the backyard. "Are you here?"

"Where's here?" Drew asks.

"Robert Hazan's party."

"Um . . . I'm not sure. The party I'm at has a lot of women dressed as cheerleaders, schoolgirls, a scantily clad owl of all things . . ."

"Drew, saying you're at a Hollywood party with a bunch of half-dressed women helps me identify the party as much as if you called asking what town you were in, and mentioned it had a Starbucks and a Gap."

"There's a woman dressed as a naked hippo," Drew continues. "Speaking of which, did you figure out what you wanted in exchange for never mentioning hippos to me again?"

"As a matter of fact, I have. Did you get a script today from CAA called . . ." I cover the phone's mouthpiece and whisper to Liam, "Wait, what's it called?"

"*A Collective Happiness,*" Liam whispers back.

"*A Collective Happiness,*" I say into the phone. "Did you get it?"

"I have no idea. Why?"

"You need to read it," I say, trying to give my voice an authoritative tone.

"Wait, she's not a hippo," Drew says, his voice suddenly sounding within earshot. "She's just a naked Komodo dragon."

Just then, Spider-Man walks over to us, talking into his iPhone.

"And what are you supposed to be?" I hear Spider-Man ask me in person as I simultaneously hear Drew's voice over the phone. "A beheaded dinosaur?"

I look up at Spider-Man, and look into his masked eyes. "Drew?" I ask.

"Yeah," he says matter-of-factly. "But only when I'm assuming the guise of my secret, crime-fighting alter ego." Drew leans his masked face in close and practically whispers, "You know, it really is liberating to appear in public with your true identity concealed. Especially when you have super powers. Did you know this costume is rigged with hand jets that shoot spider webs?" He throws his wrist out at me. "Wanna see?"

"I think I'll pass," I say, throwing my head back so as not to get covered with sticky fake spider webs.

The masked crimefighter eyes me up and down. "Why aren't you wearing your cheerleader costume?"

I roll my eyes. "For the last time. It's not a costume! It's a uniform!"

"Oh," Drew says, sounding like it's the first he's heard of it. "Well, if it's a uniform, does that mean that as your employer, I can require you to wear it to work every day?"

Drew's genuinely asking me that, by the way. There's not a hint of sarcasm in his voice. So I decide to ignore the comment. "Drew, have you met Liam O'Connor?"

"Liam," Drew says, extending a webbed hand. "You produced *Yellow Cake,* right?"

"I did."

"I loved that movie!" Drew says, his voice brightening. "I didn't understand it, but I totally loved it!"

As Drew and Liam continue their membership in the mutual admiration society, I offer to get Drew a drink, then make a hasty getaway.

I just can't see Liam for too long without needing to come up for air.

As I take a glass of champagne from the silver tray of a mummy waiter, I chant quietly to myself, "I like Jordan. I like Jordan . . ."

Even though Jordan might be boinking some Parisian slut right now.

God, I want a cigarette.

As I debate rifling through the bushes to find my spit-out piece of nicotine gum, I see my little brother Jamie talking with a naughty vampire. He's wearing a big red bow, with a giant cardboard gift tag that reads:

To: Women
From: God

As the blond Barbie doll of a vampire gives him a kiss on the cheek and heads off, I walk up to him.

"God's gift to women?" I ask, visibly horrified by the outfit.

"So far, it's been quite the conversation piece," Jamie says cheerfully. He nods to the vampire who just walked away. "She just asked me what I was doing later."

I look over at the girl. "She's a hooker," I point out.

"I know. That's why I told her I was busy. But it's nice to be asked." He takes a sip from my champagne flute. "Guess what? The editor at *Metro* finally gave me a writing job."

"You got an article published?" I asked, bursting with sisterly pride.

"Better!" Jamie says, smiling proudly. "I got my own column. You are looking at the official author of 'A Man's Eye View.' I beat out over a hundred people."

Jamie has been working at *Metro,* a women's magazine, for a couple of years as a fact checker. He has been dying to become a real writer, and has been submitting spec articles to their managing editor ever since he started.

"Wait a minute," I say, trying not to sound negative. "Isn't 'A Man's Eye View' that puff piece a guy writes every month saying stuff like 'All we men really want is someone to love us'?"

"Yeah. Load of crap, right?"

I shrug. "Well, it'd be nice if men felt that way."

"But they don't," Jamie says cheerfully. "And that's how I got the job. Everyone else was turning in bullshit pieces about how we really love weddings, and how it's okay to just cuddle on a Sunday morning, and complete stereotypes about why we like sports. I went totally the other way."

"Okay, now I'm afraid . . ."

"I called my piece 'Don't Kill the Messenger,'" Jamie says proudly. "I took every question you and Andy ever asked about boys, wrote 'em down, and then gave honest answers. I started with a man's intentions: if he is straight and he is single, he wants to sleep with you."

"Oh, for God's sake," I blurt out in a huff. "No woman is really going to want to read—"

"If he is straight and married," Jamie continues, "he may not want to sleep with you, but he still wants to know that you want to sleep with him."

"I'm not sure I ever asked that . . ."

"How can men sleep with women they're not in love with?" Jamie continues. "Duh! I believe the better question is, 'Why do women always have to be in love with the men they sleep with?' I'm making five dollars a word."

Kate walks up to us. "Hi, sweetie," she says to Jamie, giving him a quick kiss hello.

The kiss is just a quick peck on the lips—old friends who are comfortable with each other. You'd never know they had been fuck-buddies briefly last month, after Kate's breakup.

"Hey, baby," Jamie says. "You are looking sexy as hell."

"Really?" Kate asks, looking down at her outfit. "You don't think it's too slutty?"

"I'm a guy. You hear us say the words 'too slutty' about as often as the words, "No, thank you, Miss Theron, I already have a date for Saturday night."

"Hmm," Kate says, still scrutinizing her outfit. "Okay, thanks." Kate leans in to quietly ask me, "What do you think it means if a guy says he's not technically divorced, but he's leaving his wife?"

Jamie leans in and answers just as quietly,

When a man promises to leave his wife, what he really means is . . . he has no intention of leaving his wife.

"Oh," Kate says, sounding disappointed. "That's kind of what I thought."

"Wait. Who's married?" I ask Kate.

"Well, not technically divorced," Kate corrects me.

"Yeah, that," I say, my voice dripping with suspicion. "Who is it? Mike?"

Kate nods, then starts to walk away. I grab her arm. "Oh, no. You're not going back to talk to him."

Kate shrugs me off with her tone of voice. "I'm not going home with him or anything. We're just talking. . . ."

"I'll come with you," I offer.

"What am I? Fifteen?"

"Clearly not," I retort. "Fifteen-year-olds aren't stupid enough to go out with married men."

It's then that Mike magically appears in front of us, all smiles, as he puts his arms around Kate's shoulders. "I absolutely love this song," he says, referring to Britney Spears's "Gimme More" blasting from the backyard sound system. "Come dance with me."

Kate avoids my gaze, and the two trot off to the dance floor.

I turn to Jamie. " 'Gimme More'?!" I say incredulously.

"I know," Jamie says, with a defeated tone of voice. "Clearly the guy's a full-on liar. He's the type of guy who will compliment you on your shoes."

I think about that for a second. "I'm sorry . . . what about that is bad?"

"Guys don't notice shoes," Jamie says definitively. "We notice the legs in the shoes. We don't care if you're wearing Christian Louboutins. You're dressing for your female friends when you spend five hundred dollars on a pair of shoes, not us. If a man compliments your shoes, he's trying to get you into bed."

I cross my arms and glare at him. "By your theory, aren't all men who talk to us trying to get us into bed?"

"Yes, but getting a woman into bed is like getting to the end of a football field: there are a variety of techniques. A guy should have the confidence to methodically march the ball down the field, and not just throw up a Hail Mary with plenty of time left on the clock."

I narrow my eyes at him. "I think my pretending to understand even one word of that sentence would be the female equivalent of telling you, 'Nice shoes.' "

Dawn quickly walks up to us, carrying what appears to be a blood-red martini. "Okay, be subtle. Look over my shoulder."

Jamie and I look over her shoulder.

Dawn continues, "Do you see the black man wearing a firefighter's uniform?"

I do, and I want him all for myself. Unfortunately for me, I am pretty sure the six-foot-three Adonis with the perfect chin is a good friend of Rob, my cousin Jenn's husband. They are both English professors at UCLA.

Damn, he looks good tonight.

"Looks like Patrick," I whisper to Dawn.

Dawn winces. "That's what I was afraid of," she whispers. "See, he—"

"Patrick!" Jamie yells across the lawn.

Dawn's shoulders drop as Patrick turns and sees us. His face lights up. "Hey," Patrick says, walking up to us. "I haven't seen you guys in forever."

He puts out his hand and he and Jamie do the new handshake with the slightly apart hug and back pat. Then he turns to me. "Charlie. Gorgeous as ever," he says, giving me a kiss hello on the lips.

In our little Hollywood microcosm where everyone kisses each other on the lips, Patrick then kisses Dawn ever so gently on the cheek. "Dawn, how are you?" he says, in a sentence loaded with deep desire.

Huh. And the plot thickens.

Dawn, normally the belle of the ball (or at least the alpha female of the litter), forces a smile. "It's good to see you," she says, her voice catching after the word "good." "How did your English 90 class go?"

"Very well. I'm sorry you weren't able to come," he says awkwardly.

"Well, I . . . uh . . . I had to work," she returns just as awkwardly.

Patrick looks down at the ground as Dawn looks around the backyard self-consciously.

Wait a minute . . . Dawn acting awkward? Dawn acts awkward about as often as George Clooney goes on eHarmony.com—which is to say if it ever has happened, I'm not so sure I want to know about it. Did these two recently have sex without my knowledge? What's going on here?

"What's English 90?" Jamie asks Patrick, trying to break the obvious tension between them.

"Oh, it's my Shakespeare class," Patrick answers pleasantly. "I asked Dawn if she could read Juliet for one of my lectures, but she had a prior commitment."

Dawn looks away from us, uncomfortably. Patrick just stares at her, clearly trying to think of something witty to say.

Which, unfortunately, he doesn't. The four of us stand around in silence for . . . I don't know, a month? I see Jamie's eyes flit back and forth from Dawn to Patrick, trying to figure them out.

Jamie takes my champagne flute, downs the rest of my champagne in one gulp, then declares, "We need drinks." He turns to Patrick. "I understand there's a Hobbit in the kitchen with Krug, if we know the password."

Patrick looks relieved for the reprieve. "Okay," he says to Jamie. Then he gently puts his hand on Dawn's arm. "Don't go away."

And the two walk off. I watch Dawn knowingly as she watches them leave.

I've seen that look before.

"You-ou liiiike himmmm . . . ," I say, dragging out the words teasingly.

Dawn blinks once, then turns to me as though she's just realized I'm there. "What?" she says incredulously. Then she crosses her arms. "Don't be ridiculous."

As Patrick and Jamie walk away, I watch several women clearly check Patrick out. "So, to paraphrase you, how come we haven't seen that gorgeous stud in your stable yet?"

Dawn turns to me, looking alarmed. "Are you kidding?! Serious type. Wants babies."

"Pervert," I state emphatically. "Imagine wanting a wife, a family . . ." I look around as if to catch eavesdroppers, then whisper, "Commitment."

Dawn shrugs her shoulders. "Look, there's no challenge to a guy like that. One time you remember to call him back and he's yours. He's like target practice."

"Mm-hmm. Methinks the lady doth protest too much."

"Oh, please. He's an English professor. Do you see me with an English professor?" Dawn asks.

Before I can answer that yes, I can see her with an English professor, she gives me her next rationalization. "Besides, nerdy guys don't dig me."

"Sweetie," I say, putting my arm around her shoulder and trying not to sound too patronizing, "All guys dig you."

Dawn shrugs. Takes a sip of her red drink. She glances around the party, then notices Kate and Mike on the dance floor. "Wait a minute, isn't that—"

"Mm-hmm," I answer disapprovingly. "And get this, he's married."

Dawn's jaw drops slightly as she turns to me. "Oh, hell no."

Never date a married man.

Dawn determinedly marches over to the dance floor. I quickly follow her. "Be subtle," I remind Dawn. "We don't want to do anything to embarrass her."

"I wouldn't dream of it," Dawn says. I stop by the side of the dance floor to watch as Dawn walks right between the dancing couple. "Wrong!" she says to Kate emphatically, then grabs her by the hand and drags her away.

"What are you doing?" Kate seethes under her breath as she is yanked from the dance floor by Dawn. I quickly fall into step with them as we head back to our former spot.

"Saving you from six months of heartache," Dawn says sternly. "What the fuck were you thinking, flirting with a married man?"

"He's separated!" Kate says in a defensive tone. She tries to pull away her hand from Dawn's kung-fu grip, but to no avail.

"Charlie, translate 'separated' in L.A. singleton terms," Dawn says angrily.

"His wife doesn't know they're separated," I explain. "But when she finds out what he's doing behind her back, then they might really be separated."

Kate begins trying to peel Dawn's fingers off her left hand. "He's not wearing a wedding ring. I checked."

Dawn counters with, "I'm not wearing my ten-year-old sweatpants with the hole in the butt. But that don't mean I don't put 'em on the minute I get home from the party."

"Come on, seriously, you're embarrassing me. Let go."

We return to our former patch of grass, and Dawn finally lets go of Kate's hand. "What are you thinking?" Dawn grills Kate. "Do you honestly think this guy is going to leave his wife for you? And, if so, are you ready to go through a divorce that's not even your own?"

Kate responds with just as much irritation. "Look, maybe if you look like you, you can have your pick of the litter. But it's tough out there. Jack and I broke up almost two months ago, and the only date I've had has been with Mike. Beggars can't be choosers."

"Maybe that should be the new tagline for Match.com," I joke.

Kate turns to me, and her facial expression subtly changes from one of irritation to one of slight desperation. "You know, when I was with Jack all that time, I always envied you guys. You got to go out anywhere you wanted without having to run it by someone else. You got to spend four hundred dollars on a dress without anyone you love rolling their eyes and lecturing you. I used to be so jealous when you talked about your first kiss with this guy or your first date with that guy. I thought if I broke up with Jack, I'd be happy. I'd be glamorous. Instead, I'm just lonely."

I rub Kate's arm. "Sweetie, it's only been a few months. It takes time to get over a long relationship. You'll get there."

Kate shakes her head. "No, I won't. This whole breakup has made me see myself through my eyes, not Jack's, and I don't like what I see. I feel fat, I feel old, and I have no clue what I even want from my life anymore. Who the hell is going to want me?"

As if on cue, from behind us, we hear a very sexy, baritone voice ask, "Kate?"

We all turn around to see an Abercrombie and Fitch model dressed as a cowboy. Or, at least he could be a model. With perfect olive skin, piercing hazel eyes, and wavy jet-black hair, he could be anything he wants to be.

Kate's eyes bulge out of her head as though she's seen a ghost. "Will," she says breathlessly. "What are you . . . I mean . . . how did you . . ."

Will smiles widely as he pulls her into a bear hug. "My God, you look good."

"Thanks," Kate says, her body noticeably going limp.

And the two keep hugging.

Yup, just gonna keep hugging. Even though Dawn and I are exchanging glances, wondering how long a hug can go on for. A minute? Two minutes?

Dawn jerks her head toward Will and silently mouths to me, "*The* Will?"

I shrug.

Will Davies was Kate's high school sweetheart back in Houston. The two dated for three years before she went off to UCLA, and he headed to an Ivy League school. As most high school sweethearts do, they tried the long-distance thing during the fall semester of their freshman year. And their long-distance freshman romance went the way of most: he met someone else, and he broke her heart. When Kate got back from Christmas vacation, her eyes were red rimmed, and her sense of optimism about the world was shattered. She spent the next three months so heartbroken, she could barely eat. Forget about gaining the freshman ten; Kate lost fifteen.

To make matters worse, every time Kate started to date, Will would call. I have a long-standing theory that men just instinctively know when you're getting over them, and choose that moment to come back and mindfuck you all over again. That's what Will did for two years. It was always under the pretense that they were "still close friends." Will was a good guy, and I'm sure he meant well, but those calls always sent Kate spiraling down into an abyss of self-hate: "Why did he dump me? What's wrong with me? Am I fat?"

It wasn't until she met Jack, her boyfriend for the next nine years, that she stopped talking to Will.

And Jack's now gone. And Will isn't acting like a jerk. And I don't know what to think.

Dawn breaks the hugging monotony by taking Will's left hand, and lifting it up for me to inspect. "No ring, and no tan line." She turns to Kate.. "That's a step up, don't you think?"

Suddenly jolted back to reality, Kate awkwardly pulls away from the hug. "I'm sorry. Will, these are my friends Dawn and Charlie."

Will gives us the most engaging smile, and I can see why Kate fell for him so hard all those years ago. "Nice to meet you."

"So," Kate begins, searching for a topic of conversation. "How's Stephanie?"

Will's eyes squint a bit in confusion. "Who?"

The slut you dumped her for, I want to blurt out.

"Stephanie," Kate manages to eek out. She cocks her head a little. "You know the, uh . . ."

Will juts his chin forward, trying to figure out who Kate is talking about. "Steph . . ." Then he gets it. "Oh! Uh, I don't know. I haven't seen her in almost ten years. How's Jack?"

"He's good," Kate says, a little too quickly. "Running his own company now. Gets to work from home."

"So, you're still seeing him?" Will says, a trace of disappointment crossing his face as he looks at Kate's ring finger.

He's looking at her ring finger, I think to myself. *Interesting.*

Kate doesn't know how to respond to that. She looks down at the ground, then looks back up at Will. "No, actually. We broke up a few months ago."

Will's face lights up. "Really? So, are you seeing anyone?"

I watch Kate as she notices Mike from the corner of her eye. She smiles confidently as she says to Will, "Nope. It's just me for now."

Five

Overall, the party was a total waste of dinosaur. By midnight, everyone had abandoned me. Dawn was flirting with Patrick, but vehemently denying she was doing any such thing. Kate had disappeared with Will, who had single-handedly rid her of Mike. Liam had to take a very drunk Megan home, and Drew was trying to convince me to come with him to a trapeze class. By one o'clock, I had cabbed it out of there.

I'll admit, I had an ulterior motive. Although I knew from my iPhone that I had no new e-mails, calls, or text messages from Jordan, that wouldn't stop me from composing a light and breezy e-mail to Jordan to subtly show him that I had not picked up anyone at the party, and that I had gone home to snuggle up in my best red negligee, to have a glass of wine, and to think of him. And when I say *think* of him, I will make it obvious that I mean I am *thinking* of him. . . .

The second I get home, I change out of my dinosaur costume and into my favorite old Eeyore nightshirt that's shredded at the collar and a comfy pair of UCLA sweatpants. I know . . . how kitten-with-a-whip, right? I kill what's left of a bottle of cabernet and head to my computer.

Never mix wine and e-mail.

I take a sip of wine, and prepare to send off an erotic e-mail.

First, I check my inbox, just in case something happened in the five minutes since I've checked my iPhone. Still nothing from Jordan. One from my sister Andy, recently back from her honeymoon in Europe.

> I have news. It's huge. I will call you tomorrow at precisely nine in the morning.
> Love,
> Andy

I hate it when people say "I have news," but don't tell me what the news is. The worst is when you get a message on your machine where someone says, "Call me. I have big news. It's huge. Call me back." And then you spend the next hour tracking down someone, only to hear that they've won in fantasy baseball or saw something on *Dr. Phil* that applies to you.

The next e-mail is from my cousin Jenn. It has an attachment, probably of her ridiculously adorable boys Alex and Sean, or the latest ultrasound of her baby girl, due in late November. I open the e-mail.

> Subject: Well, isn't that always the problem?
> To: Charlie Edwards
> From: Jenn Smith
>
> With a three-year-old and a four-year-old comes a proliferation of birthday parties. And birthday parties mean birthday gifts. Which brings us to Barbie. The hot gift this season is "Wedding Barbie": she is blonde, she has a killer body, and she has an engagement ring that is so big, it takes up her entire finger. And it lights up. 'Cuz nothin' says class like a light-up ring.

Anyway, on the back of the box are other toys to go with Barbie to make her wedding complete: the flower girl, the ring boy, and, of course, the groom. Which brings me to my favorite picture of the year. . . .

I click on the picture of the pink Barbie box. On the box is "Ken Groom," wearing a tuxedo and dancing with Barbie. Underneath the picture of the happy couple is the caption: THE GROOM (SOLD SEPARATELY, SUBJECT TO AVAILABILITY.)

Isn't that just always the problem with grooms—you need one for a wedding, but they're subject to availability?

On another subject, Rob just got a text from Patrick that he saw you guys tonight. Ah, you glamorous single people and your glamorous Hollywood parties. So Rob wants to know, does Patrick have a shot with Dawn?

As for the Jordan e-mail you forwarded—I think Rob said it best. We're not sure what it means, but if he is not hurling himself at your door over and over again until he's a bloody pulp, he's a Goddamn fool. ☺

Love,
Jenn

I look at the *Love, Jenn,* and wonder: Had e-mail been around when she was first dating her husband, how long it would have taken Rob to write *Love, Rob.* Then I remember. . . .

Try to avoid being jealous. The only jealousy that is productive is the kind that tells you what you really want in your life. If you are jealous of someone's house, this is your mind's way of saying you want a house. If you are jealous of someone's success in a chosen field, in anything from acting to zoology, that is your mind's way of saying

you want to be an actress or a zoologist. If you are jealous of some-
one's relationship—you are in trouble. Knock it off, and stay away
from your friend's boyfriend.

And if you are jealous of a *Love, Jenn* in the middle of the night, it
means you are a complete lunatic.

I click REPLY.

> Subject: Re: Well, isn't that always the problem?
> To: Jenn Smith
> From: Charlie Edwards
>
> And not only are those grooms subject to availability, but
> they also don't have penises.☹
> Remember the Pregnant Barbie that Wal-Mart pulled from
> its shelves? I wonder if the Dad doll that was sold separately
> was also listed as "Subject to Availability." Perhaps that was
> the problem.
> I have no clue what is going on with Patrick and Dawn. They
> were still together when I left them at one.
> I have no clue what is going on with Jordan, either.
> Be happy you're married and never have to wait by the phone
> again.
> Love,
> Charlie
> P.S. Patrick probably doesn't have a shot in hell, though. Sorry.

I leave it at that. I think about elaborating by writing, "She'll play
with him for a while, the way a cat plays with a mouse. But remember what always happens to that mouse." But I decide against it.

As I hit SEND, a new e-mail beeps in, this one from Jamie. I click it
open.

Subject: For my great-grandniece
To: Charlie Edwards
From: Jamie Edwards

Hey, here's my first article for the mag. I think you should put it in your book of advice.

I quickly read the article and decide, yes, it's worth repeating to my great-granddaughter.

This is from your great-granduncle. It was an article he wrote for Metro magazine, a woman's magazine from the twenty-first century.

Lines Men Will Use to Get You Into Bed.
By James Edwards

First of all, know that everything men say, from "Hello" to "Looks like rain," is designed to get you into bed. And every teenage girl who has ever been on a fifth date has heard the line, "If you loved me, you would." But here are some other classics you might want to avoid:

1. *I have an amazing bottle of Dom Pérignon (Opus One, Cristal) at home. I keep waiting for a reason to open it, but maybe tonight should just be "Open that Bottle Saturday." Would you like to join me?*
2. *Oh, I have a print from that artist, over my couch at home. He's so (deep, real, interesting—insert your favorite adjective here). Would you like to come see it?*
3. *I don't use lines per se, because they are transparent and I think women are smarter than that. (This, if you haven't realized already, is a line.)*
4. *For you teenagers out there: Just let me for one minute— I'll pull out.*

5. I've always wanted a Christmas wedding. (June wedding, etc.)
6. I can't wait to meet your family.
7. I want to fill our house with our laughing babies.
8. Would you like to hit the beach with me and see the midnight submarine races?
9. At the bank: I'm making a deposit. Does $100,000 have the comma after the second zero, or the third?
10. I love you. (By the way, this last line, if we've waited more than two weeks, will get any nonvirgin into bed. However, we try to use it judiciously. If we say it on the first date, sometimes we freak you out.)

Just then, Jamie IMs me.

> CalienteJamie: Well, what do you think?
> AngelCharlie: Mom's going to be mad when she sees you stole her Dom Pérignon line.
> CalienteJamie: Who do you think edited this and gave me notes? She thought it would class up the piece. I had opened with number four.

"Eewwww . . . ," I say out loud, dragging the word out. Then I type in:

> AngelCharlie: Eeeeewwwwwww . . .
> CalienteJamie: You mean to tell me no guy has ever said that to you?
> AngelCharlie: Of course they have, but it's still Eww . . .
> CalienteJamie: Hold on, I think I'm getting a booty call.

While I wait for Jamie to get back to me, I decide to begin composing my e-mail to Jordan.

To: Jordan1313
From: AngelCharlie

Dear Jordan,
It's about 1:30, and I just got home. I wish you could have
been there. I went as a cheerleader.

Well, that's lame. He knows I was planning to go as a dinosaur.
And he can see from the time stamp it's 1:30.
I erase everything, and begin again.

Hey, Sweetie,
Got your message. Sorry I missed your calls. I got stuck at
Drew's neighbor's house dealing with this hippo

I stop typing, and stare at my screen. Should I really be sending
an e-mail that will end with me describing myself covered in hippo
poop? The story might be funny now, but I'm not going for funny,
I'm going for sexy. I erase, and start over.
Jamie IMs me.

CalienteJamie: Make fun of my costume all you want—I've
just been invited to Swingers Coffee Shop to meet a gaggle of
drunken women.
AngelCharlie: Have fun. Quick—before you go. If I were
sending an e-mail to Jordan to make him miss me, should I go
with humor or sex?
CalienteJamie: Humor. Gotta go. Love you.

And he signs off.
Humor. He wrote that immediately. Must be the way to go. I begin
again:

Hello my love,

Backspace, backspace, backspace.

Hi Babe,

No . . . .

Dear Reason for Living,

All right, that's just going to freak him out.

Dear Sex God,
I've just thought about you—twice. I have some fun ideas about what we can do with whipped cream, a hot tub of Jell-O, and a cattle prod.

Delete, delete, delete.
Then again, it might be funny.

With Katie Couric and a cattle prod.

Now I'm freaking myself out. Backspace, Backspace.

My home phone rings.
     I pick up on the first ring without bothering to look at the caller ID. "Hello?"
     "Do you think I have a Peter Pan complex?" someone asks me.
     "Yes," I answer without hesitation.
     There's a pause. "Do you even know who this is?"
     "No, but I know it's a male voice, so you do."

"It's Drew."

"Then I stand by my answer."

"Okay, then, what exactly is a Peter Pan complex?"

"Go to bed," I order.

"Well, I'd like to," Drew tells me. "But there's this girl in my bed right now, and at first she was very charming and really into me. But then she started crying about her ex-boyfriend, who just dumped her, and now she's saying I have a Peter Pan complex."

I start to respond, but he interrupts me. "And I need to know what that is, because if it has to do with flying during sex, I just can't. Maybe the Spider-Man thing confused her. The webs might be realistically sticky, but I don't think they'd support my weight. Certainly not both of ours." Drew sighs loudly. "I think I'm getting too old for the new sex."

I furrow my brow, and look up at my ceiling, confused. "I . . . um . . . what exactly is the new sex?"

"Oh, shit!" Drew exclaims. "She just found the harness—I gotta go. Love you."

And Drew's gone.

Great—a man who calls me right before he has sex with another woman can say he loves me, but the guy I'm dating can't. Perfect. My life is right on schedule.

I backspace myself back to an empty screen, and stare at the page.

Then, following in the footsteps of great writers everywhere, I decide to find inspiration by raiding my fridge.

Don't eat unless you're hungry.

A few minutes later, I realize I have nothing fun to eat in this house. No candy, no ice cream—not even an old can of Duncan Hines frosting hiding behind a jar of mustard. I decide I can't face a

2 A.M. Ralph's run, so instead I open a bottle of Guenoc Claret, micro-
wave some popcorn, and head back to my computer screen.

Ten minutes later, I'm still at my computer screen, staring at my
empty e-mail box. Other than a job offer from the Bank of Kenya,
and yet another ad for a penile implant, no one wants to talk to me.

I take another sip of wine, hit COMPOSE, then type.

> Dear Jordan,
> I miss you. I'm sorry I missed your calls. Call me again some-
> time when you're free.
> Love,
> Charlie

It's probably best to go with the classics.
I hit SEND.

Six

Get plenty of sleep.

I spent the rest of the night with terrible insomnia. I didn't mean to wait by the phone, but I kept expecting Jordan to call the minute he woke up. He didn't. Instead, when the phone finally rings at a little before nine in the morning, I look at the caller ID to see it's my mom's house. Probably my dad—he tends to call early in the morning.

Dad's temporarily staying with Mom, his ex-wife, while he divorces Jeannine, his current wife.

Yup—my parents are divorced, but living together. I mean, not living together, living together—just living together as roommates. They have separate bedrooms. Mom shares her bed with Chris, her thirty-year-old yoga instructor.

One big happy family.

Did I mention I grew up in Los Angeles? Did I have to mention it? Is there anyone outside of California who can utter the phrase, "My parents are divorced, but living together"?

Maybe a few in Oregon . . .

Anyway, hopefully it's Dad, not Mom. It's too early for Mom.

"Hello," I mumble groggily into the phone.

My father tells me over the phone:

Never get a tattoo on your lower back.

"What?" I ask, sleepily.

"It's for your book of advice to my great-great-granddaughter," Dad says. "Never get a tattoo on your lower back."

"Doesn't that sound a little old and judgmental?" I ask as I in-stinctively reach for a phantom cigarette.

"Oh, please. Last night your mother and I saw a woman wearing pink Juicy Couture sweats low enough to see the words DADDY'S LIT-TLE GIRL tattooed right above her butt. I complimented her on her costume and she almost punched me."

"Dad, lower-back tattoos are pretty common these days."

"Charliebear, the only man a girl will ever catch with that tattoo lives in a trailer park, has a beer gut and bad teeth, and wears a trucker cap with the word SKOAL emblazoned on the front."

"Probably true," I concede. "Though that's not the worst thing a tattoo could say on the lower back. Drew dated a hula dancer with the word MAHALO tattooed right above the back of her hula skirt."

"What does *Mahalo* mean?" Dad asks.

"It's Hawaiian for *Thank you.*"

"Oh, for fuck's sake," Dad mutters. "Anyway, what does this e-mail you sent me yesterday mean?"

He reads to me from his computer:

All women think they can utter the following phrase: "If I had a dime for every sane member of my family, I'd have a dime."

I cringe. "I'm sorry. That was just something I typed into my iPhone yesterday. I want to put it in my book of advice. I didn't mean to send that to you. I meant to send you Jordan's e-mail, so you can translate for me."

"Don't forward me the boy's e-mail," Dad nearly whines. "I thought you broke up with him."

"I did, but—"

"What is it about women that when they break up, what they really mean is, 'I want you to start acting like I want you to act.' When a man says he wants to break up, do you know what he means?"

"That he never wants to see you again, unless it's two in the morning, and he's drunk and horny," I answer authoritatively.

There's a pause on the other end of the line. Then Dad deadpans, "Seriously, you talk to your father with that mouth?"

"Sorry," I say. "It means he really wants to break up."

"Exactly. And, in response to your first e-mail: What makes you think you'd have a dime?"

"I'd have a dime!" I answer defensively.

"Really?" Dad responds dubiously. "So, who in our family is sane?"

"Well . . . ," I begin, stalling for time as I go through the members of my family.

Let's see, there's my mother, the fifty-five-year-old party girl who sleeps until noon, tends to date men half her age, still smokes pot every day, and makes her living as a writer.

And I've yet to meet a sane writer.

My dad, who's living with her. That doesn't exactly make him the poster boy for sane.

My sister Andrea (Andy), a recent newlywed whose wedding showed me that no woman should spend more than twelve hours preparing for a party that lasts a day.

Jamie . . . God no. I mean, he's the sweetest little brother ever. But when he filled out his job application at *Metro* a few years ago, and the questionnaire asked him to list his flaws, he wrote a list of twelve things. Followed by the phrase, "See attached Pages 2–17."

Then he attached pages two through seventeen.

"Jenn," I finally say, referring to my cousin Jenn.

"A full-time surgeon who's having a third kid? What kind of weirdo wants three kids?" my dad mutters back to me.

"*You* have three kids!"

"Hey, I never said you were getting a dime from me."

True enough. I try to remember some more relatives. "Mawv," I say confidently, referring to my great-grandmother, a ninety-five-year-old spitfire of a woman, and one of my favorite people in the world.

"Met her husband at a speakeasy at the age of sixteen," Dad reminds me.

"People got married much younger then."

"While she was dancing on a table."

Oh.

I think about that. "That means she's colorful, not insane," I point out.

"You know perfectly well that when I insist we have to call our family members colorful, what we really mean is that they're insane."

Fair enough. "Okay, what about me then?" I ask, the idea suddenly popping into my head. "Don't I get a dime for myself?"

"Need I remind you, you just tried to send your father an e-mail from your boyfriend-slash-ex-boyfriend so he can translate?"

"I'll admit, this is not my sanest moment . . ."

"And, by the way, I think this Jordan is an idiot."

What?? He can't say that about my boyf . . . about my current . . . uh, sort of . . . my . . .

I scrunch my head to the left, wedging the phone between my shoulder and left ear, and quickly jot down into a notebook:

When lending support to a friend during a breakup, always follow the one-month rule: Don't start trashing the ex until the breakup has taken for one month. Otherwise, if they get back together, you become the bad guy.

"Why would you say he's an idiot?" I ask.

"Because if the boy had any sense, he would have married you immediately, before you had time to realize that you were too good for him."

I sigh. "Thanks, Dad."

"Seriously. You're worth at least three goats. And a mule."

Mom picks up on another extension. "Charlie, darling, is that you?"

"Good morning, Mother."

"Darling, we're so sorry we missed you at Robert Hazan's party. We didn't get there until after two."

Oh God, I'm now so old my parents can crash my parties. "You went to Robert Hazan's party?"

"Oh, it was a hoot! We went as a cheerleader and a football player. Your father's legs were so cute in the skirt, and I haven't worn shoulder pads since the eighties! Anyway, I wanted to give you my two cents on Jordan's e-mail."

"You think he's an idiot," I say, sighing and ready for a maternal lecture. "Or, alternately, you think I'm an idiot for breaking up with him."

"No!" Mom says, verbally brushing me off. "I think he's lovely. He's clearly in love with you, and just wants what's best for you while he's away working."

"Really?" I ask, my voice bursting with hope.

"Absolutely!" Mom assures me.

Finally—vindication! My face lights up. All is well with the world again.

"Now, have you thought about taking a lover while he's out of the country?" Mom then asks.

And my face falls.

"That's what I used to do when your father was out of town, and it worked wonders."

It's then that I begin smacking my head slowly into my hand over and over again.

"You know, I *am* still on the phone," Dad points out to Mom.

"Oh please, like I don't know about your mistress of twenty-five years," Mom says offhandedly. "I only took lovers when you were out of town seeing her."

"Touché," Dad concedes.

"And, on that happy note," I say, wondering what a stroke feels like, "I think I need to hang up now . . . ."

"Oh, what, you're shocked I had a mistress?" Dad says, sounding a bit perplexed by my lack of open-mindedness.

"How could I be?" I say dryly. "She was my babysitter."

"And a damn good one, too!" Mom says, in a tone of voice like she's lifting a glass for a toast. "I don't know how I would have made it through those first six weeks after having your brother without her. Ed, get off the phone. I need to talk to your daughter about the *thing.*"

"What thing?" Dad asks.

"You know, the *thing* . . ." Mom answers back.

No response from Dad.

"My news," Mom clarifies.

"Oh, *that,*" Dad says. "Bear, be nice to your mother."

He means me. "Uh . . . okay."

"Love you."

"Um . . . love you, too," I say.

When Dad hangs up, I say to Mom, "Okay, Mom, what's up?"

"I slept with your father," Mom begins.

I open my mouth a few times, trying to force words to come out, but it's no use. My mother has managed to render me speechless.

I am shocked. Shocked and appalled.

Yes, I'm shocked that my parents slept together. And, no, not because I'm some weirdo who thinks her parents have only had sex three times (to conceive me, my sister Andy, and my brother Jamie). But because they've been divorced for . . . gosh, I'm not even sure how long. And my father has been married and separated since then, and my mother is sleeping with a thirty-year-old "yummy little snack cake of a thing" (her words, not mine). So the parents-sleeping-together thing—that is kind of news.

I mean, not big news—this is my family. They could announce I had a half-sister in Paris, and all I'd ask is, "Can she get me a discount at the fashion houses?"

I sit up in bed, and, out of habit, reach for my pack of Marlboro Lights again. "What? When?" I ask.

"After your sister's wedding," Mom says definitively, as though the sentence ends there.

I sigh heavily, while looking over at my nightstand to see that I have replaced my cigarettes with a fresh pack of nicotine gum. "Well, I guess that's understandable," I finally say. "I'm sure you guys were just emotional after—"

"And then the next day . . ."

"Mom . . ."

"And three times the day after that. Then last night, I guess I nailed a cheerleader . . ."

"All right, Mom. Stop!" I command. "That's a visual I'm gonna need at least three drinks to get rid of . . . ."

"The point is, I needed a sperm donor . . . ," Mom tells me.

What a lovely way to put it. "Mom—"

"And now I think I'm pregnant."

"Mom, I—"

Whoa. Wait a fucking minute.

"What do you mean pregnant?" I ask, alarm permeating my voice.

"Pregnant. As in the nine-month period of time when a woman is carrying a child . . ."

My call waiting beeps.

"Can you hold on a sec?" I ask.

"But I—"

"Just hold on for one second. I have another call," I say to Mom.

I click over. "Hello."

"I just want you to know that I had nothing to do with this," Dad insists.

"Dad, where are you?"

"I'm in the backyard, calling from my cell. It occurred to me that I should give you my side of the story."

"Uh-huh," I say, ripping open the new box of gum, and quickly popping a piece out of its foil, and into my mouth. "So, in what twisted world do you live in that you think sleeping with Mom is somehow 'having nothing to do with it'?"

"Oh, not that," Dad says dismissively. "I had sex with her. I take full responsibility for that. I just meant I have nothing to do with the pregnancy. Well, I mean, other than going to a sperm bank for her. But that was just a favor between old friends."

I pull the phone away from my ear to stare at it.

After a few moments, I put the phone back to my ear, and sternly say to Dad, "Don't even *think* about hanging up on me!" I click back to Mom. "Three words, Mom: What. The. Fuck."

"I think I might be pregnant," Mom repeats.

It's nine in the morning in the *Twilight Zone* when our heroine must say to her mother with complete authority . . .

"Mom, you're not pregnant."

"How do *you* know?" Mom asks defensively.

"Uh . . . because you're fifty-five years old?" I say, dragging out the sentence and phrasing it in the form of a question, so she knows my answer is obvious.

"My friend Susan's grandmother had her mother when she was fifty-seven years old," Mom tells me smugly.

Uh, yeah.

"Explain to me why it is that people now understand that back in the nineteen hundreds, a 'premature baby' who came out weighing nine pounds should have been called a 'shotgun wedding baby,' yet we still cling to the myth that a fifty-something woman could have a baby, rather than a 'non–shotgun wedding' grandbaby?"

"Helen Fielding had a baby at forty-eight. Geena Davis had twins at forty-eight."

"And you think that happened naturally," I say, crossing my arms despite the fact that she can't see me, and giving her my best *roll your eyes like a teenager* voice.

"Don't you take that tone with me, young lady," Mom warns. "You shouldn't upset a woman in my condition."

What condition would that be? Mentally deranged?

"What do you think of the name Claire?" Mom asks.

Mom goes on to explain to me that she and her young boyfriend Chris have decided to have a baby, that she has been taking fertility drugs for months in preparation for this latest project, and that she went to the fertility clinic to be transferred with donor eggs yesterday. It turns out young Chris, all of thirty years old, had too low of a sperm count to conceive, so she asked my fifty-five-year-old dad to—and I'm quoting her verbatim—"help us out here."

"Hold on," I say to Mom. I click back to Dad. "And in what twisted world do you live in that you're giving Mom sperm?"

"Please, she's fifty-five years old," Dad says. "It's like giving apples to a dead horse. This isn't going to take. Plus, I think Chris and her are breaking up."

"What was your first clue?!" I blurt out. "That she's cheating on him with you or that she wants another baby with you?"

"Sleeping with exes doesn't count as cheating," Dad says offhandedly. "Don't be such a Puritan. Anyway, she talked about shopping at a sperm bank, and I didn't want her wasting a lot of money and doing anything stupid."

Yeah, we wouldn't want her doing anything stupid, I think to myself.

"Dad, she took hormones," I begin. "She isn't using her own eggs . . ."

"Fifty-five," he answers back. "Now get back to your mother. I'm due at the Four Seasons in half an hour for brunch. I love you."

"I love you, too," I tell him through an exhausted sigh, then click back to Mom. "Mom, I—"

"I'm sorry, dear, but I must go. I'm interviewing designers for the new nursery. I'll call you later. Bye."

"I love you, too," I say, sighing. "Bye."

I hang up the phone, and look over at my book of advice on the nightstand. I open the book, and jot down in blue pen:

You don't get to choose the chimney the stork drops you down, so get over it.

I say this, even though right now I really wish I had been born to a couple of professors teaching at a college in Iowa who didn't divorce to improve their sex life. Not sure why I choose Iowa. It just seems so normal.

My home phone rings again, and I check the caller ID. It's my sister Andy.

This call I'm actually happy to take. I pick up immediately.

"Well, good morning, Mrs. Masters!" I say cheerfully. "So what's your news?"

"I think I might be pregnant," my sister Andy tells me quickly.

I don't mean to, but I wince. "Have you talked to Mom?" I ask.

"No. You're the first one I've told. Don't tell Mom, or anyone else yet, because it's not definite. Okay?"

"Not a problem," I say quickly, relieved not to be put in the middle of a pregnancy war. "So, why do you think you might be pregnant?"

Andy sighs. "Well, my period's late. And my breasts are hurting so much, I want to rip them off my body. Plus, I'm staring at my third pregnancy test, and there are two pink lines on it."

"Mazel tov!" I scream, even though we're not Jewish. "How far along do you think you are?"

"Oh, I'm gonna go with eight weeks," Andy says, and I'm just starting to notice a distinct tension in her voice. "But before you start doing the math, I want to remind you that pregnancy really only lasts thirty-eight weeks, not forty weeks. The first two weeks don't count. The first two weeks of your cycle, you're not pregnant. You're having your period, and then you're waiting to ovulate. Those weeks are only tacked on so women can be one day late, but still tell everyone they're four weeks along. So, *really*, I've only been pregnant for six weeks, which is *exactly* how long I've been married."

"Thank you for the biology lesson," I say dryly. "And what exactly are you afraid of, that people are going to do the math and declare you a slut?"

"That's what Grandma did with Mom," Andy reminds me.

"Mom was five months pregnant when she got married," I remind Andy. "Besides, the first baby always comes out late anyway, so the point is moot. Have you thought of names? I personally like the name Charlie if it's a girl. . . ."

I hear Andy let out a tense breath.

"Are you okay?" I ask.

"Well . . . ," Andy squeaks out, her voice catching a little.

"You planned this, right?"

"Not exactly. I mean, technically we were trying. But whoever heard of getting pregnant the first month you try?"

"Need I remind you, Mom and Dad got pregnant three times without trying at all."

"Actually, I'm kind of freaked. Hunter went out last night and bought me this book about pregnancy. I know this doesn't make any logical sense, but I keep trying to figure out a way to not have that big head go through this tiny space."

"Women have been having babies for thousands and thousands of years," I say reassuringly. "If labor were really awful, we'd all be only children."

"What about all those women who have only had C-sections?" Andy counters. Before I can answer, Andy asks me in a slightly panicked voice, "Did you know there's such a thing as age-appropriate nipples?"

I rack my brain. "I can't say as I did."

Andy continues, "After the labor book freaked me out, I decided to get online and start looking at cute baby stuff to buy. You know, to sort of get myself in the mood. Find things like cute cribs from Bellini. Cute sheets from Pottery Barn Kids. Fun stuff. But then I got this checklist from a registry at Target. And there were things on it like age-appropriate nipples. I mean, I have no idea how to even shop for those, much less how to use them. And then there are, like, fifty different types of infant car seats, and they all look like you need a PhD in physics to figure them out. . . ."

"Well, you've got about eight months to—"

Andy's voice then gets a bit shrill. "Plus there's this thing in the book about all the different kinds of baby cries! The 'I want to be changed' cry. The 'I want to be held' cry. All I hear when a baby is crying is shrieking."

"All right, take a breath," I say calmly. "After all, you're breathing for two."

"And to top it all off, Hunter wants to name the baby after his great-grandmother!"

I don't even want to ask. "What's his—"

"Zelda!" she shrieks. "And I'm almost positive that name was outlawed during the Geneva Convention."

Andy attempting a bit of humor was a good sign that mostly she thought that her pregnancy was good news. After a few more minutes of listening to the dramas of cribs, infant car seats, and preschool applications (seriously?!), I suggest to Andy that if she has any major concerns about parenting, she should call our cousin Jenn. I specifically don't have her call Mom, as I don't think she needs to hear about Mom's latest project just yet.

Two more minutes of talking and I hang up the phone, and start thinking about my life.

Babies. Now I'm behind schedule with babies. It was bad enough that it seemed like all of my friends were either married, or were on track with their perfect careers, or both. Now I'm behind on the parenthood track as well.

Everyone else has figured out their lives. They've gone on to become doctors, professors, radio show hosts, producers, actors, writers: whatever it was they set out to be. I have a golden handcuff kind of job that I got by accident, that I like just enough to not look for anything else.

That's not true, I like my job. But it's definitely been a glass-half-full kind of week. Most women my age are married, or have babies, and I can't even figure out if I'm dating a man.

I snuggle up in my new white down comforter and white six-hundred-thread-count sheets, and try to fall back asleep.

How can I? I bought these sheets just so the bed would be so luxurious and fantastic that Jordan wouldn't want to leave it.

My God, when did I become this pathetic?

A shower seems too ambitious this early, but I do manage to putter downstairs for a cup of coffee, and a masochistic few minutes with my e-mail.

Jordan hasn't written. I know this because my phone has e-mail, but I check my computer anyway.

Sigh.

I spit out my gum, take a sip of coffee, and spend the next ten minutes trying to distract myself by coming up with more good advice for my great-granddaughter. They're just a bunch of non sequiturs I've thought about in the last few days:

Don't ever hit.

Whether you're religious or not, let me give you my definition of sin: Sin is when you do something that hurts someone else, or hurts yourself. Try never to sin.

Men don't like ponytails.

Get a dog because you want a dog, not because you're depressed and trying to fill a hole in your life.

All meter maids should be shot. Seriously, there should be a hunting season.

Don't gamble. The light bill in Las Vegas is not paid every month because their gamblers win.

If you have to ask, "Do you know who I am?" you're not important enough to ask that.

Huge diamonds do not make you a great person.

I don't know why I write that last one. It's doubtful my great-granddaughter will grow up to be a rap star, but I might as well throw that in.

Never let how a man feels about you determine how you feel about yourself.

I stare at this one. Why do I never seem capable of taking my own advice?

As I stare at those words, my phone rings.

It's Drew. I pick up. "Good morning."

"Oh my God! I love this script!" Drew says without preamble. "The Ben character is fantastic! The part has Oscar written all over it! The only problem is, the character is a self-involved actor. I just don't know where I'm going to draw from. Do we know any self-involved actors who I could watch and research for a few days?"

Note to self: Make Drew look up the words "Irony" and "Delusional."

"I already called my agent, and we're signed on," Drew continues excitedly. "I start shooting Monday. Tell Jordan, 'We're going to Paris, baby!'"

I am mad at myself for being so relieved to hear that. Maybe if Jordan and I could just be in the same room together for a few days, we could have a great time, have great sex, and maybe we wouldn't need to break up because . . .

"I don't see why you need a man around," Drew says. "You're so busy mindfucking yourself."

"Excuse me?" I say, startled out of my thoughts.

"That's my favorite line in the script," Drew says. "That and 'Murdered children are a cheat for serious writers who can't think of anything else to write that will freak out their audience. Just like weddings are a cheat for chick-lit writers.' I'm telling you, doing this movie is going to be so much fun. Oh, that reminds me: I don't have twenty-five million dollars."

I don't know how to respond to that. "You mean on you, or in the bank?"

"In the bank," Drew answers. "Before I got this script, I was thinking about becoming a space tourist in Russia. You know, like Martha
Stewart's boyfriend did. For twenty-five million dollars, you get to
train with a bunch of Russian cosmonauts, then fly up to the International Space Station. Just a few years ago, it was only twenty million. I
thought I could swing that. But inflation gets us all. . . ."

"Wait. Since when do you want to be an astronaut?" I ask, confused. I mean, I've been working for the man for several years, and
this is the first I've heard of it.

"Oh, I don't," Drew quickly clarifies. "That requires a college degree, maybe even post grad work. Who's got that kind of time? But a
space tourist—that I can get into. Anyone can say they got away
from it all by heading to an over-water bungalow in Bora Bora. Who
do you know who can say they flew over two hundred miles into
space to drink Tang?"

He says that with such joie de vivre, I envy him.

Then I think about what I've read about space tourism. "The International Space Station is only two hundred miles in space?" I ask.

"Two hundred and forty, actually."

"That's over one hundred thousand dollars a mile," I point out,
trying to show him how ridiculous this conversation is becoming.

"Beat that, Bill Gates!" Drew answers.

Too late.

"Anyway," Drew continues, "I called my money manager this
morning to ask him if I could afford to take a pay cut and do this
movie, and he said yes. Then I asked him if I could afford to go up
to the Space Station. He suggested that if I ever want to go into
space, I should seriously consider going on a budget I can live
with."

A budget Drew can live with. This idea has about as much chance
of becoming reality as finding a unicorn in nature. I hate to sound
pessimistic, but this is a man who spent over one hundred thousand

dollars decorating and redecorating his dressing-room trailers last year.

"I went to this Web site on stretching your paycheck," Drew continues excitedly, "and I have some thoughts. For example, did you know that if I got a library card, I could check books out of the library for free?"

What's a tactful way to put this? "Drew, you don't read."

"Okay, bad example," he cheerfully admits. "But I can shop at Costco and buy in bulk. And I can sell one of my cars—apparently I'll save on insurance if I only have nine cars. Plus, there's a bunch of other stuff I can do. My money manager was getting too lecture-y, which I think is downright rude, considering I'm paying him five hundred dollars an hour. So, I need you to go to his office and pick up copies of all of my financial records, then come over here, and help me put together a budget."

I wonder how much it's costing him to pay someone at his money manager's office to copy all of his financial records on a Sunday. I'm going to guess five hundred dollars an hour.

"After you get the records, head over to Starbucks and pick up a couple of Venti lattes and a Sunday paper. Apparently, the Sunday paper has coupons."

I try to tell him that since he recently bought a three-thousand-dollar espresso machine, then hired a personal chef to make him lattes, perhaps he should save the nine dollars he's about to spend on coffee. But he's already hung up the phone.

I look down at my notebook for one final thought for the day:

Spend less than you make.

A more cynical person would have said, "A movie star and his money are soon parted."

Seven

An hour later, I put my key into the lock of Drew's front door, and let myself into his foyer. The room is empty.

"Hello?" I yell up toward the stairs, tossing the key into my purse as I balance two Venti lattes, a bag of chocolate croissants, and a Sunday paper in my arms. "They had those croissants you like, so I picked up two."

Suddenly, Drew flies over the stairwell banister, and sails above me. "I'm king of the world!" he yells, flying right over me, and scaring the shit out of me.

I instinctively hit the floor, careful not to spill the coffees. "Ahh!" I scream as his feet miss my head by inches.

"Isn't it fantastic?" Drew says as he flies higher into the air, and over to his chandelier. "I'm learning all about weightlessness."

From his marble floor, I look up to see that Drew is fastened in a harness, with pulleys surrounding him, being flown around by Joe, the stunt coordinator from our last movie, and several of Joe's assistants.

"Hey, Charlie," Joe says pleasantly.

"Hey, Joe," I force myself to say. "Should I bother to ask why Drew is flying around his front hall?"

Joe shrugs. "Don't know, and don't care. I just go where they pay me. Baby needs shoes."

"I wanted to learn what weightlessness felt like before I went ahead with my cosmonaut trip," Drew says. "Wait, watch this. Dive!"

As Joe and his stunt riggers pull, slide, and hold various wires, Drew dives right at me. I crouch, bracing for a crash until I hear, "And up!" and he flies over me again.

I have got to find a new line of work.

"Joe, how much is this stunt costing Drew?" I yell to Joe as I stand up again.

"It's not a stunt," Joe explains. "It has nothing to do with the movie."

"I'm not arguing semantics with you, Joe. Seriously, how much is this setting Drew back?"

As Joe opens his mouth to answer, Drew interrupts. "If you have to ask, I can't afford it. Watch me do a somersault!"

Joe and his crew oblige, and Drew gleefully spreads his arms, then flips around like an eight-year-old in a pool of water. "Did you get the coupons?" he asks me.

"I did."

"Okay, guys," Drew says cheerfully. "My old lady is making me hit the books. Let's call it a day."

There are just so many things that are wrong with that sentence.

Never buy a mansion—there's just too much to clean.

Twenty minutes later, I am sitting in Drew's lavishly appointed dining room, armed with computer printouts of his various assets, as well as his money manager's log of Drew's expenses.

It's not pretty. One entry completely baffles me. "You spent over three thousand dollars on worms last year?"

"Earthworms," Drew says, in a tone of voice that makes it clear he thinks that explains everything.

"And you spent more money last year on rocks than I spent on my mortgage payments."

"That was for my Zen garden." Drew reminds me.

"You don't have a Zen garden," I point out.

"That's why I needed the earthworms."

I look up at Drew for clarification. He looks deeply into my eyes and begs me, "This is your life. Try to give it a happy ending."

"I'm sorry. What?" I ask, confused.

Drew perks up. "It's from the new movie. Isn't that great dialogue?!" He pulls the coupon section out of the newspaper. "Hey, look. They've got seventy-five cents off rice."

I go back to his expenses. "Six hundred dollars for a haircut?!" I ask, shocked.

"That's including tip," Drew says offhandedly as he rifles through the coupon section. "Oh, and here's one for a dollar off gum."

"You don't chew gum," I point out, frowning, as I go through his expenses. I look up. "Seven hundred dollars for highlights?"

Drew continues his reading. "Really, I'm covering gray. Hairdressers gossip. Four hundred dollars of that is hush money." His face lights up. "Do I eat shredded wheat?"

"No," I answer. "Drew, why don't you just have Vic cut your hair when you're working?" I say, referring to Drew's personal hair and makeup guy on every shoot. "Then it's free."

"Oh, I wouldn't want to impose," Drew says offhandedly. "Poor man has a very complicated life without me interfering, begging for a haircut. Has a bipolar boyfriend and an ex-wife with self-esteem issues."

"The studio pays him about a thousand dollars a day when you're shooting. For that kind of money, he can . . ." I think about Drew's statement. "Vic has an ex-wife?"

Drew waves it off. "They dated back in college. Very few women have honed their gaydar in college. What's probiotic fiber?"

"I don't know. Why?"

"I can get a dollar off cottage cheese, as long as I don't mind that they've added probiotic fiber."

I pull the coupons away from him. "You're not going to save twenty-five million dollars by saving a dollar on cottage cheese—which, by the way, you don't eat. We need to get rid of some of your larger expenses. For example, you said you'd sell one of your cars. How about really saving money, and selling five of them?"

"But I have a garage for twelve," Drew reasons.

"I have China for twelve, that doesn't mean I'll ever use it. You could get rid of the Ferrari, for example, not to mention the damn Koenigsegg."

"The what?" Drew says, his face leaning into mine, trying to decipher the word.

"I may be pronouncing it wrong. The black car you bought in Vegas."

Drew leans back and whines, "Oh, but that's such a futuristic car . . ."

"That car cost you six hundred thousand dollars. The only future you'll have with it is throwing buckets of money at it, and being afraid to drive it in rush hour traffic, or east of La Cienega. It needs to go." I give him a list of his other cars. "Now I want you to choose five of the cars from this list that you want to keep. We sell the rest. Next up: staff. Who is Gladys?"

Drew looks at me blankly. "I don't know a Gladys."

"Well, she's costing you eight hundred dollars a week."

Drew furrows his brow, thinking. Finally, he yells aloud, "Gladys?!"

"Yes sir," I hear from somewhere in his behemoth of a house.

"Well, there you go," Drew says.

I try to suppress the urge to roll my eyes, but fail miserably. "Do you even need a maid here on Sundays?"

"Do I even need an assistant here on Sundays?"

"Apparently, yes!" I retort.

"Oh, right," Drew concedes. Suddenly, he gets up and heads to his refrigerator. "I'm bored."

As Drew pulls a bottle of Ace of Spades champagne from his refrigerator, I continue reading. "Why do you have three nutritionists on your payroll?"

"Each one lets me eat different things."

I fight the urge to let my forehead fall into the palm of my hand. Again, I fail miserably. "Is that the same reason you have four different personal trainers?"

"One trainer, two masseuses, and Chris, the yoga instructor. You know, your stepdad."

"He's *not* my stepdad," I say sternly.

"By the way, how are he and your Mom doing on the baby track?"

I look up, startled. "You know about that?"

"Oh, he's been talking about it for months. Poor guy, shooting blanks. Thank goodness your dad is there to pinch-hit, if you know what I mean."

I sigh. "You leave little to the imagination."

Drew pops the cork on the champagne. "I'm toying with the idea of buying a castle in Ireland. Any thoughts?"

None that I can say aloud if I want to keep my job.

Two hours, three pieces of Nicorette, and a glass of overpriced champagne later, I have put Drew on a budget he is sure to ignore by this evening, and made my way home.

As I pull up to my driveway, I see a dozen pink roses in a glass vase on my doorstep.

And my heart floats.

I recently wrote to my great-granddaughter:

It's better to receive a single rose from a man at your door than a dozen roses delivered to your office. The single rose comes from a man who took the time to pick the rose. The other comes from the man's assistant calling the florist. Always treasure a man's time more than his money.

But since Jordan is more than five thousand miles away, I race out of my car and over to the flowers excitedly. I pick up the vase, and smell the slightly budding blooms. Ah . . . bliss.

I rip open the card.

Thank you so much for all your help. I owe you dinner in Paris.
Best,
Liam

Sigh. I've been bested. Not that I expected *Love, Liam* or anything. But an *xoxo* would have been nice.

Oh well. I still got flowers from a hot guy. How many women can say that today? I bring the flowers inside, and check my answering machine. My machine tells me, "You have five messages."

I hit PLAY.

"Message one," the automated voice continues. "Sent at 12:52 P.M."

"Hey, it's Kate. I have big news. Call me back. Bye."

"I have big news." Argh. She sent me a text saying, "I have big news," when I was at Drew's, but I ignored it. The last time she had "big news," I dropped everything to call her and find out she got front row tickets to "Former Olympians on Ice."

"Message two," the automated voice continues. "Sent at 12:54 P.M."

"Damn it! I can't get ahold of you on your cell. I've called and sent you an e-mail," Kate continues excitedly. "Call me back!"

Well, okay, maybe it is big.

"Message three. Sent at 2:07 P.M."

"Oh fuck," Dawn says. "I just got Kate's messages. Call me back."

"Message four. Sent at 2:20 P.M."

"I just talked to your parents. Hoped you were there, but you weren't," Kate says, her face practically beaming over the phone. "Call me back."

She called my parents? Shit—I don't like the sound of that. I pick up the phone to call Kate as I hear the last message.

"Message five. Sent at 2:22 P.M."

"Darling," Mom says excitedly. "Your father just popped some champagne, and lit up the pipe. Isn't it fabulous?"

By now I've dialed Kate, who picks up on the first ring. "Finally! Where have you been all day?"

"I've been at Drew's listening to his thoughts about living on a budget."

"I'm getting married!" Kate blurts out gleefully.

Uh . . .

I try to think of something to say to that.

I got nothin'.

"Isn't that great news?!" Kate asks me, so deliriously happy that she obviously hasn't picked up on my stunned silence.

"Um . . . sure," I say, thoroughly confused. "Who's the lucky groom? Jack?"

"No. Will, of course," Kate says, still not noticing my complete lack of any type of enthusiasm.

"From the party?" I ask, taking my phone up to my room to find my nicotine gum.

"Of course from the party. Okay, now, I know I'm supposed to be seeing you guys Thursday night, but instead of doing the thing we were going to do, could I get you to come to that bridal salon your sister went to so we can pick your bridesmaids' dresses?"

"The thing we were going to do?" I ask, still confused. "You mean the New Year's resolutions?"

"Ssshh," Kate whispers into the phone. "Will doesn't know about my self-help books. I hid them all in a box when he was taking a shower."

"What else did you hide when he was taking a shower?!" I ask, ready to lurch into a lecture. "Nine years' worth of Jack photos? Does he know you just got out of a nine-year relationship?"

"Yes, he does," Kate says, sounding surprised at my outburst. "Why are you taking that tone with me?"

"Um . . . because you're telling me you're marrying a man you've known for less than twenty-four hours?" I say in the form of a rhetorical question.

"I've known him for fifteen years," Kate reminds me, with a level, even voice. "That's half my life."

"Okay, well then, you've been dating him for less than twenty-four hours."

"I dated him for three years," Kate says, using that same *don't fuck with me* voice. "What's the longest you've ever dated someone?"

Ouch. I'm stunned. Not to mention speechless.

Kate uses my silence as an invitation to continue. "We've decided on a June wedding—"

"Wait," I stop her. "June when?"

"June of next year," Kate answers, her tone of voice making it obvious she thinks that's a stupid question. "Oh, it's going to be gorgeous! Will has a ton of money, so I can do whatever I want. And, I can't wait to show you my ring! We went to Tiffany's this morning. It's a two-carat baguette cut with smaller baguettes on both sides, set in platinum . . . . Oh, and what do you think of Billy Joel's "Just the Way You Are" for a first dance?"

I'm too stunned to speak. Finally, I come up with, "I think you should avoid any song sung by a man married four times."

"Damn," Kate says, sounding disappointed. "That throws out

Sinatra, too, then." Her voice perks up. "On the plus side, Harry Connick Jr. is still in contention."

My phone beeps. "Can you hold on a second?" I say. "It's Dawn."

"Okay," Kate answers cheerfully, not the least bit upset I've cut her off.

"Hello."

"Did you hear?" Dawn asks me without preamble.

"Just now," I say, popping a piece of gum in my mouth. "I don't know what to say."

"I say we throw a sack over her head and lock her up in a hotel room until she comes to her senses."

I hear Kate's line click off.

Then I hear a click on Dawn's phone. "Hold on," Dawn says.

She clicks off. As I hold, I start thinking about this odd turn of events. Kate's getting married? To the guy who dumped her for years on end? Why? What emotional hold could he possibly have over her after all these years?

Or am I being cynical? Maybe you only get one true love. She found hers early, but for some reason, she blew it. Now she has a second chance at happiness.

Dawn clicks back. "What the fuck are ranunculus, and why do we want to avoid the orange ones like the plague?"

Oh God. I'm back in Wedding Hell.

Eight

Don't watch more than an hour of television per night.

Around ten o'clock that evening, as I'm watching my fourth hour of TiVoed television (and trying not to think about the fact that Jordan never e-mailed or called me), Kate calls me, frantic.

"Promise me you're still coming to the wedding salon Thursday no matter what!" Kate demands, sounding beside herself with anxiety.

"Please tell me you're not stressing out about the wedding already," I beg.

"Oh, there's so much to do," Kate begins. "We've set the date for the third Saturday in June, and I've already booked the reception site, which is this lovely estate in Malibu. Thursday, we do the dress thing, the following week we'll do cakes . . . ."

"Honey, if you're not stressing out, then why do you sound like you're about to burst into tears?"

"Well . . . um . . . ," Kate continues, "it's just that . . ." She struggles to find the right words. "I'm thinking of asking Dawn to be my maid of honor!" Kate blurts out, clearly wracked with guilt.

"Oh?" I ask hopefully.

"I'm sorry!" she says, speaking a mile a minute, "I love you both so much, and of course I really want you to be a maid of honor, too. It's just, well, Dawn has never been a maid of honor, and you just got to be one a few weeks ago. And it just seems more fair if I ask her to do the honors. But I haven't decided for sure yet. Are you mad?"

I take a moment to collect my thoughts.

Am I mad?

Is she kidding?

"So," I begin, "would that mean that Dawn would get to throw the bridal shower, and the bachelorette party?"

I say 'get to,' when what I really mean is 'has to.' As in, *has to* hold your hand every step of the way, even when you fight with your family, even when you use words like *hyacinth* and *hydrangea,* even when you put her in a prom dress that costs her four hundred dollars. As in, *has to* be at your beck and call the entire day of your wedding, guaranteeing she can't enjoy herself at all.

"Well . . . ," Kate begins, stalling. "Maybe. I don't know for sure."

"Huh," I say, almost to myself.

Apparently, some days life is unfair in my favor.

"You know what Kate, it's your day," I say diplomatically. "Do whatever makes you happiest. As your friend, I just want you to be happy."

"Oh, thank you!" Kate gushes. "I love you. I knew you'd understand. I'm going to call Dawn right now. And of course I want you to be a bridesmaid."

"Thank you. I'd be honored."

"We're putting you in red and pink taffeta. Oh, it's gonna be beautiful. Long ballroom-type dresses. Very quinceanera, very debutante ball . . ."

Oh, dear. She's making that sound like a good thing . . . .

Kate continues excitedly. "Don't worry, it won't be polyester, but I think you should indulge me by allowing something with two layers of tulle. I figure we'll put flowers in your hair to match the gowns . . ."

I think I need a cookie. . . .

". . . and I'm learning all about dyed-to-match shoes!"

A very big cookie.

I listen to Kate talk about caterers, and invitations, and seating charts for another few minutes, then I let her get off the phone so she can call Dawn to gleefully announce the horror . . . wait, no, I meant the honor . . . that is about to be bestowed upon her.

Then I hit PLAY on my TiVo, and prepare for Dawn's wrath.

Nine

It's only good to be up at four in the morning if you are still up from the night before, you are not alone, and you have nowhere to go in the morning but brunch.

My phone rings at four o'clock in the fucking morning. Actually, 3:58 in the fucking morning. I pick up groggily.

"Hello," I mumble.

"Wakey, wakey," I hear Drew say to me, sounding as ecstatic as a nerd at a high-school science fair.

I sit up, confused. "What on earth are you doing up?"

"I'm doing a low-budget movie!" Drew says excitedly. "Actors who do low-budget movies get up early, go running, eat a healthy breakfast, then drive themselves to work!"

It's just too early . . .

I take ten seconds for a nice long yawn. "Drew, your call time isn't until seven A.M."

"That's high budget, wasteful thinking," Drew says, trying to sound like a drill sergeant (and failing miserably). "Now get over here. I need a jogging partner."

That wakes me up. "What? Why?"

"I can't go out running alone at this time of the morning. I could get killed. Haven't you ever seen *Law & Order*?"

"I don't think the jogger ever gets killed in *Law & Order*. I think the jogger's the one who finds the body," I say, not bothering to suppress another yawn.

"Come on, it'll be fun," Drew assures me.

"No," I say definitively. "Fun is going to the Neiman Marcus half-off sale. Let me call a personal trainer, and get someone out there for you."

"I can't afford a personal trainer," Drew insists. "Remember? I'm on a budget. But you're already on the take . . ."

It's too early to tell him if I were on the take, I would tell him to go to—

". . . and frankly, it's time to take off the tonnage you've gained since you quit smoking," Drew finishes.

Always be respectful of your boss.

I press the red button on my phone and hang up on him.

I close my eyes, and try to go back to sleep. My phone rings again.

I pick up. "What?"

"Too much?" Drew asks sweetly. "Because all I meant to say was that you're not getting any younger, your clock is ticking, and you can't be a size ten in the world we inhabit, which is what you're getting dangerously close to . . ."

I press the red button again.

Take two: Close eyes, phone rings . . .

"What?!" I hiss.

"When we get to Paris, do you really want Jordan to see you looking like you do right now?"

Two minutes later, I throw on some battleship gray sweatpants with holes in the knees, match them up with a raggedy T-shirt that I've had since high school, pull my unbrushed hair into a ponytail, and head to Drew's.

Never wear clothes with holes in them.

When I pull up to Drew's black metal gate about half an hour later, I realize there are a few photographers lurking nearby.

Swell. They're going to snap a bunch of pictures of him and me, and soon I'll be on page three of the *National Enquirer* listed as the "unidentified blob with no sense of style or hygiene."

I buzz Drew's intercom. All I hear is "mmm-brbrm-STATIC-mmph, mph."

"Uh . . . it's Charlie!" I scream into the intercom.

I hear more static and mumbling, but the gate slowly swings open, and I drive in.

When I see Drew and another man standing in the driveway, I am tempted to run Drew over with my Prius.

Liam waves to me as I pull up to Drew's garage, and park behind his soon-to-be disposed-of Koenigsegg.

"Charlie!" Liam says brightly, walking over to open my door after I park. He looks amazing. His hair isn't brushed, but that makes him look pleasantly rumpled. And he's wearing a black tracksuit with red stripes that look very utilitarian, but also very hot.

And I look like a troll. Damn it! Why, oh why didn't I wear the Juicy Couture velour sweats I bought a few years ago, even though they're already out of style? Why didn't I at least wear a pair of cute running shorts with no holes in them? Why didn't I brush my hair? Put on some makeup? Not eat like an elephant with PMS for the past six weeks?

"You look lovely," Liam says, giving me a tap kiss on the lips after I get out of my car. "Did you get the flowers?"

"Yes, I did. Thank you," I say, my voice catching from nervousness.

Why didn't I brush my teeth?

Twice?

And, seriously, would some Listerine have killed me?

I turn to Drew, and try to force a smile on my face. "Drew," I begin stiffly, "if you already had a running partner, why did you call *me?*"

"Because I didn't remember Liam was a runner until after I called you," he answers innocently. "Besides, I hate to bug you with details."

Sigh.

The three of us stretch for about ten minutes, then Drew opens his gate with a remote, and we take off jogging.

As we turn the corner and head slightly downhill, I can hear photographers snap-snap-snapping away.

Perfect.

For the first few minutes, I do okay. Liam has set the pace, and we seem to be going rather slowly. A nice slow pace, our knees barely rising. This isn't so bad—I can do this. Good thing I quit smoking.

I start to imagine my new life as a size four, and I am happy. I will shop for bikinis with Dawn, and not feel the least bit self-conscious in the dressing room. My legs will look sculpted, and will give Fergie's legs a run for their money. I will eat healthier, get slimmer, and finally be able to try on lingerie at the mall without the image in the mirror depressing me so much, it sends me scurrying to the food court.

Wait. I think my chest is tightening. And my knees are starting to hurt.

That's okay. No pain, no gain. If jogging were easy, everyone would do it. Think legs, think bikini . . .

I think I'm going to have a heart attack. As Drew picks up the pace, and Liam effortlessly follows him, I lag behind a step or two, and try to figure out if I can make a quick right into the bushes and hide.

No. I'm going to do this. I don't want Liam thinking I'm so out of shape that I'm incapable of running down to the Village and back. I think to myself, "Fight or flight," and get an adrenaline surge that allows me to run a little faster and catch up to the two of them.

"So, how is Ian to work with as a director?" Drew asks, his breathing completely normal.

"He's a bit demanding," Liam admits (also in a normal voice), "but the finished product is so gripping, it's an emotional price most actors pay gladly."

I want to seem witty and droll and make a joke about the emotional prices women pay gladly every day, but I don't. I can barely breathe. My throat is now burning, my calves are mooing, I feel like I'm about to be called to the light and—

"Aaaahhh!" I scream as I trip on a big rock, twist my ankle, and fall sideways into the bushes.

Drew keeps running. Nice.

Liam, however, immediately runs to my side. "Good Lord, what happened?"

"I wasn't paying attention, and I didn't see that . . . ," I say, pointing to the big rock in the middle of the road. I grab my ankle as I wince, "Ow, ow, ow . . ."

Truth be told, I was milking this a little. I had just accidentally run into an excuse to stop running, and I wasn't giving up my injury without a fight.

Liam puts his hand on my ankle, and although I have thought about the moment when he would caress me a million times . . .

"Ow!" I scream. "Son of a—"

Liam startles ever so slightly at my outburst, and I catch myself before I accidentally curse him out. He touches my ankle one more time. "I think all you need is ice. But, just to be safe, we should get you back to Drew's, and elevate the ankle."

Drew turns around and runs back to us. "Did you get hurt?"

I stare him down for his stupid question.

"Hm," Drew says. "Maybe I shouldn't have had Liam come with us. I mean, he did win the silver medal in the Olympic marathon."

"Actually, it was only the five thousand meters," Liam says sheepishly.

Well, is that all?

It's then that I notice the subtle little logo on the left hip of his track pants: the five multicolored circles of the Olympic games.

Liam puts my arm around his shoulder, and helps me stand up.

As I begin limping back toward Drew's house with Liam at my side, I think about an article I read years ago explaining that when a man sweats, he secretes pheromones, which makes a woman want to bed him. And it must be true. Liam smells amazing. Not men's cologne yummy—rolling around in a bed with him yummy.

I, on the other hand, just remembered I failed to put on deodorant before I left the house, and probably now smell like a skunk trapped in a diaper pail.

Which reminds me to write later:

Some days are a total waste of Wakeup.

Ten

Good soap is a cheap luxury. Always splurge on it!

An hour later, my ankle is feeling better, and I am freshly scrubbed, moisturized, and slightly scented, having used several of Drew's ridiculously overpriced soaps and lotions. I'm wearing a very cute miniskirt, oversized shirt (to cover my new girth), and slight heels to show off my new runner's legs. (I say that with my tongue firmly planted in my cheek.) Truth be told, I *may* have thought about my outfit the night before on the *off chance* that Liam would be on set today.

Liam had an early production meeting, and said he'd meet us at the location. But not before he rubbed my foot several times to make sure it was okay, and also make me really wish I had treated myself to a supercute pedicure.

Drew dressed in five-hundred-dollar jeans and a two-hundred-dollar T-shirt, then insisted that as long as I was at his house, I might as well drive him to work, so he could save on gas.

Argh!

The drive turns out to be harrowing. Not because Drew is in the car reciting today's lines while simultaneously criticizing my driving, but because today is the first Monday in November.

For about half the country, the first Monday in November is crucially important, and comes with a solemn duty and obligation that should be fulfilled every year if you are a good person. Am I talking about Election Day? No, that is the first Tuesday in November, provided that the first Tuesday follows a Monday, blah, blah, blah. End of civics lesson.

Although that reminds me to write in my book later:

Read about Elizabeth Cady Stanton. She was the most important woman in American history, got women the right to vote, and was still happily married with seven kids. To read her letters is to understand what every woman goes through trying to have it all.

Anyway, in my family, the first Monday in November represents the day we all decide where we are spending Thanksgiving. It's a time-honored tradition that usually involves negotiating, tears, and, quite frankly, vodka.

As Drew reads through his lines for the day, and I brave Los Angeles traffic, the first shot of the season rings out.

I expected my mother—longtime scheduler of all things evil. But my dashboard display shows it's just my dad's cell.

I pop on my earpiece, and answer, "Good morning."

"Your bastard grandfather has invited me to Thanksgiving," Dad says without so much as a hello.

I hate myself for having to ask this. "Which one?"

"My father. And you know I can't stand him or his kin. Marrying that little zygote of a thing, then making his own great-grandchildren. Originally I said no. But then he pointed out that he's not getting any younger, and this might be his last Thanksgiving. I mean, one can only hope. . . ."

"What about Mom?" I ask nervously. "I thought you were spending Thanksgiving with her this year."

"What about your mother? Let Chris go. He's the father of her child."

"You're the father of her children!" I yell, exasperated.

"Yeah, for now. But you know women. The minute they go on to the new family with the much younger Dad, they just forget all about the first husband."

My phone beeps in. I check the caller ID. "That's Mom," I say. "Hold on while I get her off the phone."

"No need," Dad says. "Love you. Bye."

"No, but Dad, before I talk to her I need to know where . . . Dad . . . hello?"

My father hangs up on me. Rrrr . . . . I click over to the next call. "Good morning, Mother. What are you doing up so early?"

"Just basking in the glow of my impending grandma-hood," my mother says pleasantly. "Did you hear?"

"Yes, I did," I say noncommittally. Truth is, I wanted to avoid Mom until Andy told her the good news. I didn't know if Mom would be thrilled to be a grandma, or start screaming about how if you successfully got past the velvet rope at Studio 54 without ever fucking the doorman, you shouldn't ever have to be called Nana.

I also didn't know if Mom was going to tell Andy about her attempts to make some grandchildren of her own (just ones that would call her Mom).

"I can't decide which T-shirt to wear today," Mom continues. "The one that says MILF in Training, or the one that says GILF in Training?"

Ugh. I visibly wince at that. "Mom, what did Dad tell you about that fashion choice?" I ask pointedly.

Mom says to me:

Don't wear T-shirts with words on them.

"And it's good advice," I tell her.

"Maybe," Mom concedes. "But right now, as much as I adore your father, he's on my shit list. The minute he found out we were going to St. Louis for Thanksgiving, he bailed on me just to go see his mistress."

"Wait . . . what?!" I stammer. "He told me he was spending it with Grandpa."

"Well, of course he did, darling. What was he going to do, tell you he was abandoning you to spend the holidays with his whore?"

"That's what he said verbatim last year," I point out.

"Yes, and I told him that was very poor form, and not to do it again. I mean, where would our civilization be without the ample use of white lies: the bride is beautiful, what an adorable baby, it was a mutual breakup . . ."

"Mom, there's a motorcycle cop behind me, I'm gonna have to call you back," I lie, hanging up the phone.

I promptly say into my Bluetooth, "Call Dad's cell."

Dad picks up on the first ring. "Did she tell you she wanted me to go to St. Louis to see those awful people?"

"You can't call Grandma and Grandpa that. They're my family, too."

"I'm sorry," Dad says, not the least bit sorry. "But I cannot stand by another year, and watch them treat your mother like shit. I'm one step away from punching your grandfather dead in the face."

Mom calls back in. "Hold on," I say to Dad.

"No need," Dad says cheerfully. "I'm calling from the seventh hole, and everyone's waiting for me to tee off. Love you, bye."

"Dad don't hang . . ."

And he's gone.

Damn.

I click back to Mom. "Yes?"

"Don't be mad at your father. My father has always rubbed him the wrong way, and Thanksgiving is unpleasant enough without a fistfight breaking out."

"I never realized your family was Irish Catholic," Drew says offhandedly, his eyes still glued to his script.

I turn to him. "What?"

"I can hear your mom on the phone." Drew says, not looking up from his work. "Fistfights breaking out at a family function. I didn't know you guys were Irish Catholic."

I furrow my brow at him. "That's a stereotypical—"

Drew puts his foot on the dashboard, and lifts the jeans on his left leg to reveal a two-inch scar. "I got this one at the Boston Thanksgiving, 2005."

Stereotyping is wrong.

Though, when talking about your own family, it is freakishly tempting.

"Oh, is that Drew?" my Mom asks, her voice suddenly lilting and cheery. "Hi, Drew!"

"Hi, Mrs.—"

I vigorously shake my head no. Drew notices.

"Miss—" he corrects himself.

More mad head shaking from me.

"Ms.—" Drew thinks a moment, then says in his most seductive voice, "Hey, sexy."

To my mother. Oh, puke. Someone find me a bucket.

Mom giggles like a geisha. "Ask Drew if he wants to come with us to St. Louis."

"No, he doesn't," I say firmly. "He's spending it with his family."

"Damn," Mom says. "So I guess it's just you and me this year. Anyway, I talked to your grandmother, and we've decided that we'll go to St. Louis for Thanksgiving, and then your grandparents and your Mawv will come here for Christmas."

"Whoa. What do you mean it's just you and me this year?" I say, trying not to let the panic creep into my voice. "What happened to Jamie and Andy?"

"Andy can't come this year. She and Hunter are going to New York for the holiday so they can tell his parents about the baby in person."

"Wait a minute. Why do I have to go to St. Louis and sleep on a fold-out couch while she gets to lounge around the Upper East Side of Manhattan?"

"Because she's carrying around my genetic material and you're not," Mom answers succinctly.

"So, Dad gets to go to New York with her, but I don't?" I ask incredulously.

"Don't be silly. Your father's not going to be with Andy on Thanksgiving. He's seeing his mistress in Brooklyn," Mom reminds me.

"Okay, well, I'd still rather go to New York and see everyone . . ."

"Honey, don't be hurt, but your dad is going to need a little private time with Catherine. He hasn't told her yet that I might be pregnant, and you know how much it upset her the last time, when I was pregnant with Jamie."

Drew laughs out loud at that. I turn to him and glare.

He immediately shuts up.

Wise man.

"And to answer your next question," Mom continues, "Jamie has to go to Aspen to meet his new girlfriend's parents."

"Jamie doesn't have a new girlfriend!" I insist.

Mom responds by ticking off a list. "You've lost weight. You're the biggest I've ever had. Oh, your choice to live in a trailer is so offbeat and whimsical . . ."

"Are we back to acceptable white lies again?" I ask my mom irritably.

"Yes. And you know your brother. I love him, but let's face it, he's a slut who can't stand to be hated by any of his former paramours. I'm sure he'll meet *someone's* parents this Thanksgiving. Now, I've got us booked for the Sunday of Thanksgiving week . . ."

"Sunday?" I whine. "Why do we have to go so early?"

"You said Drew wasn't working that week, so I figured that would give us some quality time, just the two of us."

What could I have possibly said in the past fifteen years or so that would make her think I'd want that?

"Besides, the only first-class tickets I could book were for Sunday," Mom continues. "And there's no way in hell I'm getting off that plane and into my mother's soul-crushing universe without a lot of glasses of Veuve Clicquot under my belt."

"Okay, Mom: In the first place, on the off chance you're pregnant, you shouldn't be drinking."

I can practically hear my Mom's head fall. "Crap," she whispers to herself. After a few moments collecting her thoughts, Mom begins again, a resolve I haven't heard in her voice since she vowed to take up skydiving. "Okay, still not a problem. I have booked us a suite at the Ritz-Carlton for six nights. This year, for the first time in my fifty-five years on this planet, we are doing Thanksgiving my way."

Famous last words.

"And what do you plan to tell Grandma when she insists that you sleep in your old bedroom, and I sleep on her fold-out couch?" I ask Mom.

"She won't find out what I'm doing until it's too late. As far as she knows, we're not coming until Wednesday. By the time she knows what's up, we'll already be settled in the hotel, eating room service instead of Spam. When she huffs and puffs, I'll just calmly tell her that, what with your grandmother's aunt Ethel staying with them, not to mention all the grandchildren and great grandchildren running around, I didn't want to impose."

"At which time, she'll ask how much money you're wasting on a hotel."

"Look," Mom snaps at me. "St. Louis is an absolutely elegant, beautiful city. They have an art museum, a symphony, a Neiman Marcus. Everything we'll need for a perfect Thanksgiving week. And I am not going to let my family fuck it up for me again this year."

I shake my head. "Mom, the words 'perfect' and 'Thanksgiving' bump up against each other in this family about as often as the words "transgender" and "Republican.""

"You leave your Uncle Colin out of this. Anyway, lots of people have perfectly lovely, drama-free family holidays."

"Not in our family they don't!" I blurt out, trying to suppress an amused chortle.

Dead silence from the other end of the line.

Shit. I can practically *hear* my mother glaring at me through the phone.

"Be at my house at eight A.M. sharp that Sunday," Mom finally says, signaling to me that the discussion is over. "And pack for rain."

"Mom, you won't know what the weather will be like until at least a few days before the trip."

"I know what the weather will be in my heart."

At this point, I finally stand up to my mother. "Mom, I'm not going."

Mom's silent on her end, so I take a deep breath and continue. "I know your feelings are hurt, and I'm sorry. But I am not going to put myself through a week of hell just to make you feel better. Let's just stop the annual insanity and have Thanksgiving here, with just our immediate family."

I can hear Mom take a deep breath over the phone. When she speaks, her voice is much softer, almost that of a little girl. "If we have Thanksgiving here, your grandparents won't bring Mawv here for Christmas. Mawv is ninety-five. I don't know how many more times I will be able to see her before, you know . . . ."

There comes a moment in every fight, a time of silence, where the next one who speaks, loses. Learn to recognize that moment.

Our moment of mutual silence has come. I am determined to win this argument, and I know if I say anything else, I will lose. So the two of us stay deadlocked in silence as I drive for a block and a half.

Finally, Drew breaks the silence. "No matter how famous you are, or how significant your mark on the world is, one day you will be forgotten. It may take a hundred days, or a million years, but eventually we will all be forgotten."

I turn to look at Drew, who says to me sincerely, "What matters in our lifetime—the only thing that matters—is who we touch when we're here. The rest is just footprints in the sand."

I narrow my eyes at him. Bastard.

"Fine," I practically growl to my mother. "I'll go to St. Louis. But I'm not drinking in the garage again this year!"

"Oh, I love you!" Mom says brightly. "I'm calling the airline right now to confirm."

"I love you, too," I say angrily, in a tone that makes it clear I am snarling one of those gracious white lies she's been talking about. "E-mail me the confirmation. Bye."

As I click off my phone Drew looks at me quizzically. "Why would you drink in the garage?"

"Grandma has a rule: No drinking in the house," I explain. "Grandpa has had a few bottles of Budweiser every night of his life. At some point during their sixty years of marriage, they compromised: people can drink, but only on the porch, or in the garage."

Drew just looks confused by this.

"I know. They're nuts. But I'm sure you're right, and that the only thing that matters is who I touch while I'm here. So I'll go."

Drew knits his brows together. "When did I say that?"

"Just now."

Drew looks at me like this is the first he's heard of it.

Then suddenly he remembers. "Oh, that!" he says. "I was just reading one of my lines." He holds up the script for me to see. And I read his character's line:

BEN

No matter how famous you are, or how
significant your mark on the world, one day
you will be forgotten. It may take a hundred
days, or a million years, but eventually we will
all be forgotten. What matters in our lifetime—
the only thing that matters—is who we touch
when we're here. The rest is just footprints in
the sand.

Oh, for the love of . . .

Drew flips through his script. "Here's another line I like: 'Trying to write on a deadline is like trying to have an orgasm with a gun to your head.'"

Drew gives the line some thought. "Actually, that's not as tough as it sounds."

Eleven

Avoid the 101 Freeway.

I spend the next hour driving from Drew's house through the crush of downtown traffic to Angelino Heights, a residential neighborhood located a bit off the 101 Freeway, and famous for its nineteenth-century Victorian houses.

Shooting a low-budget movie is very different from shooting a blockbuster. With a blockbuster, the studio will pay a few million dollars for script rewrites alone, and that's after paying the original screenwriter a seven-figure salary. You have a month or two of rehearsal time. You get five or six months to get the best performances out of the actors.

In a low budget movie such as *A Collective Happiness,* the few million dollars pays for your entire crew: the writer, the director, all of the actors, and all of the "below the line" people, meaning your grips, your costume department, makeup, sound, props, and so on.

A blockbuster film budget also allocates millions of dollars for locations and sets: If you're spending more than a hundred million dollars to make a movie, you can afford to shut down Griffith Observatory for a few days, maybe even close off a freeway or two. And when you're ready to shoot your "interiors"—which basically just means the insides of houses, offices, and such—you head back to the studio, and get a production designer (basically, what we call the movie's interior designer) to make a soundstage on the lot look like anything from a 1950s kitchen, to a 1980s real-estate office, to the perfect spaceship from the future.

Not so with a low-budget movie. Many low-budget movies are shot completely on location, usually in the houses of people who rent out their homes to film crews in exchange for thousands of dollars a day. (Still what I consider a lot of money, but chump change by Hollywood standards.)

And if the movie is really on a shoestring budget (like *A Collective Happiness*), someone on the crew inevitably gets talked into letting the crew use their house for free.

I'm not sure who that sucker is. Personally, I would never allow a bunch of crew guys to scratch up my floors while they move around cables, pockmark my walls while they move around furniture and props, and clog up my toilets doing God knows what they do.

But whoever it is who got talked into housing Armageddon has a truly exquisite three-story, gingerbread Victorian, complete with round tower and wraparound porch.

As I pull up to the large house, I am struck by its intricate beauty. Like most of the neighboring houses, this Victorian is painted in a bright color (purple), with blue and white trim throughout, and dark blue shingles atop its tower and roof.

However, unlike most of the houses in the area, this one also contains at least a dozen cars parked in the front yard, and a grip-electric truck, a camera truck, a generator, and a catering van parked in the backyard.

As I pull my car up to the house and park, a woman wearing jeans, black Prada boots, and a black Prada jacket over a crisp white T-shirt, walks up to Drew's side of the car, and waits for him to open his door so she can attack him with her eagerness.

"Good morning, Mr. Stanton. I'm Whitney. I'm one of the film's producers," she says efficiently as she takes Drew by the arm and begins pulling him toward the house. "Our director, Mr. Donovan, would like me to show you to the costume department. He's made a few changes to the script, and we start shooting in an hour, so we need to get you through there, then into the makeup chair."

I try not to be offended that Whitney not only doesn't introduce herself to me, she doesn't even acknowledge me.

"Drew, do you need coffee?" I say as I get out of my car.

Drew turns around to face me. "Triple vanilla latte with soy." He tells me. Then he turns to Whitney. "Where's your craft service?"

Whitney's face screws up ever so slightly. "Um, it's over there," she says, pointing to a twenty-two-year-old production assistant standing in front of a fold-out table that holds a coffee urn, paper cups, and a few dozen Krispy Kremes in their boxes. "But we don't have lattes. Just regular drip coffee."

Drew walks over to me quickly, Whitney following half a step behind. "They don't have lattes!" he whispers loudly, the panic storm about to hit.

"It's okay," I say to him calmly. "I'll just go to Starbucks, and get you a latte."

Now he's even more panicked. "You're going to drive around this neighborhood? Alone?! I can't let you do that!"

"Why not?" I ask.

Drew darts his head this way and that, looking around at the sleepy neighborhood. "This area is very sketchy. Do you know we're east of La Brea?"

"I *live* east of La Brea!" I point out, huffily.

"And I have offered you countless times to sell your place, and come live with me," Drew counters, sounding like a mother who's just seen her daughter's home in Berkeley for the first time.

I sigh loudly, then try a different tack. "Listen, you start shooting in an hour. I'm sure there's a Starbucks within two miles of here."

"How do you know that?"

"We live in Los Angeles. There's a Starbucks within two miles of anywhere," I say dryly. "Now let me go, I'll get your coffee while you're in wardrobe, and I'll have it here for you before Vic gets you in makeup . . . ."

"Susan," Whitney corrects me.

"I'm sorry?" I say to Whitney.

"The makeup artist's name is Susan," Whitney tells Drew and me.

Drew's eyes widen, but he keeps himself from hyperventilating. "What? Where's Vic?"

"I'm afraid we couldn't afford him," Whitney says offhandedly. (I note by her tone of voice that what she really means is, "There's no fucking way we're paying a thousand dollars a day for someone to smear down your face with foundation.")

Drew grabs my arm, his eyes wide as he leans into me. "I can't do a movie without Vic," he says under his breath.

"Yes, you can," I whisper back, noticing Whitney craning her head as she tries to eavesdrop on our conversation. "You're a handsome man, you'll be fine."

"But I'm supposed to look like a movie star for this role," Drew whines back.

"You *are* a movie star!"

"Not at seven o'clock in the morning, I'm not."

Whitney places herself between us. "Mr. Stanton, Susan has worked on everyone from Affleck to Vaughn. Trust me, you're in good hands." Whitney gently pulls Drew off of me, and leads him away as she turns to me. "As long as you're going to Starbucks, I'll take a Venti latte, nonfat, low foam, with whip. And get Mr. Donovan a half-caf tall cappuccino with skim, Miss Tavers a tall nonfat mocha, and Mr. O'Connor a Venti cappuccino."

As I head back to my car to track down a Starbucks, I decide I hate that bitch already.

After finding a Starbucks (one point two miles, thank you very much) and filling and delivering the coffee order like I'm Whitney's PA, I walk around the house and try to get a feel for the place.

The few Victorian homes I've been in have always been dark and gloomy. But this one is light and cheery. I walk into the kitchen, which has been transformed into a makeshift production office. The room has a bright, airy feel to it, and the appliances were clearly bought by a gourmet: a stainless steel Sub-Zero refrigerator; a Viking stove; All-Clad cookware hanging from a ceiling pot rack. Even the various production people and their various piles of papers stacked all over the counters and kitchen table do little to detract from the room's beauty.

I walk through the hallway and over to the drawing room, home to the first shot of the day.

The production designer has done an amazing job with this room. The cast will be shooting mostly interiors until they get to Paris, and one of the running jokes of the movie is that despite the home's exterior being Victorian, each room in the house is decorated in a different decade: this room is from the sixties, complete with beanbag chairs, lava lamps, and peace posters.

As I look up to see some grips rigging the lighting, and blasting a giant searchlight over the pinstripe velour couch, I hear my cell phone ring.

Drew.

I pick up. "Hello?"

"I have no trailer," Drew whispers to me.

"What?" I say, leaning into my phone. "I can't hear you."

"I said I have no trailer," Drew whispers again. "I have a bathroom."

"Well, of course you have a bathroom. SAG rules require—"

"Come up to the third floor, make a right, then an immediate left."

I run up the two flights of hardwood stairs, make a right, then an immediate left, and open the door to find . . .

Okay, yes, I do find a bathroom. A fairly small bathroom, but exquisitely refurbished, complete with a black-and-white checkerboard floor, and a bright red stand-alone tub with gold claws.

The room would be right out of *Architectural Digest* if it didn't have Drew sitting on the floor, wearing nothing but silk boxer shorts, and with his hand stuck in the toilet.

I'm not sure which is worse: the fact that I have to ask my boss, "Why is your hand stuck in the toilet?" in a completely nonjudgmental tone of voice, or the fact that this is the second time I've had to ask him that question during my illustrious career as his assistant.

Drew waves his good hand at me. "Get in here and shut the door," he tells me in a stage whisper.

I do.

"I think I may have done something stupid," Drew says.

I squelch my desire to either ask, "What was your first clue?" or state, "You have an amazing command of the obvious."

Instead, I go with, "What happened?"

"What happened is that they don't have enough money for star trailers, so instead, each cast member gets a room on the top floor of the house," Drew answers.

And that's it. That's all he says to me. Apparently, in Drew's world, the answer to the question, "How the fuck did you get your hand stuck in the toilet *again*?" is, "The film doesn't have the budget for trailers."

Sure. That makes sense. And the answer to, "What is the capitol of Zimbabwe?" is, "Sauté the shrimp for two minutes in lemon butter."

Drew and I engage in a staring contest for another minute or so before I cave.

"Aaaannndddd?" I ask, dragging out the word three syllables.

"And you know how I normally like to decorate my trailer to match my religious mood?" Drew asks.

"Sure," I answer.

"Well, *that's* why I got my hand stuck in the toilet," Drew concludes.

I should have gone to law school.

"Drew, do you remember geometry?" I ask him, starting to lose my patience.

"Vaguely," Drew answers, not sure where I'm going with this.

"And do you remember how they have the theorems that state: If A, then B. If B, then C. If C, then D . . . ?"

"Yeah," Drew says.

"You've missed giving me B and C again."

"Oh, right," Drew says, pointing to me with his good hand. "So, you know the amulet that goes through every character's life at some point, the really expensive one they got on loan with all the ornate diamonds, and rubies, and stuff? Well, I asked the prop master if I could see it for a bit, just to sort of get the feeling you have when you hold it. I figured I'd do the room up in faux jewels, maybe get sort of a *Breakfast at Tiffany*'s vibe going. Some blue-lit glass cases with necklaces and earrings displayed on nice velvet. Audrey Hepburn's character talks about the feeling she has when she's in Tiffany's. I thought I'd go for that feeling, but with a masculine twist of . . ."

I can't help but interrupt. "You dropped the amulet down the toilet, didn't you?"

"You're jumping to the end of my story . . ."

"Shit," I mutter, walking behind Drew, putting my arms around his bare chest, and trying to rip him out of the toilet. "I left you alone for five minutes!"

"You know technically, you left me alone for thirty minutes,"

Drew says in his defense, as though this is really all my fault. "You were out getting coffee when the prop master loaned me the amulet."

"That thing is worth at least fifty thousand dollars," I tell him through labored breath as I yank on him to no avail.

"Why do you think I went in after it? I don't have that kind of money lying around."

This from the man who once spent forty-five thousand dollars on a foosball table.

After unsuccessfully trying to pull Drew out two more times, I take a break, and take a seat on the checkerboard floor.

"I think you need more leverage," Drew says, his naked back to me. "What if you put your right leg up against the wall, and your left leg up against the bathroom cabinet? Then you can use your legs' strength to pull me out."

The fact that we're also going to look like a picture from a book on Kama Sutra positions hasn't even crossed his radar.

"Can I just say one thing before I try that?" I say from behind him.

"I'm not exactly in a position to oppose . . ."

"When we get to Paris, this is going to cost you two nights at the Hotel Ritz."

"A bargain," Drew states. "Now, get to doing the splits behind me. I'm due in makeup in less than five minutes."

Clown college. I could have gone to clown college. Or maybe become a fisherman in Alaska. . . .

I bend my right knee, and put my right leg up waist level against the wall. Then I bend my left knee, put my left leg waist level against the cabinet, grab Drew's chest tightly, then push off with my feet.

We land with a thud on the floor, and he's out.

Drew opens his fist, and sees that his hand is empty. "Wait. Dropped it again," he says, lunging for the toilet.

As I yell, "Drew, no!" he puts his hand right back in the toilet, and gets stuck again.

Oh, for Christ's sake . . .

"Why did you do that?" I scream at him.

"I still need to get the amulet out!" Drew yells back. "Otherwise, that's fifty thousand dollars of my money literally down the toilet!"

"Yes, but my hand is smaller," I say, sighing in exasperation, as I spread my legs, put my arms around Drew's chest again, and prepare for rescue number two of the day. (No pun intended.)

"I couldn't ask you to put your hand down a toilet," Drew says.

"You did last month!" I remind him angrily.

Drew face lights up. "Oh, that's right," he says brightly. With my legs sprawled about, and my arms still around him, Drew twists his upper body to face me. "What does something like that run? A third night at the Hotel Ritz?"

Before I can answer, there's a knock on the door. "Drew, are you in there?" I hear a concerned Liam call out through the door.

I let my head fall onto Drew's bare shoulder.

"Uuuhhh . . . yeah . . . ," he admits.

"Is everything okay in there?" Liam asks.

"Not exactly," Drew admits. "Maybe you should come in."

I stammer out a quick "No!" into Drew's ear just as Liam opens the door.

Oh, just the sight of Liam walking into a room makes me lose my breath a little. He looks positively doable in a light blue button-down shirt and nicely fitting jeans. I can't help but picture him in nothing but boxer shorts.

Speaking of nothing but boxer shorts . . .

"This is not what it looks like," I insist to Liam, who clearly doesn't know what to make of the sight of me with my arms and legs around my almost naked boss.

"I can't even imagine what it looks like," Liam says diplomatically.

"I can," Drew offers. "But, then again, I watch a lot of porn."

"You want to make it a week?" I ask Drew, smacking him on the shoulder.

"Hey! I'm a starving actor," Drew answers. "I can't afford it."

Liam scratches his neck self-consciously. "Can I ask what's going on?"

"Henry over in the prop department gave me the amulet to look at." Drew answers succinctly. "And I dropped it down the toilet."

Liam waits for more. Nothing from Drew. I shake my head slowly. "B and C, Drew."

"Oh, right," Drew says, then turns to Liam. "Obviously, since it's worth so much money, I thought I'd better go in and get it. But I got stuck. So I asked Charlie to come in here and pull me out."

"I see," Liam says. "Well, that sounds reasonable. But, if I'm not being too bold, can I ask you . . . why are you almost naked?"

Drew seems confused by the question. "Well, this is my dressing room. I needed to change." He points up to an outfit hanging on the shower rod.

Just then, Whitney shoots past the doorway, carrying a clipboard and wearing a headset. "Mr. Stanton should be finished changing. I'm going to his dressing room now. . . ."

I hear her stop midsentence. She backs up a few steps, reappearing in the doorway, and looks at Drew. "Oh!" she says. "Mr. Stanton, what are you doing in here?"

It turned out that the amulet that Drew had borrowed was one of seven copies made for the movie: the original amulet was back in the shop of the jeweler who designed it. It also turned out that one of the grips had some sort of tool that got the faux amulet out of the toilet in ten seconds flat. So, crisis averted.

Finally, it turned out Drew's dressing room was not a bathroom. He misheard Whitney's instructions, and when he got to the third floor, he went to the right, then to the left. He was told to go left, then right. Actually, he got the master suite of the house.

Ten minutes later, we had him all moved in, dressed, and ready for makeup.

I now have five minutes to myself, and a promise extracted from Drew that he was still good for a two-night stay at the Hotel Ritz in Paris.

Ah, Paris. I decide to head outside for a few minutes to make a phone call.

I speed dial Jordan, and prepare to leave a message on his voice mail. I had rehearsed it several times in my head. I would sound sexy, yet sweet, purring like a kitten as I said, "Hey, baby, it's me. Guess what? Drew took a job in Paris. Call me back."

And then I would wait for him to call me back. I'd be flirty, but nonchalant. I'd leave him wanting more. I'd make him miss me, and make him dream of the moment when we'd be back in each other's arms, drinking champagne in a romantic hotel room, making passionate love in the middle of the night, whispering sweet nothings in the Latin Quarter, holding hands as we walked along the Seine . . .

"Hello," I hear Jordan whisper.

Wait—he wasn't supposed to pick up.

"Uh . . . hi," I stammer.

"Hold on," Jordan whispers.

"Who's that?" I hear a girl whisper on Jordan's end.

"It's Charlie," Jordan whispers back. "Give me a minute. I'll be right back."

I wait for him to . . . what? Walk away from his set? Walk out of the girl's bedroom?

Breathe, Edwards. Let it go.

About twenty seconds later, Jordan returns to the phone with his normal voice. "Hey, what's up? Is everything okay?"

"Who was that?" I hate myself for asking.

"Genevieve," he says, pronouncing it with a French accent, and acting as though I've heard that name before. "So, what's up?"

"I'm coming to Paris!" I tell him gleefully.

"What?" Jordan says, sounding confused.

"I'm coming to Paris. Drew just took this low-budget movie, and part of it shoots in Paris. I'll be there at the beginning of next month!"

There's only a few seconds pause, but I wonder if that's because of the delay during long-distance calls, or a complete lack of excitement on Jordan's part.

"Oh," Jordan says. "Well, that's . . . um . . . that's great."

If you want to know what someone means, listen to how they sound when they speak. We've all trained ourselves to listen to the words, rather than the tone of voice inflected in the words. That's to protect ourselves. We all know from a man's tone of voice when "No," means "Yes." When "All right," means "I don't want to." And when "I Love You," means "Don't hate me, but I need you to go away."

I take a deep breath before I go on. "You don't sound like you think it's great."

"No, I do," Jordan says quickly. "I'm just in the middle of something. Can I call you back tonight?"

"Yeah. I guess," I say sheepishly, trying not to let the hurt creep into my voice.

"Are you mad?" Jordan asks me, sounding concerned. "You sound mad."

"No. It's just . . . I thought you'd be excited."

"I am," Jordan assures me. "I meant to call you yesterday. I have some news of my own I want to talk about. Can I call you later?"

My lungs are feeling constricted. I'm getting nauseated. My mind races with all the news he might give me, and all of it leads to our permanent breakup.

"Can't you just tell me the news now?" I beg.

Jordan sighs. "I really should be back on set. I shouldn't have taken the call, but when I saw it was you, I decided to pick up."

"Hey, sweetie," I hear behind me as Liam's hands wrap around my shoulders. "You know, in all the excitement, I forgot to ask how your ankle is doing."

I turn to face Liam, and force a smile. "Great," I mouth silently, giving him a thumbs-up.

"Oh, sorry. Didn't see you were on the phone," Liam whispers, smiling brightly as he pulls away from me. "I'll see you back inside."

"I'll be right there," I say cheerfully. Then I turn my back to him so he won't hear how pathetic I sound talking to Jordan.

"Who was that?" Jordan asks, with what I think might be a tinge of jealousy.

"One of the producers," I say a little too quickly, hoping to God he can't tell in my voice how much lust I have in my heart (or another part of my body anyway). "Why?"

There's a pause on Jordan's end. "No reason. Listen, I really have to go. Can I call you later?"

"Look, if you're going to dump me, please just do it now," I say sadly. "Otherwise, I'm just going to spend all afternoon waiting for the other shoe to drop, and dreading your phone call."

There's another pause on his end. "Charlie, I can't really dump you. I've been trying to stay a nice guy about this, but you do remember breaking up with me, don't you?"

There it is. I force myself to breathe, "I didn't break up with you. I said we should see how things go when you're away, and then decide what we're going to do once you get back."

"All right. Well, first of all, to a guy, that's a breakup."

"It's not really a breakup—"

"Yes, it is," he says a bit angrily. "And that's fine. I probably deserved it for all I put you through before. But don't act like you weren't just keeping your options open. The minute I left, I'm sure all of your doe-eyed suitors came back out to sniff around."

"Options?!" I say, completely flummoxed. "I don't have doe-eyed suitors. Name one doe-eyed suitor."

His voice is sarcastic. "Um . . . the guy who just asked how your ankle is doing. Should I even ask what that was all about?"

"Liam is a friend. You accusing him of liking me is right up there with my accusing Genevieve of liking you."

There's silence on the other end. Uh-oh.

"She likes you?" I ask sadly.

Jordan laughs a little. "No. Genevieve is gay."

A weight has been lifted from my lungs long enough to let me breathe.

Then Jordan hits me with his news. "But I've been offered another job. Starting in February. For a film shooting in Germany."

And the weight is back. "Oh," I manage to stammer out. "So . . . what did you tell the people who offered you the job?"

"I told them I'd think about it."

I think I'm going to throw up. "Oh." I take a deep breath, and try to barrel through the rest of the conversation as quickly as possible. "Okay. Well, um . . . I should let you get back to work."

"This is why I didn't want to tell you while we were both at work. I want to talk to you about this."

"No. It's fine," I say quickly, hoping to get off the phone before my eyes start watering. "Take the job. I get it."

"Charlie . . ."

I hear Drew behind me. "Charlie, what do you think of me turning my dressing room into a space station? I found this catalog that sells freeze-dried ice cream . . ."

I turn around to face Drew, and I must look pretty bad, because he stops talking.

"Oh shoot, that's Drew," I say into the phone, as I look right at Drew. "I gotta go."

Jordan sighs. "Okay. But can we talk about this later?"

"Sure," I lie. "But I gotta go."

There's more dead air between us before Jordan finally says, "Go to it then. Call me when you're ready to talk."

"Yeah. You, too. Bye."

I click off the phone. I force a smile as I say to Drew, "So, freeze-dried ice cream. I'm on it. What flavor?"

Drew cocks his head, and looks at me oddly. "Was that Jordan?"

I avoid the question. "Because I know where I can get Mint Chip or Ice Cream Sandwich. Any other flavor requires I get on the Internet and . . ."

Drew pulls me into a hug. He pats my back, and says, "It's okay, baby. Let it all out."

Ick. I don't want to get into this with my boss. I let my arms dangle to the sides, refusing to hug him back.

"I don't want to let it all out," I say, my voice muffled deep in his chest. "I'm fine."

"No, you're not," he says in a voice dripping in sympathy. "You're thirty, you're alone, you have a dead-end job, and your biological clock is ticking like a time bomb in the middle of Manhattan."

I pull away from him and glare. "That'd better be a line from your script."

Twelve

Men send confusing messages. Don't waste your money on books try-
ing to simplify or decode the messages. Sometimes, even other men
don't know how to translate the mixed messages. The only authors in
my day and age who claimed to know what men really wanted were
usually unattractive, wimpy, or both.

By late that afternoon, Jordan had already sent me two messages
telling me he missed me, and that he'd really like to talk to me. The
first one, a text, was brief:

> Are we still friends?

To which I responded:

> Of course.

Even though I think he made it very clear in those four words
that we were no longer dating.

The second one, an e-mail, was more confusing:

> Can I call you tonight? I miss you.
> xoxo
> J

Argh . . . I didn't respond to that one. I mean, I am completely within my rights to hate him now, right?

After driving Drew home, I head back into hideous Los Angeles traffic, and debate my options.

Well, there are the obvious ones: Ice cream. A bottle of wine. Enough cigarettes to fill a petting zoo.

Or, there is a more proactive approach. Go out and find a nice guy to flirt with.

But where does one find a truly nice guy in his natural habitat on a Monday night? Okay, we all know:

Karaoke is never a good idea.

But here's a thought: a sports bar.

I call Jamie.

He picks up on the first ring. "I do, too, have a girlfriend."

"You do not," I insist.

"Do, too—"

"Do not—"

"Do—"

"Okay, fine!" I interrupt, knowing my brother well enough to know we'll go twelve more rounds otherwise. "How long have you had this girlfriend?"

"Since the Halloween party."

"That's two days. You mean to say that after a two-day relationship she's already invited you to Thanksgiving?"

"Well, she has abandonment issues."

"Don't they all?" I say dryly.

"Yes. But I'm not gay, so I'll just have to deal with that. By the way, I'm writing my next article for *Metro*. Is it funny or offensive if I say I could hear a girl's knees snap shut over the phone?"

I sigh loudly. "Both, I suppose."

"Excellent!" Jamie says, audibly typing on his computer keyboard. "So, why are you calling? Obsessing about Jordan again?"

"Actually, no," I say firmly. "But I talked to him this morning. He's been offered a job in Germany this February, and I suspect he'll take it."

"Oh, that sucks," Jamie says sympathetically. "I'm sorry. Are you okay?"

"I will be," I say, and I mean it. "And part of my recovery is to go out and be social tonight. Do people still play Monday Night Football?"

"People?" Jamie repeats. "Well, twenty-two *men* play. The rest of us watch them."

"Good. I want you to come with me to Tonight Let's Score!"

"The fake sports bar?" Jamie says with a tone of disgust.

"It's not fake. You just hate it because it's trendy, and it has a decent wine list."

"Sweetheart, if you knew anything about men, you'd know we don't care about a sports bar having a decent wine list. We care about lots of large plasma TVs, cute little waitresses in tight little outfits, buffalo wings, and beer."

"There are also twenty-seven beers on tap," I tell him.

"I'm in."

I call Andy, Dawn, and Kate to invite them to join us at Tonight Let's Score! at 7:00 P.M., just in time for the second game of the night to begin. Andy and Dawn can come, but Kate can't make it: She and Will are going out to register for gifts tonight. After a momentary bout of jealousy (followed by the standard, "What's wrong with me that nobody wants to register for gifts with me?" self-hatred I've come to know and love), I decide it's time to focus on sports.

Or, at least the men who love them.

When I get home, I throw on some nice jeans, a yellow fitted T-shirt with the word LAKERS written in faux amethysts, and a matching baseball cap. (Why do they make baseball caps with basketball logos on them? And why do I even own such a thing?) Then I head out to Hollywood.

Beauty is only a light switch away.

Tonight Let's Score! (nicknamed Score by the locals) recently opened in Hollywood to become the trendiest local sports bar in town. Well, okay, other than the fake sports bar at Staples Center, this place is probably the only sports bar in town. For whatever reason (maybe our lack of a football team, maybe our lack of caring), Los Angeles does not have that many sports bars. Oh, we have bars all right: trendy bars to be seen in (think Hyde a few years ago), classic hotel bars that have become trendy, (like Stone Rose, or the Polo Lounge). We've got funky urban bars in downtown for the new condo set living there, and we've got divey bars on the Westside with a beach theme. But we don't have a local sports bar on every corner, like they do in San Francisco, Boston, or New York. Which is a shame, because we also don't have any kind of decent public transportation in L.A., so if a sports bar opened in Silverlake, I'd go some nights just so that I could walk home.

But I digress.

I valet my car, show my ID to Score's doorman, and walk in to find Jamie, who has snagged us a table in the middle of the room, and has already ordered a pitcher of beer, buffalo wings, nachos, and curly fries.

I look around the room. There are at least fifteen giant TVs showing everything from professional basketball and hockey to what I think might be a national cheerleader tournament. The waitresses are dressed in tight little referee uniforms.

I hate them. But I take a cleansing breath, throw my shoulders back, and walk confidently up to Jamie.

He looks at me disapprovingly. "The Lakers aren't playing tonight."

"I know," I say, taking a seat. "I did this on purpose. I don't want any guy hating me just because he thinks I'm rooting for the . . ." I grasp at straws to try and finish my sentence. "For the . . ." Finally, I have to admit my ignorance and ask, "Okay, who's playing?"

"The 49ers and the Chargers," Jamie says, pouring me a beer. "It was supposed to be a more interesting game, but since the Chargers' quarterback is out with bruised ribs, and the 49ers' top receiver broke his hand last week, I just don't know how much action we're going to see."

"None for me. I'm going to get some wine," I say.

Jamie continues to pour. "Rule number one in trying to get a man's attention tonight: have a beer. It implies you're low maintenance although . . ." The thought makes Jamie burst out laughing. "I can't imagine."

"The ratio of men to women here is eight to one. I'll take my chances," I insist.

"No, you won't," Jamie says, sounding authoritative, as though he's imitating some old coach talking to his players in a locker room. "Tonight you are in my house. I'm the coach. I've got the game plan. And you need to follow it to the letter."

I look at him blankly.

He rolls his eyes to the ceiling, then leans in toward me and whispers, "I know how these places work. You don't. This is my turf. You want a guy, fine, but do as I say, and don't embarrass me."

I nod. That seems fair.

Before Jamie can continue with his game plan, Dawn comes in, wearing a 49ers jersey and a look of contempt. She takes a seat next to me, and throws down a bridal magazine, which I immediately pick up. "In the past twenty-four hours, I have concluded that the three words, 'maid of honor,' are about as incongruous together as the words, 'great Bavarian food.'"

"Rule number two," Jamie instructs me sternly. "Do not read a bridal magazine in a sports bar."

Dawn waves him off. "Look up page one hundred and forty-eight," she says to me.

I turn the pages to 148, and see what might be the most hideous bridesmaid's dress ever: a neon pink satin ball gown, complete with hoops.

Jamie leans over to check out the dress. "Who would wear that?"

"Scarlett O'Hara's trailer-trash cousin," Dawn practically spits out.

"Wow," Jamie says, squinting his eyes, and moving his head in for a better look. "I think that might be the ugliest dress I've ever seen."

"Turn to page two sixty-four," Dawn says, pouring herself a beer. I do.

Jamie actually shudders as his body involuntarily pulls away from the magazine. "Wait, no, *that's* the ugliest—"

"Turn to page three twelve," Dawn interrupts, shaking her head.

This reminds me to write in my book of advice later:

One day you will get married. There will never be a time when bubblegum pink will be a fashionable bridal color. Ever.

"And that's just the beginning of her whole bridal craziness," Dawn chastises. "She demands that I read this article on guest list etiquette because her future MIL, whatever the fuck that means—"

Suddenly, Andy appears at our table, carrying a baby book in one hand, and several pregnancy and parenting magazines in the other. "What do you think of the name Dalton?" she says, throwing down her magazines.

"Addendum to Rule number two," Jamie says. "Do not read baby magazines in a bar."

"Oh, I love that little outfit," Dawn says, referring to a cute little sweater set worn by the cover baby of one of the magazines. She picks up the magazine and asks Andy, "Do you think that's Baby Gap?"

"Actually, it's Target," Andy tells her.

"Get out," Dawn says.

"Apparently, they do a lot of baby stuff now," Andy informs her. "I have been learning so much." She turns to me proudly. "Hey, did I tell you, I figured out what age-appropriate nipples are."

"Jesus Christ!" Jamie says, nearly choking on his beer. "Don't say things like that in front of your little brother."

"It's not dirty, you moron. It has to do with baby bottles."

"Oh," Jamie says sheepishly. "Well, anyway, moratorium on the wedding and baby talk. We've only got a few minutes until kick off. I need to give you your game plan."

Dawn looks at me for translation. I enlighten her as I continue to leaf through the wedding magazine. "Jamie has a bunch of stupid theories about how to catch a man at a sports bar, and we're indulging him."

Dawn shrugs. "I suppose knowledge is power." She points to Jamie. "Go."

"Okay, to start with, don't spout off about hating this team or that team until you know where his team loyalties stand. Same goes with players. You might hate Reggie Bush, but if he just got traded to your guy's team, you've already got a strike against you."

"You're implying I know or care who Reggie Bush is."

Jamie pays no attention to my remark, and continues, "You don't have to agree with everything your target says, but guys are sensitive if they think their allegiances are being impugned by someone they don't know well. This would be the same if the insults came from another guy, but presumably that other guy wouldn't be hoping to hook up later."

"I'm sorry. Did you just say *impugned?*" I ask Jamie. "At a sports bar?"

Dawn cracks up. "You know, that would be a good test for the guys here. Don't tell me Kobe Bryant's stats. Just use *impugne* in a sentence."

Jamie ignores us, and pushes on. "Next, don't act overly flirtatious or romantic right in the middle of an important play. At best, you'll be wasting your time, and at worst, annoying him. Make yourself known during the game, do the eye contact thing, but don't make your move until afterward.

"It'll be a breeze to approach him if his team has won the game. He'll be in a good mood and everyone around him will seem like great people. If his team has lost, his mood, and your romantic prospects, won't be as good. Unless it was a particularly devastating loss, in which case, you can console him over numerous Jägermeister shots and you're in if you want to be."

"Of course, if you do that, you'll forever be associated with the guy's miserable sports evening and corresponding hangover the next morning," Dawn points out.

"I didn't say my game plan was foolproof," Jamie concedes. "Now, quiet. The game's on!"

Dawn apparently has some interest in the game because she immediately turns around to face the TV screen.

And the game begins.

I ignore Jamie's rule number two, and go back to the magazine.

I have to! Wedding magazines are like porn for women. Pretty dresses, shoes, and lots of pictures of Tahiti. What's not to love?

As the center snaps the ball to the quarterback, I flip open to the magazine's first article: "Answers to your burning questions about shoes, veils, and lingerie."

Here's a basic rule on lingerie: if it's pretty, and doesn't have holes in it (except in strategically placed areas), men love you in it. They don't care about the color, or where you got it, or if you think it makes you look fat.

I may sound a little like Jamie here, but come on—this is not rocket science.

I flip through to the next article. Oh, good, a quiz. Turns out that because I want to sleep with Johnny Depp, I need a really modern Baccarat crystal bowl.

Hey, if I thought that bowl would give me a shot in hell of sleeping with Johnny Depp, I'd buy a dozen.

"When do you think Smith will be back?" Dawn says to Jamie, her eyes glued to the screen as she takes a swig of beer from her glass.

"Hard to say," Jamie concedes, eyes trained on the same screen. "I would guess they'll keep him out at least a few more weeks."

I read the quiz out loud to Dawn and Andy. "Who would you want more: Justin Timberlake, Johnny Depp, or Brad Pitt?"

Dawn turns to me. "To marry or sleep with?"

"Marry."

"What moron would answer 'Brad Pitt' to that?"

I hold up the magazine, and show her some suggested registry pieces. "A woman who needs flatware that looks like bamboo shoots with tines."

"Did you know the name Brad came from some World War I general?" Andy asks while reading her baby book.

Jamie leans into the table and quietly admonishes, "Ssh!"

Jamie then sternly informs us that we are only allowed to talk during commercials, unless it's about football.

I find out about a minute later that asking if Jamie knows if the cute quarterback is married does not count as talking about football.

The moment a commercial begins, my face lights up as I rest my chin in my hands and cheerfully ask Dawn, "So, has the whole maid-of-honor thing been horrible?"

Dawn glares at me, "Do you know that little heifer called me last night, while I was on a date, mind you, to talk about possible wedding favors. Like anyone really gives a damn if they get dragées at the end of the night."

"Dragées?" Jamie asks, squinting his eyes in confusion.

"It's a polished silver candy-coated almond," Andy tells him.

Dawn shakes her head like it's the stupidest thing she's ever heard of. "Yeah, like anybody over the age of six is going to want to bring *that* home. So I tell Kate that. She thanks me and hangs up."

"Point is moot," Andy tells Dawn. "Dragées are illegal in the state of California."

"Seriously?" I ask, "Why?"

"Some lawyer sued, alleging that the candies were toxic. It's not illegal to bring them into the state. You can consume them here. You just can't buy them here."

"I am not smuggling candy across state lines," Dawn vows.

I try to keep from laughing. "So I'm guessing, having been a maid of honor recently, Kate called you back *again* ten minutes later . . ."

"Five!" Dawn exclaims, thrusting out her left hand, and spreading apart all five fingers. "I'm on a date, which she knows, so I don't answer. So she calls me back. Again and again until I pick up."

I smirk.

"Are you smirking?" Dawn asks me suspiciously.

"No," I assure her, while still smirking.

"Good. Because then she asks what do I think of measuring spoons . . ."

I'll admit, now I'm lost. "Measuring spoons?"

"Yeah. Apparently some people give them to their guests as wedding favors. They include a spoon that says, 'A spoonful of laughter,' and one that says, 'A dollop of kindness.' At this point, I lose it. I say,

'Kate, you want your guests happy? Send them home with a half bottle of champagne, and a straw.' Then I hang up on her."

The game begins again, and Dawn and Jamie immediately turn their attention back to the screen. Andy is still engrossed in her baby name book, so I decide to take this time to scope out the men in the bar.

Ah . . . what a nice assortment to choose from: there's Lawyer Guy, complete with slightly undone tie (pulled to the side to reveal an unbuttoned top button) and perfectly tailored suit. He's good-looking, coiffed, looks like he wears Chanel for Men or Hugo Boss.

Then there's Writer Guy: He's with a group of friends, all of whom look like writers (they're all wearing some version of a team jersey and jeans). His hair looks a little unkempt, but that's okay. This is the type of low-maintenance guy who thinks it's weird that you spend twenty dollars on a scented candle, but not enough to withhold sex or anything.

In between the cute slob and Michael Clayton we have everyone else: We have the guys in oxford cloth shirts, some in bowling shirts (God, why was that ever a popular style, and when is it finally going away?), and many more wearing team jerseys. Two men are wearing Hawaiian shirts. Or, as I like to call them, "I've gained twenty pounds, and I think I'm fooling everyone" shirts.

Leggings are for women what Hawaiian shirts are for men: comfy, sloppy, and never sexy.

Most of the men look cute tonight.
And none of them is Jordan, my subconscious reminds me.
I drink some beer to try and drown her voice out.

Almost one and a half mind-numbingly boring hours later, Andy has already cited pregnancy exhaustion, and called it a night. I have made eye contact with a few cute guys, a few more have cheerfully high-fived me when their teams scored, and I have had various "conversations" (although I use that term loosely) about various football and basketball players with various good-looking men (but only during time-outs and commercial breaks, per Jamie's instructions).

But I've yet to strike up a love connection, so when halftime hits, I'm depressed.

"Do you realize how many of these guys have wedding rings?" I ask Dawn, dejected. "Which is a shame, because everyone here seems so genuinely nice."

"Well, of course they're nice," Dawn says, using the downtime to open her compact and check her lipstick. "These are the guys someone already picked and put a leash on. We need to go back to the shelter, and by that I mean the clubs we frequent, to go get one some other girl threw away."

Jamie sighs. "Guys, this is not a club, it's a sports bar. These guys did not come tonight hoping to meet a woman. They came hoping to watch a game."

"Yes, well, I go to bars hoping to meet the perfect martini, but that doesn't mean I'm adverse to an Abercrombie and Fitch model coming to say hello," Dawn says, clicking closed her compact. "Order another pitcher. I'm going to make the rounds."

Dawn hops off her seat, and sashays her way to the ladies' room.

Jamie looks confused. "Why doesn't she just admit she has to pee?"

"Because she doesn't," I explain. "She's pretending to go to the ladies' room to separate herself from the herd."

Jamie laughs and shakes his head. "God, I love that woman."

"Me, too," I say. Then I pull out my phone, and check it absentmindedly. No new e-mails.

As Jamie flags down the waitress for another pitcher, I stare at my beer.

"What's wrong with me?" I ask Jamie.

Jamie does this half-sigh thing he does when he doesn't know what to say. "Nothing wrong's with you," he tells me for the millionth time. "It's him. You only had a few weeks together. They meant something. Just not as much as you thought they did. . . ."

"But why didn't it mean as much to him as it did to me?" I half say/half whine.

Jamie shrugs his shoulders as if to say, "Sorry, sweetie."

I start playing with my cocktail napkin. "What's wrong with me that no one wants to stay with me? It's not just Jordan. It's Dave before him, and Marshall before him. Doug, Jim, Nick, Spencer . . ."

Jamie grimaces. "You really wanted to keep Spencer?"

"No. Okay, I got rid of Spencer," I admit. "Jim, too. But only because it was obvious that he was just killing time with me until someone better came along." I start mindlessly shredding my napkin as I ask, "What am I doing wrong that the guys I want don't want me?"

Jamie rolls his eyes. "You're not doing anything wrong."

I shrug as I continue to stare at my napkin, and away from the perfect guys in the bar with their perfect wedding rings and their perfect wives and their happy lives. I look over to see a beautiful blonde reporting for ESPN on the game. "Why can't I be like her?" I say, jutting my chin in the direction of the TV.

Jamie turns to look at the reporter. "Kelly Timbers? Why would you want to be Kelly Timbers?"

"Because every guy in this place is watching her," I say.

"That's because she's interviewing the Chargers coach."

"No, it isn't," I insist. "It's because she's Cameron Diaz."

"Huh?"

"In *Something About Mary*: Cameron Diaz is the perfect woman, she's a beautiful blonde who loves sports. Which I always said there was no such woman, she's a figment of men's imaginations designed to make the rest of us feel bad about ourselves." I point to the screen. "But there she is! That little hussy is a beautiful blonde with big breasts who can effortlessly flirt with a middle-aged guy as she asks about special teams and turnover differential. I hate her."

Jamie glances at the screen, then back to me. "Do you really think you're not married yet because you don't know enough about turnover differential?"

"No, I think I'm not married because I don't know what men want." I take the last gulp of my beer. "Though they all seem to be in universal agreement that they don't want me."

As I renew my interest in my cocktail napkin, Jamie looks at me sympathetically, then rubs my arm. He tries another approach. "Look, why do you think people make such a big deal about weddings? Do you think girls would make such a big thing out of the wedding, and the dress, and the party, and all that stuff if they found ten right guys and they had to do it ten times?"

I look up at Jamie, then nod my head.

"Okay, yes," he concedes, "you all probably would throw the party ten times. But that's because all women are bat-shit insane. My point is, it only happens once. There's nothing wrong with you. You just haven't met your guy yet."

"Do you think I'm fat?" I let slip out.

"Yes," Jamie says immediately, clearly kidding.

I laugh a little. Then I sink back into my depression. "I just don't know why this has to be so hard. Why can't I just find a guy who's cute, and funny, and nice to me?"

"Well, you have," Jamie deadpans, "but I'm related to you."

I give Jamie a snarky smile just as Drew and Liam suddenly appear at our table. "I'm sorry we're so late," Drew says cheerfully. "I left my phone on the set, so I had to go retrieve it. Fortunately, I ran into Liam there, and he had the game on, so I invited him to come with."

Liam turns to me, smiles, and gives me a quick kiss on the lips. "Hello, dear. I hope it's all right I've joined you."

"Of course," I say, confused, but not altogether unhappy to see him. He looks so good in a blue and green rugby shirt that it makes me want to take up the sport.

"What's the score now?" he asks.

At this moment, I have no idea. What are they doing here? How did they know we were here?

"Six to three." Jamie tells Liam. "It's been a bit like a soccer match. Everyone moves up the field—then nothing. Everyone down the field, then nothing."

"Sounds like my dating life," Liam jokes as he flags down the waitress, and signals he and Drew need beer glasses.

Is he joking? Was that a joke? Are men who look like that ever let out of a woman's bedroom once she's got him trapped?

"Will you excuse us a moment?" I say to Jamie and Liam as I pull Drew away from the table.

With the eyes of the bar following us, and people subtly using their cell phones to snap a photo of Drew, I yank him into a private corner.

"What are you doing here?" I say quietly, but urgently. "In the first place, I saw you leave with your phone. And in the second place, when do you ever drive yourself anywhere?"

"You know, I *do* have a driver's license," Drew says snippily.

"Yeah. And I have a treadmill," I counter sarcastically. "What are you doing here?"

"I was bored," Drew says cheerfully. "Dawn said you guys were here, so I figured I'd do you a favor, and bring Liam over. I checked, and he's totally available."

Drew smiles, gives me two thumbs-up, and starts to head back to our table.

I grab his arm and yank him back. "What are you talking about? Why do you think I want Liam?"

"Come on. Jordan dumped you today by phone. By phone! If that doesn't deserve a revenge sump-mmm, sump-mmm, I don't know what does."

"He didn't dump me. He is thinking about taking a job in Germany next year, that's all."

"You know, men are totally okay with being the rebound," Drew tells me. "We get sex, and we don't have to break up with you afterwards. So for us it's a win-win."

"I don't need a rebound. I have Jordan."

"No, you don't."

"Yes, I do!"

"No, you don't."

"Yes, I . . ." I stop mid-sentence. "You know, there's a reason someone needs to write your dialogue. It's not exactly riveting."

Drew crosses his arms, and looks at me accusingly. "You yelled at your iPhone."

I stare at him, confused. "What?"

"In the car," he clarifies. "When you were driving me home. Your iPhone beeped. You read the e-mail, then you made a yelly kind of grunt sound, turned off the phone, and threw it into your console so hard you nearly broke it."

That's weird. I don't remember my reaction to Jordan's e-mail being quite so violent.

"That was my mother," I quickly lie.

Drew flashes me a self-satisfied smile. "Darling, I'm an actor. I know behavior. If it had been your mother, you would have made a nasty comment about your family under your breath, then ignored the e-mail. But you wouldn't have turned off your phone. After all, you always need to be available for me and what if I was calling?"

I glare at him, not quite believing his story.

He shrugs. "Okay, fine. I saw his e-mail address at the top of the e-mail when you read it."

I nod. Yeah, that sounds more like what happened.

"Then I called Dawn to find out what was going on with you two, and she told me everything, including that you were here tonight trying to find a new man. So, I figured, why waste time finding a new man, when there's a perfectly good 'old' man you already want to do the horizontal mambo with?"

Ouch. He nailed me. I try to cover. "I never said I want Liam—"

"Oh, please. You want Liam like a shoe wants the other foot. Why else would you have me read the script for his movie?"

I decide to ignore the botched metaphor completely. "I told you to read the script because it shoots in Paris. Which is where Jordan is working until the end of January."

"Oooohhhhhh," Drew says, suddenly understanding. He looks over at Liam, casually conversing with Jamie and Dawn at the table. Then Drew turns back to me. "But you like Liam."

"No, I don't," I insist.

Drew looks at me suspiciously. "Do you want me to make him go away?"

I turn to watch Liam with the others. Damn, he is hot. "No, he can stay," I concede. "But I don't want you trying to set me up anymore."

"What if Orlando Bloom was asking about you?" Drew asks me.

"Was Orlando Bloom asking about me?" I ask, kind of intrigued.

"No. But I'm asking, if he was, am I allowed to set you up?" Drew says. "It's sort of like asking a woman if she'll sleep with you for ten million dollars. She says yes. Then you ask if she'll sleep with you for a dollar. If she says no, really she's open to the idea, but you have to negotiate. So, if I could set you up with Orlando Bloom, that means really I could set you up with Liam."

I've been working for Drew too long. I'm starting to follow his logic.

Drew looks up at the ceiling, thinking. "Wait a minute. Or was I supposed to ask you if you would sleep with Liam for ten million dollars?" He looks at me. "Or maybe it's me. . . . Would you sleep with me for ten million dollars?"

I roll my eyes, and can't help but throw one back at him. "I guess since you're economizing, you'll never know."

Before Drew can respond, I grab his arm and pull him back to our table.

After we take our seats again, Liam leans into me. "So, who's your team?"

I quickly glance over at Jamie for an answer. He mimes something that's completely foreign to me. I guess I let my eyes stay on him too long, because Liam turns to see Jamie pretending to shoot a gun.

"I was gonna have you tell him the Cowboys," Jamie tells me, smiling.

"Why?" I ask.

Jamie shrugs. "For my own amusement." Jamie looks at Liam. "Charlie doesn't know much about football."

"Oh," Liam says, turning to me. "So what is your favorite sport?"

Tonsil hockey. Naked wrestling in six hundred thread count sheets . . .

"Truthfully, I like playing sports more than watching them," I lie. "But Jamie invited us out tonight, so we decided to come out and see how the other half lives."

"Other half?" Liam asks.

"She means men," Dawn quips.

Liam gives her an appreciative nod, then turns back to me. "So how is it you were a cheerleader, but you don't know much about football?"

Dawn guffaws at that. I glare at her, then turn my attention back to Liam. "At my high school, the cheerleaders did a lot of dancing, so we were always focused on what the next dance or cheer was. We didn't really have much time to watch the game, we were always setting up for the next big cheer." Then I can't help but ask. "How did you know I was a cheerleader?"

"The night of the Halloween party: everyone kept asking you why you weren't wearing your cheerleader costume."

"Oh, that," I say, sighing. "I guess I should have just worn the cheerleader uniform again. It's just that I wear it every year, and I wanted to do something different. Of course, it made me look like a ten-month pregnant elephant amidst a horde of size-zero swans, but I hadn't completely thought that through."

"Nonsense. I thought your costume was delightful," Liam says, smiling as he takes a sip of his beer. "To me, it showed a woman filled with self-confidence, and a dash of whimsy."

Could the man *get* any more charming?

"Oh, *that* is an awesome closer," Jamie says, pointing at Liam appreciatively. "I gotta write that one down."

Jamie uses the wedding magazine as scratch paper, and writes down what Liam said. "I've already turned in my 'Lines Men Will Use to Get You Into Bed" article, but I can put that somewhere."

Liam notices the wedding magazine. "Who's getting married?"

"Oh," I say, trying not to be obvious about grabbing the magazine out of Jamie's hand. "Just my friend Kate. Dawn and I are bridesmaids." I roll up the magazine, and try to force it into my purse.

"Really?" Liam says, seemingly charmed by this information. "I love weddings."

What the hell does that mean?

Men are impossible to read. Make peace with it.

"Do you get a plus one?" Drew asks me. "Because I'm sure Liam would like to . . ."

"Halftime's over!" Dawn says. "Everybody quiet!"

I silently thank Dawn for the save, as Drew actually quiets down and watches the game.

Liam and I spend the next few hours talking during commercial breaks, which is the first time we've ever really done that. I learned that before he went to business school in Boston, he studied litera-ture and writing in college back in Dublin. He ran track in the Olympics, coming in sixth and eighth for a few races, then second place in the five thousand meter. He spent several years living all over the world putting together film financing, but bought a house here last year, hoping to settle down. No girlfriend as of four months ago (I can thank Dawn for getting that information out of him). Two brothers, one in Ireland, one in Boston. Likes Cuban cigars, Ten-nessee Whiskey, and playing soccer every Saturday morning with a group of guys who are all expatriates from Europe.

Favorite book: *Ulysses*. (Okay, but he's so cute, how can I hold that against him?)

All in all, good, solid boyfriend material.

Which, oddly enough, makes me sad.

Why? Because I have no self-confidence when it comes to guys like him. Particularly not when my last boyfriend has acted in a way that has made me feel old, and chubby, and completely worthless.

After the game, we continue talking. Once I have calmed down, and stopped thinking about him so much as "out-of-my-league guy," it becomes effortless to talk to him. He seems to really be en-gaged in everything I'm saying. Our conversation ebbs and flows, we talk about everything from Guinness brewing techniques to Shake-speare's "The Taming of the Shrew." Of course, several times during the evening, I think about leaning in to kiss him. But for the first time since I met him, I'm starting to think that if I took a chance and leaned in, he might kiss me back.

And just as Liam is hinting that he might want to bring me to see "Shrew" this weekend at the Taper, my iPhone rings.

I ignore it. Four rings, and it goes to voice mail.

Liam doesn't ignore it completely. I can tell he's made a mental note of the fact that I just got a call at eleven o'clock at night.

And before I can offer up some excuse, the phone rings again.

Jamie, who has been flirting with the waitress, watches me as I pull the phone out of my purse. "That's not Mom, is it?" he asks me, sounding irked.

Before I can answer, he saves me with Liam. "Because she just called me, and I didn't pick up. You know she's just calling to argue about Thanksgiving."

I check the caller ID. "You know what? It is," I lie. "I'm sure she'll just leave a message and go to bed." I hop off my seat as I say to Liam, "I need to use the ladies' room. Can you order me another drink? I'll be right back."

Liam says, "Of course," and rubs my arm as I grab my purse, and take my leave.

I walk quickly across the crowded bar, then around the corner, and into a long hallway leading toward the ladies' room.

The moment I have turned the corner and am out of Liam's eyeline, I key in my code to check my message.

I already know who it's from.

Message one begins. "Hey, it's me," Jordan says. "It's about eight A.M. here, eleven your time. I tried you at home, but you're not there. Or maybe you're just not answering. Listen, I know this is last minute, and I'm not exactly number one on your list right now, but do you have any interest in meeting me in New York this weekend? Turns out they want me to shoot some promo stuff there for the movie Thursday and Friday, and then they're giving me the weekend off. My flight leaves for Paris at about five Sunday night. Call we when you get this and tell me if you want to come out."

I have to say: I didn't see that one coming.

I peep my head around the hallway corner to see everyone happily chatting at the table, not seeming to notice my absence yet. Liam looks so good tonight, and he does seem interested in me. But just hearing Jordan's voice makes me want to crawl into his arms and stay there forever.

I have no idea what the right answer is.

I hide in the hallway again, and quickly dial my sister's number. She picks up. "Hello," she answers groggily.

"Were you asleep?"

"I'm in my first trimester of pregnancy. I'm always asleep. What's up?"

"Liam's here."

"Oh," she says disappointedly. "Had I known he was coming, I would have stayed. How is he?"

"He's fine," I say quickly. "So, can I ask . . . how come you never dated him?"

"Oh, God," Andy says, suddenly waking up. "You're not thinking of hooking up with him, are you?"

"Why? Is that a bad idea?"

"Mind-numbingly bad. At Harvard, he made Don Juan look like a wallflower."

"Oh," I say, both surprised and saddened by that information. "I suppose that shouldn't surprise me. Okay, thanks for the heads-up. One more question: Jordan just called to ask me to meet him in New York for the weekend. Should I go?"

Andy thinks about that. When she answers, there's a hesitancy in her voice. "Honestly, if it's a choice between Jordan or Liam, I'd go with Jordan."

"But . . ." I say, stretching out the word.

"But what?"

"Your sentence had a 'but' in it. You'd choose Jordan, but . . ."

Another hesitant pause from Andy. "Just ask yourself this: What would Jamie do?"

I thank Andy for the advice, apologize for waking her, and we say our good-byes. I click off my phone and think about her last question, "What would Jamie do?"

Oh, for fuck's sake. Jamie is a twenty-five-year-old single male. He'd sleep with both of them, and deal with the fallout later.

I dial Jordan's number.

He answers the phone on the second ring, "Hey, stranger," he says cheerfully.

"Hey, you," I respond anxiously.

"So, do you want to go?"

"Of course!" I say, surprising myself a little with my exuberance. What the hell am I doing?

"Good," he says. "It'll be really good to see you."

We spend the next few minutes making plans, but then Jordan has to get off the phone to head out to work. Which is good, because I've been gone from my group for more than ten minutes, and already I don't know how I will explain my absence to the table.

After we hang up, I debate what to do about Liam. I call Drew.

He picks up on the first ring. "Where are you?" he asks. "Is it a place to be seen? Are there paparazzi there?"

"I'm in front of the ladies' room, and, God, I hope not," I say quickly. "Don't let on to Liam it's me, okay?"

"Um, okay."

"I just figured out what I want in exchange for the toilet fiasco. I need Friday off."

"Okay," Drew says.

"And instead of a hotel in Paris, I want a first-class ticket to New York."

"But I'm economizing . . ." Drew whines.

"Business?" I suggest.

"Done," Drew says cheerfully.

"Good," I whisper. "Don't tell anyone it was me on the phone. I'll be right there."

I hang up the phone, then quickly head back to the table.

"Sorry," I say to Liam as I take my seat. "That was Andy calling, so I called her back. She sends her love." I look around to see Drew having his picture taken with some fans at the bar, Dawn talking to a good-looking man in the corner, and Jamie talking to one of the referee waitresses. "Did we leave you alone at the table?"

"Yeah, but it's fine," Liam assures me as our waitress hands him his credit card, and a check to sign.

"Wait," I say, as he signs the tab, leaving her a twenty-five percent tip. "You don't have to get that."

"It's not a problem. I brought one of our stars out to dinner. I'll charge it to the production."

"But that check goes back to when we got here at seven," I say, pulling out my wallet, and handing him a couple of twenties. "At least let me get some of it."

"Don't be silly. You can get the next time."

Pay attention to how a man divvies up the tab with his friends. A guy who throws an extra five dollars on the table for his meal is way hotter than the one who asks who ordered the extra side of fries.

I protest for a few moments more, then Drew, Dawn, and Jamie join me in trying to throw twenties at him (or, in Drew's case, hundreds; but he's economizing). Liam insists it's his treat, and he won't hear another word about it. Within minutes, our group collects our things, and heads out.

As the five of us leave the bar, Drew makes a big deal of stretching his arms out for a big yawn. "Man, I'm beat," he says, suddenly sounding exhausted. "Charlie, Liam and I came in my car. Since you're going to Silverlake, would you mind driving him home?"

Damn him.

"Uh, sure . . ." I stammer.

Normally, I would be thrilled with this turn of events, but right now I'm just torn and confused. I'm excited to see Jordan, but things are so wonky with him right now. And, meanwhile, I never thought I'd ever have a shot in hell with Liam, but for tonight at least, he seems interested in me.

Liam can sense my unease, and assures me, "I can grab a cab."

"No, no," I say quickly. "It's not a problem. Where do you live?"

Liam seems a bit confused by my question. "Angelino Heights," he says, with a tone of voice like I should already know the answer.

"We're shooting the film in Liam's house," Drew tells me. "Didn't you know that?"

"That beautiful Victorian house is yours?" I say, surprised.

"Indeed," Liam says.

I agree to take Liam home, and we say our good-byes. I am conscious of how he says good-bye to Dawn. First he says, "Lovely to see you again," and then he kisses her good-bye.

Right. This is Hollywood. Everyone kisses everyone hello and good-bye.

So why did the tiniest spark of jealousy just fly through me?

I'm a terrible person, I think to myself as Liam walks me to my Prius. As we chat about his Victorian home—when he bought it, all he's done to improve it, why he wishes he had never bought a house with sixty-year-old plumbing—my mind wanders, and I can't help but think about kissing him again . . .

If a man has walked you to your car or your door, and you want to linger (and hint that you want a kiss), pretend not to be able to find your keys.

I get my keys from my purse before we get to the car. I beep my alarm, then beep it a second time to open all the doors.

Even though I'm still thinking about kissing him.

As I drive Liam home, the conversation flows freely. He's funny and interesting, and normally this would be the end of a really great first date.

A tangential thought occurs to me: Has anyone ever had a really great first date that started out as a first date? I'm just curious. My experience with really great first dates is that either I've been out with the guy several times before I even realized I was on a date or, alternately, I met the guy that first night, and made out with him that first night, which means by the time we actually got around to the first date, really it was a second date. So the whole idea of a great first date: fact, or one of those urban myths comparable to the Mexican pet or the emotionally available single man over thirty?

As we pull up to Liam's house, he cuts into my thoughts.

"So," Liam says pleasantly, "are we on for 'Taming of the Shrew' this weekend?"

I'm awful. I'm a dreadful person. I went out fishing tonight, and now I'm playing catch and release.

"Uh . . . I can't," I say awkwardly. "I'm afraid I have to go to New York this weekend."

Liam looks a bit confused. "Oh. I'm sorry. I didn't realize that." His face immediately brightens. "What's the occasion? Visiting friends?"

"Actually, my boyfriend," I find myself saying.

Liam's eyes open a bit wider, so I quickly rush to explain. "I don't even know if I can call him my boyfriend. He's a guy I date. Sort of. He's working in Europe right now, but he's in New York this weekend, so I'm going to go visit him, and see how things go."

Liam smiles and gives me a quick nod of the head. "Well, he's a very lucky man. See you tomorrow?"

"Absolutely," I say, trying to sound cheery and casual.

"Great," he says, disarming me with his easy smile.

I get my "friends only" nonromantic kiss good-bye, and then Liam gets out of my car, and walks up the pathway toward his house.

I watch him as he unlocks the door, turns to me, and waves good night.

I wave back.

Hmmm. Seems like I may have just tackled myself on the two-yard line.

Thirteen

I spend the next two days running various errands for Drew. I went to college for four years so I could pick up dry cleaning, deal with fan mail, and buy birthday gifts for all of his close personal friends who were born in the month of November. (Although, in all fairness, a morning shopping at Tiffany's really is more pleasant than a lot of other jobs.)

I didn't see Liam, and frankly, I didn't know what I'd have said if I had. I hadn't wanted him to know about Jordan. I'm not sure if I wanted to keep my options open because things with Jordan weren't working out, or because I was so used to being chronically single that I was sure I'd be single again soon.

Side note: When are any of us absolutely sure that we're never going to be single again? Does anyone over the age of sixteen ever really have that love-at-first-sight moment when they see the guy next to the barbecue at a friend's house doling out hamburgers, and they know he's the one they'll be holding hands with at eighty? Or do we know after the first date? The third? After we've been proposed to? Walked down the aisle? Or had his first child?

Speaking of people who know they'll never be single again, the day before I leave for New York, I take a few hours in the afternoon to slip away from the set, and head to Beverly Hills to help Kate pick out her wedding gown.

I drive to the same bridal salon I graced with my presence a little more than two months ago, when I was the maid of honor for Andy's wedding. That time, the bride put me in a silver dress that made me look like a baked potato in dyed-to-match heels. On the plus side, how much worse can it get?

The secret to happiness is low expectations.

I walk into the posh salon, and look around. There's a twentysomething girl in a pastel pink suit quietly taking an order over the phone in a hushed, "soothing" tone of voice, and other than that, the place is empty. The clerk looks over to me, smiles brightly, and silently raises her index finger to indicate that she'll be with me in a moment.

I smile back, then seat myself at one of the spotless white overstuffed chairs that perfectly match the unsullied white plush carpeting, and the immaculate white damask walls. I pick up a bridal magazine from the sparklingly clean glass table, and flip open to the first article: A guide to making the perfect bridesmaid's tote bag. (Because God knows how one's nearest and dearest have lived so long without a lime green tote bag that says "Janet and Ted: Soulmates Forever" in pink embroidery.)

I flip a few pages to the next article: the ins and outs of designing the perfect wedding program guide. (Frankly, I think it's a bad idea to let your guests know in advance that right after your processional, your great-aunt Doris plans to solo "You Light Up My Life." This information tends to encourage guests to sneak out mid-ceremony).

And finally, why it's a good idea for brides to carry moneybags at their wedding.

Classy.

I would later write in my journal of advice:

Some advice for your future wedding:
1. *It's NEVER a good idea to carry a moneybag at your wedding. Nor is it a good idea to register for mortgages or stock certificates. Nor can you tell your guests you want cash for your gift. This is a wedding, not a charity event.*
2. *Don't have a cash bar.*
3. *Don't wear a miniskirt on your wedding day. Unless you're in Vegas. And on wedding #4 or higher.*

Finally, I get to an article debating the pros and cons of a honeymoon in Hawaii. Apparently, there are cons to vacationing in Hawaii. Right. I suppose there are also cons to two-hour massages, any kind of chocolate, and twenty-two-year-old models you don't have to call the next day. Before I can read too much, I hear Dawn's voice above me: "Explain to me how it is that an intelligent women with all of her faculties can send her black friend a PDF of bridesmaids' dresses that begins with the title, 'You Can Never Have Too Much Black in Your Closet'?"

"Oh, please," I say, referring to yet another set of pictures of hideous dresses Kate e-mailed to both of us last night. "I'd kill to wear one of those. Did you see the PDF of the dresses that included the phrase 'The Joy of Sex'?"

Dawn's face falls into an oh-my-God look. "I missed that one. Though I did get the attachment of the ones where we'll look like decorated Christmas trees. I wrote back, 'You put us in anything taffeta, I swear to God, I'm putting a hit out on you.'"

Dawn falls into the seat next to me. She leans in and whispers, "This is the guy who dumped her seventeen times. What is she thinking anyway?"

The salesclerk quietly hangs up the phone, then perkily walks over to one of the dressing rooms, and knocks on the door. "What do we think of the Monique Lhuillier?"

The dressing room doors open, and we see Will's body pressing a half-zipped (unzipped?) Kate against the wall. The two have just broken from a passionate kiss as Will moves his hand out from under Kate's white gown.

"And the plot sickens," Dawn says, shaking her head.

"Uh, it's very nice," Kate says to the clerk, averting her eyes as she zips up the beaded gown.

Kate and Will smile, and exchange a "knowing glance" at each other (I hate that.) As they smooth down their clothes, I notice Kate is actually blushing.

Hell, Will is actually blushing. "Ladies," he says, walking out of the dressing room, then slightly bowing. "So sorry about that. We were just talking about . . ."—Will turns to Kate and smiles a conspiratorial smile—"wedding favors."

"I would say she was about thirty seconds from giving you a big wedding favor," Dawn says jokingly.

Kate looks away from us coyly as she smoothes down her hair.

My friend, my political-talk-show-host friend—the one who asked Bill Clinton point-blank what his exact definition of sex was, then a week later asked Tom DeLay who his ideal prisonmate would be—is actually coyly looking away from us.

I think I might be ill.

"Okay, I'm going to call the Biltmore right now. I'll see you in a few hours," Will says to Kate.

Kate nods.

Will kisses her lightly on the lips. "You're sure you'd rather do a hotel downtown, instead of the beach?"

"Of course," Kate says, her face brightening. "I loved the Emerald Room. And it's going to look magical with all the green and white flowers."

Will looks her over lasciviously, and brushes his hand over her left hip. "And I think we should book the bridal suite."

Again with the coy look. Puke.

"I love you," Will nearly whispers.

"I love you more," Kate says in that half baby talk/half-whisper thing couples do that I loathe and despise.

"I can't wait to marry you," Will whispers.

They kiss again, and Will turns to us. "Ladies, Kate and I have decided on your dresses. You can blame me if you hate them."

"I just might," I attempt to joke. "How many layers of tulle have you allowed her to drape us in?"

Will looks confused, so Dawn clarifies. "Ugly netting that goes over dresses."

Still confused, will turns to Kate for an explanation. "I'll handle this," she assures him. "You go book the hotel."

Will smiles, waves good-bye to all of us, and leaves.

We watch him pull out his cell phone as he walks out the glass double doors, and onto the sidewalk. Once the doors are shut, and Kate's sure he's out of hearing range, she turns to us excitedly.

She beams. "Can you believe it?" she asks. "And check this out."

Kate puts out her left hand to show off her new engagement ring.

"Wow," I say, stunned (and, admittedly, a little jealous) as I take her left hand, and lift it up to the light.

The center stone is a rectangular emerald-cut diamond that's at least two carats—probably two and a half—with three smaller rectangular emerald-cut diamonds on each side, all set in shiny platinum. It is stunningly beautiful.

Dawn looks at it, and cocks her head. "I thought you always wanted a Royal Asscher cut."

This is true. Back in our freshman year of college, we all talked about our dream engagement rings. (Are women pathetic, or what?) Dawn wanted what I thought was uncharacteristic for her: a vintage diamond ring from the 1940s with lots of small stones that sparkle. I wanted a one carat round diamond, set in platinum.

Kate was even more specific: she wanted a Royal Asscher cut—the antique cut, not the newest Asscher cut with the sixteen extra facets. It basically looked to me like a puffy octagon but a little bit more sparkly. And she wanted it set in white gold—not platinum—because she thought that made it look the tiniest bit antique-y.

"I did," Kate admits to Dawn. "But when we were actually at Tiffany's I decided I liked this one better."

Dawn continues with her interrogation. "And why is Will calling the Biltmore Hotel? I thought you booked an estate in Malibu."

"I did." Kate says, pinching up her nose, "but we've decided to move up the wedding to New Year's Eve, and I wasn't sure if the place in Malibu was available. Plus, I started thinking about how many guests are coming from the Eastside. You, Charlie, all of Will's friends . . . so I thought a nice downtown hotel would be easier on the guests. Plus, you can't really do elegant at the beach, and we're spending so much, I really want everything to be perfect."

Now don't me wrong: I love the Biltmore. It's one of the prettiest hotels in town, and I've gone to weddings there that were exquisitely beautiful. But Kate has always wanted a beach wedding. And a Royal Asscher–cut diamond. And a June wedding.

The salesgirl distracts my thoughts by appearing with a dark green, strapless velvet gown with a satin ribbon that wraps around the hip into a bow.

"Kate and Will have chosen this dress for Kate's maids," the salesgirl says in a bubbly voice. "The maids will be in forest green, the maid of honor in emerald green. The dress has a bias cut, emphasizing the waist, and a slit up the left leg to make walking and dancing a breeze. The bow is subtle, yet dramatic, and the top area is fitted with a built-in corset. This dress makes any woman look like she has the perfect figure."

"How can something be subtle yet dramatic?" Dawn asks.

"We love it!" I say emphatically. "We'll take it!"

Dawn is unconvinced. She turns to Kate. "Kate, this is beautiful, but it doesn't look like any of the dresses you've been talking about."

"I know," Kate concedes, "but I've decided that the dresses I was looking at don't really fit in with the tone of our wedding. We're going for sophisticated. Classic. My ideas for bridesmaids' dresses came from being a flower girl twenty-five years ago. Styles change." She smirks. "And, besides that, one day I'm going to be your bridesmaid, and I don't want you trying to get even."

Dawn smiles, and does what every maid of honor has done at least twice before a wedding: She bites her tongue. "It's perfect. I love it."

"Yay," Kate says, clapping her hands a little. Then her look turns somber. "Okay, now I have a serious wedding problem that only my dearest friends can help me solve."

Uh-oh. I've seen my sister Andy with that look: Are Kate's divorced parents refusing to sit together? Is her grandma so sick she can't fly to the wedding? Will one of us be assigned to keep Uncle Harry away from the bar?

Kate looks at us in all seriousness. "Sometime in the next few weeks, I will need to pick a cake. Will doesn't like sweets, and he has no interest in learning the difference between ganache and buttercream. Can I count on you guys to help me taste cakes?"

"Oh, sweetie," I say sarcastically as I put my hand over my heart. "You know you never need to ask."

As Kate smiles, her cell phone rings. She walks to her purse to get it. She checks the caller ID, then opens her phone. "Hey, Jack," she nearly purrs.

Yes, I said *purrs*.

Then she quickly tries to walk away from us to talk.

"Whoa, whoa, whoa," I say, grabbing Kate before she can make her escape. "Why are you on the phone with Jack if you're marrying Will?"

Kate quickly covers the phone. "Shh!" she whispers. "I haven't told Jack about the marriage yet."

"You what?" Dawn exclaims.

"I haven't told him yet," she repeats in a whisper. "I called him yesterday to tell him, but we had this really great talk, and I didn't have the heart to tell him then. I'm gonna tell him Sunday night, over dinner."

"Dinner?" I ask, trying not to sound alarmed.

"Yes. We're having dinner at Mario's. I need to get him in a public place, so he won't make a scene."

You don't need to take a man out to dinner so he won't cause a public scene. Men don't cause scenes in public—women do.

Kate quickly walks away from us to finish her conversation. I turn to Dawn, who turns away from Kate to inspect our new brides-maids' dresses. "Which part did you find more interesting?" I ask Dawn. "The fact that her favorite color is red, but her wedding is in two shades of green? Or the fact that she's on the phone with her ex-boyfriend of nine years?"

Dawn shakes her head. "Oh, I'd say the fact that she's meeting her ex for dinner at the restaurant where they shared their first kiss."

Fourteen

Some nights are a total waste of new lingerie.

The weekend should have gone off without a hitch. I had booked a red-eye flight Thursday night, and played the romantic weekend over and over again in my head to get me through the lonely nights of my week.

I was to leave LAX at 11:25 P.M., have a cocktail and some nuts on the plane, then fall asleep to awake refreshed and ready for romance when the plane landed at JFK at 7:48 the next morning. I would take my time getting my luggage, hail a cab, then drop off my luggage at Room 2516 of the W hotel in Times Square, where Jordan was already staying. At that point, I would have a leisurely lunch at Pastis, then cab it over to the West Village to do a little lingerie shopping at La Petite Coquette before meeting Jordan back at the room.

Woman plans, God laughs.

I called the limo service to pick me up at my house in Silverlake at 8:30. Sharp. Which theoretically should have given me plenty of time to get to the airport, go through security, blah, blah, blah.

The limo does come to my house at exactly 8:30.

And that is the last thing that goes right for the next twenty-four hours.

When we get to LAX at nine o'clock, we come to a long line of stopped cars. The driver turns on KFWB News to hear that LAX is completely shut down due to a bomb scare.

Not one car moves for the next twenty minutes.

Ten minutes of non-movement after that, I call Jordan.

He picks up. "Are you here already?"

"Hardly," I say, trying to cover my panic. "LAX is completely shut down."

"What do you mean it's shut down?" Jordan asks, concerned.

"Bomb scare."

"Oh," he says, his voice relaxing. "Well then, it'll probably be half an hour, forty minutes tops. We're fine for time. Listen, when you get to the W, the room key is waiting for you at the front desk. Promise me you'll just drop off your stuff, and not snoop around."

"Okay," I say, my voice brightening as I decide to sound a little kittenish. "Why?"

"I may have ordered a few things to begin our weekend on a romantic note," Jordan says mysteriously.

"Really?" I say, intrigued. "Like what? Champagne? Strawberries? A pink satin blindfold?"

"Ma'am, I can hear you up here," my driver informs me in his nondescript foreign accent.

Jordan's phone is cutting out, so we say our good-byes.

Fifteen minutes later, I call him back to say we still haven't been allowed into the airport. I go right to his voice mail.

When you're heading down the wrong path, there are usually lots of signs warning you along the way. Be intelligent. Pay attention to the signs.

I don't even vaguely pay attention to the obvious signs of doom. At eleven o'clock, cars are finally allowed to start coming into the airport.

But security is heightened, so it takes me another two hours to get through security. All flights are leaving late, so at least I don't miss my plane. But by the time I'm finally on the plane and ready for takeoff, it's almost two in the morning.

No matter, I will still be in New York by ten o'clock in the morning. I'll just drop off my stuff at the hotel then, instead of Pastis, I'll hit a street vendor for a falafel or a hot dog, then go to Petite Coquette.

And tonight I will finally get to see Jordan again. The thought puts butterflies in my stomach.

As I settle in my seat, the airline attendant offers me a glass of Pommery Brut champagne and some peanuts.

I calm myself down. Okay, so things didn't go according to plan: I am in a business-class seat with a glass of champagne in my hand, preparing for a fabulously romantic weekend with my fabulously sexy boyfriend. Life is good.

I smile to myself as I pull out the copy of *War and Peace* I've been reading for the past few months, and begin reading.

Twenty minutes, and twelve pages, later, the plane still hasn't left the gate.

Ten minutes after that, I hear our captain over the loudspeaker. "Ladies and gentleman, this is your captain speaking. We're having a small problem with one of the parts of our left engine. We're just gonna have our mechanics look at it, and we should be on our way momentarily."

Noooo . . .

An hour and a half after that, I am off the plane, calling Jordan, and getting his voice mail again. "Okay, we've had a slight setback,"

I say, trying to sound cheerful despite the fact that I want to rip out my hair. "It's almost four here, something was wrong with the engine, and we all needed to get off the plane. But they're bringing us another plane now, and we should take off soon."

Then at five o'clock: "Okay, I'm boarding now. I can't wait to see you."

And at 6:30: "Did you know that if all of the passengers get off a plane, but then not all of the passengers get back on, they have to rifle through everyone's luggage to find the missing person's luggage, and throw it off the plane?"

At 7:45 in the morning, we are finally on the runway, and heading to New York.

By way of Connecticut.

Because apparently, even in November, a hurricane can hit New York. I'm sorry—I'm exaggerating. As my local weatherman had cheerfully told me on the Six o'clock News the night before, Hurricane Steven had been downgraded to a tropical storm as it headed toward New York, and because it was November, it would be nothing more than a lot of rain.

Wrong. We landed in Hartford, Connecticut, at four in the afternoon. I immediately turned on my phone to two messages from Jordan.

"Hey, it's me," Jordan says, sounding relaxed and cheerful. "I'm done with the job, and heading back to the W. I'm calling from a pay phone. Something is wrong with my cell. I got your messages. I'm sorry you're having such a hard time, but I promise things will be great once you get here. So, just call me at the hotel when you land, and we'll take it from there."

"Me again," Jordan says, now sounding a bit stressed. "I think you're flight number 668, in which case, you're still up in the air. I'm going to go out for a while. I have to pick up the tickets to *The Coast of Utopia* I bought for tonight. I hope you'll be here by then. Bye."

I call the hotel immediately, but Jordan isn't in his room. I leave a message that the airline is bringing us back down to New York in a bus, and that I should be to JFK in two and a half hours, and to him within three and a half.

Only I didn't take into account that a bus driving through a tropical storm might take longer to get where it's going than, say, a crazed and horny thirty-year-old in a rental car.

I finally see Jordan at nine o'clock that evening.

The moment Jordan opens the door to our hotel room, my gut tells me that I shouldn't have come.

Oh, he looks perfect in his jeans and cable-knit sweater. He's still his usual dark-haired, green-eyed, breathtakingly handsome self.

But he also looks pensive. Nervous (and not in the good way). And, frankly, a little pissed.

Meanwhile, I am sopping wet, freezing cold, and I haven't slept in forty-two hours. I want to be excited to see him. I really do. But my eyes are stinging and heavy, my feet feel so frozen I'm afraid I may have to amputate my little toe, and all I'd be excited to see right now is a glass of Merlot resting by a steaming lavender bubble bath.

Jordan tries to put a smile on his face, but the smile looks a little like the awkward artwork of a five-year-old. "Well, at least you finally made it," he tries to say cheerfully.

He pulls me into a hug, and I sink deep into his arms, and begin a mental fantasy of getting him into bed—so that we can sleep for fifteen straight hours. "I'm pretty sure I saw an old man out there with long gray hair, several pairs of animals, and a set of boat blueprints," I whine.

As I feel Jordan rubbing my back through my Burberry trench coat, I start to feel a little more comfortable. Okay, so far, this has been a complete disaster. But, then again, just a few days ago, I thought I might never get myself into these arms again. And I like the feeling of these arms.

I continue to lounge in Jordan's arms as I apologize, "I'm sorry we missed *The Coast of Utopia*."

"That's okay," Jordan says, pulling out of the hug, and giving me an awkward kiss. "I've got reservations for Aureole at ten."

"Oh. Great!" I force myself to say.

Jordan knits his brows together. "You don't look like you think it's great."

"Oh no! I do!" I say in exhaustion as I fall into a velvet chair next to the bed. "It's just that I . . . I . . . um thought maybe we could . . ."

Think, Edwards. Give some valid reason not to go back out into that weather again tonight. Mention the restaurant downstairs . . . room service . . . the elevator leading to an ice skating rink . . . trapeze artists . . . Barack Obama . . .

"Charlie?" Jordan says.

"Hm?" I ask, startled awake.

"You fell asleep," Jordan tells me.

"I did?" I ask in a spacy voice. Then I turn to see I'm still in the chair. "That explains the trapeze artists."

"Are you going to be okay going out?" Jordan asks me.

Black Labrador puppies dancing with chocolate chip cookies and Christmas wreaths . . . and everyone's happily playing a Monopoly game . . .

"Charlie!" Jordan yells.

"I'm up!" I yell back, jumping out of my seat. I quickly throw off my coat. "I'm going to be fine. Just give me ten minutes to jump in the shower, change into the fabulous outfit I bought just for tonight, and then I'll . . ."

It's at that moment that I notice our room for the first time. It is stunningly romantic: a king-size bed overlooking a view of the hustle and bustle of Times Square. Next to it is a silver bucket dripping with condensation from the melted ice surrounding a bottle of champagne. There is a plethora of white candles that have been lit and placed all around the room, giving off the lovely scent of roses.

Everything is perfect. Absolutely perfect. I couldn't ask for more if I were a princess on her wedding night.

But my nose is clogged, I'm achy everywhere, and I just want to crawl into bed.

"This is really beautiful," I say, smiling.

I think I notice Jordan exhale a sigh of relief. "Good. Since you took so many hours to get here, I had a lot of time to think about how this might be overkill. So I'm glad you like it."

He walks over to the champagne bucket, pulls out a bottle of Dom Pérignon, and prepares to pop the cork. "Would you like some champagne?"

"I'd love some," I say, happily walking up to him, and giving him a hug.

As Jordan opens the bottle and pours the bubbly, I look out the window to our amazing view of Times Square. The pouring rain blurs the neon signs bidding us to buy from Gap and Coca Cola.

Jordan is about to hand me a glass of champagne when he notices my teeth chattering. "Oh my God. You're shivering."

As I take the glass, I tell him, "Honestly, my fingers are so frozen I could keep that bottle cold better than the bucket." I take a sip. "This is phenomenal. Thank you."

Jordan and I hug again. We begin kissing. Oh, it feels so magical and wonderful to be back in his arms, I feel like I'm going to drift off into a cloud . . .

Which is exactly what I do.

But not in a good way. Within five minutes, I had drifted off into a deep sleep.

I found out later, I was actually snoring.

Fifteen

The next morning, I open my eyes to see sunlight pouring through the hotel curtains.

Oh, shit.

I look over at Jordan, who is shirtless, and under the covers.

I look down at myself. I'm still wearing the jeans I put on two days ago. No, no, no.

I sit up in bed and sigh. The last thing I remember was kissing Jordan at the window. I fell asleep mid-kiss, and must have fallen backwards, because I spilled some of my champagne as Jordan caught me.

Jordan then suggested I might be too tired and cold for a big night out on the town, and suggested we get some really great room service.

I told him I loved him for suggesting we stay in the room in this horrible weather. Although it wasn't a real "I love you" so much as an "I love you" that I might say to the caterer on set for giving me an extra helping of chocolate cake. Then I grabbed the room service menu, opened it to decide if I wanted filet mignon or salmon . . .

Then fell asleep again.

Shit.

Jordan stretches and opens his eyes. "Good morning," I say sheepishly to him.

"Good morning, sleepyhead," Jordan says, smiling as he asks, "are you feeling better?"

He doesn't say it in a bad way at all, but I feel like shit anyway. "I'm so sorry," I say. "I totally blew it."

Jordan shrugs, then sits up to face me. "You were exhausted. I understand."

I look over at the nightstand, where my glass of champagne is still almost full, and two white candles have burned down their wicks. "What can I do to salvage this weekend?" I ask.

"I can think of a few things," Jordan says flirtatiously.

He leans over to kiss me. As the two of us begin making out, Jordan moves to unzip my jeans, and reveal my sexy black underwear.

Which I've now been wearing for over forty-eight hours.

Ew.

I grab his hand. "Wait," I say, then slither myself out from under him. "I need to go change," I say as I get up, and head for my suitcase.

Jordan sits up. "Change? I think you're a little unclear on what I'm trying to do here."

"No, no," I say as I unzip my bag, and rifle through my things. "You see, I specifically wore this fabulous bra-and-panty set under my clothes so you could rip them off me yesterday in a mad, passionate frenzy. But now I've been wearing them for two days. They're probably seriously funky."

At the thought of that, I instinctively raise my arm and smell my pits. "Oh, Jesus. How could you stand to be in the bed with me last night?"

Jordan gets out of bed to reveal his washboard abs, and my favorite pair of his boxers. He laughs as he says, "Have we really hit the comfort level in our relationship where you're sniffing yourself in front of me?"

Jordan donuts his arms around my waist just as I find my decidedly unsexy plain cotton underwear. (Why on earth did I pack that?) "Just give me five minutes to shower," I say, grabbing it anyway, and heading for the bathroom.

As I climb into the hotel's famous "voyeur" shower, and lather up with Bliss soap, I wonder what the hell is the matter with me? Why am I acting like such a freak? Why can't I act like my usual confident (for the most part), happy self? Why am I coming across as Jekyll and Hyde?

It takes until after I'm out of the shower that my answer hits me. I wrap a towel around my body, then turban another around my head, and walk out of the bathroom to find Jordan, now dressed in jeans and a nice sweater, casually lying on the bed and watching ESPN on the room's flat-screen TV.

"I am just so nervous around you!" I can't help but blurt out.

Jordan looks confused. I seem to do that to him a lot.

"Do you want to know why I think guys like us when we don't care about them?" I ask.

Jordan gives me a shrug, which I take as encouragement to go on.

"Because we don't care about them!" I say, throwing my arms up in the air. "We can be witty, and glib, and cheerful, and energetic around some random five-on-a-scale-of-one-to-ten guy. And we don't walk into walls, because we don't care what Mr. Five Guy thinks of us. But you!" I say, pointing to him. "You make me walk into walls."

I sit down on the bed next to him, then sigh loudly. "I wanted this weekend to be perfect."

Jordan starts rubbing my arm. "Yeah, me, too," he says sympathetically. "And it hasn't been, but that's okay."

"No, it's not okay. I haven't seen you in almost a month. You haven't seen *me* in almost a month. You need to remember why you dated me in the first place, so everything needs to be perfect."

Jordan chuckles. "No pressure," he jokes.

I smile back. "None at all."

Jordan rubs my shoulder. "So . . . what would make today perfect for you?"

I look up at the ceiling and think. "I don't know," I say, shrugging. "A carriage ride in Central Park . . . skating at Rockefeller Center . . . Dinner at the Russian Tea Room . . . taking in a Broadway show . . . . Why are you shaking your head?"

"I'm sorry," Jordan says, laughing lightly as he shakes his head. "Those things are all fine, and we'll do them if you want. It's just . . . that's such a standard, carbon-copy way to spend a day in New York. Any couple can go where the tourists go. I want to go where the locals go."

I smile as a thought suddenly occurs to me. "I forget. Didn't you live in New York briefly?"

"Yeah. I went to Columbia for about a year. Which may only make me a semi-local. But if you'll allow me"—Jordan stands up and puts out his hand—"I would like you to bundle up, and get ready for a day of unexpected romance."

"Really?" I say, suddenly feeling like the burden of our entire future has been lifted from my shoulders (if only for today). "Do I get a hint about where we're going?"

Jordan grins. "Get dressed. We're going to Brooklyn."

I eye him suspiciously. "Seriously. Have I pissed you off that much?"

Sixteen

At least one day of every year, think about the most obvious thing you can do on that day—and then go do something completely different.

Ten minutes later, I am bundled up in a heavy sweater, a scarf, gloves, and a Burberry coat, and walking hand in hand with Jordan down Forty-second Street. The weather is cold, but the sky is blue, and the air is spectacularly clear. We walk to the Times Square Station, take the subway to the F train, then take the F train out to Brooklyn.

Yes, Brooklyn.

Our "romantic" day begins at York Street Station, the first stop in Brooklyn.

"Welcome to DUMBO," Jordan says cheerfully as he takes my hand, and leads me out of the train car.

I've heard of DUMBO from my bohemian friends here in the east. An acronym for "Down Under the Manhattan Bridge Overpass" (although some people claim it's really "Down Under the Manhattan Brooklyn Overpass"). The area began as an artist's haven (for those artists not successful enough to afford the rents in Manhattan), and in the past ten years its denizens had progressed from artists, to commercial artists, to doctors and lawyers and hedge-fund managers (oh my).

"I'm dubious," I say as we climb up the subway station stairs and head up to York Street. "Is this really going to be more romantic than a hansom carriage ride?"

"I have never been completely clear on why women think sitting behind a horse's ass is so romantic," Jordan counters.

We exit the station and walk over to the East River, to see the view of the New York City skyline I've seen a million times in movies and on TV. You know, the shot of New York City that they have on all the sitcoms about New York City, which someone shot next to a river, slightly under a bridge, and with a small building off to the left? That picture was taken in DUMBO. Who knew?

We take a few minutes to look at the river and, without thinking, I snuggle into Jordan for warmth. He hugs me back, and I start to feel like we might be okay after all.

"Okay," Jordan announces, clapping. "First stop: We need to find a good wine shop."

Jordan takes my hand, and we turn around to walk amongst the shops and natives of Brooklyn.

I can't help but smile as Jordan and I walk hand in hand along a cobblestone street. We're not talking. I think we're both contentedly taking in the sights and smells of the city. Our silence is peaceful and happy. For the first time in almost a month, I'm peaceful and happy. I feel the uncontrollable urge to kiss Jordan on the cheek. So I do. It's not a romantic kiss. It's better than that. It's decidedly . . . comfortable.

Jordan smiles, lifts my hand, and gives it a light kiss in return.

Which is wonderful. I haven't felt this comfortable around him since before he left for Paris.

"So, tell me again . . . when did you go to Columbia?" I ask as I lean my head into him, and snuggle up against his sweatered chest.

Jordan smiles devilishly as he pulls his head back to see me. "What do you mean 'again'? I never told you I went to Columbia."

Damn it, he got me. I never knew he went to Columbia. But it seemed like the kind of thing you're supposed to know about your boyfriend. "Touché," I admit, smirking. "Let me rephrase. When did you go to Columbia? Wait, more important, why were you at Columbia? Do they teach photography?"

"Uh . . . they might," he says cryptically. "But that wasn't why I was there. Ah!"

Jordan's face lights up at the sight of a small wine shop on the first floor of a tall, red brick building. He leads me in, then immediately walks up to the proprietor at the counter. "I was wondering if you could help me. I'm looking for a full-bodied red, preferably Italian, and a good demi-sec champagne. Could you make some suggestions?"

A few minutes later, the owner of the wine shop has sent us off with a robust cabernet from Veneto, Italy, a bottle of Veuve Clicquot demi-sec, a bottle opener, and four plastic cups, all in an unmarked paper bag.

As we exit the store, I shrug my shoulders demurely and say, "So, he deflects my question, then shows me he plans to ply me with booze."

"Good booze," Jordan reminds me.

"Great booze," I concur, "but we were talking about Columbia . . . ."

"I'm told it's a beautiful country," Jordan jokes, smiling as he takes my hand, and leads me down another street. "Good coffee."

Pick your battles.

I decide to drop the subject of Columbia in favor of hugging Jordan as we walk around the borough looking like a couple of newlyweds.

We pass some pretty fabulous shops. As we pass the ABC Carpet and Home Warehouse, the outlet of a wonderful furniture store I thought only existed in Manhattan and London, Jordan stops at the front window and points to the bright red sofa on display. "I'm thinking of buying a new couch when I get back to L.A.," Jordan says. "What do you think of something like that?"

"Seems very . . . New York," I say noncommittally.

Jordan turns to me. "Does that mean you like it or hate it?"

I shrug. "It just means it strikes me as a piece of furniture I'd see in a New York apartment."

Jordan thinks about that. "I like the color. It would photograph beautifully." He turns to me, then asks out of the blue, "Do you ever think about moving to another city?"

Uh-oh.

"Ummm . . . sometimes," I say.

"But you have a house in L.A.," Jordan answers for me. "So you're probably planning on settling there."

I don't like the way this conversation is going. "I don't know. Maybe," I say, not knowing what the right answer to his question should be.

"Would you ever think about moving to New York?" Jordan asks me.

Uh-oh.

I give Jordan's hand a gentle squeeze. "Are you thinking about moving here?" I ask, trying to sound as sweet and nonjudgmental as possible.

Jordan shrugs. "It didn't work out so well the last time I lived here. But . . . I don't know . . . I like it here. I kind of miss the place."

"Why don't you want to talk about Columbia?" I ask him. "What, did you flunk out or something?"

I can tell from the pinch in Jordan's face that he's uncomfortable. "I went to law school there. For one year."

I think about that. "Okay. So why the mystery? Why the discomfort?"

Jordan stares at the sidewalk for a few moments before answering. "It wasn't a very good time in my life. It turned out I hated law school. And there was a girl involved . . ."

He lets his voice drift off.

I never know what to do with the ex conversations. If you don't ask, it looks like you don't care, but if you do ask, sometimes you're poking at a pretty big wound. I decide to show interest, but tread lightly. "Did you go to law school for the girl?"

"No," Jordan says definitively. "I went to law school because that was what I always thought I'd do with my life: become a lawyer, make a lot of money, buy a house at the beach, raise kids. It's what my dad did, and he seemed happy with it, so it's what I had always planned to do."

He looks at me kind of sadly.

"And . . . ," I ask sympathetically.

"And there's a big difference between waiting for your life to begin, and actually living it. I hated law school. And frankly, I wasn't very good at it. By the time I came home for Christmas, I knew I had to get out."

I wait for him to elaborate, but he doesn't. Instead, we begin walking again. The two of us walk hand in hand, passing brightly lit windows scattered among buildings of condos and artist's lofts, and I try to remain comfortable in our silence.

Eventually, I can't help but prod. Hopefully with a safe question. "So, what made you choose Columbia?"

"I had always wanted to live in New York. My dad's family is here. We used to come every other Christmas, and I had this childhood memory of skating at Rockefeller Center while looking at the giant Christmas tree, watching snow silently fall over the city, looking at all the Christmas windows. . . ." Jordan lets his voice drift away. "I don't know, the whole city was magical to me in a way that it only can be when you're a kid."

We turn a corner, and head back toward the East River, more toward the Brooklyn Bridge side.

"So, what happened?" I ask.

"I don't know. Everything was different. To see the Christmas windows these days, you have to wait in a line with a bunch of tourists, then walk quickly between the window and a velvet rope. If you stop and look for too long, a security guard tells you to move it along. And that tree in Rockefeller Center isn't as big as I remembered. And it's no longer the biggest in the country. The one at The Grove in L.A. is bigger, as is one in Newport Beach, and another in Florida. And the skating rink is small. And snow is great for the first few days. But then it becomes gray slush. Or, even worse, yellow slush."

I nod my head and listen.

"Plus, I hated law school. I could not imagine practicing law for the rest of my life. Talk about your golden handcuffs. What would happen when I got used to the money, had my house and my family, but dreaded every Monday morning for the next forty years? I mean, photography hasn't always been very lucrative. But at least I like going to work."

As we walk along the riverfront, I am flattered that he's opening up to me, and letting me into the parts of his world that aren't so perfect. But I can also sort of tell he's not telling me everything. Call it women's intuition.

Actually, no. Call it fifteen years in the dating trenches.

When listening to stories from men, if the stories don't completely make sense: Cherchez La Femme.

Jordan doesn't say anything else for a few minutes. He gives me hugs, forces smiles, and clearly debates in his mind how much more to tell me.

I decide to go for broke. "So, who was the woman?"

"What?"

"You said there was a girl involved. Who was she?"

"Her name was Stacey. We dated my senior year in college. She moved to New York to be an actress, and I guess, at least according to my parents, I found an excuse to follow her."

"I take it that relationship didn't go well."

Jordan stops to face me. "Raise your left arm up, over your head for a minute."

I do.

"Okay, now keep it there as long as you can," Jordan says.

I stare at him dubiously as I keep my left arm raised over my head for what feels like an hour.

"Getting tired yet?" Jordan asks me.

I nod my head.

"Keep it up there. Are you getting so tired your arm hurts, and you can't stand it anymore?"

I nod my head again.

"That's what dating an actress is like," Jordan concludes.

I chuckle as I put down my arm.

We begin to walk under the Brooklyn Bridge. Jordan suddenly stops, and happily announces, "Ah . . . we're here."

I look over at a green awning announcing Grimaldi's Pizzeria, with a red sign underneath stating, COAL BRICK OVEN. Outside the windowed door, a line of people patiently wait in their overcoats, sweaters, and sweatshirts.

"Have you ever had coal brick oven pizza?" Jordan asks, his face now beaming.

"I don't think so," I say, trying to be cheerful. Even though all I can think about is an ex-girlfriend I know nothing about (except that he moved three thousand miles from home to be with her), and his confession to thinking about moving three thousand miles away from me.

"Now, before we begin," Jordan says, pulling out the Italian red wine he bought earlier, "We need to have our provisions." He opens the bottle with the corkscrew, and quickly pours some wine into two of the plastic cups we got from the wine store. "This is the best pizza in the world. But the line takes a while."

We wait in line outside for forty-five minutes, polishing off the bottle during that time. Jordan says nothing more of his New York past, and I decide not to push any further. For now. Frankly, I'm having too much fun talking to other people in line, and stealing kisses from my boyfriend when no one seems to be paying attention.

When we get inside the restaurant, I bask in the warmth of the air, and the smells of the thin crust.

It's another twenty minutes before we get our pizza, but all that time waiting gives us lots of time for talking. But instead of discussions of moving, and the failures of our youth, we stay on the safe topics: other people. We gossip about Drew and the new movie. I talk about how I am to be a bridesmaid yet again. He tells me about his shooting schedule in Paris, and how he hasn't seen much of the city yet.

I forgot how funny he can be. I spend most of my time with him either laughing or kissing him. And by the time our sausage and basil thin-crust pizza gets to our table, I am in heaven.

When we walk out of Grimaldi's a half hour or so later, I am pleasantly drunk, and wonderfully well fed. I have completely put our earlier conversation out of my mind, and am now thinking about all of the good things in our relationship, and all of the good things yet to come.

I'm back in love.

A rose by any other name . . . still has thorns.

As I look around at the old red brick buildings on the Brooklyn waterfront, I am continually struck by the unexpected romance of the place. Maybe I *could* move to a place like this. I mean, after all, I like my job, but I don't think I'm going to want to be an assistant for the rest of my life. At some point, I'd like to have a family. And most personal assistants don't have families: they're already so busy catering to the whims of a child (that would be their celebrity boss) that they don't have the time or energy or patience to have a real child. Before my mind wanders too much, I remind myself:

Don't jump ahead in a relationship. While on a first date, most women are thinking ahead to whether or not they see themselves married to the guy. Meanwhile, all the men are thinking about is getting their date into bed.

Besides, for all intents and purposes, a week ago we were broken up. I have to remember that. The only guarantee I have is of this weekend.

We head down Water Street, and I see our next destination: The Jacques Torres Chocolate Shop.

My God, can the man get any more romantic?

As we enter the lower level of the red brick building, I am once again enveloped not only in warmth (it's getting pretty cold out here in Brooklyn) but in my favorite aromatherapy scent: chocolate.

When we get to the front of the line, Jordan orders the twenty-five-piece boxed assortment, and two hot cocoas. We sip our hot cocoas at one of the three mosaic tables in the store, then head back out into the bracing cold of November autumn.

As the November air nips at my ears, I can't help but ask greedily, "Okay, so when do we get to tear into that box?"

"Not until we get to a bench," Jordan tells me. "There's only one thing that would be better than great chocolate right now."

"I'm not having sex on a bench," I say sternly, but jokingly.

Jordan juts out his bottom lip in a mock pout. "No? Why not?"

"Too cold. Check back with me in June around noon."

Jordan laughs. We walk to a metal bench, and have a seat.

"Brrrr . . . ,"I say, referring to the cold metal beneath my bottom.

"I've got something to warm you up," Jordan says, smiling as he pops the cork of the demi-sec champagne. He pours the champagne into the other two plastic cups, and hands one to me. "What do you think?" he asks.

I take a taste and . . .

"Yuck," I can't help but stammer. "What, did you put Maniechewitz in the bottle when I wasn't looking?"

Jordan laughs. "Too sweet for you?"

"Well, demi-sec isn't usually my first choice."

"Ah, but it goes perfectly with this," Jordan says, opening the chocolate box, pulling out a milk chocolate heart, and feeding it to me.

I open my mouth, and let him slip the tasty morsel onto my tongue. The creamy milk chocolate dissolves, then bursts into . . . what? What the hell is that flavor? "Tastes like passion fruit," I say with my mouth full.

Jordan laughs. "From the look on your face, I can't tell if that's a good thing, or a bad thing."

I start laughing. "I'm not sure yet," I say.

Jordan leans in and kisses me. We begin to make out under the leafless trees, and I feel like a teenager necking with her boyfriend. The world is good.

After another minute or two of making out, we drink our champagne (which actually becomes very tasty with the chocolate) and make our way through the box. The box has combinations I'd never thought of: ginger with dark chocolate ganache, melon puree with port wine . . . one is even made with Chipotle chiles.

A little while later, we make our way back to York Street Station, onto the F train, and back to our hotel.

My fingers feel frostbitten by the time Jordan slips his key card in to let us into our room, but my heart is on fire.

And so is the rest of me.

Don't discuss your love life in vivid detail. No one really needs the blow-by-blow account.

Several delicious hours later, Jordan indulges me in a romantic, five-course meal at Le Cirque, followed by drinks at The Plaza. Yes, we decided to go a bit touristy. We even skated at Rockefeller Center.

And that night, after we made love for the third time, I felt like we were finally back on track.

Seventeen

Tempting though it always is, try never to rest on your laurels. The universe is not stagnant.

I woke up the next morning blissfully happy . . . wildly in love . . . And alone in my bed.

Wait, no, I'm not. I can hear Jordan in the bathroom. Whew. Dodged a bullet there.

As I listen, I realize he's talking to someone on the phone.

Being the idiot that I am, I don't think anything of it as I take the top sheet, wrap it around my body, and get out of bed to tell him I'm awake, I'm naked, and I'm feeling amorous.

"No, I haven't told her yet," I hear Jordan whisper into the phone.

Oh. Shit. Why am I always the "her" in the "I haven't told her yet"? Why do I never get to be the girl on the other end of the phone?

That's right—because I have ethics. I actually believe the adage:

Work hard. Be nice. Hurt no one.

Of course, that may be why I'm thirty, and still single.

I get as close to the slightly opened door as possible and listen in.

"Yeah, well, I don't know where it's going anymore. And she is going to freak when she finds out," Jordan continues to his mystery woman (I'm assuming it's a woman) on the other end of the phone. He listens to her for a moment, then answers, "No. The first day was a disaster . . . No, it's not that easy. Yesterday was—"

But before Jordan can finish his sentence, he sees me at the doorway.

"Gotta go," Jordan says abruptly into the phone. "I'll see you tomorrow . . . . Yeah, me, too. Bye."

And he clicks off the phone. "Good morning," he tries to say brightly.

I don't bother mincing words. "Yesterday was what?"

"Hm?" Jordan says, clearly stalling for time.

"You were telling the girl on the phone that yesterday was something. I'm wondering what yesterday was."

There's a half-second pause while Jordan debates what to do next. It's that half second I never picked up on in college. (There are some advantages to battle scars.) Jordan looks at me seductively as he wraps his arms around my waist. "Yesterday was phenomenal," he says, pulling me into a sexy kiss.

Or, what would have been a sexy kiss, if I hadn't started talking through it. "Who was on the phone?" I ask, my voice a little muffled from his tongue in my mouth.

Jordan stops kissing me. "No one," he says, then begins kissing my neck and making me crazy.

"Sure didn't sound like no one," I manage to eek out (although I must admit, he's wearing me down with those kisses). "And what haven't you told me yet?"

"Can we talk about it later?" Jordan moans. "I want to make love to you."

"Yeah, right," I say, pulling away from him, and putting my hands on my hips. "You think I'm so stupid, I don't know men can fake moans, too?"

Jordan sighs. Rolls his eyes a bit. "Charlie, do you really want to ruin what little time we have left talking about something that will almost certainly make you angry?"

"No. I'd much prefer spending the day with someone wondering when the guillotine is going to hit my neck," I answer sarcastically.

Jordan heavily sighs. "Okay, fine. Have a seat."

For one brief moment, I debate waiting until the end of the day for that guillotine. But I force myself to sit down on the bed, and get whatever bad news he has over with.

Jordan takes a deep breath, clearly bracing for a blowup from me. "The girl who was on the phone was Stacey. The ex I told you about yesterday."

Shit. "The actress?" I ask, already getting mad.

"Yeah. She's one of the stars of the movie I'm working on right now. Which, before you freak out, she's only, like, the sixth lead in the thing; I did not know she was going to be in it, and she's happily married now. As a matter of fact, her husband is a producer on the movie. He's the one who offered me the film in Germany in February."

"Oh," I say noncommittally, unsure of where this is going.

"I'm taking the job," Jordan says.

"Oh," I repeat.

"It's a huge studio picture," Jordan continues. "It shoots for five months. So, other than the weeks before and after Christmas, I'll be gone until the end of June."

I don't say anything for a while. Finally, I have to ask, "So what does that mean? We do long-distance for another seven months? You're breaking up with me? What?"

Jordan doesn't answer me at first. He rubs his neck, and takes a deep, tired breath. "I don't know. You haven't exactly been very happy lately. I don't really see what our future is if our conversations and e-mails continue the way they've been going."

I don't know what he means by that: Does he mean that we're

breaking up, or is he just issuing me an ultimatum—be nicer and more patient in this long-distance relationship, or I'm out of here.

Jordan sighs. He looks battle weary. "I need to ask you something, and I'd like the truth."

"Okay," I say nervously.

Jordan walks over to his suitcase, and pulls out a British tabloid, which he hands to me. "Check out page five."

I open the tabloid to page five. Underneath the screaming headline, "Sexiest Man Alive Drew Stanton Afraid of Winding Up Alone" is a picture of Drew, Liam, and me coming home from our "run" earlier this week. The run where I tripped, and had to have Liam help me limp back to Drew's house. Of course, you can't tell I'm limping and hurt from the picture. No, no . . . the story is all about how Drew is still pining for his ex-wife, and how he's afraid he may not find anyone. The picture makes it look like Liam and I are cooing little lovebirds, cuddling in each other's arms as a frowning Drew runs ahead of us and looks pathetic.

"Who's the guy?" Jordan asks me.

I decide to come clean. Sort of. "His name's Liam," I say in a tone of voice designed to assure Jordan that Liam is no big deal. "He's a producer on Drew's movie. He went running with us, I hurt my ankle, he helped me back to Drew's house."

Jordan eyes me suspiciously. "The guy I heard on the phone?"

Shit. I think I unconsciously wince. "Yeah."

Jordan nods ever so slightly. "Okay."

Then he turns to pack. He deliberately does not look at me as he says, "You were right in the first place. I think we should see other people."

"Meaning what? Is that your toe-in-the-water way of breaking up with me?"

Jordan turns to me. He looks sad. "No. That is my way of saying I'm going to be working for the next seven months out of the country, and I think we should see other people. But if you think it's a breakup, I guess it is."

Oh, God. I think I'm going to throw up. I spend the next thirty seconds forcing myself to breathe, and watching him pack his black duffel bag.

Needless to say, I call the airline, and immediately change my flight to the next one out of town. Jordan goes with me to the airport, and we say good-bye as exes. For the few hours I was still with him I would tear up, then force myself not to cry. All that time Jordan looked pained. But he never suggested that he wanted to reconsider, so I never asked him to. Because in my heart of hearts I knew:

Never beg a man to take you back. The only thing worse than having a man leave you is having his last memory of you crying and begging.

And when he kissed me good-bye at the security line at JFK, I knew it really was good-bye.

Eighteen

Sometimes you just need to cry it out. That's okay.

When I got to my gate at the airport, I locked myself in a stall in the ladies' room, and cried for twenty minutes straight. I felt a little better when I was done. There is a certain sense of relief in knowing how the relationship turned out, in not being in limbo anymore.

My iPhone rang four times during that time, but none of the calls were from Jordan: instead my caller ID showed three were from Drew, and one was from Liam. I didn't want either of them to hear me crying, so I didn't pick up.

After my crying jag, I wipe away my tears, walk to a seat at my gate, and check my messages.

Message one: "We're not going to Paris!" I hear Drew wailing into the phone. "Now my contract specifically states I get to go somewhere on per diem, so I think I can quit. But I don't really want to, since I think I read somewhere that an Academy Award nomination can be worth an extra ten thousand dollars or so on a film, and I am trying to get to space. So I'm torn. How do you feel about Rancho Cucamonga? Call me back." Beep.

Message two: "Me again. Listen, I just slept with Whitney. You know, that producer you hate. I'm pretty sure she just came over because I threatened to pull out of the film. She started out by saying wouldn't it be more fun if I pulled out . . . actually, that's not really the important part of the story. Question is, has she sexually harassed me here, or have I sexually harassed her? I told her I need to talk to you, and that I might not report for work tomorrow. You need to call me back ASAP. I'm having a moral breakdown." Beep.

Message three: "Or is it a nervous breakdown? Because I'm thinking maybe I'm having one of those. In which case, do I qualify for any cool drugs? Anyway, call me back." Beep.

Message four: "Charlie, it's Liam. Listen, I am so sorry to disturb you during your romantic weekend, but I'm afraid we've got a problem. It would appear that we're not going to be able to shoot in Paris. I'll explain later. But Drew is absolutely apoplectic. He's threatening to pull himself from the project, and nothing we've been able to do has reassured him that the film will be fine. If I could maybe get your help talking to him, that would be great. Call me back." Beep.

I call Drew first. He answers on the first ring.

"We're not going to Paris!" Drew says in a panic.

"Okay, calm down," I say. "What happened?"

"Apparently the director was arrested last night for soliciting, and now we can't shoot in Paris."

Huh?

"Soliciting what?" I ask, confused. "Drugs?"

"No. Sex," Drew says, like the idea of a director soliciting drugs was out of the question. "He was dressed up as a transvestite on Santa Monica Boulevard, and got pulled in. I mean, you expect this kind of thing from a Republican senator, but not from a respected artist in the community. Anyway, how was your weekend?"

"Um . . . fine," I lie. "So, unfortunate as this is, why aren't we shooting in Paris?"

Drew gives me his answer in an incessant monologue. "Apparently, because the director is applying for citizenship here, he's not allowed to leave the state before the trial, much less the country. Which means the writer is doing a massive rewrite on the movie, and we're shooting everything here in the States, and . . . hey, wait a minute. Are you crying?"

Shit. I guess I am. I pause to take a deep breath. "No."

Drew stops talking. He knows I'm lying. When he does speak, his voice is soft and comforting, "Aw, sweetie. I'm sorry."

That one response makes me water up again. "It's okay," I lie. "Things weren't working out anyway. Better I know now." I try to sound upbeat when I joke, "And, hey, now I won't be trying to avoid anyone in Paris."

Drew's silent on the other end.

Which kills me. So I change the subject. "Liam called me. They want to know what it's going to take to make you happy again."

"What's it going to take to make you happy again?" Drew asks me.

Having Jordan call me and beg forgiveness? Being able to go back in time, and at least not spend all morning with him trying to act like nothing's wrong. Being able to go back in time and never meet him at all?

"I'm gonna be okay," I say, literally swallowing some tears down the back of my throat. "But the flight is about to board, and I need to call Liam. What are your demands?"

Drew considers my question a moment before answering, "I want to be able to decorate my dressing room however it makes me feel the most inspired."

"Okay."

"Whitney told me last week that since I was assigned Liam's bedroom, I couldn't do anything with the décor. If I'm going to be there for several more weeks, I need to feel the room is my sanctuary."

I grab a tissue from my purse, wipe my drippy nose, take another deep breath, then say, "I'm sure that won't be a problem. I'll call them now."

"Do you need anything?" Drew asks. "Can I send you something?"

"I'd really like the rest of the day off," I say, and Drew agrees not to call me again until tomorrow.

I finish up with Drew, then call Liam to let him know Drew has been calmed down, but wanted free rein to decorate his dressing room however he wished. Liam said that was no problem, and thanked me for my time.

He also asked how my weekend went. I lied and said it was good.

Never admit to a man that another man dumped you.

My final calls were to my girls: Dawn and Kate. I told them both what happened. Both immediately cancelled their plans for the evening to pick me up, bring me out for Thai food, then languish around my home to join me for a self-pity night.

And for that, I worship them.

Nineteen

The next morning, my iPhone is beeping a text message:

> You don't need to pick me up this morning. Had to go to my dressing room early to meet my interior designer. Wait until you see it! It's going to be magical!
> Love,
> Drew

Let's hope that when he says magical, he doesn't mean the room will be swamped with white rabbits.

I look at the clock. It's only six o'clock in the morning. I decide I should get ten minutes to myself before I call my boss. It's getting cold in the mornings here, so I put on a robe, putter down to my kitchen, brew up a pot of Starbucks Winter Blend, and check my e-mail from my office computer.

Okay, yes, I was also checking to see if Jordan had written.

He hadn't.

I do get Jamie's latest article, which I pore over, hoping for some inside information about men.

To: AngelCharlie
From: CalienteJamie

What do you think of this?

Things You Girls Should Know About Us Guys: And No, The First Answer Is Not "Be a Little More Adventurous in the Bedroom"

Do you want to know the biggest lie men tell? It isn't, "I want two kids: a boy and a girl," or "I really like your mother." Nope, the biggest lie men tell is, "I really like your shoes." No man really cares about a woman's shoes. A man may love to see you in five-inch heels, but we really have no idea if you spent five hundred dollars on them at the Beverly Center, or twenty dollars at the stripper shoe store on Sunset.

Here are some other things you might not know about men:

1. When we ask you how your day was, we want you to answer in three sentences or less. And we certainly don't want to know how your friend's day was. Seriously—the game is on in two minutes.

2. When you ask us, "What are you thinking about?" try to remember that once every forty-four seconds, we are thinking about sex. So, the odds are not in our favor here that we're going to look good in front of you when you ask that question.

3. We want to know how much you spent on clothes this month about as much as you want to know how much we spent on lap dances the last time we were in Vegas.

4. We do not notice if you gain five pounds. We very much notice if you gain fifty. But seriously, men do not notice

bodies as much as women think they do. What we notice is if you're confident, and happy with yourself, and at ease around us.

5. On the subject of fifty pounds: If you're going on a diet, fine. But don't talk about it all the time.

6. We don't send mixed signals. If you say, "How about Chinese food tonight?" and we say "Fine," we mean "Fine." So you can stop giving us ten more meal options.

7. Most of us truly suck at the romantic gesture. Those that don't are not to be trusted.

8. We really don't want to take the *Cosmo* quiz. If it's important to you, we will, but just know that in the back of our minds it's just to kill time before we can have sex with you again.

9. We have female friends. Ignore *When Harry Met Sally*: we don't want to sleep with all of our female friends. As a matter of fact, we chose the women we wanted as friends specifically because we didn't want them sexually.

10. We really don't like *Sex and the City*. Sarah Jessica Parker scares us.

11. We would like to see you wear more than once the lingerie you bought. Frankly, we'd like to see you walk around the house in it all the time.

12. Be a little more adventurous in the bedroom.

Before I can write back to argue point six, I get a call on my iPhone. I check the caller ID. It's Whitney, from the movie. I pick up anyway. "Hello?"

"Good morning, Charlie. This is Whitney. I'm afraid we have a bit of a situation here."

. . .

Ten minutes later, I am parking in the driveway of Liam's Victorian house, ready to avert a crisis. I am dressed in jeans for the day, I haven't showered, and I have on no makeup. While this is the last way in the world I want Liam to see me, I have no choice.

My boss has gone mad.

I toss my keys over to the PA organizing the cars, and run into the house. I race through the kitchen bustling with the day's catering staff, through the chaos of the dining room turned production office, past the living room (now transformed into a sleek vision of glass and chrome for the eighties scenes), and up the stairs. Once up the stairs I make a left, then a quick right, open the door to Drew's dressing room/Liam's bedroom . . .

And am immediately smacked in the face with a snowball.

Yes, a snowball. In the middle of someone's house. In the middle of Los Angeles. In the middle of November.

"Sorry," Drew says cheerfully. "Coats are to your right. Come on in and close the door."

I shiver as I walk into Drew's newly decorated dressing room, and close the door behind me. It's fucking freezing in here—and I mean freezing. Like below thirty-two degrees Fahrenheit, zero degrees Celsius. I look to my right, where Drew has set up several full length fur coats, muffs, scarves, and gloves.

"What on earth have you done?" I ask. "It must be fifteen degrees in here."

"Actually, it's twenty-eight," Drew corrects me. "I couldn't get the extra generator I brought in to bring the temperature any lower, and Whitney says we can't have two extra generators on the set without blowing out Liam's wiring, so we're just going to have to make do."

Whitney, fully decked out in fur to resemble Lara in *Dr. Zhivago,* walks up to me and whispers, "If Liam sees this, he's going to blow a totally different kind of fuse. Do something."

I rub my arms with my hands quickly as I say sweetly, "Drew, can I see you in the hall for a minute?"

"No. It's hot out there. Throw on a coat, and have a seat."

He motions to a chair that looks like a small block of ice atop a larger block of ice.

"Is that real ice?" I ask him.

"Nah, it's fake. All of the fur is fake, too, not to mention biodegradable. I don't want to get spray-painted again."

Whitney looks aghast. "Someone spray-painted you for wearing fur?!"

"No, not for that." Drew and I admit in unison.

At this point, Liam walks in. "Oh, good Lord," he says, trying to suppress his shock. "What have you done to my bedroom?"

"Isn't it awe-inspiring?" Drew asks gleefully. "It's Paris at Christmas! Can you believe I got my interior designer to put this all together on twelve hours' notice?"

At this point, snow flurries silently descend upon us. "Where is that coming from?" Liam asks, covering his alarm as he looks around his bedroom.

"Ice machine, attached to a snow-cone machine, attached to a windblower," Drew says, his face beaming. "I know what you're thinking: the wiring in this house is too old to hook up all my stuff on. That's why I have an electrician upgrading everything as we speak. Oh, and I had an extra generator brought in."

Liam puts on a pair of leather gloves as he says, "So I can hear. Drew we need to talk. When I said you could decorate my bedroom however you wished for the duration of the shoot, I was under the impression you were going to bring in glass boxes with fake necklaces and such. I thought we discussed *Breakfast at Tiffany's*."

"Well, yeah," Drew admits, his tone of voice creeping up a notch.

"But suddenly that struck me as mundane. I mean, anyone can turn a bedroom into a department store. How many people can turn one into a snowstorm? Charlie, your lips are turning blue. Put on a coat."

I haven't come up with a plan of attack yet, so I slink over to the coats, and grab a fake dark-brown mink with a matching fake mink muff.

Liam walks over to inspect his closet. "Where are all my clothes?" he asks, surprisingly without a hint of anger. As though it's just a nonjudgmental question, you know, just curious, what happened to all my stuff?

"I had it moved to wardrobe. I need that room for my meditation."

Whitney's phone rings. She answers. "This is Whitney." She listens for a moment. "Okay, I'm coming down." She hangs up, then says to Liam, "Apparently craft services tapped into the same circuit as Drew's AC, and blew all the power out on the ground floor. I'll be right back."

She takes off her fake fur, throws it to me, and walks out. As I put the fur coat back on the coatrack, Liam tries to reason with my boss. As Drew happily strings some white lights around a window, Liam tries another approach. "Drew, although this is . . . absolutely breathtaking, I don't think you've worked out all of the logistics."

"Don't you think white lights are festive?" Drew asks.

"Incredibly celebratory," Liam assures him before returning to his point. "For example, where am I going to sleep at night if my bedroom is twenty-two degrees? I mean," he tries for a lighthearted joke, "I left Europe for a reason."

Drew hands him a fake sequined snowman. "That's right! You're from Europe! What do you think of this? Do they have fake snowmen like this in Paris?"

Liam closes his eyes, and shakes the cobwebs from his head. "About my bedroom . . ."

"Not a problem. Charlie lives a few miles from here, and she has a wonderful guest room. I'm sure she wouldn't mind you staying with her, just until the shoot is over. Charlie, have Liam's clothes moved from wardrobe to your house. Your guest room has a big closet, right?"

I'm too stunned at that suggestion to speak. Liam on the other hand, is starting to lose it. "Don't you think that would be putting her out a bit?" he asks Drew.

"I pay to put her out a bit."

"I'm sorry," I say to Liam. "Can I have a minute with Drew?"

"Go check out what we've done in the bathroom!" Drew says proudly to Liam.

I can hear Liam suppress a sigh as he leaves us. The moment he is out of earshot I whisper to Drew, "What the hell are you doing?"

"Getting you a comforter," Drew says like it's the most obvious thing in the world.

"A what?"

"A comforter. You know, like, a guy who can comfort you, help you get over Jordan. What better way to get a guy in your bed than to actually own the bed?"

Oh, for God's sake.

"Drew, I don't think I'm ready to jump right back into dating right now. But, even if I was, I'm pretty sure the way to attract a guy does not include letting him see me brush my teeth in the morning, or wash out my underwear in the sink."

I hear Liam yell, "Shit!" Followed by a thud. Followed by Liam yelling, "Fuckity-fuck, fuck, fuck!"

Actually, he's Irish, so it sounds more like, "Feckity-feck, feck, feck."

I run into the bathroom to find Liam flat on his back. "What happened?"

Liam sits up. "Somehow, my bathroom flooded, and due to Drew's bedroom fantasy, the flood froze into a sheet of ice."

Drew walks into the doorway. "You like it? I had the room turned into an ice rink. Kind of like the outdoor one I saw in Paris a few years ago."

I happen to look in the toilet. "The toilet water is completely frozen," I tell Drew. "Was that your intention?"

"No, but there are no mistakes in art," Drew reasons.

I offer my hand to Liam, who takes it to help himself stand up. He sighs, then walks out of the bathroom. "I'm afraid I'm going to have to put my foot down here," Liam says to Drew patiently, but sternly. "You cannot have a winter wonderland in the middle of my bedroom."

It's kind of cute, really, the way people try to stand up for themselves around Drew, and think they can get away with it.

Drew and Liam engage in a mild staring contest before Drew says to Liam in his most nonconfrontational voice, "I'm afraid you need to leave."

Liam looks confused. "You need me to leave my own bedroom?"

Drew nods. "Yes. Because right now I need to lock myself in my trailer, and pout until you give me my way. And since I don't have a trailer, I need to lock myself in here."

Twenty

Some days it's all about the drink.

Around nine o'clock that night, Liam follows me in his car, and I introduce my new roommate to his new digs for the next few weeks.

The argument went just as I thought it would. Drew wouldn't stay in the film without his frozen dressing room, and after losing their Paris location, the movie's financial backers were going to pull the plug if Liam lost Drew as well.

Liam spent almost a year of his life putting this movie together. It was his passion. So there was no doubt about it: for the next few weeks, as far as living companions went, he was all mine.

As I unlock my door and let him in, I fret over what he'll think of where I live. I had raced home for an hour in the middle of the day to clean up, so the place didn't look too bad. At the same time, it wasn't exactly a sexy stewardess bachelorette pad that would make me look like the type of woman I figured a guy like Liam would date: jet set, perfect, sexy, perfect, funky, perfect. It was a boring little home with furniture cobbled together from all the castoffs my boss didn't want anymore.

Of course, some of those castoffs were things like a ten-thousand-dollar sofa and love-seat set, so it's all relative.

"We're home!" I say brightly, trying not to sound nervous. I turn on my living room light, and watch as Liam comes in, puts down his black Tumi overnight bag, and looks around. "It's charming," Liam says. "I love the Noguchi."

I look around my living room. "The what?"

Liam points to my wood and glass coffee table. "The coffee table. Isamu Noguchi created that design in the 1940s. My parents have one in their living room. My mother tells me it looks very futuristic, in a kitchy mod kind of way. I still have no idea what she means by that, but I like it."

"Thank you," I say, relieved that he likes my (Drew's) taste. "Can I get you a glass of wine, or should I just show you to the bedroom?"

That came out wrong. "I mean . . . *your* bedroom. I mean . . . would you like some wine?"

Before he can answer me, my home phone rings. I look over at the caller ID. It's Whitney. She's been pissing me off for days, so I decide not to answer.

My machine, however, does. "Hi, it's Charlie. Leave a message." Beep.

"Charlie, it's Whitney. Listen, I'm sorry to bother you at home, but I tried Liam on his cell, and he's not picking up, and we have a check that was supposed to go to Sejeune prop house by the end of the day, but no one can find it, and I'm kind of panicking. Can you have him call me the second you get this?"

She hangs up as Liam checks his cell phone. "That's weird. I'm not getting cell reception up here."

"Yeah, that can be a problem in Silverlake," I tell him. "The phone companies want to put up a tower in the neighborhood for better reception, but the residents won't allow it. So, some phones work and some don't. You can use my home line to call her back if you like."

"Ah, the glamour of moviemaking," Liam jokes. "I'll only be a minute. In the meantime, here," he says, opening his overnight bag.

"I brought you this. A sort of 'Thank you for having me / My God, do you need a drink as much as I do after today?' present."

Liam hands me a bottle of Clos du Val Cabernet.

"Wow. That's a really nice bottle," I say, impressed. "Let me get this open while you make your call."

Hmm . . . the man brings over wine, compliments my taste in furniture. Maybe this whole roommate thing won't be so bad.

Eww. Don't think of him as a roommate. That would be gross. Think of him as a guy who wants to bring you wine and spend the night.

As I enter the kitchen, and pull out some glasses, I can hear Liam on the phone saying, "Hey, it's me . . . No, the check was already sent to them yesterday. It's in their office. . . . Hold on." Then I hear him call from the other room, "Charlie, that's your call waiting. Should I pick up?!"

"Answer, and tell them I'll call them back!" I yell back as I pull out a corkscrew from the drawer.

"Charlie Edwards's residence," Liam answers in that adorable little accent of his. "No, she's not available at the moment. Can I take a message? . . . Excellent. I've got it . . . . Hi, Whitney, I'm back. . . . They haven't? Feck . . . well then, check with Monica and see if her . . . wait a minute, Charlie has another call . . . Charlie Edwards's residence. This is Liam, who's this? . . . Oh, I'm so sorry. Let me get off my line . . . Whitney, Charlie needs to take this call. Her friend just lost a baby. Let me call you right back."

I nearly drop the wine bottle when I hear that. I run into the living room as Liam hands me the phone. Not knowing if it's Jenn or Andy, I urgently say into the phone, "What happened? Are you okay? Do you need me to come over?"

"I'm fine," my Mom answers matter-of-factly. "I'm just not pregnant yet. I did the test, and I'll have to try again next month. It was a long shot. I knew that. Mostly, I was calling to check up on you.

You sounded pretty down last night from the breakup, and I wanted to make sure you were okay. But the Irishman sounds adorable, so I'm hanging up now. Love you, bye."

"Wait. Mom. Are you really okay?" I ask, realizing she's already hung up the phone. Which is very unlike my mother—normally she talks for a month.

I immediately call her back. She answers on the first ring. "Darling, I said I'm fine."

"I know," I say. "And I say I'm fine about the breakup. And we both know we're lying. Do you want me to come over?"

"No. Your father's here, Chris is here. I'm fine. I was just checking up on you."

"You're checking up on me?" I ask. "But you just . . ."

"Sweetie, the chances that a woman my age gets pregnant on the first round are not as high as the press makes it sound. But I'm a tough old broad. I'll be fine. And Chris and I will try again next month. Meanwhile, get back to your guest. I've monopolized your time enough this evening."

"But Mom—"

"I'm sorry dear, but I really must go. Chris and I are off to Hyde for drinks. Thank God I can drink again. It'll make Thanksgiving so much easier."

Then she hangs up on me again.

When I hang up, Liam looks at me sympathetically. "Was that your stepmom?"

"No, it was my real mom. But I guess she's okay."

"Your biological mother thought she was pregnant?" Liam asks, clearly stunned. "What, did she have you at twelve?"

I shake my head. "No. But if you ever meet her, say that. She'll worship you." I try to change the subject. "Did someone else call?"

"Oh, yes. Your friend Kate. She wanted to tell you that Jordan is an asshole, that there are plenty of fish in the sea, that she's confirming tomorrow night's cake tasting, and also to let you know that she is getting rid of all of her self-help books so Will doesn't see them, and that she has a fabulous diet book for you. Oh, and she wanted to encourage you to give online dating another try, and said, and I quote, 'Okay, so the first guy lied about his age, and showed up in a walker. That could happen to anyone.'"

I roll my eyes at that. "Oh, good Lord."

"I have to say, and I mean this with love, you don't strike me as the online dating type," Liam says.

Okay, debate time: Do I focus on the words, "I mean this with love," or the statement, "You don't strike me as the online dating type."

I can't help myself. "What exactly *is* the online dating type?" I ask Liam.

Liam shrugs. "I'm not sure. But definitely not *you*."

Before I can decipher *that* sentence's hidden meaning, Liam throws me a curveball. "So, when did you break up?"

No, no, no. I don't want Hot Guy knowing I'm used goods.

"I really don't want to talk about it," I say, turning back toward the kitchen, so I don't have to look him right in the eye. "Can I get you that wine?"

"That would be lovely," Liam says, wisely deciding not to press me on the breakup, and opting to lighten the mood with a joke. "You know what they say: 'Misery Loves Cabernet.'"

"Really? I had always heard it was Misery Loves Merlot." I joke back.

Liam laughs. "Ah, you Americans . . . always corrupting our language. Let me call Whitney back real quick, and I'll be right with you."

As I head back to the kitchen, I can hear Liam talking on the phone again. "Hi, Whitney, me again. . . . She did? Excellent . . . no, no, if we do that, we'll need a fire marshal on set . . . you can check with the permitting office, but I'm almost positive. . . . Hold on, Charlie has another call. . . . Hello, Charlie Edwards's residence . . . Um, let me think. Once we pass the age of fifteen, we no longer think with our penises . . . well, okay then, eighteen . . ."

"Tell Jamie to write his own material!" I yell from the kitchen as I pull the cork from the bottle.

"Oh!" Liam exclaims into the phone, "and there is no good answer to the question, 'How many women have you slept with?' So please stop asking. . . . Not a problem. Thank you." I hear him click back over. "Whitney? Yes, the general rule with the fire marshal is . . . oh wait, that's for Charlie again. Hold on. . . . Hello? This is Liam, who's this? . . . Hold on . . ."

Liam yells to me. "It's your friend Dawn. She says to get off me, and pick up this phone right now!"

"Tell her I'm not on you and I'll call her tomorrow!" I yell back as I pour the wine into the glasses.

"She's says she's not on me, and she'll call you tomorrow. . . . Well, you have a gorgeous voice, too, thank you . . . Hello, Whitney? No, it doesn't matter if we went out of the thirty-mile zone, we'd still need one. So just call them tomorrow morning, and book . . . hold on. . . . Edwards's residence. . . . This is Liam. Who's this?" He listens. "Oh, you must be the boyfriend. Let me get rid of my other line. I'm sure she's anxious to speak with you."

Oh shit!

I race out of the kitchen as Liam says into the phone, "No, no. Let me get off my other line. She'll be right with you. . . ." He looks up at me as he listens to the other end. "I can, but she's right here. I . . ." Liam stops talking. He presses a button on the phone, then says, "Whitney, just go ahead with everything we talked about, and I'll see you in the morning . . . you, too . . . good night."

Liam clicks off the phone, and then hands it to me. "I'm afraid he hung up."

I look down at the phone. I'm torn between wanting to talk to Jordan, and not wanting to be completely humiliated in front of Liam. At that moment, I think of two new things to write in my book of advice:

Always keep your dignity during breakups. Even if it's killing you inside, let him leave.

and

Tolerance for other races, cultures, or religions is a sign of intelligence. Tolerance for staying in a bad relationship is a sign of stupidity.

I put up the palms of my hands to show that I'm not taking the phone. "No. You know what? If he wants to talk to me, he'll call back."

"Absolutely," Liam says, trying to give me moral support.

"How about that wine?" I ask, determined not to let Jordan get to me.

"Excellent idea," Liam says cheerfully.

I turn back toward my kitchen to get the wine. Liam puts the phone back on the charger, then follows me. "Do you want to talk about it?" he asks sympathetically.

"No," I say, picking up the filled glasses. "We broke up, I'm single again, and that's all I'm going to say about it."

"Then I won't mention it again."

"Good," I say, handing him his glass, then raising my glass for a toast. "Here's to the movie."

Liam raises his glass, "Here's to my gracious hostess, who kept me from killing the star of my movie."

My face falls as I lower my hand before drinking the toast. Liam notices my reaction. "I'm sorry," he says. "It's just your boss is really getting to me. I know we're lucky to have him working for scale and all, but to kick someone out of his own home . . ."

"I just don't understand why men give off such completely mixed signals!" I say in exasperation.

Liam narrows his eyes. "Are we talking about Drew, or the boyfriend?"

"Ex-boyfriend," I correct him.

"Ex-boyfriend. Jordan, is it?" Liam asks.

"I said I don't want to talk about it," I say again. I take a sip of wine, then try to brighten my voice as I ask, "Can I give you a tour of the house?"

"That would be lovely," Liam says. "And let me thank you again for taking me in. I suppose I could have booked a hotel room . . ."

"It's just that he wouldn't make a commitment, so he basically wanted us to be in this dating limbo . . . ," I blurt out.

"And we're back to the boyfriend?" Liam asks.

"*Ex*-boyfriend," I remind him.

"Ex-boyfriend," Liam starts to say, but I interrupt him.

"I mean, it's one thing to take a job in Paris in the fall for a couple of months. But he took a job in Germany in February! Even though he gets job offers in Southern California all the time, he'd rather be in the dead of winter in Germany with Stacey than in balmy Southern California with me. What does that say about me?"

"I don't think it says anything about you," Liam responds. "He might just—"

"And even if Stacey really is happily married," I interrupt, "which I doubt, I'm not convinced Genevieve is really a lesbian. He could have just been saying that."

Liam furrows his brow. "I'm sorry. Who's Genevieve?"

"This girl in Paris who may or may not be trying to sleep with him."

"There's a girl trying to sleep with him?"

"There are probably two," I reason, taking another sip of my wine before I continue. "The problem with dating an attractive man is that there are always at least two girls trying to sleep with him."

Liam thinks about my statement a moment. Then he asks, "So how long were you two dating before his wanderlust became a problem?"

I sigh. "Oh, I don't want to talk about it," I repeat. Then I take my wineglass and walk out of the kitchen, toward my stairs. "Want to see the guest room?"

Liam nods his head "yes," then follows. As I walk up the stairs, I can't help thinking about Jordan again. "And what was up with that phone call? He calls me, then hangs up. I mean, that's so 'ball's in my corner,' right?"

I turn around to Liam, who shrugs. I decide to continue ranting as we walk into my guest room. "And, you know, I know you answered the phone, and we had that picture in the paper. But I'm caught between a rock and a hard place, because if I call him back, then I lose any power I had. But if I don't call him back, then in his mind, we're either having raucous sex right now, or I am plying you with wine, and trying to seduce you. And, either way, once again, He-llo! we just broke up yesterday, I'd at least wait until the body was cold. I mean what kind of a slut does he think I am?"

I sit down on my guest bed, and wait for an answer from Liam, who stands in the doorway, wine in hand. "Were we in the paper?" Liam asks. "What paper?"

"It's not important. I don't want to talk about it," I say, sighing, and taking another sip of wine. "This is really good wine, by the way."

"Thank you," Liam says, walking into the room completely, then taking a look around.

As he looks out the window to admire my view, I notice an open pack of Marlboros on the side table. Without thinking, I pull a cigarette out, and pop it into my mouth as I lie down on the made bed.

"This room is fantastic!" Liam says, turning around. "I love your view of . . . what on earth are you doing?"

"Drysucking a cigarette," I say, then close my eyes, and deeply inhale my unlit cigarette. After a few blissful moments, I open my eyes to see Liam watching me with an unreadable expression on his face. "I quit smoking recently. That's why I've gained so much weight."

Liam jolts his head back a little. "Have you gained weight?"

That makes me sit up. "How are you not married?"

Liam laughs, "Oh, I'd tell you, but we haven't got that kind of time. Now I know you don't want to talk about it, but can I offer my opinion?"

I'm not sure I want to hear it, but I nod.

"Men who actually want to break up don't tend to call the next day. Unless you still have their key." Liam reconsiders. "And even then, some men just pay a locksmith to change the locks."

I fall onto the bed again. "Never mind. I don't want to talk about it."

"Wait, I'm not done. If he doesn't know what he has, then he's a fool."

Why is it the only hot men who ever say this to me out loud are the ones who only want to be friends?

Twenty-one

I spent the rest of the evening absolutely enchanted with my new houseguest. Besides being gorgeous, he was also ridiculously well traveled and well read. He had been everywhere, and done everything, from skiing in Gstaad to wine-tasting in South Africa. He had stayed in a hotel made entirely of ice in Sweden, and a hotel made entirely of salt in Bolivia. He was fluent in five languages. He was very funny, and he watched Food Network.

He was totally out of my league.

It was weird: At the beginning of the evening, no matter what Liam and I talked about, all I kept thinking about in the back of my mind was Jordan. I kept wondering if he'd call back, what he wanted to say, what he was thinking about.

But then he didn't call back. And as the night wore on, and I talked to Liam longer and longer, I stopped trying to guess what Jordan might be thinking and feeling, and started concentrating again on what I was thinking and feeling.

It had been a while since I had done that.

Which was good and bad. Because unfortunately I have a condition many single women my age face: I have OCDR: Obsessive Compulsive Disorder in the Romance department. My condition is chronic. So now, instead of obsessing over Jordan, I have started obsessing over Liam.

Earlier in the evening, Liam and I finished off the wine, and said our good nights. He didn't kiss me. Instead, he walked into his room, smiled, and said good night. I said good night back, then went into my room.

And then the nocturnal obsession began.

First of all, what happened tonight? We spent most of the night laughing, and within two feet of each other. On several occasions, he touched my shoulder. Why is it that he didn't suggest we open another bottle of wine? And if we were having such a good time, why is it he suddenly announced that we both had an early day, and should get to bed? What did I do wrong?

Or is it that he doesn't think I'm very cute?

Maybe he thinks I'm old. A guy like that could have any twenty-two-year-old model he wanted. Why would I even think he'd give me the time of day?

And I'm sure he thinks I'm a tubbo. This is a guy who runs every day of his life. He's going to want a Liam equivalent. And, unfortunately, I am a Charlie equivalent.

Man, why did I let this guy into my house? So I can feel bad about myself, and completely unworthy, for the next three weeks?

I hear water running in my bathroom.

Good, he's still up.

Why is it good he's still up? What am I going to do? Ambush him in the bathroom? Pin him against the light blue tiled walls, and show him who's boss?

I wonder what he's wearing. Probably boxers. He seems like a sexy boxer guy to me.

As my mind wanders into a fantasy of Liam with a bare chest allowing me to reach into his boxers, the water stops. I strain to hear him walk quietly through my hallway, then close his door.

I listen for more, but can't hear much. A clock radio being set. Then my guest bed creaking as he climbs in.

I'm in my own version of Hell.

I wonder what he would do if I knocked on his door right now? Well, answer it, of course. But what if, when he did, I just kissed him. What if I just put my arms around him, tilted my head, closed my eyes, and . . .

Oh, for God's sake Edwards, the poor man is captive in your house. At this point he'd kiss you back just to be polite, then find a new place to stay in the morning. And then he'd be out of your life for good.

And I don't want that. So: plan B. What if I knocked, and asked if I could stay with him tonight? I could just say I'm upset about Jordan, but don't want to talk about it, and could we just snuggle? Then if he wanted to try something . . .

It would only be because he had a half-naked woman in his bed.

I sit up in my bed, and sigh. I can't sleep. Not this worked up. I decide to go downstairs, and check my e-mail.

I try to silently open my door, but it creaks as I slowly pull it open. I tippy toe past Liam's room, and silently walk down the stairs.

Never drink alone.

Before heading into my office, I decide I want some chamomile tea. I head into my kitchen, fill my kettle with water, then silently open the cabinet where I keep the tea bags.

I hear Liam's door open. Hope swells: maybe he'll come downstairs and talk to me.

I strain to listen for upstairs foot traffic, but all is silent.

Oh well. Maybe it was my imagination. As I pull a tea bag from a box of Tazo Calm, an infusion of chamomile and rose petals, Liam appears in the doorway.

He's wearing nothing but boxers, (I knew it!) and looks even more doable than I could have imagined. It's at that moment, I suddenly remember that I'm in my favorite pair of Eeyore pajama bottoms with matching Eeyore T-shirt and big yellow, furry slippers (they look like big Tweety birds).

"Are you okay?" Liam asks, not sounding wildly worried about me, but definitely concerned.

"I'm fine," I say, a little confused. "I just can't sleep. Why?"

"No reason."

He stands in the doorway for a moment, crossing his arms, not saying anything. Finally, he says, "Okay, Good night then."

"Good night."

Liam turns to leave.

"Do you want some decaf tea before we go to bed?" I ask quickly. "I have Chamomile and Rose, or Sweet Orange."

"The orange sounds good. Let me go throw on a robe, and I'll meet you back down here."

Yay.

As the kettle boils, I happily grab another mug and tea bag, and internally praise myself for managing to keep the evening going. I fill the mugs with boiling water, then practically trot over to my living-room couch.

I put down the mugs on the coffee table, then have a seat. I'm so nervous, my back is ramrod straight. I take a deep breath to try and relax, but as I lean back on the couch, I realize I look like I'm trying too hard. Before I can decide on a look, I see Liam heading back down the stairs, wearing a terrycloth robe.

Liam sits. I hand him his tea. "Thank you," he says.

"Did you need cream or sugar?"

"No, no. This is good," Liam says.

And we're both silent.

There's nothing wrong with silence. Don't always race to fill up the silence with words.

As I watch him blow on his tea, I debate what to do. Lean over and softly kiss his cheek, then hope he gets the hint and makes his move? Treat his lips like a bull's eye, and make mine an arrow to be shot right at him at a hundred miles per hour? Coyly untie his robe, and grab him by his . . .

As I lean in coyly toward Liam, he furrows his brow and asks, "Can I ask you a personal question?"

I pull my body back. "Sure," I say awkwardly.

"If it's none of my business, you can tell me."

I don't like the sound of that. "Okay," I say.

"What did you want to be when you grew up?"

I stare at Liam. When did the evening go in this direction? "Catwoman," I finally answer. Off his dubious look, I elaborate. "Seriously. She was hot. She was confident. She never had to hold down a real job, and she could have Batman in two shakes of a cat's tail."

Liam smiles. "Okay, fair enough. I suppose I wanted to be a fireman when I grew up. What I mean is, what do you see yourself doing in ten years?"

I sigh. "That's a great question for a Monday night after I've broken up with my boyfriend. Thanks."

"I'm sorry," Liam apologizes. "It's just something I've been thinking about ever since I ran into you at the Halloween party. Have you ever thought about producing?"

"Movies?" I sputter out. "God, no."

"Why not?"

"Because I have no interest in being a money-grubbing sociopath who got into the business to get rich, terrorize employees, and get laid by would-be starlets," I blurt out. Then I backtrack. "No offense."

"None taken," Liam says, quietly chuckling at my assessment. "Although permit me to argue another side. As a producer, I track down screenplays that really speak to me, and pair them up with actors and directors who can make me laugh, or choke me up inside. Then I find someone with the money to get a film made with all of those talented people. And by handling all the countless other details in getting a film made, I become the glue that brings all of these people together to tell a story that might otherwise go untold. I think that's kind of a cool calling in life. Don't you?"

As I pick up my mug, I chuckle at a private thought.

"What?" Liam asks.

"Oh nothing. I just started thinking about all of the countless details I handle for Drew. If you ever suddenly need a hippo wrangler, a 1968 Jaguar XJ6, or a professional window washer willing to work at three A.M., I'm your girl."

Liam smiles. "Which is exactly what a producer does. He or she finds whatever his or her people need to get a movie made. By the way, can you really track down old cars like the 1968 Jaguar XJ6?"

"Sure."

"Because we need to find a 1966 Mercedes 250SL by next Monday morning. Would you be able to locate one of those?"

"I'll give you Sid Falco's number. He rents restored cars. If he doesn't have it, he'll find it in twenty-four hours or less."

Liam breaks into a proud smile.

"What?" I ask.

"You're a producer. You just don't know it yet."

I turn away from him, embarrassed. "Yeah, right. I'm not even vaguely qualified to be a producer."

Liam furrows his brow at me. "You not only managed to get one of the biggest stars in the world to read a script in a day, but you convinced him to commit to a movie that shot the next day, which is lightning speed by Hollywood standards. My lead took eight months to read it, and another four to commit. And that was with his agent bugging him every other day."

I shrug. "Drew owed me a favor."

Liam shakes his head. "You know, on the one hand, it's great to see someone who has so much going for her, and doesn't know it. On the other hand, it's incredibly frustrating. On any movie, attaching a star entitles you to at least an associate producer credit. Which, by the way, I secured for you the moment Drew signed on. But if you want to watch what I do, and get some hands-on training, I can make you a producer."

I take a teeny sip of tea to stall for time. I'll admit, it's a tempting offer. And producing is something I've always thought about doing; I just never had the nerve to voice that to anyone in a position to help me.

"Let me think about it," I say to Liam.

And for the rest of the night, I do.

Twenty-two

I wake up the next morning to the heavenly smell of gourmet coffee.

Half asleep, I putter into the kitchen (still wearing my Eeyore pajamas) to see Liam, looking perfect, dressed in a black T-shirt and workout pants, sitting at the dining room table, drinking coffee, and reading the paper.

"Good morning!" he says cheerfully.

"Good morning," I say, yawning. "Did you already go for your run?"

"Yes. It was wonderful. I love this time of year. It's so brisk at sunrise."

"Oh," I say, a little disappointed. "Why didn't you wake me? I would have gone with you."

Liam chuckles. "I did. You hit me on the arm and said, 'Go away. I'm a lover, not a runner.' "

Crap.

"Sorry," I say, wincing. "I'm not much of a morning person."

Liam laughs again. "It's okay. You don't have to be."

No, I don't have to be, I think to myself. *But I'd be more attractive to you if I was.*

"What's that coffee you made?" I ask, suppressing another yawn. "It smells amazing."

"Have some," Liam says brightly. "I brought a pound from home as another hostess gift. It's a Colombian blend from the farmer's market here."

As I walk into my kitchen to pour myself a cup, I have to ask, "We have a farmer's market here?"

"Yes, and they're excellent," he answers from the dining room. "They're here every Saturday from eight until one. I go whenever I can. Freshest eggs in town, and a different species of apple sold every week."

"Good to know," I say noncommittally as I pour my coffee. (Because, I don't care how cute the guy is, I am not getting up at eight in the morning to wander around a pile of fruit.)

I look down. Good God, I'm so tired, I forgot what I was wearing. Not that I really could have casually walked into the kitchen decked out in La Perla, but perhaps I could have killed the bird slippers, and maybe put on some cute jeans.

I pour some milk into my coffee as Liam comes into the kitchen, and rinses his coffee cup in the sink. "Do you have plans for Saturday?"

Oh no. Not the farmer's market. "As I said, I'm really not much of a morning person," I force myself to admit. "Though if you want to pick up some eggs, I'll be happy to give you money—"

Liam laughs. "No, no. I thought we might try to catch 'The Taming of the Shrew' this weekend if you're free."

I frown. "Oh," I say sadly. "I'm kind of busy."

I can't read his face as he says, "Oh. Well, maybe next weekend . . ."

I wince. "Actually, next weekend I have my friend Kate's engagement party."

Liam gives a quick nod. "Okay. Another time then."

"It's kind of a girls' night," I stammer out. "The Saturday thing, I mean. It's um . . . well, how would I put this?"

Liam's eyes widen as he waits for me to explain.

"We're going to a *Charlie's Angels* drag show."

Liam's eyes widen further, so I rush to explain. "It's called *Chico's Angels*. It's an episode of the TV show *Charlie's Angels,* performed as a musical by a bunch of Latin drag queens." I'm not sure if saying that out loud makes me sound weird or cool. "My cousin Jenn is a big fan, and we always go with her when a new episode comes out. So, um, that's why I'm busy."

Liam nods. "So, girls' night. No men allowed unless they wear dresses."

"Well, no. Actually, I guess guys can come . . ." I say, letting the sentence peter out. "Would you like to go with us?" I ask, in my head already coming up with a myriad of reasons for why he'll say no.

Liam smiles. "I'd be delighted."

I smile back, almost sheepishly. I don't know why, but I almost feel like I may have a date.

With my roommate.

And several of my closest female friends.

And some very fabulous and funky ladies.

Okay, so maybe I don't have a date. I still get to spend Saturday night with a hot guy.

"Oh, would it trouble you too much if I made a copy of your key today?" Liam asks me. "I have a date tonight, and I don't want you to have to wait up."

And the plot sickens.

Twenty-three

That night, I head out to Kate's apartment in Santa Monica to help her pick a wedding cake. Just what I want to be doing when I'm doing such a bang-up job with my own love life, right? Although I try to remember:

If you can't be with the cake you love, love the cake you're with.

"I'm so glad you're here," Kate says to me as she opens the door that night. "We have so much to cover tonight, and not a lot of time."

As I walk into Kate's large living-room/dining-room area, I can see Dawn leafing through a self-help book called *You and Improved.*

"Listen to this one," Dawn says, laughing. "Places to meet men: the line at the DMV. Right, because we're all so in the dating mood then. Oh, and an Al-Anon meeting. Yeah, that doesn't scream codependent or anything."

Dawn throws down the book, then picks up a pink hardcover entitled, *Good Women: Poor Choices.* She flips through the book. "Man-hating chapter . . ." She turns another few pages. "Man-hating chapter . . ." Dawn opens the back cover to check out the author's photo. "Yikes! If I looked like that, I'd be bitter, too. Hey, Charlie, I got something for your book of advice."

"Shoot," I say.

Just because you can perm, doesn't mean you should.

"Trust," Dawn says, putting up her hand to indicate the words *Trust me*. "Much like blind dates, and Jim Carrey in dramatic roles, it never ends well."

Kate opens her coat closet, and pulls out an open box of self-help books. "Okay, I'm getting rid of all of these. Anyone need a diet book? I have South Beach, Weight Watchers, the Cake Diet . . ."

"There's a cake diet?" I ask, taking the book and leafing through it with the false (yet eternal) hope that I can find a way to stuff myself with Twinkies, and still lose weight.

"Yeah, but it wasn't what I thought," Kate admits. "It told me how to make things like carrot cake with fake sugar, and zucchini bread. Life is too short not to eat real cake. And, with that in mind"—Kate stands in front of her dining room table like a *Price is Right* girl, and demonstrates—"I present to you . . . your dinner."

Kate's table can only be described as Wedding Central: every available surface is littered with plates and bowls filled with wedding-cake paraphernalia. Each plate has a different type of cake on it: chocolate, white, marble, lemon, mocha (which looked like chocolate, but Kate had stuck a pink Post-it on the plate saying it was mocha), a few other flavors I couldn't recognize by sight, and carrot.

Next to the plates were bowls of potential fillings: cream-cheese filling, chocolate ganache, chocolate mousse (again, another Post-it), vanilla cream with chocolate chips—I could go on. Total, there were about a dozen fillings.

Finally, there were four plates of potential frostings, each plate with three scoops of frosting (a scoop from each of the three bakeries Kate was considering).

This is where Kate asks us to begin.

"Now, I want you to taste the frostings by themselves first," Kate says. "The first priority is to make sure they don't taste like Crisco.

That's my first way to eliminate potential bakeries—crappy frosting means a crappy wedding cake. While you taste, I'm going to show you pictures I've cut out of various wedding cakes that I like."

Dawn is still fascinated with her book. "Here's another bit of advice I like: Give yourself a timetable: you will be engaged within the year, and married within two. Don't be halfhearted about it." She looks up from the book. "Because nothing eases a guy into a relationship faster than a woman with a biological clock and a deadline."

Kate turns to Dawn. "Hey! Maid of honor! I got at least twelve thousand calories with your name on it. Help me out here."

"Sorry," Dawn says, tossing the book down, and standing up to meet us in the dining room.

"Okay, ladies, stay with me," Kate says with a look of determination as she looks over her sea of wedding cake. "The next few hours won't be pretty. But we have a mission to accomplish, and we take no prisoners. What are we?"

"Women of action," Dawn and I say in unison.

"I said, What are we?!"

"Women of action!" Dawn and I yell like privates addressing a sergeant.

"Excellent," Kate says, grinning widely as she gives us a thumbs-up.

Kate hands us each a fork, then takes the first magazine cutout from a pile of cutouts, and hands it to us. The wedding cake in the photo looks like a big lamp shade. "This is a rolled fondant cake. The ruffles are made of white chocolate—"

"Let me stop you right there," I say, in all seriousness. "White chocolate is a lie perpetuated by the candy-making industry. It's waxy, gross, and not even real chocolate. You can't have a cake made with that stuff."

Kate shrugs her shoulders. "Okay." She crumples up her cutout picture, and throws it into the trash. "Moving on . . ."

Dawn decides to follow my lead. "As long as we're on the subject of cakes not to be considered until hell freezes over," she says, pointing to one of the plates, "is that carrot cake I see on your wedding-cake table?"

Kate examines the plates, trying to figure out which one is the carrot. "Oh, that. Yeah, Will likes carrot cake, so I . . ." She lets her sentence peter out after she looks back up to see Dawn and me slowly shaking our heads "no" in unison. "All right," Kate says, slightly exasperated. "No need to get snippy."

Kate shows us another picture she cut out of a magazine, this time of a four-tiered confection of square shaped cakes, with little white flowers all over. It is beautiful.

"Now this is also a rolled fondant cake . . ." Kate begins.

Dawn takes her fork, and prepares to dig in to a white scoop of heaven. "Which of these frostings is the rolled fondant?"

"The off-white one," Kate tells her.

Dawn is about to dip her fork into one of the white frostings to officially begin the tasting, but Kate stops her.

"No," Kate says. "That's the royal icing. It's white white."

"I thought you said the white was the fondant," Dawn says.

"I said the off-white. But you put your fork in the white white, not the off-white. The white white is royal icing."

Dawn bugs her eyes out at me in a mild panic, and I am so enjoying not being the maid of honor. Dawn moves her fork over a different plate, then lets it dangle in midair.

"No," says Kate. "That's pale yellow. That's the buttercream."

Dawn glares at Kate, but she is determined to be on her best behavior. She moves her fork over the next plate, and leaves it hanging in midair, waiting for approval.

"That's cream-colored," Kate says.

"Oh, for God's sake!" Dawn says, dropping her fork and starting to lose it. "How the hell do you know that's cream-colored, and not off-white?"

"Because that's whipped cream," Kate answers.

I suppress a giggle. Kate writes the numbers one through four on Post-its, then sticks them on the four plates of frosting. "Start with plate number four," she instructs us.

Number four is the rolled fondant, and Dawn and I take a taste as Kate moves on to show us the four-squared cake in the picture. "Now this cake is made of a pale, pale green rolled fondant," she begins cheerfully, "with what they call 'embroidered' flowers, made of royal icing all around . . ." She turns to us, and her face drops. "Why are you both making that face?"

Because this is the most disgusting food I've ever eaten, I think to myself.

But I'm not going to say it. I am determined to be a good bridesmaid.

Dawn daintily dabs the corner of her mouth with a paper napkin, clearly trying to suppress her gagging reflex. "Sweetie," she asks, her mouth still full, "do you happen to know what rolled fondant is?"

"Umm . . ." Kate grabs a dictionary, and looks it up. "Sugar paste."

Dawn and I spit the rolled fondant into our napkins. Then we wipe our tongues with the napkins for good measure. Ick.

"Okay," Kate says cheerfully. "No cakes with rolled fondant. How about the next one . . ." Kate hands us a picture of an all white, three-layered circular cake with red flowers decorating the top and bottom. "This is a white buttercream cake with red flowers made of royal icing."

"Which one's the royal icing?" I ask.

"Plate number one," Kate says, grabbing the dictionary again as Dawn and I each take a forkful from plate number one. "According to this, royal icing is," she reads, "a viscous substance secreted from the pharyngeal gland of honeybees . . ."

Dawn and I spit that one out into our napkins even quicker as Kate continues reading. "Wait, no, that's royal jelly. Royal icing's not in here."

"Why don't we think 'buttercream?'" Dawn suggests. "After all, everyone loves buttercream."

"Okay," Kate says, flipping through her pile of magazine clippings. Flip, flip, flip. "Oh, here's one I like."

She shows us a three-layer cake with buttercream lace and buttercream flowers over a white buttercream canvas.

"Now, see, that's nice," I say.

"You like that?" Kate says, "I also like this one."

She hands us another picture, and it is stunning: a three-tiered white cake with green and white flowers piled on top, then cascading down the white cake.

"The flowers are made of sugar," Kate explains. "But you don't have to eat them."

"It's gorgeous," Dawn says, and I tell Kate I agree wholeheartedly.

"Well, we've got a finalist," Kate says happily.

She made us look at more than thirty other cake pictures, but we all knew: that was the one.

Now it was on to my favorite part: the cake tasting!

We spent the next hour sampling the cakes. It wasn't hard to decide on the baker. The problem was agreeing on which kind of cake to have for each layer, as well as which fillings.

Heated debates ensued (I'll admit, initially as an excuse to eat more cake). We tried every possible combination of cake and filling possible: chocolate with chocolate, chocolate with cream cheese, lemon with cream cheese, lemon with strawberries and cream, white with strawberries and cream—you name it, we ate it. By the time we were done eating, I think we were all about ten pounds heavier, and in dire need of a cup of black coffee.

Finally, we agreed on a chocolate-bottom layer with a cream-cheese filling, a white middle layer with a chocolate ganache filling, and a top layer of whatever Kate wanted, even though:

The tradition of saving the top layer of your wedding cake for your first anniversary leads to stale, frostbitten cake. Eat it on your wedding night.

After another hour of helping pick flower arrangements, Dawn and I said our good-byes to Kate, and called it a night.

After I got into my car, I made the mistake of checking my iPhone. Jordan had texted me:

> Hey. I'm sorry I hung up last night when I called. I miss you. How are you doing?

I sit in my car, staring at the text for a good three or four minutes.

What is it about men that they seem to instinctively know when you're okay with them going away, and then they come back to pursue you?

I hit reply, and begin texting back:

> I'm OK.

I stare at the screen. There are so many things I want to say, but I don't know how he'll react: I'm not okay, I miss you. I'm better than okay, I'm pissed at you. There's someone new. There's no one else. I hate you for treating me like this. I ache for you.

I stick with 'I'm OK.'

But, instead of sending it, I turn off my phone.

Twenty-four

Half an hour later, I unlock my door to my lit-up, though empty, living room. Hoping Liam is back from his date early, I yell, "Honey, I'm home!"

"Be right down!" Liam yells from upstairs. "I have wine for you in the kitchen!"

Still reeling from Jordan's message, I go into my kitchen to see a bottle of Clos du Val Chardonnay, opened and breathing, and an empty glass next to it. Next to the wine is a cheese platter consisting of what looks like a triangle of Brie and a triangle of blue, accompanied by some crackers and fruit. "What's all this?" I yell from the kitchen as I pour myself a glass of wine.

Liam appears in my doorway, wearing boxer shorts and a white cotton T-shirt, and looking ridiculously hot, as always. "I figured that after dining on cake samples all night, you might want some real food when you got home."

I use a cheese spreader I didn't know I owned to spread some Brie on a cracker. "I love Brie," I say enthusiastically.

As I put it into my mouth and experience a C.O. (culinary orgasm), Liam tells me, "That's actually a Camembert from Normandy. I remember how much you said you liked Brie, so I thought this would be a fun way to expand your palette. The other is a Valdeón from Spain."

I try the Valdeón, and I am in heaven. "My God, this is so good. Where did you find these?"

"From the cheese shop next to Trader Joe's," he says, referring to the gourmet cheese shop I have within a mile of me that I've never set foot in. "I'm still torn between that one and the one on Sunset."

"There's a cheese shop on Sunset?" I say, surprised.

Liam smiles and shakes his head as he pulls a can of Guinness out of the refrigerator for himself. "You really never have explored your neighborhood, have you?"

I shrug sheepishly as I sip the wine. "I will now." Then I force myself to pleasantly ask, "So, how was your date?"

Liam pours the Guinness into a large glass. "Well, it's ten o'clock, and I'm already home. So that should tell you something. How was your evening?"

I shrug. "Oh . . . fine."

Liam cocks his head. "Doesn't sound like it was fine."

"It was fine," I reiterate.

I can tell from the look on Liam's face, he doesn't buy it.

I want to tell him about the text from Jordan. but I want to keep my options open with him. And nothing says, "About as sexy as a dead fish," quite as much as a mopey girl still hooked on her ex-boyfriend.

"Sometimes it's hard to be happy for your friends," I say, thinking out loud. I stop myself. Take a nervous sip of wine. "My God. I must just sound like this really horrible, awful person now. I just mean . . . I don't know. It just seems like all my friends live their lives so much more effortlessly than I do."

Liam doesn't take his eyes off me as he leans against my counter. "How do you mean?"

"Well, Kate was with a guy for nine years. She finally has the courage to break up with him and . . . bam! The universe gives her a husband. Andy just got married, and bam! She's already pregnant. Drew decides he wants to go to space; I guarantee you through some bizarre turn of events he will go into space. Meanwhile, I languish around in my life, never quite doing what I set out to do. I'm tired of being a silver medalist, and tired of fighting uphill battles that I only sort of win."

Liam takes a cracker, and spreads it with the Valdeón. "I'm sorry. Why is it bad to be a silver medalist?"

I let my head fall into my hands. "Crap. You actually are a silver medalist. So, that came out wrong."

For some reason, it's really important to me that Liam understand what I'm talking about. I take a sip of wine, and try again. "Aren't you ever jealous of the guy who won the gold medal in your event?"

Liam shrugs. "Sure." He smiles as he takes a sip of his beer. "But that doesn't mean I regret going after my goal. I love running. I loved being in the Olympics. Silver's pretty good."

"Didn't you ever get tired of going after your goal?'

"Of course. But what's the alternative? Eating potato chips on the couch, and hoping people will come to you with life's big rewards?"

I make a big show of eyeing the ceiling and thinking about that. "I don't know. But can we try that for a while and see how it works out?"

Liam laughs. "If this is your way of trying to get out of becoming a producer, I won't let you." He rubs my arm in a friendly way. "What you're feeling is normal. Don't beat yourself up over it. Particularly not tonight. You just broke up with your boyfriend. Of course you don't want to think about a wedding."

"Right," I say. "And I certainly didn't want to be given diet books by my helpful friend right before I gorged myself on cake."

"You don't need to go on a diet," Liam says, sounding like the thought of it is the most ridiculous thing he's ever heard.

"I'm sorry," I say, smiling and flirting a bit. "Tell me again how you're single?"

Liam laughs. "You sound like my mother. Of course, what she says is usually something more like, 'Why can't you keep a woman around?' and it's followed with expressions like, 'Carrying on the family name,' and 'Not getting any younger.'"

I laugh. "Meaning you or her?" I ask.

"Both, actually," Liam says, smiling warmly at me.

Liam and I spent the next hour on the perfect date: we were comfortable together, we laughed a lot, we had great food and wine.

At the end of the evening, Liam hugged me good night, gave me a kiss on the forehead, told me how much he adored me, then went to bed in his room.

It's at that point that I realized that no matter what I did, no matter how funny I was, how cute or how clever, he saw me as a friend. At this point a good friend, a lovable friend, but just a friend.

And he became the second man this week to break my heart.

Twenty-five

I can't sleep. I'm Ping-Ponging between two thoughts: whether or not to seduce Liam, and have him see me as more than a roommate, and whether or not to text Jordan back, and try to make things work with us.

Do I pursue Liam—just go knock on his door and act all coquettish until he suddenly sees what he's been missing, sweeps me off my feet, then carries me to my guest bed so we can share a night of conjugal bliss?

Or, do I pursue Jordan? Text him back and act like nothing's wrong? Call him tomorrow and act like Sunday morning never happened? Keep everything status quo, and hope things get better once he gets home?

It's like I'm trying to run to the destination of "relationship," but I can't figure out which direction I'm supposed to be running toward. So I just end up running in circles, fretting.

As I ponder my dilemma, I putter downstairs, pull a pint of vanilla Häagen-Dazs from the freezer, grab a spoon, and head upstairs to call Jamie.

"Here's a novel idea," Jamie deadpans. "How about letting one of them pursue you?"

"God, that's just too depressing," I say, with my mouth full. "I'd like to think I have more control over my destiny than waiting around, hoping I don't get picked last for the basketball team."

"Are you eating again?" Jamie asks incredulously.

"No," I lie with my mouth still full. "But do you think that's why Liam isn't interested in me? Because I'm eating too much?"

"No. I think he's not interested in you because he's living in your guest room, because he knows you just broke up with your boyfriend, and because you're working for a man who is a nut who could pull out of his movie at any time for any reason, including, 'You banged my assistant and now she's in tears, and we can't possibly come to work to finish your movie.'"

I'm relieved to hear this. "So, you don't think he doesn't want me because I'm fat, or a loser, or a neurotic mess?"

"Do you open with that when talking to new men?"

My phone beeps. I see it's Andy, and put Jamie on hold. "Hey, Mommy. What are you doing up so late?"

"Jamie just e-mailed me that you have a crush on Liam," Andy says with a concerned tone.

"I don't have a crush on Liam," I insist, trying to sound as irritated as possible. "He's just staying with me for a few days. Why Jamie would jump to the conclusion—"

"Jamie is e-mailing me that you're lying right now," Andy interrupts.

"Hold on," I say to my sister.

I click back over to my brother. "How do you even know what I'm saying?"

"Hi, I'm Jamie. I'll be your brother today," Jamie deadpans. "Oh, Andy is e-mailing me that she's going to throw up soon, and to have you click back over to her."

"How do you people type so fast?" I ask, exasperated. "Okay, bye."

Jamie says good-bye, and I click back to Andy. "Sorry. I don't exactly have a crush, it's just—"

"I know," Andy says quickly. "Jordan just dumped you and you're vulnerable. Just trust me: Liam is not a good rebound guy. He's had more conquests than William."

I think about that for a moment. "Kate's William?"

"No, William the Conqueror. As a matter of fact, we used to call him Liam the Conqueror. Why? Has Kate's fiancé had a lot of conquests?"

Before I can answer, Andy continues, "Seriously, I love Liam like a brother, but the truth is, he goes through women as fast as . . . our brother."

"Ew," I can't help but snicker, the left half of my upper lip moving up like Lucy Ricardo in *I Love Lucy*.

"Yeah," Andy agrees. "Oh God, I gotta go throw up again. I have no idea why they call it 'morning sickness;' I'm nauseous all the Goddamn time. Promise me you won't do anything stupid."

"Okay, I promise," I say, probably even meaning it. "Why do you think they call it morning sickness at midnight?"

I hear Andy heave on the other end of the phone. "I'm sorry. Can we discuss semantics another day?" she asks.

"Sorry," I say. "Love you, bye."

"Love you, too. Bye," she says, then hangs up.

Lots of conquests. Yuck. I mean, I guess it doesn't surprise me: men who look like that don't need to do much pursuing.

Still, he seemed nicer than that.

My phone rings again. I check the caller ID. Argh . . .

I pick up. "Hello, Drew."

"I need you to give me directions," Drew says, "I'm lost. I'm driving in some town just outside L.A., and I don't know what it's called, but it sounds like a cheese."

"You're going to have to be more specific," I offer gently.

"Fine. I'm passing a Wal-Mart on my right."

"Thank you. That narrows it down to everywhere except your dining room."

"Wait. I also passed a gas station. Oh, and does a McDonalds help?"

I ignore his other identifying landmarks, call LoJack, and find out where my boss's car is. Then I patch them through to Drew to give him directions home.

I don't even want to know.

Twenty-six

Learn to cook.

The following morning, I awake to the smell of bacon.

Really . . . is there any better smell in the world?

I head downstairs to find my new roommate slaving over my hot stove. He's got three jets working: sausage sizzles in one pan, while hash browns cook in another. And in the final pan, Liam fries up some eggs. Off to the side, bacon and some sort of sausage rest on paper towels, getting degreased.

"Good morning!" he says brightly. "Hope you don't mind. I've been rifling through your kitchen. Coffee's in your coffee thermos."

"I have a coffee thermos?" I ask.

"Yeeeessss . . . ," Liam says, smiling as he drags out the word. He grabs a medium-sized silver jug, pours me a wonderfully smelling brew, quickly hands it to me, then goes back to the eggs. "I found it stored in your oven. Along with your frying pans."

I look at the thermos. "So that's what this is. I always thought it was for making monstrously big Jell-O shots."

Liam chuckles at my joke. "I'm making us Irish fry-ups. You're not one of those women who needs a sliced tomato on her plate, are you?"

"I never need vegetables on my plate," I answer.

"Excellent. The newspapers are already on the table. Have a seat, breakfast will be ready in a moment."

I take a sip of coffee as I walk into my dining room. On the table is a *New York Times,* a *Los Angeles Times,* and a *Wall Street Journal,* all folded neatly, ready to be opened.

If it weren't for Andy's information last night, I think I'd be tempted to take an arm and push everything off the table, then when Liam walked in, throw him down on the table, and take advantage of his virtue.

But now that I have Andy's information, I know that Liam's "perfect guy" act is just an act, designed to get women into bed before they realize he's not perfect, he won't call them later, and that he will be the catalyst for a month of ice cream and self-pity binges.

Actually, Andy didn't tell me that—I'm just assuming.

Liam walks in, carrying two plates, each with a pile of bacon, two types of sausage, runny fried eggs, greasy hash browns, and some starchy-looking concoction that appears to be fried in grease.

"I know how much you like bacon," Liam says, putting the plate with the big pile of bacon in front of me. "So I made extra."

"Thank you," I say.

Things that seem too good to be true usually are. This is especially true with men.

I look at the greasy mess on my plate. "It smells heavenly," I lie. I point to the starchy bready-looking thing. "What is that?"

"Irish soda bread, cooked in sausage drippings."

What is this? Some kind of test to see what I'll put in my mouth? "Uh-huh," I say. "And this?" I ask, pointing to . . . um . . . well, some kind of fried meat?

"Black pudding," he answers.

"Oh," I say, feeling that one is safe to have a bite of.

I put a forkful in my mouth. Oh, yuck. I think I'm going to throw up. With my mouth still full, I ask, "What exactly is black pudding?"

"It's a traditional Irish sausage. I think Americans call it blood sausage."

"Feckity, feck, feck, feck," I blurt out, running to the kitchen to spit it out in the garbage.

Liam yells from the other room, "You didn't even give it a chance."

"I won't give anal sex a chance either, but I'm comfortable with that, too!" I yell back. I return to the table to stare at the runny eggs. They look like they have the consistency of snot. "Aren't you supposed to cook the eggs a little more?"

Liam smiles as he dips his greasy soda bread into his runny egg yolk. "Nah. Puts some hair on your chest."

"I don't want hair on my chest," I say, trying not to look too disgusted as I pick around the food with my fork.

"At least give them a try. I added the Fleur de Sel from your spice cabinet."

"Fleur de Sel? That's salt, right?" I say, furrowing my brow, and feeling like a seven year old just three Brussels sprouts away from dessert.

"Just try it," Liam implores.

I take a small bite of runny egg, and chew it quickly. Then I wash down my small piece of food with about a half gallon of coffee. "It's great," I lie, taking a piece of bacon, relieved to find one thing on this entire plate I can stomach.

Liam laughs. "The hash browns are cooked in bacon fat. You might want to try them."

I look at the potatoes and debate. "I'd ask why on earth would someone want to cook hash browns in bacon fat. But I must admit, it sounds kind of inspired." I break off a piece of potato with my fork and tentatively put it in my mouth.

Not bad. I take a bigger bite.

Liam smiles at me, then slices off a piece of sausage and pops it into his mouth. "So, did you hear where we found the perfect location for the final few weeks of filming?" he asks with a full mouth.

"No," I say, continuing to pick at my food. "Where?"

"Lake Arrowhead."

Lake Arrowhead is a picturesque little community located in the San Bernardino mountains, about two hours outside of the city. It is positively magical at Christmastime: the whole town decorates, and there's usually snow. There's hot chocolate available almost everywhere, at least three stores that sell Christmas ornaments, and even a candy shop. Not a bad place to work at Christmas.

"I need to scout a few of the locations today and tomorrow," Liam says, taking another bite of runny egg. "Need to make sure we can get all the permits we need, reserve the necessary hotel rooms, things like that. Why don't you come with me? Think of it as the first few days of learning to be a producer."

"Hah!" I blurt out, smirking.

Liam looks startled by my response.

"I'm sorry," I say. "It's just Drew would never let me leave his side while he's shooting. What if his cup ran out of coffee, or his toilet melted in his dressing room?"

As if on cue, my phone rings. As I walk over to pick it up, Liam says to me, "Well, if you could swing it, I've reserved two rooms at the Lake Arrowhead Resort, and I'd be happy to buy you a fabulous dinner at BIN189."

I see from the caller ID, it's Drew. I pick up. "Good morning," I say cheerfully.

"See if the suites are really only twelve hundred square feet," Drew says without preamble.

"Excuse me?"

"I mean, I know it's a low-budget movie, but doesn't that strike you as a bit tiny for a presidential suite?" Drew asks.

"Drew, that's the same size as my whole house."

"Which is why I keep telling you that you don't have to keep slumming it. You can move in with me. Anyway, go up there with Liam, see if you can get me anything bigger than the presidential suite, and I'll see you tomorrow."

"I don't think that's a good idea," I say carefully, painfully aware that Liam is watching me.

"Why?" Drew asks. "Afraid the romantic ambience of the place is going to inspire you to do the horizontal hokey pokey?"

"No," I say, trying to sound disgusted. "It's just . . ." I struggle to find a reason to stay in the city that will insult neither the man on the phone nor the man in my dining room. "What are you going to do for coffee while I'm gone?"

"Whitney already said she can send a PA out for my Starbucks."

"What if you get lost in a small town outside of the city, and you're not sure of the name, but it sounds like a kind of lunch meat?"

Drew considers that possibility for a moment. "Then I'll call your cell up in Lake Arrowhead."

"What if you get the uncontrollable urge to rescue a rabbit from a nest of vipers? And there's no one to talk you out of it? Or no one to call the proper doctor to get you the proper antivenom?"

There's silence on Drew's end.

"It's no wonder you're not in a long-term relationship," Drew finally says snippily. "You have a very nasty habit of rehashing a man's past mistakes. That's my yoga instructor. Gotta go! Namaste."

And he hangs up on me.

Two hours of brutal traffic later, Liam and I are in his Z3, driving east on the 210 Freeway, toward the San Bernardino mountains, and up to Lake Arrowhead.

We haven't talked much. Part of the reason is because Liam has been on his headset most of the morning talking to various people from the movie. But part of it is because I don't feel like talking.

I'm feeling a bit betrayed, which I know makes no sense because Liam hasn't actually done anything to me. But still—it sure seemed like he was flirting with me. You don't make a girl breakfast, even a disgusting frat-boy breakfast, without knowing she's going to develop a crush on you. Or bring her a bottle of wine twice in two days. Or walk around in your purple paisley silk boxer shorts looking ridiculously fuc . . .

Oh, I'm so mad at myself right now. Why am I so tempted by yet another guy I know is bad for me? I don't need to be another notch on someone's belt, and frankly I'm offended that he has chosen to see me that way.

Well, if he's chosen to see me that way.

But, come on, do you take a woman to a hotel out of the city for a night if you don't see her that way?

"You're awfully quiet," Liam says, rescuing me from my thoughts.

"Oh, I'm sorry," I say. "I've got a lot on my mind."

"Want to talk about it?" he inquires.

I shake my head "no."

As traffic finally clears up, Liam drives us onto the 15 Freeway North. As we drive on the overpass, I stare out over three thousand unit tract houses that all look exactly the same, dotting a landscape of desert. As I stare at the pile of tumbleweeds that have blown into the tract's outer wall, I wonder why I'm out here at all. What exactly am I hoping for? That he will forgo his harem, and decide that I'm his one and only?

Hah!

"Isn't the American West fascinating?" Liam says with wonder as he pulls his car into the fast lane of the 15. "Shades of Billy the Kid, Jesse James, Wyatt Earp . . ."

I try not to look too horrified and confused as I look at the houses around us. "It's nothing but ugly houses in shades of chewing-gum beige and baby-poop brown."

Liam tries another approach. "But look at all the wide open space—"

"Yeah, right. People who live out here have all of seventeen inches of space between their McMansion and the McMansion next door."

Liam eyes me, then jokes, "Someone's cranky."

"I'm sorry," I say.

Then I go for broke. "So, what's up with this dating thing?" I ask in an accusatory fashion. "How many women are you dating?"

I can't read Liam's face: Is he startled by my question? Confused? He takes a moment to respond, and his answer completely emulates that of a presidential candidate. "I don't know. A few?"

"Well, you brought a bombshell to the Halloween party," I point out, doing my best to sound like a lawyer showing the jury Exhibit A. "You had a date last night. I know you were a Lothario in college. I'm just wondering what the deal is. Are you juggling three women? Four? Do you have a girl on the side who thinks she's your girlfriend that you don't want anyone to know about? What's up?"

Liam seems stunned by my lengthy accusation, but not insulted. "I can see my reputation from business school precedes me," he jokes.

I shrug. "Andy was a little concerned that I was rooming with you. She was afraid I might wind up having a crush on you."

"And I can certainly see why that would keep her up nights," he says with a slight amount of sarcasm creeping into his voice. "Is that why you've been acting strangely all morning?"

"I haven't been acting strangely," I snap. "I'm just curious. Men who look like you are either taken, gay, or both. They're not just wandering the streets, ready to be picked up at a moment's notice."

Liam turns to me, smirking. "How *do* I look?"

I cross my arms and turn away from him. "Don't change the subject."

"You just said, that men who look like me—"

"Just answer the question," I interrupt.

"Okay," Liam says, shrugging, and clearly irked with me. "I was dating a woman off and on for several years. She was on the road so much of the year that we might as well have been in a long-distance relationship, which was dreadful. She broke up with me several months ago to take a job in Connecticut. I've been on a few dates since then, but my experience with women is that if you ask them out once, they want to see where it's going, and I'm not ready to see where anything is going yet. Which I always tell women on the first date. Which usually means there is no second date. But I don't want a rerun of my first year of business school, when the love of my life broke up with me, and I responded by seducing anything that would move." He turns to me. "Is that an acceptable response?"

My voice softens. "Yeah," I say, turning to look at the road in front of us.

We're both silent for a minute or two. All I can think is dammit, he doesn't want a relationship. There's no point in liking him now, because he's just admitted it will lead to my assured heartbreak. Which really sucks, because I'm really beginning to like the guy.

And not the perfect guy, either. I mean, the guy who walks around in boxer shorts, speaks in a sexy accent, and brings me wine and cheese—I'm loving him. But in the past few days I've really gotten to know Liam, and he's really funny and really fun to listen to. And, most of the time, incredibly easy to be with. It's been so long since I've been around someone who was incredibly easy to be with. I forgot there were relationships out there that weren't hard.

That said, if we do anything romantic, the relationship would get really hard really quickly.

Like I said, dammit.

Then my brain suddenly switches gears. I start thinking about how nice it has been to have Liam around. And, once again, how effortless. I always have room in my life for another low-maintenance friendship. What girl doesn't? And, if the sexual chemistry is taken out of the mix, I still get a pretty great friend.

Overall, not a bad deal for me.

"Thank you for answering me," I finally say. "I'm sorry I was being so cranky."

"I'm sorry your sister still remembers things people did almost ten years ago. Not that I don't take full responsibility. I was an asshole."

I try to come up with something supportive to say, but I'm at a loss. Liam interrupts my thoughts. "Oh my God. Look at all the snow up there."

I look up at the mountains ahead of us. It would appear from the clouds surrounding the peaks and the white stuff under those clouds, that the town is in the middle of the season's first snowstorm. "Uh-oh," I say. "You brought snow chains, right?"

Liam gives me a weird look. "I think so."

Forty minutes later, we are heading up the mountain, and waiting in line to cross a roadblock set up by the California Highway Patrol. An officer walks up to Liam's window as Liam rolls it down. "Good afternoon, sir," the officer says to us.

"Good afternoon, officer," Liam responds ever so politely. "Are we allowed to continue on?"

"You can," the officer assures him. "But the storm's been kind of rough, so we're requiring snow chains. Are they in your trunk?"

"I'm not sure," Liam says. "If I opened my trunk, would you mind showing me what they look like?"

I turn to Liam. "Oh my God. You don't know what snow chains are, do you?"

"Can't say as I do," Liam says. "But I bought the car with a complete maintenance kit in the trunk. Every wrench, tire iron, liquid rubber, and spare known to man. I'm sure they're back there somewhere."

Before I can tell him that if he doesn't know what snow chains are, he doesn't have them, Liam jumps out of his car, and he and the CHP officer head back to the trunk. I wait as they discuss the fact that Liam doesn't have snow chains.

A minute later, he returns to the driver's side and gets back in. "They're turning me around. I need to go get snow chains, and come back."

"Actually," I say, trying not to sound too cocky, "you need to buy them, put them on your car, and then come back."

Liam nods slightly. "Fair enough. Do you know what snow chains look like?"

"Yes."

"Can you show me how I can put them on my car?"

"Yes."

"Well, then . . ." Liam says cheerfully. "An extra perk to bringing you along."

Liam turns his car around, and we head to a road stand where a local entrepreneur is selling snow chains for about five times what you'd pay for them at Pep Boys.

We pull over.

"These are actual chains," Liam says, seemingly flabbergasted as we look at the selection of sizes a few moments later.

"Of course they're actual chains," I say as I peruse the assortment of different size chains. "What did you think they were?"

"Well, I don't know. I figured it was like the term *bear claw*. It's a donut, not the actual hand of a bear."

I laugh. "No, they're chains. And you're holding the biggest ones."

Liam looks down at the web of thick chains he holds. "Well, I figure nothing but the best. We want to be safe."

"Those are chains designed for an eighteen-wheeler. You drive a sportscar." I pick up four smaller chains. "You need these."

I hand Liam the four smaller chains, he pays for them, and we walk over to his car. As I place the first two chains down in front of Liam's two front tires, I explain the process to my little Irishman. "Most people in Southern California never have to deal with snow. So we never put snow tires on our cars. However, we do occasionally use chains." Liam looks down at the chains, then back up to me. He seems fascinated, so I continue. "Now, what I'm going to do is slowly roll my tires over the chains. Then, once the tires are completely in the middle of the weave of the chains, I'm going to pull each chain up over the tire, thereby causing each tire to be completely covered in a chain, which will keep the tires from sliding on the snowy and icy roads. Then we're going to do the same thing on the rear tires. Okay?"

"How can I help?" Liam asks.

"You can stand back and look pretty," I say, jumping into his car, and starting it up.

"It's a stick shift," Liam warns me.

"Not to worry," I say as I turn on the car and roll his tires over the chains. "My daddy raised girls who can drive a stick, shoot a gun, and beat you up."

I spend the next few minutes getting all the chains on the car, and we're back on the road in no time. We clear the roadblock in a few minutes.

I am so proud of myself, I am practically beaming.

"Why are you smiling like that?" Liam asks, smiling to himself at the sight of glowing little me.

I shrug. "I don't know," I say, practically giggling.

"Yes, you do," he says, amused by me. "It's like this little private joke in your head. Make fun of the guy who comes from a country of rain—"

"No, it's not that," I assure him. I take a few moments to try and put it into words. "I just love that after all this time, I finally found something that I knew how to do that you didn't do better."

"Ah . . . incompetence," he jokes. "Gets the women every time."

"No," I say, laughing and lightly punching him on the arm. "The fact that you didn't know how to do something, but you were so open to letting me help you . . . I don't know . . . It's like you're perfect, but you're not perfect. I like that. It's very charming."

"Okay, so if I am to understand this, you like me better because I didn't know what a snow chain was, or how to put one on my car?"

I smile and blush a little as I shrug. "Actually, yeah."

Liam chuckles, and shakes his head. "Charlie, I love ya, but American women are so strange."

Twenty-seven

Take two-day vacations when you can fit them in.

The drive up the mountain was stunning. I'm not used to seeing so many trees, and all of them are covered in glittering snow. I'm struck by how much the snow appears to glitter. Southern Californians don't get to see snow much. So when we do, it seems almost magical. I open the window to smell the clean, noncity air. I take a deep (albeit chilly) breath and I am relaxed, and in heaven.

Soon, we are driving slowly through the town of Lake Arrowhead, and around its scenic Lake Arrowhead Village, a collection of shops with architecture ranging from early log cabin to German cookie cutter. As I watch the snow silently fall onto us in the quiet town, I am struck by how clean the air is, how polite the other drivers are, how uncrowded everything is.

Don't get me wrong—I'm a city girl. I always will be. But it's wonderful to be able to take a day or two and just forget about the day-to-day problems of your regular life, and to recharge your batteries.

Liam pulls into the Lake Arrowhead Resort, which was built to look like a massive log cabin. A valet runs up to open Liam's door. Liam hands him his keys, and tells him, "O'Connor and Edwards, checking in."

He does that so effortlessly, I think to myself as he walks around to my side of the car, and we walk into the lobby. I have never been good at checking into four-star resorts. I always try to park my car myself, for fear the valet might lose it. And I always start to carry in my own bags before a bellhop offers to do it for me.

We walk into the expansive lobby, which is also designed to look like a giant rustic cabin, but with an artistic flair: Instead of real mounted animal heads (a decorating trend I always found disturbing), hanging above the front desk are sculpted white animal heads made to appear as though they have magically emerged from the white walls to see what the guests are doing. The hardwood floors are clean and shiny. Tasteful brown leather couches and chairs complement tables of various sizes carved from solid chunks of tree. And I'm not sure which adds the more romantic touch: the stone fireplace, or the floor-to-ceiling windows with spectacular views of the lake.

We walk up to the woman at the front desk with the name tag MARY, and Liam checks us in. He gets us connecting rooms, each with a king-size bed, each with views of the lake.

Then he says to Mary, "Miss Edwards will need to see the presidential suite, just to make sure it meets with Andrew Stanton's specifications."

Mary turns to me. "Oh, our manager, Ms. Owens, will show it to you personally. We are so excited to have your company coming here to film. And, if there's anything I can do to make your stay more enjoyable, you just let me know."

"Thank you," I say, pleasantly surprised by her friendliness.

I sometimes forget that people outside of Los Angeles actually like moviemakers. They're actually nice to us. In Los Angeles, filming on location brings out restrictive neighborhood associations, fuming commuters passing by and yelling, and irate neighbors calling the cops at 10:01 P.M. with noise complaints. But in places like Lake Arrowhead, Las Vegas, and St. Louis, people welcome the extra money a crew of a hundred can bring in. (Or, in our case, at least thirty.) Film permits are cheap, and accommodating. The locals have fun being extras, and see the free food from craft service and the hundred-dollar check at the end of the day as a fun bonus of an enjoyable day. People are excited to meet the actors. They don't go around sniping about how inconvenient it is that Will Smith had to park a trailer near their house. Residents tend to be friendly. They'll walk past to say "Hi," to the crew, and ask questions about the film. And the local camera crews, set decorators, and grips welcome a job working on a big movie.

Truth be told, I'm surprised Los Angeles continues to keep as much work in town as it does. Other parts of the country don't resent us.

The bellhop shows us to our rooms. My room has a similar feel to the lobby—very rustic, but also nice. Most everything is done in shades of brown: the desk and chair, the couch (although there is a muted quilt pattern on the ottoman.) My bedspread is even a muted shade of bronze. The bathroom is nicely sized, and comes with my own soft waffle weave robe. There is a lovely view of the lake that on another day I could have spent hours gazing at. But as much as I would have enjoyed throwing on the soft robe, and cozying up in here with a good book, I am here to work.

And work I do.

The next six hours are the most exhilarating I've had in I don't know how long. Liam and I ran around doing all the "boring" things a producer does, and I couldn't have been happier. After years of making restaurant reservations, and scheduling private plane pickups, I was actually doing something that mattered to me.

We scouted various locations that Liam had seen pictures of, but needed to look at in person. I eliminated one of them immediately by insisting no ten-ton grip truck was going to get down a three-hundred-yard gravel road—that only went one way. When we scouted the Village, I secured the parking we'd need for the crew, not to mention found some locals who could drive trailer hitches in snow, and would be available to work on the movie. When Liam found a house that matched the protagonist's childhood home from the 1950s, I pointed to the modern glass and metal monstrosity next door that could not be shot around. I then walked up to a home down the street that was perfect, knocked on the door, and secured the location for half of what Liam had budgeted in exchange for securing an introduction between Drew and, quote, "his biggest fan." (By the way, she was ninety if she was a day, and was going to fawn all over him. Drew loves crap like that.)

Throughout the day, I was glowing. I felt useful. I felt like I was doing something new and interesting. And I realized, as I happily trotted back to my room that evening, that this was something I desperately wanted.

We get back to the hotel around six-thirty, and agree to meet at the hotel bar at eight. I decide to take a long, leisurely soak in the tub before dressing for the evening.

Unfortunately, I make the mistake of bringing my cell into the bathroom with me. Before I can close my eyes and inhale the smell of Ginger Citrus bubbles, my first call comes through.

Truthfully, I was surprised it had taken Drew all day to call. Usually he calls me every twelve minutes. Which is why I have nicknamed myself his "beck-and-call girl."

I pick up on the first ring. "Hello?"

"So who's there? Is it a place to be seen? How's the lighting?"

I look around my bathroom. "No one you'll recognize, no, and very natural."

"Did you get together with Liam yet?"

"I'm not going to dignify that with a response."

"Is that an 'I'm not going to dignify that with a response,' meaning, 'Yes, but I don't want you to think I'm a slut,' or, 'No, he doesn't want me and I'm hiding in my room eating whatever I can scrounge up from the minibar'?"

If Drew hadn't actually caught me once in a room with a Mallo-mar in one hand, and a small can of roasted cashews in the other, I'd take offense.

"It means that it's none of your business," I respond.

"You know what you need to do? Take him to the bar and get him drunk. With straight men, that's pretty much a closer."

"Thank you," I say dryly. "How'd the shoot go today?"

"Okay, except they had to replace the focus puller. Hey, do I like olives?"

"You like the black kind, but not the green kind. Unless the green kind are Cerignola."

"Thanks. Bye."

And he hangs up on me.

Whatever.

I lie back in my steamy bath, revel in the bubbles, and think about Liam.

I'm back to being torn about what to do about him. We just had such a phenomenal day. And not only do we work well together, but he's so fun to be with. I mean, on the one hand, he says he's not ready for a relationship. And I'm not ready to get hurt again, so the point is probably moot.

But, on the other hand, most men are not ready for a relationship when they get into one. While women see relationships like a heated pool on a chilly day—something to dive into headfirst—men usually see relationships like garages: they have to back in slowly.

So, do I take him at his word, or not?

My phone rings again. It's Drew. I pick up. "Hello?"

"What's a knish?" Drew asks me.

"It's basically a baked turnover," I answer.

"Uh-huh," Drew says, sounding like he's writing down my answer. "And do I eat gefilte fish?"

"No."

"Okkaayy," he says, drawing out his words. "Kippered salmon, yes. Pastrami, oh yes . . . What do you think? Chocolate chip bagels? Yummy or weird?"

"Drew, are you trying to order dinner?"

"No. I was reading this article about breaking through your mental blocks to achieve greatness, and I need to change my dressing room again. According to the article, I should 'surround myself with things I love.' And for me, that's deli food."

I sit up in the tub. "I'm confused. What does that mean? You want to change your dressing room to a deli?"

"Yeah. I'm not sure if I thought this winter wonderland completely through," Drew answers. "I nearly got frostbite yesterday using the bathroom. So, I've decided to turn the room into a deli. Either that, or a gift-wrapping room."

"Oh, I don't think that's a good idea," I say urgently. "You love that dressing room. And we're only there another week and a half; why change things now?"

"That, plus you still want Liam staying with you," Drew offers.

Caught.

"I didn't say that," I say awkwardly.

"Get 'em drunk. Show 'em who's boss. See you Friday," Drew commands, then hangs up.

I hang up the phone, and once again try to enjoy a moment to myself.

Ten seconds later, my phone rings again. I check the caller ID. Kate. I pick up. "Hello."

"Hey, it's me," Kate says, sounding totally stressed-out. "Can I bug you with a couple of quick wedding questions?"

"Shoot."

"How do you think the guests would feel if we offered them a New York steak in a peppercorn sauce, instead of the classic filet mignon in béarnaise?"

When planning a catered party, the only hard and fast rule about the menu is to avoid the rubber chicken.

"I think that sounds delicious," I tell her.

"Okay, and do you think we could replace the Chilean sea bass with salmon? I know it's boring, but since the Chilean sea bass is so overfished, I would feel more comfortable with salmon."

"Then go for it," I tell her.

"Great. And finally, what do you think it means if I may have accidentally slept with Jack?"

I sit up in the tub. "I'm sorry. You what?"

"I may have accidentally slept with Jack," Kate repeats. "What do you think it means?"

It means you're still in love with him, you moron, I think to myself.

But I answer more diplomatically. "What do *you* think it means?"

Kate's voice cracks the tiniest bit as she makes her rationalization. "I think it means that we were together for a lot of years, and we have a history. I had a weak moment when I was stressing out about my wedding, and I took comfort in the love of a friend."

"Wow. Put a joint in one hand, and a martini in another, and you could be my mom explaining to me why she keeps sleeping with my dad."

"Oh, Will's at the door. I gotta go," Kate says quickly. "Are we still on for *Charlie's Angels* Night?"

"We are."

"Great. We'll talk more then."

"Wait. Kate?"

Kate brushes me off. "Never mind," she says quickly. "I shouldn't have called you. I'll see you Saturday. Bye."

Kate hangs up on her end. I debate calling her back, but I'm tempted to yell at her and tell her she's being an idiot. And we all know:

You're never going to win an argument by telling the person they're stupid. Be nice at first, and try to win their trust.
Then nail them with the truth.

Besides, if Will is there, we won't get much accomplished. I lie back in my tub, and try to relax again.

I spend the next thirty minutes getting ready for my dinner with Liam. I wonder if men would be flattered or horrified to know we can spend fifteen minutes just trying to get our eye makeup looking perfect for them. (And let's not even get into how long a woman can spend working on her hair.)

Don't overpack.

After debating between the three dresses I packed for our one night stay, I finally opt for a little black dress I picked up at the Beverly Center and a pair of sparkly Jimmy Choo stilettos I got for my birthday.

Knowing we are not to meet until eight o'clock, I decide to sit around my hotel room until 7:56. I don't want to look too eager for the dinner, and I want to make an entrance. That said, I spent twenty minutes pacing around the room, chomping on nicotine gum, and being, well, too eager.

The room's digital clock hits 7:56, and I grab my sparkly bag, and leave the room.

I arrive at the entrance of BIN189 at precisely 8:00. I walk through the entrance, past the glass wall of displayed wine bottles, and over to the restaurant bar.

Liam is sitting in the lounge area, wearing a beautiful dark gray suit, and sipping a martini in front of a roaring fire. In the seat across from him, I see he has ordered me a glass of red wine.

"Hello, dear," Liam says, standing up to greet me. "You look lovely." He gives me a quick kiss hello on the cheek, then says, "I ordered you a Merlot."

I look *lovely?* Don't know what that means. Does it mean he thinks I look beautiful, and he can't help but notice that I recently shaved my legs? Or, is *lovely* a euphemism men use when describing blind dates with good personalities?

"Thank you," I say, taking a seat. "So, have you been here long?"

"Just long enough to fascinate myself with people-watching," he says, taking a sip of his martini. "I cannot believe how many first dates are here tonight."

I turn in my seat to check out the people in the bar, lounge, and adjoining dining room. Many of the women are dressed to the nines like me. No one wears four-inch stilettos and a short black dress to a lodge in the middle of the mountains unless they're trying to get laid.

"Actually, there aren't any first dates here," I inform him, speaking like an anthropologist, and absolutely sure of myself. "A few second dates. Mostly third dates. And, of course, some people are here for their first romantic getaway." I look around further to test my hypothesis. "Oh, except that table," I say, pointing to a slightly overweight gentleman in an ill-fitting suit and his date. "They've gone out so many times without sex, the poor guy's ready to explode."

Liam laughs. "Well, all right then." He points to the guy in the ill-fitting suit. "How can you tell with him? Do we men give out signals of desperation?"

"It's not him, it's her," I say authoritatively to Liam. "She's dressed dowdily, low white pumps, nylons, a tasteful blue dress with a way-past-the-knee hemline. Plus that, her hair is barely brushed. This is a woman who's not putting too much energy into the date. Which means she's only dating him because he's nice, not because there's any chemistry between them. And, if there's no chemistry, he might as well pack it in now."

Liam makes a show of checking out my dress. "Let's see: hemline above the knee, no nylons, insanely high heels." He smiles at me mischievously. "Am I to assume I might get lucky tonight?"

"Hey, if you hadn't just told me earlier today you weren't looking for a relationship, we might be ordering room service right now," I say lightly as I take a sip of my wine.

Liam laughs. "Fair enough." He looks around the room. "What date do you think people assume we're on?"

I ponder his question a moment. "Second," I answer.

He smiles as he takes another sip of his martini. "You seem pretty sure of yourself. What are the facts you used to come up with your hypothesis?"

"Well, first of all, we didn't arrive together. You were waiting for me," I tell him. "Therefore, we're not on a romantic together. Second, you kissed me hello when I arrived, thereby indicating that you were relaxed around me: hence, it's not a first date. However, the kiss was brief, not lingering. It was on the cheek, not on the lips. And there was no tongue involved. Ergo, you're not dying to get me into bed, and therefore, it's not a third date. The only one left was second."

"I see," said Liam. "Well, I'm afraid, my dear, that I have to disagree with you. This wouldn't be the second date, it would be the third. This would be the seduction date."

"I see," I say jokingly. "You seem pretty sure of yourself."

"I am."

"And what are the facts you've used to come up with your hypothesis?"

Liam smiles wickedly. "Well, for one thing, you've shaved your legs."

The fact that he has noticed this makes me want to hide under the table in embarrassment. Or, drag him under the table to have my way with him.

But I try to deflect how I'm really feeling by giving him a shrug as I say, "Women shave their legs for a first date."

"One would hope," Liam says, almost smirking. "However, women do not normally dress for a first date the way you have chosen to dress this evening."

I cross my arms, and glare at him. "And how exactly have I dressed this evening?"

Liam eyes me up and down. "Absolutely captivating," he says in his lilting Irish accent.

"Thank you," I say, feeling myself blush. "By the way, if you didn't have that cute little accent, there's no way you could have gotten away with saying 'absolutely captivating' to a woman without sounding like an idiot."

"Noted," Liam says. "Anyway, the second date is the date where you go do the thing you both said you like to do. For example, you talk to a girl about how you like to go running, she says she loves running, you make a Sunday morning date to go jogging in Griffith Park. Or, let's say she says she likes the theater or a certain sports team, you get tickets to a play or game you know she'd like."

I can't help but think back: Didn't he ask me to go see 'The Taming of the Shrew' with him? Twice?

Liam continues. "And, let's say the girl doesn't really like to go running, or the theater or sports, she's just yanking your chain. Well, then, the second date allows you to find out if she's telling the truth. If not, there probably won't be a third date."

"You mean just because a girl tries to show interest in something you like, she gets punished?" I ask him, a little offended.

Liam takes another sip of his martini. "Now, see, this is something I've never understood about women: why would you pretend to like something you don't? Why not just say: I'll go to the football match, but I'm dragging you to the opera the following week to make up for it?"

"Because then you won't like us as much," I answer.

"Darling, we've asked you out. That means we like you. Don't overthink it. Why is it women have to think about everything all the time?"

"Probably because we're killing time watching the game you've dragged us to," I counter.

Liam gives me an appreciative smile and a wink.

The hostess calls out Liam's name, and we follow her to a table by a window. As I look out to watch snow silently fall outside over the lake and trees, I wish I was here with someone who did want to take me somewhere romantic for a seduction date.

Or, I should say, I wish Liam was really taking me up here for a seduction date.

"So, hear from Jordan again?" Liam asks as he opens his menu.

"I'll take 'conversation killers' for a thousand, Alex," I say dryly.

"You can't blame me for being the least bit curious as to how someone could be so stupid as to let you get away."

"Speaking of, how is your ex-girlfriend?"

Liam looks up at me. Smirks. "I'm thinking about getting the rib eye . . ."

The waitress soon appears to take our orders. I start with the corn chowder, a specialty of the house. Liam goes with a standard Caesar salad.

"And with the appetizers, we'd like a bottle of your Hanzell Chardonnay," Liam tells the waitress.

Nice.

For our entrees, I order the New York steak, while he opts for the grilled Rib Eye. "And for that," Liam says, still perusing the wine list. "I think we'll go for . . ." He looks up at me. "You like Merlot, right?"

"Actually, when I'm eating steak, I kind of like Cabernet better."

"Fantastic," Liam says to me. "Do you like Chateau Montelena?"

Yeah, like I'm going to admit I've never heard of it. I smile. "That sounds wonderful."

Liam closes the wine list, and hands it and our menus to our waitress. "Let's get a bottle of that with the meal."

As she walks away, he looks over at me. "So, shall we put the exes in exile, and not speak of them again this evening?"

I smile, relieved. "That would be great."

"Do you ski?" Liam asks me out of the blue.

"Why?" I ask.

"Don't give me that look," Liam says, laughing. "I just thought before we headed back down tomorrow we might want to spend a few hours on the slopes."

"Don't tell me, let me guess," I say sarcastically. "You used to ski up in the Alps, so if someone were to ask you your skill level, you'd say you're okay. But, in reality, you're damn good, and have your own set of skis tailor made just for you."

Before Liam can respond, our sommelier arrives. "Hanzell Chardonnay," he says, showing us the bottle before he opens it. The sommelier puts a white wineglass in front of each of us. As he opens the bottle, he asks, "And who will be tasting this evening?"

"The lady," Liam says.

Damn it! Other than knowing if the wine has turned, I never know what I'm supposed to be sniffing, swirling, and tasting. It either tastes good or it doesn't.

The sommelier pours a small amount into my glass, and the two men wait for my reaction. I swirl the glass, get my nose in there to sniff, then I have a taste.

"It's wonderful," I say, smiling.

The sommelier pours for both of us, then places the wine in a silver ice bucket on a stand near the table.

"So, where were we?" I ask as the man leaves.

Liam takes a sip of his wine. "You were pretending to compliment me, yet actually insulting me, about my skiing."

"No, no," I quickly correct him. "I wasn't insulting you. I was actually trying to be self-mocking."

"First of all, why? And, secondly, how so?" he asks.

"Well," I say, taking a sip of my wine to stall for time. "The why is easy: Basically, you are intimidating as hell. However, you're so charming, that occasionally I forget how intimidating you are, and I let down my guard. But then you ask some innocuous question like, 'Do you ski?' and I'm back to being intimidated again. So I respond by being self-mocking."

Liam takes another sip of wine. Any flirtation I may have perceived before has vanished. Now he seems irritated. "I'm unclear here. How am I intimidating again?"

At that, I burst out into an awkward laugh. He seems startled. I take another nervous sip of wine. "Oh, please. I'm surprised you didn't put skis in the trunk. Oh wait, you drive the perfect car, except it won't fit skis in a trunk."

"So, I love to ski. How does that make me unapproachable?"

"I didn't say you were unapproachable. I said you were intimidating," I say, starting to feel it is very important to win this debate, and getting angry that he's not seeing my point here. "I mean, my God, who actually walks around their house wearing boxer shorts?"

"I'm sorry. I didn't realize my wearing boxer shorts made you uncomfortable."

"Well, I mean, how would you like it if I walked around the house in my bra and underwear all through breakfast?"

"You can walk around your house any way you're comfortable," he says crossly. "And, frankly, I'm a man. I will always encourage a beautiful woman to walk around in nothing but her frillies."

How can men be so dense? "No woman is comfortable wearing a bra and underwear around a guy she hasn't slept with!" I nearly yell. "Well, I mean except a Victoria's Secret model."

"I thought we weren't talking about exes tonight," Liam says angrily.

At this my jaw drops. "You actually dated a Victoria's Secret model? But you don't see why you're intimidating?"

Naturally at this moment, our waitress appears. We abruptly stop arguing. She serves us our appetizers, and refills our wineglasses. Then we sit and eat in silence.

As I eat my chowder, I will admit, I am already tipsy. Which is probably why I'm so upset he isn't seeing my point. Could also be why, maddening though he may be, I'm still considering grabbing him by the belt buckle, and pulling him into a kiss.

But then that would prove that's he's not intimidating, which would make him think he was right, and I was wrong, and for some reason that is enough to stop me.

I sip my wine again.

"So, I take it you don't ski?" Liam finally says, still angry.

"No," I say definitively.

"Would you like me to teach you tomorrow?" he asks, his tone steely.

"Fine," I say curtly.

"Fine," he says back.

And we continue to eat our appetizers in silence. Liam refills my glass, then his. "I won't wear the boxers anymore," he says softly, and I detect the smallest melt in our ice age.

I shake my head, not angry anymore. "It's not that. I was just trying to give you a compliment."

"By telling me I'm intimidating?"

"No. By . . . by trying to tell you I wish I was more like you. It came out wrong. I wish I had skied in the Alps. I wish I knew how to produce movies. I wish I liked jogging. It's like sometimes I look at you, and you're a reminder of how little I've lived up to my potential. And tomorrow, I'll go out skiing, because I want to be like you. But I won't be a cute little snow bunny out there; I'll be uncoordinated, I'll be embarrassed, and I'll be wondering how much longer before I can get to the bar at the bottom of the hill."

Liam smiles. "You've just described my first time with a woman."

I laugh.

And we're back.

"Listen, we don't have to go skiing," Liam says to me. "We didn't get a chance to go for a hike around the lake. You want to go do that in the morning?"

"No," I say, shaking my head. "We can go on a hike anytime. Let's go skiing."

Liam smiles. "Well, aren't you being a bad second date, pretending you want to go skiing when you don't?"

I laugh nervously. "All right, I'm going to use your advice from earlier, and tell you the truth: I'll go skiing with you tomorrow, but you're taking me to a drag queen show Saturday."

Liam smiles. "Deal."

The next hour flies by. We talk all throughout dinner about anything and everything. Then we head to the bar for a nightcap.

I am so drunk as we walk through the restaurant and into the bar that I fall into Liam. He caught me, and I definitely feel a spark between us as he puts his arm around me, and leads me to a couch near the fireplace.

"Are you sure you want another drink?" Liam asks. "I think maybe you've had enough."

"I'm not driving," I say. Then I rethink this. "But if you need to call it a night, we can go."

"No, no." Liam says, sounding sober to me. "I'm up for a brandy."

The waitress takes our orders, and we sit on the couch. I lean into Liam, and he puts his arm around me.

"See," Liam says, turning his face to me, "I'm not so intimidating."

I lean toward him as though I plan to kiss him. I won't actually do it, but I'm hoping he'll take the hint. "Oh, you are," I insist softly. "But you're worth it."

Liam smiles, he leans in slightly, we look deep into each other's eyes . . .

And my phone rings.

Damn it! I begrudgingly pull away from Liam and pull my iPhone from my purse. I check the caller ID, then answer. "Hello, Drew."

"Hey. Quick question: What constitutes kidnapping?"

I don't answer at first. I mean, it's Drew. The question could mean he's losing at a game of beer pong. "Is there a woman involved?" I ask him.

"Yes."

"Are you holding her against her will?"

"Don't be ridiculous."

"Is she over the age of twenty-one?"

"Of course."

"Is she incarcerated, running from the law, or mentally unstable in any way?"

"Can any woman really claim to be mentally stable?" Drew counters.

"You're fine. Go to bed."

"Wait!" Drew says. "You sound drunk. Have you done the deed yet?"

"Good night, Drew."

"Oh, fine," he pouts. "Good night."

And he hangs up.

I put the phone down next to my purse, just in case he calls back.

Then I turn my attention back to Liam, who leans back against the couch, blissfully listening to the piano in the background. "Don't you love the piano?" he asks, smiling contentedly. "Everything played sounds so romantic."

"It's very nice," I agree nervously.

He stands up. "Dance with me?"

I look at him, mildly horrified. "What? Here?"

"Yes, here."

I glance around the room. "But there's no dance floor. No one else is dancing."

Liam rolls his eyes, then pulls me up and into his arms, and we begin slow dancing.

I wish I could write advice for my future great-grandson. Besides writing the obvious:

Learn to do laundry properly. Pink underwear looks silly on men.

I would write:

If you want to meet women, take a dance class. This will also help if you want to land a bridesmaid for the night (just remember to call her the next day).

Being in Liam's arms just feels so delicious. It makes me want time to stand still.

The song ends, a few people clap for the pianist, and we sit again. This time, Liam doesn't put his arm around me, but he still sits very close to me.

Oh, to hell with it. I'm going for broke. I intentionally lean back against the couch, subliminally coaxing him into leaning into me.

Liam relaxes his whole body, leaning in toward me, and gives me that "I'm about to kiss you for the first time" smile.

And then my phone rings again. I look at the caller ID, then pick up. "Yes, Drew?"

"What about aiding and abetting? Or being an accessory to a crime? What constitutes that?"

Now I'm getting miffed. "Was there a crime committed?"

He responds as though I've asked a bizarre question. "I don't think so."

"Drew, you can't 'aid and abet' a criminal if there's no crime," I say, exasperated. "Nor can you act as an accessory to anything. Are the police at your house?"

"No."

"Do you think the police will be coming to your house anytime soon?"

"I don't see why they would."

"Have you hurt anyone in any way?"

"Of course not."

"Then you're fine. Go to bed."

"Okay," Drew says. "Speaking of bed, have you . . . ?"

"Good night, Drew," I say firmly, then hang up.

I put my phone down and turn to Liam, who once again is leaning back in his seat, totally relaxed. "Everything all right?" he asks.

"Fine," I say.

I take a sip of cognac, lean back, and try to recapture the moment.

And the phone rings again.

"What?!" I hiss into the phone.

It's my mother on the other end, and she sounds like she's been crying. "It appears your Mawv has committed suicide," she tells me through her tears.

I bolt upright in my seat. "Oh my God. When? What happened?"

Mom sniffles back tears and tells me, "Well, Andy announced her pregnancy to my family a few days ago, and when Mawv heard, she insisted she wanted to spend the holidays here, where she could be near her new great-great-grandchild. Well, your grandmother would have none of it, and they've been fighting ever since. Then one of the nurses went to check on Mawv in her room at the home, and all they found was a suicide note. It said, 'Dear Rose, I can't take another Thanksgiving in this God-forsaken place. I've gone with Jesus. Don't be mad. Love, Bernice.'"

I am stunned. Absolutely stunned.

"It's 'Hay-*Seuss*'," I angrily say to my mother.

"What?"

"She hasn't gone with 'GEE-zuss', she's gone with 'Hay-SEUSS.' Drew's part-time bodyguard, Jesus. I can't believe Drew . . . I'm going to fucking kill him."

"Sweetie," Mom says sympathetically, "the first stage of grief is disbelief—"

"Mom, didn't anyone find it the least bit odd that they found a note, and not a body? Isn't it usually the other way around?"

I quickly fill her in on my theory, then hang up to call Drew.

He answers immediately. "Hello."

"Did you kidnap my great-grandmother?" I yell/ask, even though I damn well know the answer.

"Of course I didn't kidnap your great-grandmother," Drew says, highly offended. "She wanted to leave."

With Liam looking on, I rub my eyes with my thumb and forefinger. "Jesus Christ, Drew. When did you and my Mawv even become friends?"

"After your wedding," Drew tells me. "We talk almost every day. She's like the grandmother I never had."

"*Both* of your grandmothers are still alive!" I remind him angrily.

"Yeah, but one's a judgmental alcoholic, and the other one keeps gambling away the money I give her. They don't count."

"Drew, you can't just steal an old lady from an old folk's home!"

"I didn't steal her! She specifically told me the place was like a min-imum security prison, and she was free to walk away at any time."

My iPhone beeps a call coming in from Jesus Gonzalez. "That's Jesus now. Let me call you back."

For the first time in my life, I hang up on Drew, and answer the other line. "Hello."

"Don't you dare get mad at that nice boy for springing me," Mawv says haughtily.

I sigh. "Mawv, where are you? Grandma and Mom are worried sick."

"I'm on my way to California. Andrew invited me to stay with him at his home over the holidays, and I have accepted. Andrew sent his security guard to escort me from the home. Gorgeous boy. I could bounce a quarter off his ass."

"Mawv—"

"Seriously, if I were sixty years younger . . . eh, he still wouldn't give me the time of day. But he sure is pretty to look at."

"Mawv, where are you specifically? Are you still in St. Louis?"

"No, no. Andrew rented me a private jet so that I could land with-out being hounded by the paparazzi."

I'm confused. "Why would you be hounded by the paparazzi?"

"I'm not sure. But Andrew insisted that I didn't want to fly on a commercial plane, because the moment I landed, the paps would be snapping away, and the photos are never flattering."

I'm getting a headache.

I spend the next half hour harriedly on the phone with half of my family explaining what happened, then tracking down a helicopter to take me back to the city so that I can meet Mawv at Drew's house when she lands.

Ten minutes after that, I am packed, checked out, and in front of the hotel waiting for a cab to take me to the heliport.

"Are you sure you don't mind driving home by yourself tomorrow?" I ask Liam as the cabbie puts my bag in the trunk.

"Not at all," Liam says soothingly, adjusting my coat collar so my neck stays warm. "Have snow chains, will travel."

"I really had a great time tonight," I say apologetically. "I'm sorry I ruined it."

"You didn't ruin it," he assures me. "Your boss, Mister Me Bollocks, ruined it. Story of my life for the next month."

"Story of my life for the rest of my life," I joke.

We stare at each other, each wondering the proper way to end the night. A little kiss good-bye? A big kiss good-bye? A hug?"

We continue to look into each other's eyes for a few moments.

After what seems like an eternity of a staring contest, I tilt my head and ask him coquettishly, "What?"

Liam breaks into a grin as he shrugs. "I just wanted to thank you for a truly perfect evening. I can't remember the last time I had this much fun. It was like a perfect third date."

I smile, and turn my eyes away. "Thank you," I say, almost embarrassed by my obvious feelings for him. "I had fun, too."

"And you know the best part?" Liam asks me.

I shake my head.

"Because we're not really dating, you won't even hate me in the morning."

On that note, he kisses me on the nose, then helps me into the cab.

And as I am driven away, I think of my next bit of advice to write:

Frequently we have to control our impulses. And that sucks.

Twenty-eight

All good things must someday end. Fortunately, this is also true of bad things.

"I quit," I say to Drew when he answers his door a few hours later.

"What are you talking about?" Drew asks, as I push past him and yell, "Mawv?! Mawv?!"

"In here, dear," Mawv yells from Drew's kitchen.

I walk into the kitchen to see my ninety-five-year-old great-grandmother, wearing nothing but a lace camisole and panties, playing strip poker with a shirtless Jesus, who's all of twenty-three. She has a cigarette dangling from her mouth, and a large glass of whiskey at her side.

I think seeing dogs play poker would have been less jolting.

"Hey, Charlie," Jesus says, smiling brightly at me.

I ignore his shirtless physique to ask the obvious question: "Jesus, do you mind telling me why you kidnapped my great-grandmother?"

"I wasn't commissioned to kidnap her," Jesus calmly enlightens me. "My services were enlisted to bring her safely home. And I did that." He looks up at Mawv. "Did you feel your life was in danger at any time that I was with you?"

"Well, not until now," Mawv says, eyeing me suspiciously.

"Raise you twenty," Jesus says, throwing in a red chip.

"I have a cab waiting outside," I tell Mawv purposefully.

"Now, what is twenty worth again?" she asks Jesus.

"Each hundred is worth one piece of clothing," he answers.

"You're coming home with me tonight," I continue. "And then Mom is going to bring you back to St. Louis tomorrow. Where are your things?"

Mawv takes a puff of her cigarette. "Don't you use that tone with me, young lady." She looks at Jesus. "I think you're bluffing. I'll see your twenty, and raise you fifty."

She throws a blue chip and a red chip onto a pile of chips on the counter as Drew walks in. "I paid the cabbie, and sent him on his way."

I turn to Drew. "You what?!"

"I said I paid the cabbie—"

I interrupt Drew by slapping him dead in the face.

"Ow!" Drew grabs his cheek. "You hit me."

"I'm going to do a lot more than that in about two seconds. Mawv, get your goddamned stuff! Jesus, since Drew got rid of my ride, I need you to drive us to my house."

"Can't do that, Charlie," Jesus warns me apologetically. "And, if you try to remove her from the residence, I'm going to have to call the police and have you arrested for trespassing, assault and battery, and kidnapping." He looks up at my Mawv, and throws down a blue chip. "I call."

My jaw drops as I look at Jesus. He shrugs. "I'm sorry. But there's no court order saying she's a danger to herself or anyone else. She legally had the right to leave St. Louis, and she legally has the right to be with Drew."

Drew's face lights up. "Jesus, my man! That's brilliant! What's assault and battery?"

"What Charlie's doing to you now," Jesus says. "Hitting is assault.

The yelling at you is battery." He puts down his cards, then says to Mawv, "Full house. Tens high."

"Excellent!" Drew says, smiling.

I raise my hand to hit him again, and he flinches.

As Mawv puts down a straight flush to Jesus' full house, I put down my hand, and try to soften my voice. "Seriously, Mawv, everyone is worried about you. You need to be in a place where people can give you your medication, and watch out for your safety."

"There are people here who can do that," Mawv counters as she pulls the pot of multicolored chips toward her. "Your boss has a bigger staff than the White House." She holds up her drink. "And this Gladys person who works for him makes the best drinks in the state."

I look at Mawv's highball glass of whiskey. "Isn't that just three shots of Canadian Club over crushed ice?"

"What's your point?" Mawv asks.

Drew looks at me. "Can I have Gladys whip up a little something for you?"

"Nooooo!" I yell.

"Seriously, because you reek of wine. I'll bet that's why you're so angry, you're drunk. Maybe a little pot to mellow you out?"

"I reek of wine because I was splitting bottles of the stuff—bottles!—with Liam before I got pulled away from a romantic dinner in the middle of the snowed-in mountains so I could fly home and deal with yet another one of your screwups!"

"Since when is helping out an old lady a screwup?" Drew asks.

"Since when is ninety-five an old lady?" Mawv asks, offended.

"Never get in the middle of a domestic squabble, sweetie," Jesus says to Mawv as he deals another round.

As Mawv nods her head to show she thinks that's good advice, I practically yell, "This is *not* a domestic squabble. I am not Drew's wife, I am . . . I *was* . . . his assistant." Then I turn to Drew. "And you have crossed the line for the final time. I quit."

I walk out of the kitchen, and prepare to walk out the front door. I'll call a cab once I'm out. For right now, I just need to say my exit line and go.

Unfortunately, Drew never lets anyone have the last word. He follows me. "You can't quit me!"

"Yeah? Give me one good reason why."

"Because I'm your family."

I turn around and glare at him. "In what twisted world do you live in that you could possibly ever consider yourself family?"

"Don't give me that look," Drew says offhandedly. "I'm neurotic, I'm self-involved, and you're constantly having to deal with me. I fit in beautifully."

I shake my head, and turn to leave again. "I'm so out of here."

"And because I love you," Drew says.

I stop at the door. I'm so tired of this. I turn around to Drew. "At the risk of sounding like one of your damn movies, you don't even know what love is. Love is not making your loved one deal with hippo poop. Ever. Or, making your loved one accompany you to Idaho at three A.M. because you, and I quote, 'need to see winter.' Or, making them pull you out of a toilet . . . twice. And let's not even get into the fact that I have a roommate right now because of you. . . ."

"Yeah," Drew says, pointing at me. "And you're welcome!"

"No," I say, throwing my hands up to the sides of my head in exasperation. "You don't get it. I can't like someone if . . . you know what? Never mind. Like I said, I quit. I need to lead a normal life. And this is clearly not normal."

Drew crosses his arms. "Do I get to talk before you leave?"

I sigh. The man exhausts me. "Fine."

Drew looks over at the table by his front door. He might as well have a lightbulb go on over his head, because clearly he has an idea.

"I don't love you in the way you want to be loved. But never doubt that it's there. I love you unconditionally. I love you because you're cute, I love you because you think I'm a pain in the ass but you're still here, and I love you because you have a certain Charlieness that I have not been able to find in any of my other friends. I have loved you through Dave, Danny, Steve, Jim, Jeff, John, Marshall, Patrick, Jerrys numbers 1 and 2, and Jordan. I'm gonna love you when you fuck it up with Liam, and I'm gonna love you when you fuck it up with the next guy. I'm gonna love you the day you walk down the aisle when you finally do find the right guy, and I am going to love you every Thanksgiving, Christmas, New Year's, and Fourth of July until one of us dies. And, for that reason, you can't quit." ,

I look him in the eye to see if he's lying. He doesn't look like he is. He looks like a vulnerable man who has just admitted his deepest, darkest feelings, and wants to feel like they've been reciprocated, and like he's been accepted as a caring human being.

Which is why he's an actor. I look over at his front table, and set my sights on the script on top of the highly polished wood. I quickly walk over to the script. "Which page?" I ask angrily.

"Fifty-six," Drew admits sheepishly.

I flip through to page fifty-six. As I do, Drew continues monologuing at me, a desperation creeping into his voice, "Your favorite color is something called eggplant. It's this really dark purple that you always wanted to put your bridesmaids in when you get married. . . ."

He's not getting me this time. I keep flipping through the script pages while Drew continues, "Only now you're so irritated with them, you figure you'll put them in bright orange polyester microminis with white go-go boots. You tell people your favorite sex symbol is Jared Leto, but really it's Stephen Colbert. You tell people your favorite book is *A Connecticut Yankee in King Arthur's Court,* but really it's *Oh, Not Again,* the book your mom wrote in 1979. . . ."

I get to page fifty-six, and start scanning the page. Drew continues, "And you didn't have me read this script because you thought I might get an Academy Award, you did it because you wanted to go to Paris to see Jordan."

I look up from my reading.

"Yeah," Drew says. "I figured that out, and I read it anyway. That night. I came home with a drunk woman who wanted to have sex in a harness, and instead of doing that, I read a script you told me to read. And I committed to the project the next day, guaranteeing you a second chance with Jordan, or a first chance with Liam. So, you can get mad at me for hippos, and trips to Idaho, and granting your great-grandmother her dying wish. But you are staying. You're stuck with me. Because, you know what? I am the best thing that ever happened to you. You're just too blind to see it."

I stand there, dumbfounded.

Wait a minute, the best thing that ever happened. . . . I lift my hand to slap him again. He flinches. "All right. That last line was too much. I take it back."

I put down my hand, still glaring at him.

"It was," Drew continues. "I had you after white go-go boots. But then I pushed it." He takes my hand, and kisses it. "Seriously, I fucked up, and I'm sorry. But I can make it up to you. What is it going to take to keep you from quitting?"

Good question. And I know the answer. Because, despite how badly my day ended, I think back to earlier in the day, when I was really energized. When I got to scout locations, learn about permits, read through the writer's latest script changes, and in general do something I thought was invigorating and interesting.

And, for better or for worse, continuing to work for Drew could help me do what I want to do in the future.

However, I'm not sure how Drew will handle my demand.

You want the foolproof test to see if you're in a good relationship? Tell the person the thing that you're most afraid to tell them. Then see how they react.

I take a deep breath, and say to Drew, "I want to produce a movie that you'll star in."

Drew just seems confused by my request. "Oh, I don't think you want to produce the type of crap I star in."

"No, I'm not talking about one of your blockbuster movies. I want to produce a movie like *A Collective Happiness* for you. Something that's important. Something that will be remembered. Think about it: you could be like George Clooney. You could star in an *Ocean's Seventy-two,* then star in a small movie that will be nominated for a slew of Academy Awards."

Drew smiles to himself. "I like the sound of that."

"And I could find you the script. Then help secure the financing. We could go to Sony or Universal for a development deal tomorrow, and we'd have studio offices by the end of the week."

Drew furrows his brow at me. "Nah, I've had studio development deals before. It's an ego offer that never works out. You develop scripts for years, and no one ever greenlights any of your projects."

True enough. I try a different approach. "What if I manage to secure a good script for a low-budget film, then put together outside financing? Would you do it then?"

Drew thinks about it a moment. "If I agree to star in a small movie, you don't quit?"

"No."

"And you still get me my coffee?"

I roll my eyes. "Until I find the right project for you, yes."

He shrugs. "Done." He puckers his lips together, thinking. "Can you get me a trailer for the next one?"

"Sure," I say, then I walk with him to the kitchen to announce to Mawv that she can stay. "By the way, you do realize that Liam crack is going to cost you an extra hundred dollars a week."

"Hey, you can't do that. I'm economizing."

Twenty-nine

Some men are just an itch you can't scratch. Get away from these men.

Despite our romantic evening, once Liam got home from Lake Arrowhead, we were back to being just roommates. He was a roommate who made me breakfast, who was fun to watch DVDs with on a weeknight, and who was helping me on my career path. But he was still just a roommate.

And by now, I am ready to explode.

"Maybe I should just fuck his brains out, and get it out of my system," I suggest to the girls on Saturday night.

"Yeah. Because women are so good at doing that," Dawn responds dryly.

"No, seriously," I continue. "I've had the last few days to think this through. How many gorgeous men do you know who are good in bed?"

This is followed by Dawn, Kate, Andy, and Jenn answering with, "Not many," "Good point," and "I'd say about ten percent."

I'm surprised Jenn and Andy would give the same answer, but I run with that. "Weird answer, but okay: let's go with ten percent."

"Way too optimistic," Dawn insists.

"Word," Kate concurs.

Dawn turns to her. "I'm sorry. Did you just say 'word'?"

"Guys, Liam will be back in less than five minutes. Eyes back to me." All four girls turn their attention back to me. "Okay, so ten percent. That means I have a nine-to-one shot that I'll pin him to a wall, show him who's boss, then be wildly disappointed, and lose my crush."

"Why would you pin him to a wall?" Andy asks.

"I don't know. Because he's standing right now, and I can't afford to lose time. You're missing the bigger picture. A show of hands. Am I allowed to do this?"

Naturally, this is met with a split vote of two each.

To backtrack: I spent the rest of my week utterly charmed with my new roommate, and completely hating myself for having a crush on him. And I kept thinking about kissing him at the most inopportune times. Like when he makes breakfast. Or when he was fixing my TiVo. And even though he's been wearing long flannel pajamas around the kitchen all week, I still think about wrestling him to the ground, and giving him a big smooch.

And I miss those damn boxers.

Now it's Saturday night, and I'm ready to burst, and thinking about my next move. Liam and I have met up with Jenn, Andy, Kate, and Dawn in the basement of a Mexican restaurant in Silverlake, ready to see "Chico's Angels," an episode of *Charlie's Angels* performed by a group of Latin drag queens who have turned it into a musical.

It's sentences like that that make me glad I live in Los Angeles.

The five of us girls have settled into our seats, and Liam has gone to get us drinks.

Which means I only have a few more moments to talk.

Which means I need to have everyone give me advice quickly.

"Okay, Kate, you're first. Why no?"

"Because you think you're just going to have a lovely one-night stand. And then nine years later, there he is, causing you to accidentally sleep with him and mess up your wedding plans."

Dawn shakes her head. "I disagree with you on two counts," she says to Kate. "First of all, Charlie already knows he's a dog. She just needs to satisfy her libido." Dawn turns to me. "Flip 'em over. Turn 'im out."

"Word," Jenn says jokingly.

"Stop that," Dawn tells her sternly.

"All right. I'm leaning toward Dawn's argument. Andy: your rebuttal."

"Wait," Kate says to me, then turns to Dawn. "What was the other thing you disagree with me about?"

"You accidentally hit your car. You don't accidentally sleep with someone," Dawn says.

"Treat him like a cold," Andy says. "Don't touch his hands, lips, or any part of his anatomy, and you won't get infected. Seriously, think about how many women he's been with. You don't want him bringing anything home to Mama."

"Home to Mama?!" Dawn says. "When did all you white folks start trying to sound like you got street cred?"

Jenn shakes her head at Andy. "Oh, now see, I completely disagree. I have a total married crush on Liam. I think she should go for it."

"He's totally out of her league," Andy points out with a snap in her voice.

"Women go out with men who are out of their league all the time. Look at Rob and me," Jenn counters.

"Wait a minute," I say, ignoring the obvious barb from my sister to stare at my very pregnant cousin. "You have a crush on Liam?" I ask, trying not to sound shocked.

"No," Jenn says with a *don't-be-such-a-silly* tone in her voice. "I have a *married* crush on Liam. It's not a crush—I'm almost nine months pregnant, a crush would be beyond delusional—it's a married crush."

"I see," I say, confused about the semantics. "So what exactly is a married crush?"

"A married crush is when you think the person is amazing, and you wish you had met them ten years ago, when you were both single, but who you don't have a real crush on, because you're married and you're with the person you're supposed to be with, so you've stopped having crushes."

"So you're saying if you had met Liam ten years ago, you would have dated him?" I ask, sort of surprised that my happily married cousin could ever have carnal thoughts about another man.

"Of course not, he would have been totally out of my league," she self-deprecates. "That's the other advantage of married crushes. I could flirt with Justin Timberlake and happily think to myself, 'Oh, if only I'd met him ten years ago, I could totally get him into my bed tonight.'"

I squint my eyes together. "Justin Timberlake was a teenager ten years ago. . . ."

"Now you're missing the bigger picture."

Fair enough. Fascinated, I continue my line of questioning. "But if you had dated Liam, wouldn't that mean you wouldn't have ended up with Rob?"

"No. Rob's my soul mate. Liam would have been a fun diversion, though. I mean, you should totally tap that if you get the opportunity."

Andy and I stare at her. "I'm sorry," Andy says dryly. "Did you just say 'tap that'?"

Jenn nods her head. "I'm trying to sound more hip. Wanted to know how it sounded when I said it aloud." She looks at us. "No, right?"

I widen my eyes and shake my head no vigorously.

Liam suddenly appears with a tray of multicolored margaritas.

"Okay, we've got a virgin strawberry for Jenn; a plain margarita, double tequila, for Dawn; a regular strawberry margarita for Kate; peach margarita for Charlie; and a water for Andy."

"Why didn't you get me a glass of wine?" Kate asks.

Liam visibly winces. "At the risk of being a cad, I thought we'd go a different way. A magnum is the perfect size for champagne, but not for three dollar bottles of red."

"A man after my own heart," Dawn says, taking her drink.

"Oh shit!" Kate says, seeing someone, then covering her face and scrunching into our group to hide. "Jack is here!"

Naturally, everyone but Liam cranes their necks to look and ask, "Where?"

"Don't look!" Kate commands.

Kate's command is blocked with, "Yeah, right." / "Oh, he looks good." / "Not gonna happen my friend."

Liam stands in front of Kate to block her from Jack's view. "Who is Jack, and why are we avoiding him?" he whispers.

"My ex." / "The love of her life." / "The guy who's going to blow up her wedding."

At this, Jack pops his head over Liam's shoulder. "Kate?" he says happily. "What are you doing here?"

Kate stands up. "What am I doing here? I told you I was going to a girl's night. . . ." She pushes past Liam to get to Jack. "What are you doing here?"

Jack shrugs innocently. "It's a Saturday night. I thought I'd take in a show."

"A drag show?" Kate asks him suspiciously.

"I'm trying to see more off-Broadway stuff."

"Oh my God! What did you think was going to happen? That we'd just run into each other, and sleep together again?" Kate says angrily as Jack puts his arm around her waist. "This relationship is over. It's not working. I'm getting married. . . ."

And, without the slightest hesitation, Jack kisses her. Kate kisses back, but keeps talking. "Seriously, the wedding is in December. And we have to just make a clean break of this."

"You're right," Jack says confidently. "Let's go have a drink upstairs, and we'll talk."

Kate turns to us, and actually seems to believe her own words as she whispers, "I'm just going to have one drink, and break up. And then I'll be right back."

We all wave and say good-bye, and she's gone.

Liam, still standing, observes the entire scene without commenting. Finally, he turns to us and asks, "Is she coming back?"

"No," we all say in bored unison.

"But isn't she getting married?" he asks.

"No," we all answer.

Dawn puts out her hand to Liam. "Sweetie, I'll take her drink."

The lights dim, and Liam takes a seat next to me. Liam smiles at me, and I smile back.

Ohhhh . . . I hate that I like him so much. Why can't he be overweight? Or balding? Or a lawyer or something?

Two male actresses come onto the stage, pretending to be prostitutes. One is wearing a pink frilly penoir set. My mind wanders to whether or not Liam likes that look in lingerie. Perhaps he would prefer the bright red matching bra and panties worn by the other drag queen. Perhaps if I wore something like that one evening, walking around in my own house as though this is what I'm most comfortable wearing, I'll bet I could get him to think—

"Oh shit, I'm sopping wet."

I turn to Jenn, who instinctively crosses her legs, and throws her sweater over her lap.

I look over, startled. "What?" I whisper.

"My Goddamn water broke," Jenn whispers back. "I'm sopping wet. I gotta go to the hospital."

Just then, the woman sitting in front of Jenn jumps up from her seat. "Oh, my God! There's some kind of flood!" she yells, trying to lift her Jimmy Choos off the floor, and looking like a fifties housewife afraid of a mouse.

Jenn struggles to stand up from her seat. "Sorry. That's me. Just a little amniotic fluid . . ."

A woman shrieks (or was that one of the drag queens?) as everyone in the front row jumps out of their seats, and away from the puddle of fluid forming on the concrete floor beneath them.

Drag queen Kelly, fully dressed up in seventies layered hair and a pantsuit, runs over to Jenn. "Baby, how are you feeling? Have you been having contractions?"

"Yeah," Jenn says, sighing. "But they were almost ten minutes apart, and not so painful. I thought maybe they were just Braxton Hicks, and since this was my last night out for a while, I figured I'd see the show and then see how far—" Jenn doubles over in pain. "Aaaaaarrrrrrrgggggghhhhhh . . . Son of a . . ."

"You drove yourself to the theater when you were in labor?" Andy asks, incredulous.

Jenn starts her Lamaze breathing—Hee-hee-hee—as she glares at Andy. "Don't give me that judgmental tone! It was my last night out for eighteen years."

Hee-hee-hee . . .

Drag queen Kelly and I each take one of Jenn's arms, and lead her out of the basement. "How far apart are they now, baby?" Kelly asks as we slowly walk up the steps.

"About six minutes."

"First baby?" she asks.

"Third."

Kelly looks past Jenn to me. "The third always comes quick. You need to get her to the hospital now."

The next twenty minutes were a blur. I drove Jenn's car (with her in it) to Cedars Sinai, Andy followed me in her car, and Liam followed me in my car. En route, Jenn used her cell to call her husband Rob. "Hi, it's me," she says into the phone softly. "I just wanted you to know that I'm . . ."

I can tell a contraction is hitting again, because Jenn lifts her butt off the passenger's seat and winces. But she doesn't make a noise, other than to take a deep breath. She keeps the phone to her ear, and acts like nothing is wrong. "I'm in labor."

Jenn listens to an earful on her phone. "Well, neither of the boys came out until week forty-two. I just assumed this one would also be yanked out late. . . ." Jenn takes a deep breath. "Okay, dear. You were right. I was wrong. Meanwhile, I think it would be prudent for you to get on the next flight available so that you can see your daughter being born. . . ."

Jenn is silent again as Rob continues to talk on the phone. Finally, she says, with preternatural calm, "Charlie is with me, she'll relieve the babysitter once you get here. Meanwhile, I need you to quit panicking, and get on a plane." And then Jenn's voice suddenly harshens. "Rob. I'm in labor. This is not the time to be fucking with me. I'm a urologist. I know how to make bad things happen to men." She smiles. "Good. I'll see you then."

And she hangs up.

"Rob's in San Francisco this weekend, isn't he?" I ask wearily.

"Yes. And I told him to go because neither of the boys ever came out on time. I made a mistake, but he'll be here in time. Meanwhile, would you speed it up a little? I would like to get the epidural in the parking lot on the way in."

The next hour flew by. Andy and Liam were right behind us, and we all stayed with Jenn while she got checked in, weighed, moved to a room, and, most important, given her epidural.

"Oh, that feels so much better," Jenn says from her hospital bed once the epidural had totally kicked in. "I'm telling you, Dr. John Bonica should be sainted."

"Who?" I ask.

"The guy who invented the epidural. Oh, wow. Look at the screen," Jenn says cheerfully. "I'm having another contraction."

I turn to see the screen line rapidly climbing, which I guess indicates a contraction. Jenn isn't in the least bit of pain. It makes me wonder why my mother always talks about how many hours she was in excruciating labor. Looks to me like all you do is sit in your bed, and eat Popsicles.

Andy takes Jenn's hand. "Can I get you anything?" she asks, her voice dripping with concern.

"Another orange Popsicle would be great," Jenn says cheerfully. "They're in the refrigerator to the left of the nursing station." As Andy leaves, Jenn turns to us. "I'm out of pain, I'm only five centimeters dilated." She puts her hands up behind her head. "Ah . . . what could be more relaxing than this?"

"Mommy!" Alex, Jenn's four-year-old, yells as he and his three-year-old brother Sean tear into the hospital room.

"Don't get near Mommy!" Jenn yells. "Mommy has a big needle in her back, and if you get near it, Mommy will be very, very angry."

"Darling!" my aunt Julia says, suddenly appearing behind the boys.

"Mom!" Jenn says, bolting upright in her bed. "What are you doing here?"

"Preparing to revel in the wonder of childbirth," Aunt Julia says cheerfully, placing an iPod and a speaker system onto Jenn's nightstand. "I was reading all about how important it is psychologically for the baby to hear the laughter of family members as she emerges."

Julia turns on the iPod to play the sounds of Enya just as Alex finds the hospital remote, points it at the TV, turns it on, then immediately changes the station to Cartoon Network.

"Alex, what did Mommy say about you using electronic devices before me?" Jenn asks him sternly.

"That I'm smarter, and I always figure them out first," Alex answers without turning his head away from the TV.

"And that you're the dumbest one in your own house because you can't set the clock on the VCR," Sean adds as he tries to climb into the bed with Jenn.

"Honey, there's a tube here, and if you knock it out—"

Andy walks in, not yet noticing the chaos of the room. "They didn't have orange Popsicles, so I got you a grape."

"Popsicles!" Sean yells, turning to his mother, and giving her the most cherubic look ever. "Please Mommy, can I have a treat?"

"Honey, I love you, but you need to get off the bed," Jenn says urgently. "Mom, why aren't they with the babysitter?"

"Rob called to tell me you were in labor, and needed me to relieve her. I just assumed you wanted me to come here with the boys." Julia puts her hand over her heart, and nearly cries, "My baby's having a baby."

And we hear machine gunfire from the TV.

Jenn kicks into Mommy gear, and gets her take-charge voice on. "Alex, turn off the TV. Sean, yes, you may have a treat, but only if you get off this bed right now. Mom, the boys should be in bed asleep. They can meet their new sister in the morning after all the blood and poop are cleaned up."

"There's poop?" Andy asks, shocked.

Jenn points to her. "I'll give you a book to read. Meanwhile, everybody out."

"I'm not leaving my daughter here by herself," Julia insists.

"I'm not by myself, Mother," Jenn quips. "There are nurses all over the floor."

"But what about having the whole village here to experience the wonder of the new generation?"

"Mom, to be blunt, I have a rule about childbirth: unless you were there for the conception, you can't be here for the birth. Which technically means only Sean can be here, and he needs to go home and go to sleep. So, as much as I love you all, you need to go."

Thirty

Motherhood is a thankless job.

"Bown-chicka-wow-wow," I hear from the backseat of my car.

Nineteen seventies porn music. Swell. I turn around to look at Alex in his booster seat in the back. "Where did you hear that?"

"Daddy and I heard it in a movie this week," Alex tells me. "Bown-chicka-wow-wow."

Before I can look too horrified, Liam enlightens me from the driver's seat, "It's from the *Alvin and the Chipmunks* movie a few years ago." He cheerfully yells back to the boys, "Who wants ice cream?"

"Me!" they both yell excitedly.

"Um . . . I'm not sure that's a good idea. Jenn said to take them straight home, and put them to bed."

"So that's one 'no' "—Liam says, pretending to count—"and three 'yes'es."

The boys cheer loudly in the backseat. I shrug. "Okay, but let's make it quick."

Liam drives us to a Cold Stone Creamery near the hospital. The moment we are within running distance, the boys take off for inside the store. I quickly follow them. When I open the door, they are pressed against the glass case of ice cream, and talking at about a deci-bel 10. "I want the blue one with sprinkles on top!" Alex yells.

"Alex, keep your voice down," I say nervously. "You don't want to bother the other customers."

"I want chocolate!" Sean yells, flapping his arms up and down excitedly. "With M&Ms mixed in."

"Ssh," I admonish. "Guys, seriously."

"I don't want my sprinkles mixed in!" Alex tells Liam and me urgently. "I want them on top!"

"But I don't want mine on top!" Sean insists to us with equal in-tensity. "I want mine mixed in!"

"Okay," I whisper. "But everyone needs to take it down a notch. Inside voices. There are grown-ups we don't know here."

Liam laughs. "Honey, if the other customers are bothered by kids getting excited, they should be in a bar, not an ice-cream store. What are you having?"

"Do they have anything with Marlboros mixed in?" I mutter to him.

Liam laughs. Rubs my back. "Large Sweet Cream with Oreos, right?"

"Yeah," I say, surprised.

When did I order that in his presence? And how the hell did he remember it?

When picking a man, the man who automatically orders you the large ice cream is the keeper.

We order our ice creams (Liam gets all of us larges) and take our ice cream to a little table outside. As the boys dig into their ice cream, Liam asks them, "So, do you go to school?"

"I go to Swanson Preschool," Alex says through a full mouth.

"Me, too," Sean says through his mouthful of ice cream.

"And who's your best friend there?" he asks them both.

"Sean." / "Alex."

"And what's your favorite toy at the school?" Liam continues.

My cousin Jenn once said that when you get married, foreplay changes. You no longer get hot when a man wears a suit to a date and brings you flowers. You get hot when you see him load the dishwasher, or run the vacuum cleaner. I gotta say, that is nothing compared to watching men who are good around children. Over the next twenty minutes, I watched Liam listen intently as the boys told him all about their dinosaurs and their trains. I even watched as he let them wrestle him to the ground (a sight that almost frightened me, because they were being so rough).

But that was nothing compared to when we got to Jenn's house. The sight of watching this man read them books while they sat in their pajamas, one on each side of him, their eyelids getting droopy from the late night and the sugar low. Oh man—Jenn might not be the only one suddenly sopping wet tonight.

As Liam continues reading, I walk downstairs, and call Jenn at the hospital. Her mother answers, and after we talk she hands the phone over to Jenn.

"How are they?" Jenn asks. "Are they being hideous? Have I completely ruined your chances with my married crush?"

"They're already in bed, and they've been amazing," I assure her. "We took them for ice cream. Was that okay?"

"I'm in labor. I wish you could take *me* for ice cream. Where'd you go?"

"Cold Stone."

"Oh," Jenn says, wincing. "Was Alex a terror about the sprinkles?"

"Nope. Sprinkles on top for him. M&Ms mixed in for Sean."

"You're a better woman than I."

"Thanks. Listen, would it be okay if Liam stayed with me for a while here? He's just been amazing with the boys, and I could use the help."

Jenn laughs. "Yes, babysitter, your boyfriend can stay with you."

"Yay," I say quietly. "And thank you."

"No problem. Help yourself to a bottle from the wine refrigerator. You've earned it."

"Thanks," I say. "Call me if you need anything. Love you."

"Love you, too. Good night." As Jenn hangs up, I can hear her telling her mom, "Mom, incense isn't allowed in the room. Put that out."

I hang up, then race over to Jenn's kitchen. She and Rob are such grown-ups, they actually have a wine refrigerator. I look through everything, and pull out a Guenoc Claret. I open the bottle, giving it time to breathe, while I search her cabinets for some wineglasses. I happily pour two glasses, then head upstairs to see if story time is over.

And that's when I see it: Liam out cold on the floor, sleeping between the twin beds of the boys, also asleep.

On the one hand, they all look so peaceful and cute, and my mind jumps ahead to Liam and me married, and him putting our kids to bed.

On the other hand, to quote Rod Stewart: Tonight's the night.

I tiptoe in, and kneel down next to Liam. I shake him lightly on the shoulder, "Wake up," I whisper. "The boys are asleep."

Liam smiles, his eyes still closed. He gently puts his arm around me, and tries to pull me down to sleep next to him. I suspect this is an unconscious gesture, because although I allow myself to be pulled down (Hey, I'm still lying next to the guy. That's progress, right?), I whisper, "I opened some wine. Do you want to go downstairs?"

And I get no response.

So, I just lie there like an idiot for five minutes, wanting him to wake up, but not wanting to be responsible for being the person who woke him up.

Then I go another five minutes.

Nothing great comes without some failure.

Finally, I peel Liam's arm off my body, stand up, and go look for my nicotine gum.

Thirty-one

I spend the next hour chewing orange gum, sipping beautiful wine, and checking my e-mail.

The first e-mail is from Kate. It's addressed to Dawn and me.

> Hi Guys.
>
> I haven't had a chance to talk with you guys yet, but I have news: Will is being transferred to Chicago at the end of January. He's already got his eye on a house in Naperville, which we're flying out to see after our engagement party next week. It looks pretty amazing: thirty-five-hundred square feet, good schools, close to downtown. All in all, a perfect place to raise a family.
>
> Obviously, I'm going to give notice on my job at the station. Jack keeps saying things like, "You love your work," and "You love living in California." But, honestly, my job is getting to me. I feel like I don't do enough for the political community, it's not the job I thought it was going to be when I broke into radio at twenty-two, etc. Maybe I could do more in the Midwest. Who knows?
>
> Anyway, I know I did something stupid tonight. I'm embarrassed. But nothing happened, and I'd prefer none of us men-

tion it again. The engagement party will still be at the Biltmore next Saturday. The wedding may have to move to Chicago, I don't know. But I do know my favorite women in the world will be there, and you two will always be by my side.

Love,

Kate

I pick up the phone to call Kate, but I get her answering machine. I hang up before I can leave a message.

I type back:

I'm just going to write this once, and you can ignore me, and I promise not to say another word about it. Obviously, I want you to be happy. But I've rarely seen the geographical cure work, and I don't know many people who love their job more than you. Most important, people who have been best friends for nine years know each other pretty damn well, and have a pretty good idea of what makes the other happy.

And I don't mean me. I mean Jack.

Love,

Charlie

I sit back in Jenn's reclining chair, and stare at my screen. The thought of Kate moving tears me up inside. She's been my rock for over ten years. Through all the jobs, the boyfriends, the dramas of my life, she's been there. And now she'll be gone. And e-mails and phone calls aren't the same as being there.

And just when I thought my night couldn't get worse, I get roped into an e-mail chat:

Jordan1313: Hey, how you doin'?

I stare at the instant message, and start to feel sick. I can barely breathe. Instantly, my ego is deflated, and I'm not sure what would make me feel better: getting rid of him, or getting him back.

> AngelCharlie: Hangin' in there. You?
> Jordan1313: I miss you.

Yikes! Now what? As I debate what to type next he writes:

> Jordan1313: That's me on your phone. Pick up.

I type furiously.

> AngelCharlie: I can't pick up. I'm not at home.
> Jordan1313: Oh.

A few seconds later:

> Jordan1313: Are you at that Liam guy's house?

I type back:

> AngelCharlie: No, I'm at Jenn's, watching the boys. She's at Cedars right now having her baby.
> Jordan1313. Oh, good for her. Tell her to get the epidural.

And a few seconds later:

> Jordan1313: I'm sorry I hung up when I called last week. I thought you had moved on to another guy already, and I got upset.

Is now the time to point out that he also broke up with me the day before that?

> Jordan1313: So . . . are you dating him?
> AngelCharlie: No.
> Jordan1313: Are you dating anyone else?
> AngelCharlie: Not yet. Why? Are you?
> Jordan1313: No.
> Jordan1313: Although you were right about Stacey. She made a move on me last night. I'm an idiot for not seeing it coming. It would appear the German job might not happen now, because I rebuffed her.

Well, what the hell am I supposed to say to that?

> Jordan1313: Actually, I'm not even sure if you told me she liked me, or warned me that she would hit on me. I don't really remember what we said in New York. I just remember the outcome.
> Jordan1313: Shit. I have to go. Will you e-mail me this week?

I debate for a minute before I write:

> AngelCharlie: Sure.
> Jordan1313: I'd like that. Oh, and I might be home for a few days on Thanksgiving weekend. If so, do you want to go have dinner?

I look at the screen, and realize I am sighing aloud.

> AngelCharlie: I don't know. I'll have to see how my schedule looks.

Jordan1313: I understand. Well, hopefully, the stars will align in our favor.

And then he writes the thing that really messes up my head.

Jordan1313: Love, me

Thirty-two

Men are fuckers who just want to mess with your head.

I end up falling asleep on Jenn and Rob's couch, watching a rerun of some sitcom from the nineties I don't remember. I didn't think I'd ever fall asleep; I was once again in the purgatory that is my romantic life: Who do I want? Who wants me? Who will make me happy?

The following morning, I am no further along in my pursuit of happiness.

"Get this party started on a Saturday night!" Pink loudly sings to me.

I am jolted awake by the blasting sound of a synthesizer, and Pink letting me know that everyone is waiting for her to arrive.

I pull myself off of the couch and stub my toe on a bin of Legos as I follow the music to Jenn's kitchen. There, I see Sean eating at the breakfast table, and Alex watching Liam make pancakes.

"So, you want a stegosaurus?" Liam asks.

"Yeah, and you need to put spikes on the back of its tail," Alex advises.

As I watch Liam pour the tiniest bit of batter into the frying pan, I mumble, "Good morning."

"Good morning!" Liam and the boys say in unison.

"Coffee's made," Liam tells me. "How did you sleep?"

"Oh, fine," I say, turning down the music before pouring myself coffee in the biggest mug I can find in Jenn's cupboard. "You?"

"Great. The boys and I have been making pancakes in the shapes of dinosaurs and trains."

"I got a T. rex," Sean tells me with his mouth full of pancakes.

"Great," I say, sleep still permeating my voice. "I told Jenn I'd get the boys to the hospital when visiting hours start. They're pretty excited to see their new sister," I say, as Liam lifts Alex's pancake out of the griddle with his spatula.

As Alex carefully carries his stegosaurus to the table, Liam says, "Excellent. So, what can I make you? A T. rex? An Apatosaurus? Perhaps a frisky little Composnathus?"

"Just a big circle is fine," I say, and rub his arm suggestively.

Jenn's home phone rings. I see from the caller ID it's the hospital, so I pick up. "Hello?"

"I think I'm holding someone here who'd like to meet you," Rob says in a soft voice.

We were at Cedars-Sinai within the hour. Hurricanes Sean and Alex raced through the hospital to meet their new sister, then lost all interest in about five minutes. While Rob went outside to make phone calls and to send e-mails of baby's first picture, Liam took the boys out to the Grove Shopping Center to look at the big Christmas tree, and basically wreak havoc in an outside space where running was acceptable.

Jenn's hospital room is now peaceful, and silent. As Jenn takes a quick shower, I hold the new baby. She is asleep in my arms, and I am already in love with her. She's perfect. Ten tiny fingers, ten tiny toes. These are the moments that life is all about.

Do at least one thing in your life that will outlast it.

Thirty-three

You can go entire weeks or months without anything interesting happening. And that's okay. Your life doesn't always have to be bounding forward at full speed for you to be happy.

The following week was a complete failure to communicate. I didn't have the emotional energy to call or e-mail Jordan, nor did he call or e-mail me.

The not calling was fine for now. Because, until Friday of that week, I still had Liam in my bed (and, sadly, by that I mean guest room). Unfortunately for me, that Friday, we wrapped local shooting, Drew had his dressing room defrosted, and I lost Liam as my roommate.

And, even though I knew I was on a bit of a deadline with him (could there be a more captive audience than a roommate?), I never did get up the nerve to kiss him, or to declare my feelings for him in any way.

I have excuses aplenty. We were shooting twelve-hour days all week. Then Kate would keep me on the phone for hours and hours every night describing her roller-coaster relationships with Will and Jack. And Liam was already starting to spend evenings in the editing bay looking at dailies, and preparing for finance meetings next week in New York. Plus, Drew sent me to Rancho Cucamonga for the perfect dozen donuts. (That took six hours.)

But, really, my lack of nerves stemmed more from fear. Over the course of the past few weeks, Liam had stopped being this unattainable god to me, and became this really nice, loving person. He had meshed in perfectly with my family and friends. He didn't think they were bizarre, he thought they were charming. He had gone shoe shopping with my costume-designer father. Drank shots of whiskey with my Mawv. Went to yoga with my Mom, and babysat Sean and Alex with me. My mother had even invited him to Thanksgiving and he had accepted.

Which meant that, as desperately as I wanted to kiss him, now I would risk losing him if he was alienated by my advances. And I really couldn't bear the thought of losing what we had. I liked him too much as a friend.

Cut to Saturday night. Despite her whirlwind of drama, Kate was still determined to marry Will. So, Liam picked me up that night, and we headed out to her wildly lavish engagement party downtown.

"So she's been on the phone every night this week with Jack, and Will doesn't mind?" Liam asks me as he navigates his car through Downtown traffic.

I shrug. "Apparently, Will isn't threatened by him. When I had dinner with Will and Kate on Tuesday, he specifically talked about how Jack was a total loser who would never amount to anything, or have any stability in his life. I mean, on the one hand, I guess it's great that he's so unthreatened by her ex, but on the other hand . . ."

". . . she's still sleeping with him," Liam finishes.

I shrug. "Well, they haven't slept together this week. Jack moved on from seduction, and is now onto phone skills."

"I'm sorry. What are phone skills?"

"You know, being able to talk until three in the morning. Making the woman laugh over the phone. I'm sure you're great at that."

"Not really. If I'm talking to a woman at three in the morning, I'm probably trying to convince her to check out some of my other nocturnal skills."

Liam gives me a mischievous smile.

I make a show of rolling my eyes at his hubris, but truthfully, I'm intrigued.

Liam is my date tonight. There's an open bar, free food, and a beautiful, romantic setting. If I don't have a shot here, I might as well pack my arrows and quiver, and go home.

We park the car, and head into the hotel. We walk into one of the smaller banquet rooms, where Kate and Will are receiving guests at a table toward the front of the room. Kate looks like a forties movie star in a silver lamé floor-length gown, and Will looks positively elegant in a navy blue suit.

The room is decorated in light and dark green: the colors of Kate's wedding. There are white flowers of all sorts everywhere. The center of the room has been transformed into a dance floor, where I see Dawn dancing with a man I'm sure is yet another stud from her stable.

Liam and I each take a glass of champagne from a wandering waiter, just as Dawn finishes her dance, gives a hug to her partner, and walks over to us. "How's it going so far?" I ask her.

"Jack's here," Dawn says, nodding her head toward a table where Jack sits in an ill-fitting suit by his lonesome.

"Good God," I say. Then I look at Liam. "You're a guy, you tell me: What on earth would possess a man to show up at his ex-girlfriend's engagement party?"

"Never underestimate the power of the out-on-a-limb gesture," Liam answers.

He looks over at Jack. "Frankly, I hope he wins. That's a gold medalist, right there."

"You told him your silver medalist analogy?" Dawn asks me.

"Yeah, but I think I explained it wrong," I say to her. "Liam, a silver medalist is the one who tries and tries, and never quite gets what they're working for. No offense."

"None taken," Liam says, smiling.

"Why would you take offense?" Dawn asks Liam.

"He actually has an Olympic silver medal," I tell her.

Dawn shakes her head. "Girl, you really do have the worst luck with what comes out of your mouth around good-looking men."

"Anyway," I say, glaring at Dawn while I talk to Liam, "a gold medalist is what you want to be. And, frankly, as much as I love Jack, Will is the gold medalist. Not Jack."

Liam smiles at me. "Darling, I adore you. But I'm going to have to disagree. You're missing the point of the silver medal. Yes, I would have loved winning a gold medal in track. But I love running. I do it every day, because it makes me happy. So, it doesn't really matter if things didn't turn out exactly as I thought they would in my head. I went after the thing I really wanted, and I got it. Just in a different form than I thought I would."

Liam looks at Will for a moment. "Fear of failure is an insidious thing. Leads people to pretend they never wanted a medal in the first place."

I look over at Will, than back at Liam. "Huh?"

Liam gestures with his champagne glass toward Will. "That guy is a lawyer, right?"

I nod.

"He's not doing what he really wants to do in his life. But it's a safe choice," Liam asserts. "And he's marrying a woman he knew in high school, who he had the nerve to break up with ten years ago, when he still had the energy to go after what he really wanted in life. But now he's afraid of failing. He's lost his nerve in life, he's lost his way in the world, and he's not happy. Don't let the expensive suit, the polished shoes, the money or the charm fool you: that guy doesn't even have a medal. Whereas Jack"—Liam points to Jack—"that guy knows what makes him happy in his life. And he's balls out about getting it."

Kate and Will walk up to us, hand in hand. "How is everyone enjoying the party?" Kate asks, beaming.

"It's wonderful," I say nervously. I motion toward Jack. "I see Jack is here."

Kate gets a nervous look on her face. "Yeah, I invited him. He seemed kind of lonely."

"What a loser!" Will says, laughing. He turns to Liam. "Can you believe a guy who would come to the engagement party of the woman who never wanted to marry him? What kind of a masochist is that?"

Liam smiles at Will. "Positively Olympian," he tells him, while giving me a "private joke" look.

"Uh . . . yeah," Will says, not knowing quite what Liam's statement means. "Hey, did Kate tell you for our honeymoon we're going trekking in Mongolia?"

I made the mistake of taking a sip of my champagne while he said that. Which means I choked on my champagne, while trying to suppress a spit take.

"Now see, that's comedy," Dawn says to Will, laughing. "You should really think about doing stand-up."

"Actually, the tour we're going on looks amazing," Kate insists to us. "It's not all camping out and hiking. We're going horseback riding for two weeks."

Dawn crosses her arms. "I forget. Is 'equinophobia' spelled with one 'I' or two?"

"There's no such word," Kate says, glaring at Dawn.

"If there isn't, there should be," Dawn says, glaring back.

Kate grabs Dawn by the arm, and forces a smile at Will. "Can you guys excuse us for one moment?"

Kate drags Dawn away from Liam and Will, and over to another part of the room. Naturally, I follow them, and try to diffuse the situation.

"Kate, calm down. She was only kidding," I begin.

"What the hell is your problem?!" Kate snaps at Dawn.

"*My* problem?" Dawn says. "What the fuck is *your* problem? You're not having the wedding you always wanted, you're not wearing the engagement ring you always wanted, you're quitting your job and moving out of the city you love, and now you'll be spending your honeymoon on a horse. Even though you have a deathly fear of horses."

"It's more of a hesitation than a fear," Kate barks back.

"Oh please. It would be like Charlie spending her honeymoon in a room full of commitment-phobes and snakes. And I've had it. I'm not standing by anymore to watch you make the biggest mistake of your life just because I'm afraid you'll be mad at me. You are not this person, and the man you love is sitting in a corner by himself. Deal with it, before we have a wedding where Jack is screaming your name through a plate-glass window at the church."

Kate looks like she's about to burst into tears. I try to alleviate the tension. "Look," I begin gently. "Dawn's not really saying it's going to come to that. She's just trying to make a point. But I think we're both wondering, if you're spending all night talking to Jack, if you still want to sleep with Jack, and if you want him here now . . . why don't you love Jack?"

Kate doesn't answer me for a moment. "I do love him," she squeaks out. "Very much." Her eyes start to glisten with tears. "But I don't like who I am when I'm with him."

"Why?" Dawn asks, rubbing Kate's arm gently. "What is so bad about you when you're around him?"

"What's so bad is that I'm me when I'm around him. I'm awful. I sleep until noon when I can, I eat too many Cheetos, I don't exercise, and I'm constantly worried about how I'm going to pay my rent. I don't want to be that person. I want to be the other person. I want to be the girl who wakes up early and goes jogging, and isn't an artist, and who makes lots of money. A girl who loves lavish weddings, loves Chicago, and can't wait to go horseback riding in Mongolia. I want to be the girl who deserves to be loved by Will."

My face must have shown how much pain I was in just listening to her pain. This wedding was just so wrong. And it wasn't even anyone's fault. Will wasn't a bad guy, he just wasn't the man for Kate. The man for Kate was a graphic artist who took too long to paint his living room, who didn't know the first thing about clothing, who also slept until noon, and who lived from paycheck to paycheck. Kate never wanted to marry him not because she didn't love him, but because he wasn't Will. She had spent nine years breaking up with him every week because he wasn't perfect: he was a silver medalist, just like her.

I wish I could say that I gave her the perfect speech about self-acceptance. About how the guy that you dream about at fifteen isn't the same guy you dream about at thirty. About how eventually your boyfriends—when you're lucky—become family. And, take it from me, every family is fucked up.

But, in the end, nothing I could have said mattered. Because a moment later, a not-so-perfect guy walked up to Kate wearing an ill-fitting suit and the wrong color tie. And he pulled out a small velvet box, and flipped it open to reveal a tiny Assher cut diamond ring.

And Jack said the one thing Kate needed to hear.

"Come home."

Thirty-four

You reap what you sow. This applies to your career, your relationships, your financial life, everything. Some days it may not feel like it. But whatever you put out there eventually comes back—so be careful what you put out there.

A little while later, Liam and I have parked his car at my house and taken a cab to Tiki Ti, a dive bar in Silverlake known for its crazy rum drinks and for still permitting its patrons to smoke. (Side note: now that I haven't been smoking for a while, the smell of smoke is getting kind of gross.)

Anyway, although I was very happy for Kate, I was disappointed that my plans to intoxicate Liam with both my charm and her booze at the party had not materialized. Within the hour, Jack had disappeared, Kate had said she needed to talk to Will, and the party had petered out.

However, this was my last night with Liam until Thanksgiving, and I was determined that tonight was the night.

I wasn't pussyfooting around. We each ordered a rum drink, and then I suggested a drinking contest. Liam agreed. Instead of Truth or Dare, we would play Truth or Drink.

I am such an idiot.

Never play Truth or Drink with a man.

I won't get into the "why" with my teenage great-granddaughter, but I really should have thought this through. Obviously, Liam, being a guy, wasn't going to ask questions like, "Who was your first kiss?" or "Have you ever fired a gun?" He was going to ask sex questions. And my truthful answers either made me sound too innocent, or like a total slut. Either way, I was drinking, not answering.

Now, one would think a sip of a rum drink wouldn't be as bad as a shot. You can kind of cheat by lifting the bottom of your glass up high, keeping your lips almost closed, and pretending to drink more than you do. That can buy you some time.

But when the question is the fourth incarnation of, "How many men have you slept with?" in effect you are drinking four times to not answer the same question.

Which can lead a girl to do bad things.

Three massive rum drinks later, I was rather drunk. Okay, I was drunk out of my mind.

And here's where everything turned. Liam was just taking a sip of his drink after not answering my question, "How many women have you slept with?" when I looked him in the eye. And he looked back. And all I could think about was leaning over and kissing him.

I turn away nervously. "Wow, I never get to do that," I slur at him.

Liam looks mildly amused. "Do what?"

I lean over, almost falling into his lap. "Look you right in the eye." I start waving my finger around, trying to make a point, but my index finger sort of spins around in an imaginary circle, never quite landing anywhere. "Okay, if I stare at that smile anymore, I might climax, so I better look away."

Liam narrows his eyes at me and tilts his head, smirking. "I'm not sure how to take that. Thank you?"

"De nada," I say, waving him off.

Then I lean in closer to look at his beautiful smile. "You have very nice teeth. Very white. I'll bet you've never smoked."

"Uh . . . not really. Are you okay? Maybe we should get you home."

"No," I say definitively, smiling back at him. "Have you ever cheated on a girlfriend?" I ask Liam.

Liam thinks a moment, then takes a sip of his drink.

"Oh, come on!" I challenge. "I answered the question that really embarrassed me."

"Which question that embarrassed you?"

I open my eyes wide. "You know . . . ," I say under my breath. "Question number three."

Liam laughs. "But you answered no."

"Yeah, but I still can't even believe you asked me that," I say, my eyes still wide from the shock of his question. "Come on," I say seriously. "I've heard all these rumors. Have you ever cheated on a girlfriend?"

"Hm," Liam says, giving it some thought. "Well, I suppose there are women out there who would say I have, but I didn't think they were girlfriends at the time, so I'm not sure what answer to give."

"Good," I slur. "Because Andy says you're a slut. Which is bad. But Jamie says all men are sluts. Which is good." I look up at the ceiling. "Well, not good, exactly. Can I have a hug?" I blurt out, then I fall into him.

Liam gently hugs me, letting me lay in his arms. My God, that feels good. I could be in these arms all night.

"You smell good," I mumble into his chest.

"What?" Liam asks, pulling away from me slightly so he can hear me.

"No, don't do that," I say, pulling him back to me. I lean up to him, trying to give my best "kiss me" face. "I said you smell good," I repeat. "What is that? Chanel for Men? Lavender soap?"

"Right Guard Deodorant."

Is it that men *try* to be dense, or does it just come naturally?

"Well, it is nice deodorant," I say, still trying to hint for a kiss. I look up at him, doe-eyed. "So, if you had met me ten years ago, would I be your married crush?"

"Um . . . you're not married," Liam points out.

"Right!" I say a little too loudly, then point at him. "Men. Are. Dense."

Liam motions for the tab, and the bartender throws down a piece of paper. Liam puts cash onto the bar without looking at the bill. "Thanks," he says to the bartender. "And can you call us a cab?"

"Right outside," the bartender tells us, taking the cash, then thanking Liam for the generous tip.

"Oooh," I say. "He's picking up the tab. He's buying me drinks. Maybe he'll ask to take me home. And since his car is in front of my house, maybe he'd like to stay the night."

Liam smiles. "Is that an offer?"

I smile back. "Well, my roommate recently moved out, so we'll have the place all to ourselves."

Liam laughs. "Well, when you put it that way, I'd be delighted."

My face lights up. "Oh . . . ," I say, excitedly hitting him on the arm. "You know what you should do tomorrow morning?"

Liam continues to smile at me as he shakes his head "no."

"Make me an Irish fry-up. Except maybe you could cook the eggs this time. And wear nothing but your boxer shorts when you make it."

I feel so proud of myself for my suggestion. Liam, on the other hand, chooses to ignore me. "Okay. And do I get to pick the lingerie you'll be wearing?"

"Flirt!" I exclaim, throwing my index finger in the air. Then I give the question some thought. "Wait. Was that a 'Truth or Drink' question? Was I supposed to drink to that?"

"I definitely think we need to get you home."

I like him. I really like him. It's probably a bad idea, but I just can't help myself.

"Can I ask you a question?" I say in all seriousness.

Liam smiles. "Braces when I was twelve, and a Beverly Hills dentist who bleaches my teeth," he jokes.

I laugh. Then I look down. My question is rather serious, and right now my ego is riding on his answer. "No, that's not it." I watch my feet shuffle about nervously before looking back up at him, then looking away toward the dartboard. "I'm always with someone, or you're always with someone, so I know I shouldn't ask but . . ." I turn to look Liam straight in the eye. "I just want to know . . . if we had both been single when we met, would you have thought I was cute?"

Liam and I keep eye contact for what feels like several hours. He puts his forehead against mine. "I think you are way cute," he says quietly. "Why, if your sister hadn't threatened me with bodily injury, I would have tried to bed you the night we met."

"Oh, that is so sweet!" I drunkenly say, putting my hand to my heart. "Is Ireland just an island full of James Bonds?"

"James Bond is British."

"Pierce Brosnan isn't."

Liam smiles. "Truth or Drink: Would you have sex with Pierce Brosnan?"

"Yes," I answer immediately.

Liam laughs. "You won't even consider drinking to that question?"

"Oh, I'll drink to that," I joke.

Liam laughs. I gulp the rest of my drink before he takes my hand and leads me outside to a cab.

"Did you know I'm neurotic?" I ask as we walk out.

Liam smiles. Opens the cab door for me. "All women are neurotic. Don't apologize for it. Own it."

"I need to write that down," I say. Before I step into the cab, I look at him sadly and say, "If I slept with you, I'd fall in love with you."

He looks pained that I've told him that.

But I'm drunk, so I continue. "And then it would end badly, and I'd wait by the phone, and I'd check to see if your e-mails were more than two sentences long, and I'd try to translate how you signed your name. Only now that you've become my friend, I'd want to call you and ask you to translate what the e-mails mean. And I'd think about the time we made out, and how great it was to kiss you, and I'd wonder why you didn't want to kiss me like that anymore. What was wrong with me that I wasn't enough for you?"

We have a moment where we look into each other's eyes. I can't take the intimacy anymore, so I climb into the back of the cab. Liam follows, closes his door, then gives the cabbie my address. Next he turns to me and asks softly, "How on earth did you jump ahead from us making out to me never talking to you again?"

I shrug. "Women always think ahead. We think about the first kiss, then we either think about the wedding, or we think about the breakup. Men, on the other hand, think in the middle: they're thinking about sexual positions, and trying to figure out how to get us into bed. It guarantees procreation really: one sex thinks about the beginning and the end. The other thinks about the middle."

Liam nods his head. "I think you've given this way too much thought."

"And I think you have beautiful lips," I say, gently putting my finger up to his bottom lip.

Before he can say thank you, I continue. "They match your eyes, which is funny, because they're not the same color or anything. Blue lips would be bad."

The backseat is starting to spin. Liam gently takes my finger from his lips, takes my hand in his, and gives me a soft gentlemanly kiss on the hand. "We really need to get you home."

"You know what I wish? I wish I could see pictures of you as a little kid. I wish I could watch . . . wait. What's your favorite movie?"

"*I Went Down.*"

I blink at him a few times. "Is that a porn movie?"

"Yes, Charlie, I just told you my favorite movie of all time is a porn movie," he deadpans. "It's an Irish road movie."

I furrow my brow at him. "Isn't Ireland all of sixty miles across?"

"Yes. But we still have roads."

He is so taking away from my romantic moment here. I forge ahead with my confession.

"I wish I could watch *I Went Down* with you. I wish I could ask you your favorite color, and your favorite food, and what your first pet's name was, and if you've ever been in love. I wish I knew how you got that scar on your chin. I wish I had the courage to tell you that I want to know everything about you."

I lean in, and kiss him gently on the lips. Then I pull back and admit, "I wish I had the courage to say how much I've been thinking about you."

Which sounds like it could have been a promising prelude to an enchanted evening.

Unfortunately, I have no idea.

Thirty-five

Some days are a total "What the Hell was I thinking?"

Oh. God.

Ow, ow, ow, head throbbing. Eyelids feel like sandpaper . . . glued shut to pupils made of broken glass. Too much rum . . .

All right, open your eyelids now, Edwards . . .

I force my eyes open. Ow, ow, ow . . .

I look around. I'm in my own bedroom.

Which probably means I went home with Liam, and he's in the guest room.

Or he ran screaming back to Ireland.

I look down. All clothes still on. That's good, I suppose.

Oh God, I'm thirsty. I feel like I could drink a swimming pool. I look over at the nightstand. There's a glass pitcher of water with a water glass next to it. I start to pour the water into the glass.

Oh, to hell with it, I just grab the pitcher and guzzle it.

I hear a key in my lock downstairs. I quickly put down the pitcher, and head downstairs to see Liam, looking ridiculously fantastic in a gray cotton T-shirt and blue jeans. He walks to my dining room, carrying a tray of coffees and a white paper bag.

"Good morning," he says brightly, flashing an altogether unhung-over smile. "How are you feeling?"

That's a very good question.

And, of course, I have two options to that very good question: be a charming little minx, and act like I'm lovely, thank you very much. Last night was wonderful, thank you very much. Oh, and, by the way, did we sleep together? And should I be thanking you? And by how much?

Or I could go for the truth.

"Well . . . ," I begin, looking around and trying to piece together the evening, "I finally found something to replace my cigarette cravings—I'd give up a kidney for a bottle of fruit punch Gatorade right now."

Liam smiles, and pulls a bottle of fruit punch Gatorade from the white bag. "Oh, I think you'll be needing both of those today to keep your poor liver company."

"Oh God!" I say, letting my head fall.

Liam laughs. "I'm kidding. Man, you were funny last night."

I open the bottle of Gatorade, and chug down half of it in one greedy gulp as Liam pulls a bottle of Advil from the bag. "I'm just going to jump right in," I say to Liam. "How fun was I?"

"I said funny," Liam says, chuckling as he opens the Advil bottle and hands me three tablets. "I think you would have been fun. But you were pretty inebriated. And there are rules against that. Although after you insisted to me for the third time that there's a nine-to-one shot I must be bad in bed, I must say I was tempted to prove you wrong."

"Oh, God!" I whine as I take the tablets from him. "I swear there was a compliment buried in there somewhere."

"Well, it would have to be buried, wouldn't it?" he jokes. "So, how much do you remember?"

"Oh, enough," I lie, then throw the Advil into my mouth, and chug the rest of the Gatorade.

Liam smiles, and looks deep into my pink eyes. "Good," he says, then gives me a quick kiss on the lips. "Are you still up for taking me to the airport this morning?"

"Sure."

"Because I can take a cab."

"Don't be silly," I say. "I have to be at LAX in a few hours anyway. My mother is making all of us kids meet the grandparents when they get in from St. Louis."

"I'm so sorry I'm gonna miss that," Liam says. "But I'm taking the red-eye back Wednesday night, so I'll be bright-eyed and bushy-tailed Thursday morning for your mother's dinner. I can't wait to meet the rest of your family."

He can't wait to meet my family?!

Okay, what in God's name happened last night?

Thirty-six

There are no such things as mistakes, just lessons.

"I'm never drinking again," I whine as I let my head fall between my knees at the airport baggage claim a few hours later.

"He can't wait to meet your family?" Jamie asks me from the blue plastic chair on my left.

"Yeah, I know, right?" I respond nonlinearly, lifting my head, and rubbing my temples to try and rub out the pain of a full-blown headache.

"Well, then, obviously you slept with him, and just can't remember," Andy tells me from the blue plastic chair to my right.

"No," Jamie says, shaking his head. "If she had slept with him, he'd have been in her bed trying to get in a quickie before his flight. Instead, he was fully clothed, not in bed, and talking about being excited to meet everyone. That means he's still in full-on 'lying to get her into her pants' mode."

Jamie, Andy, and I are sitting around baggage claim, waiting for our grandparents to arrive for Thanksgiving week. Once it was determined that no one could get Mawv back home to St. Louis against her will, Grandma and Grandpa decided that they would come out to Los Angeles for Thanksgiving, and stay at my mother's house to enjoy the holidays with her.

Enjoy. Destroy. Same difference.

"Do you want me to just call him, and ask how you guys are doing?" Andy asks me.

"I think he's smart enough to figure out I put you up to that," I tell her.

"It's okay. We can figure this out on our own," Andy says. "Did he have you park and walk him all the way to the security line, or did you just drop him off at the airport?"

Jamie shakes his head. "You know, *When Harry Met Sally* was, like, a billion light-years ago. That proves nothing."

"False," Andy counters. "If he had her drop him off at the curb, it would mean he wanted to get away from her, no matter what he said about her family."

"Or, it could mean that he was being polite, and didn't want to trouble her," Jamie points out.

"Guys, it doesn't matter. I had to be here anyway, so I parked."

"Well then, the next question is the kiss," Jamie suggests.

"What about it?" I ask.

"Well, for one thing, did it exist?" Jamie asks.

"And, if so, was it great?" Andy asks, possibly a little dreamy-eyed.

"Why are you looking at me like that?" I ask her.

"I'm married. From now on, I have to live first kisses vicariously through you."

"Great," I mutter.

"It was great?" Andy asks hopefully.

"No. I meant great that you . . . forget it."

"So it wasn't great?" Andy asks.

"I don't know," I say, torn. "I'm not even sure what kind of kiss it was."

"Meaning what?" Andy asks.

"Well, I'm not sure if—" I stop and look at Jamie. Embarrassed, I lean into Andy and whisper, "I'm not sure if it was a French kiss or not."

"You don't know if he slipped you the tongue?" Jamie asks incredulously.

"I think he did," I say to Jamie, embarrassed and unsure of myself. "Possibly."

Off Andy's look I add, "It's like he sort of opened his mouth, but sort of didn't. And then afterwards he pulled away, looked at me with concern, and said, 'You look like you're going to throw up.'"

Jamie shakes his head slowly. Andy just purses her lips together so much they disappear.

"In his defense, I was planning to do so within five minutes of leaving him. I was starting to get that baking-soda taste in my mouth . . ."

"Yummy," Jamie says dryly. "Who wouldn't want a piece of that?"

I shake my head. "I knew I shouldn't have had that last Ray's Mistake."

"That what?" Andy asks.

"It's a rum drink. Which reminds me." I take out a little notepad, and jot down:

Never have that last rum drink.

My mother walks up to us, carrying four Venti Starbucks cups in a brown four-cup carrier.

"Okay," Mom says, putting down the cardboard tray, and handing us each a cup. "I have decaf vanilla latte for Andy; Christmas blend, nothing added, for Jamie; and a mocha for Charlie."

Mom hands me my cup, and I take a sip.

Then I gag. "Ew! This takes awful!"

"I added a shot of bourbon to yours," Mom says. "I would have added brandy, but it was all I had in my flask. Hair of the dog." She sits down. "So, what did I miss?"

"Nothing," all three of us kids say in unison.

Mom eyes us suspiciously. "Were you talking about your father and me?"

"Yes." / "Of course." / "Caught."

Dad walks up to us. "Okay, Jacquie, wanna give the kids a quick rundown on what your parents don't know as of late?"

Mom points to Dad. "Good idea," she says as she turns back to us. "Okay, first of all, they don't know your father and I were trying to have a baby."

Andy's chin juts out. "What are you talking—"

I lean into her and whisper, "Don't ask. I'll explain later."

"They also don't know Chris and I split up," Mom continues.

"Do we know Chris and you split up?" I ask.

"Well, you do now. It happened two weeks ago, and I don't want to talk about it."

"He found out you were still sleeping with Dad, didn't he?" Jamie surmises.

"No," Mom says nonchalantly. "I found out he was sleeping with our dog walker."

Andy looks thoroughly confused. "Dad, when did you start sleeping with Mom?"

"When we had that one-night stand back in the late seventies," Dad answers.

"Why did Chris need a dog walker?" I ask Mom. "He doesn't own a dog."

"Yes, but he used to," Mom explains. "And when the dog died, he couldn't bear to fire the dog walker. So, they would go on walks together instead."

"No," Andy clarifies to Dad, "I mean when did you and Mom start sleeping together again, post divorce?"

"You mean post our divorce, or post my divorce with my second wife?" Dad asks her.

"I never trusted Chad," Mom says.

"Who?" Jamie asks.

"Chris's dog walker," Mom answers.

"Let's go with your second divorce," Andy says.

"Um . . . your wedding, I guess. Your mother needed my sperm," Dad explains.

Andy looks at Mom in disgust. "This isn't like the lamb placenta moisturizer you tried to make at home last year, is it?"

"Oh, it's so much worse than that," Jamie tells her.

And from behind us we hear my grandmother's irritated voice. "Well, we're finally here."

All five of us turn to see my grandmother Rose, wearing a light blue sweatshirt with a picture of a turkey wrapped in an American flag, light blue polyester knit pants, and a look of scorn.

Never wear polyester.

My mother is as confused as the rest of us as to how Grandma snuck right past us. "Mom, where did you come from?"

"We decided to take the Winnebago, so we could see Vegas on the way home. Your father's parked at the meters."

Use public transportation, and carpool whenever you can.

And so the eight of us proceeded to drive to my mother's house in a typical Los Angeles caravan of four cars and one thirty-foot-long Winnebago. (Okay, I'll admit that part isn't typical.)

When we get to my mother's home, Grandpa parks his Winnebago in front, and the rest of us find spaces in the garage, driveway, and street.

I get out of my car, and walk up to my mother, staring at the back bumper of Grandma and Grandpa's RV. Mom glares at the bumper sticker of a red, white, and blue ribbon with the words FREEDOM ISN'T FREE.

Don't put a bumper sticker on your car. You will never change any-one's political or cultural opinions based on what your fender is telling them.

"I thought you weren't going to put bumper stickers on the new 'Bago," Mom says to Grandma as she walks out to meet us.

"I only used that to cover up the sticker your Mawv put on the car!" Grandma screeches.

I turn to Grandma. "What did she—"

Grandma glares at me. "'My letter got published in *Penthouse*. Ask me how.' Where is she, anyway?"

"Drew took her parachute-jumping in the desert," I tell Grandma. Off her horrified look, I add, "Only he's going to jump. She's just go-ing along to keep him company so I can be with you."

Mom leans into me. "Lost the coin toss, huh?"

"Best two out of three," I confirm.

Dad walks into the Winnebago, and emerges carrying Grandma's luggage. Grandpa pops his head out the door. "What the hell are you doing?" he asks my dad.

"Basking in the glow of your unconditional family love," Dad re-torts as he begins lugging the bags toward my mother's house.

"Excuse me?"

"I'm just bringing the bags inside," Dad answers.

"Oh, you don't have to bring the bags inside," Grandma says. "We're staying in the Winnebago."

Dad turns around to return the bags.

Mom looks mortified. "You're going to sleep on my street?"

"Don't use that tone of voice with me, young lady," Grandma warns. "Now, everyone inside the Winnebago. I've made a tuna casserole and a big macaroni salad for lunch."

"But Mom, I've made a lovely lobster salad for our lunch."

"So you can freeze yours," Grandma says, disappearing into the motor home.

Mom turns to me as Andy and Jamie get out of their cars to join us. "You kids are so lucky you don't have parents who embarrass you."

Jamie puts his hand over Andy's mouth just as she opens it to respond.

We all follow Grandma into the Winnebago, fill up blue plastic plates with tuna casserole and macaroni salad, grab canned sodas from the refrigerator, and take seats where we can find them.

Before our first family meal of the week can officially begin, Grandma hands each of us two stapled sheets of paper. I look down at the top sheet to read:

Thanksgiving List

1. Abortion
2. Any politician with the last name Clinton or Bush
3. Gay Rights
4. L.L. Bean
5. Paris, France
6. Any war—from Gulf to Vietnam
7. Paul Lynde, the center square from the *Hollywood Squares*
8. Cats

I blink several times. Hm. As Grandma hands us each a ballpoint pen, I turn to see my mother scrutinize the list, then take her pen and add a word to the bottom of page two.

"You're going to have to add 'Catherine,'" Mom says.

Grandma mutters, "Right," and pulls out her own pen to write down "Catherine" in blue ink.

Grandpa lights up a Camel, then leans over to look at Grandma's paper. "Who's Catherine again?"

"Ed's mistress," Grandma says.

"She's not his mistress!" Mom yells, frantically waving away Grandpa's secondhand smoke as she explains, "She's his—"

"Didn't you just say she's on the list?" Dad asks as he reads his copy.

"Hold it," Andy asks. "What is this list?"

Grandma turns to her, "This year, in order to promote family harmony, we have come up with a list of topics that no one is to discuss over Thanksgiving week, and then throughout the Christmas season."

Mom smiles. "All of the topics on this list are subjects that have brought acrimony to past family get-togethers. We figure we'll head that off at the pass with this list."

I continue perusing the list:

9. The expansion of the strike zone
10. Global warming
11. Tattoos
12. Gerbils
13. Dr. Phil

"What strike zone are we talking about?" I ask, confused. "From which country?"

"I specifically said we were not to argue about the strike zone at all this year," Grandpa admonishes firmly. "Let's not limit it to the expansion."

"Don't even get him started about the Cardinals last season . . . ," Grandma mutters.

"They were robbed," Grandpa's voice booms.

"Grandpa, do you really want to compare the Cardinals to the Angels this past year?" Jamie asks innocently.

"Listen, young man, you are not too big that I can't still put you over my knee."

"Better put Cardinals on the list . . . ," Mom says.

And we all write Cardinals at the bottom of the second page.

I flip back to page one of the list:

14. Priests, Pedophiles, and Popes

"Isn't number fourteen three things?" I ask.

"All the same scandal," Mom reasons.

"How did you decide on what's on the list?" Jamie asks. "Because I'd like to put down why I'm not married yet."

"Why? Are you one of the gays?" Grandma asks him.

"No, he's a slut, Mother," Mom counters matter-of-factly. She turns to Jamie. "Although apparently there was a young lady he was so enamored with that he planned to miss Thanksgiving with us just to meet her parents. I was so excited for this new addition to the family that I insisted we have a brunch together before they left for Aspen."

"Unfortunately, we broke up," Jamie admits, mentally kicking himself for getting caught in his lie.

Mom can't help but give him a self-satisfied smile before saying, "Anyway, darling, the list started as any topic that has caused a brawl, temper tantrum, or crying at the Thanksgiving table in the past thirty years."

"Or, grabbing car keys, leaving the table, and slamming out the door," Grandpa reminds Mom.

"Right. That too." Mom agrees.

"Actually, the year that white-trash in-law of yours with the missing front teeth did that was pretty funny," Dad says.

"Are you kidding?!" Grandma gasps. "That Thanksgiving was our family's personal low."

"I got to go with Ed on that one," Grandpa says. "Anything that gets someone who lives in a trailer out of my house is a good thing."

Mom looks around. "Dad, aren't you staying in a trailer?"

"It's a recreational vehicle, not a trailer," Grandpa admonishes Mom. "If you had stayed in St. Louis instead of moving to this den of sin, you'd know that."

"If I had stayed in St. Louis, I'd have killed myself."

15. Leviticus 18:22, 19:1-35

Okay, this argument I remember. My great-aunt Doris told my uncle Colin, who is gay, that he is going to hell. And to read Leviticus 18:22. Then she quoted the phrase: "You shall not lie with a male as with a female: it is an abomination." Colin assured her that he had never lied with a female, so this was really beside the point. An argument ensued, which led my Jesuit-educated uncle to quote Leviticus 19 in its entirety, thus damning her to hell for wearing a cotton/poly blend sweatshirt adorned with a faux jewel turkey.

"If you're not taking out all of Leviticus," Dad asks, "can I damn everyone to hell with the quote about touching unclean pigskin again this year?"

"Oh, that was so cool how you quoted it right before the traditional touch football game," Jamie tells Dad approvingly.

"Forget it. Let's just say all of Leviticus, and leave it at that," Grandma says.

"Why don't we just agree to throw out the whole Bible?" Mom asks.

"You can't throw out the whole Bible!" Grandma nearly shrieks.

"Fine," Mom mutters. "I'm adding a number forty-two. I don't want to hear about Ruth."

"What's wrong with the Book of Ruth?" Grandpa asks.

"Nothing. I mean Aunt Ruth."

I continue reading:

16. String theory

Did I mention that not one of the members of my family is a physicist?

17. John Maynard Keynes

Nor do we have any economists . . .

18. Arthur Schlessinger

Nor any historians . . .

19. Illegal immigration
20. Secondhand smoke
21. Yogi Bear

"When did anyone ever have a fight about Yogi Bear?" I ask.

"It's not Yogi Bear! It's Yogi Berra," Grandpa says, scratching out the word *Bear* and writing *Berra*. "Why would anyone ever have a fight about Yogi Bear?"

"Oh, but throwing down over Yogi Berra, that's healthy," Jamie mutters.

"I don't know what kind of rap slang, "throwing down" is, young man," Grandma admonishes Jamie as she lights up a cigarette, "but I think number thirty-eight shows it's clearly banned."

I zone out from the argument for a moment to inhale deeply. Aaaaahhhhhh . . . secondhand smoke. With all the stress of today, I suddenly find the scent appealing again. Maybe if I can inhale deeply enough, I can get enough fumes into my lungs to make me calm.

"Don't open the window!" I yell at my mother as she opens a window.

"I need to let the poison out," Mom says, scrunching her nose up.

"Are you referring to your mother's smoke, or this conversation?" Dad asks her dryly.

Mom looks at Dad a moment while she decides on an answer. Finally, she shrugs. "Well, six in one . . ."

"Close the damn window, Jacquie. I'm not heating the entire neighborhood!" Grandpa bitches.

"Dad, it's seventy-eight degrees outside," Mom reminds him.

"Oh, that's right," Grandpa nearly spits as he puffs on his cigarette. "I can't believe we're thinking about spending Christmas in seventy-eight-degree weather. Honestly, what kind of Christmas are we gonna have with no snow?"

"Jesus lived in a desert, Dad," Mom reminds him for the millionth time. "Wait a minute," she says, eyeing him suspiciously. "Since when are you staying until Christmas?"

And Grandma pipes in, "Well, dear, with the price of gas the way it is, we're thinking about just staying parked here until after the New Year."

For the next minute, I watch my mother carefully. I'm pretty sure she just had a minor stroke.

Thirty-seven

The chances of having the happiest Thanksgiving of your life with your family present are 0 in 100.

I spend the next four days chauffeuring various extended family members to and from the airport, Disneyland, the beach, Hollywood, various hotels and motels, and my mother's house (now filled to capacity with—count 'em—twelve guests, plus an additional four guests in Grandma and Grandpa's Winnebago).

So many highlights of my week. Hard to pick one for the top spot.

In contention for the top prize was the time my grandmother complained about all of the cooking and cleaning she had to do to prepare for the Thanksgiving meal (even though Mom was technically the hostess) and wondered aloud, "If it's all worth it."

"Probably not," Grandma decided. "But I guess I need to keep putting myself through the hassle. After all, I could be dead tomorrow. This might be my last Thanksgiving."

To which my mother muttered to me, "She keeps making promises she won't keep."

Then there was the argument between my Mom and my grandfather over her Pratesi napkins, which began when Grandpa admonished, "Why the hell would you spend over a hundred dollars on napkins?"

"Because they are elegant and fabulous," Mom explained.

"Seriously, Jacqueline, do you have too much money lying around? Decided that when you die, instead of an inheritance, you should force your kids to kick in a little to bury you?"

Which was followed by Mawv telling her son-in-law sternly, "I'm warning you: Leave my family out of this."

Or, the delightful evening we had en famille at the Olive Garden. You know that restaurant that advertises when you're here, you're family? I wonder who on earth ever thought *that* was a selling point? Do you think people want to walk in to have the maître d' tell them they never lived up to their potential? Then be seated to have the waiter ask them why they're not married yet, then remind them that their biological clock is ticking?

This is why in general I believe:

Don't eat at a publicly traded restaurant.

Which is the broader version of another piece of advice:

Never go to a chain restaurant with an apostrophe "S" at the end of its name.

Although I have to admit it was better than Grandpa's original idea of a restaurant in the Valley that advertised, "We deep-fry all our sushi." Or the restaurant they chose the night before where the waitress pronounced "crudités" phonetically.

All of these events were irritating as hell, and worthy of a notable mention.

But I'd have to say the highlight came Wednesday afternoon, when four generations of Geoghen women (Mawv, Grandma, Mom, and me) came home from grocery shopping to see my great-great-aunt Ethel, ninety-eight and deaf as a post, sitting on Grandpa's La-Z-Boy in the middle of Mom's living room, blaring a rerun of the 1980s game show *Super Password.*

Don't waste your time watching reality or game shows.

How she even got there, we didn't know. Where Grandpa's La-Z-Boy came from, we're not sure. But Mom just took her bags and walked into the kitchen as if nothing was out of the ordinary. "It's amazing," Mom says, as she passes the TV and observes Dick Sargent give a clue about Elizabeth Montgomery. "Now that we know Dick Sargent was gay, it's so obvious. He's definitely got the vibe."

"Dick Sargent was not gay!" Grandma insists.

This was the sequel to last year's Thanksgiving argument, which is how Paul Lynde got on the list in the first place.

Mawv follows us through the living room, then out the back door, without even acknowledging her sister Ethel.

"Mom!" Grandma yells toward Mawv. "Aren't you going to at least say hello to your sister?"

"Of course not," Mawv responds as she lights up a cigarette in the backyard.

"Mother!" Grandma admonishes.

Mawv rolls her eyes. "Fine."

She puts her cigarette in the ashtray, walks back inside, goes into the living room, and stands between her sister and the TV screen to loudly ask, "How are you doing, Ethel?"

"You stole my husband, you little slut!" Ethel says in her old-woman voice, while Mawv nods as if to say, "See, I knew that would happen."

Mawv walks back up to us in the kitchen. "I'd love to have her killed. But of course that would make her sympathetic."

Also on Wednesday, Mom managed to convince Jamie and me to spend the night, in order to "water down all the tension in this house."

I had no choice. Mom wrote down some advice in my great-granddaughter's book that guilt-tripped me into it. The first two weren't bad:

Never compete with your children. Always be their biggest fan. If you do your job right, they will not only be younger than you, they will be happier than you.

And:

Any mother who says she never bribes her children is lying.

But the last one nailed me:

Honor thy mother, even if she drives you crazy. Yes, I know how hard it is—I have a mother, too.

I didn't even get my old room. No, my room was given to my two- and three-year-old aunt and uncle from my paternal grandfather's fifth marriage. Instead, I got to sleep on my mother's pull-out couch. Why is it, no matter how much money you spend on a fold-out sofa, it still feels like you're sleeping over a balance beam?

On a more positive note, as disastrous as the week had been family-wise, it was bliss Liam-wise.

He had called me every day this week, and tonight is no exception. As I do a slight back-bend over the metal bar crossing my fold-out bed, I regale him with today's edition of, "In the sanity department of my family, clearing the bar usually is accomplished by tripping over it."

Fortunately, he can't stop laughing.

I'm in mid-story, ". . . So there's Mom and Grandma arguing in the middle of Gelson's over the virtues of red wine versus pink wine, and, of course, Grandma keeps pronouncing it Mer-LOT."

Liam continues guffawing. "Something to pair with the kruh-DITE?" he asks.

"Exactly," I say. "And, no one asks me, but my opinion is firmly . . ."

Never drink pink wine.

"Actually, there are some lovely rosés coming out of Italy . . ." Liam begins.

"Are any of them coming out of a box?" I ask.

He laughs again.

"I mean, seriously," I continue, "throw that stuff over some crushed ice, and call it a Slurpee. Then we move to aisle five, so they can have the cranberry-sauce argument—"

"Do Americans have a cranberry-sauce argument?" Liam asks.

"These Americans do. Some of them want fresh, with the zest of an orange, slow-boiled to perfection. Others want it straight from the can, complete with an indentation to make it look like a mini Jell-O mold. And it is to be sliced into circles, not mixed in any way. Speaking of Jell-O molds . . ."

I hear an announcement over Liam's line. "Oh, that's my flight," he says. "I better go."

"Wait," I say. "I've been babbling this whole time, I didn't even ask you how dinner with your ex went."

"It wasn't dinner with my ex," he says, sounding a bit tired. "It was dinner with my friends, who my ex is trying to take custody of in the breakup." Liam takes a deep breath. "It was fine, I guess. She has a new boyfriend. A football player who could snap me in half." He pauses to listen to another announcement. "Okay, we're definitely boarding. I should go." He sighs loudly. "I hope I can sleep on the plane."

"You can always nap in your own bed before you get here."

"That's not a bad idea. What time is dinner?"

"Well, depending on who you ask, it's either at one, or at four."

"Let me guess," Liam says. "Your grandmother wants it at one, your mom wants it at four."

"Very good," I say, impressed. "Apparently, Grandma thinks if we wait until four to have dinner, everyone will, and I quote, 'sleep all day,' and by that she means until eight in the morning."

Liam laughs again. "So, should I be there at one, just in case?"

I smile. He read my mind. "That would be great," I say, my voice a little softer now.

"And for the hostess gift, I'll bring a nice Sauvignon Blanc," Liam says brightly.

"Because you know what they say . . ." I begin.

"Misery loves Sauvignon Blanc?" Liam says, playing along.

"Exactly," I say, smiling.

I'm infatuated all over again.

"I'll see you tomorrow," Liam says to me softly.

"Yeah. See you tomorrow," I respond, just as softly.

But neither of us hangs up.

Liam laughs. "Okay, one of us had better hang up."

"You first," I say.

"I never hang up on a lady," Liam says.

"Well, I never hang up on a—"

"Charlie, can you come up and look at something for me?" I hear my great-great-aunt Ethel yell.

"Shit!" I whisper into the phone. "Gotta pretend I'm asleep now. Bye," I say quickly, then click off the phone, and throw it under my pillow. I close my eyes, and pretend to snore.

All I can hear upstairs is the quiet nocturnal puttering of people finishing up their hygiene rituals, then returning to their bedrooms to whisper about everyone else.

I keep my eyes closed, and dream of kissing Liam.

Liam having to be in New York this week has allowed me to give him the phone test. Back in college, when Dawn, Kate, and I would sum up potential partners, one of the first questions we always asked (okay, after "Is he cute?") was, "Did he pass the phone test?"

What is the phone test? Simple, really. If a guy really likes you, he will talk to you on the phone for hours, and you'll talk about everything from vegetable juicers to Chihuahuas to why you hate Valentine's Day. If he calls you relatively late at night, you'll stay up talking until three A.M. He won't try to get you to come over, he won't try to come over. This isn't a booty call. This guy really likes you.

Two nights ago, Liam and I talked on the phone until six in the morning. My time.

As I dreamily think back to all of the topics we've covered in the last few days (and how much more fun it would be to talk at three A.M. in bed), I hear my mother quietly putter down her stairs, and over to my couch. I open my eyes, and look up to see her wearing her nightgown, robe, and slippers, and lighting up her water pipe.

"What are you doing up?" I ask her.

"Marinating in the juices of my family's vitriol," Mom says with held breath. "I need you to do me a favor. I need you to go buy hemorrhoid cream for Ethel."

I cringe. "Why can't you go?"

"Darling, I'm stoned. How irresponsible would it be to have me on the road?" she says, still holding her breath.

I glare at her. "You specifically just lit up now so you could—"

"And, as long as you're out, can you get me a bottle of personal lubricant? Oh, and your dad needs a one-pound Hershey bar."

So I drive to the twenty-four-hour grocery store in search of hemorrhoid cream, personal lubricant, and Hershey bars.

There's a country-western song in there somewhere.

Thirty-eight

Have yourself a merry little Christmas—no matter how many drinks it takes to get you there.

Okay, for today, I mean Thanksgiving. But drink early and drink often.

I awaken at seven in the morning to my two-year-old aunt Jasmine, and my-three-year-old uncle Bodhi, racing around the fold-out bed in my mother's living room. "Charlie! Charlie! The Wiggles are on!"

I force my eyes open to see the Macy's Thanksgiving parade on TV, and a quartet of men wearing brightly colored shirts and singing something about a pirate.

I throw the pillow over my head to block out reality.

After Bodhi begins jumping on my bed, I realize my attempt at one more minute of rest is futile, so I drag myself out of bed. I walk into my mother's kitchen to get some of my grandmother's MJB coffee: fresh from her burnt-orange coffee percolator, circa 1972, which she brings into Mom's kitchen every morning from the Winnebago in order to make, and I quote, "Real American put-some-hair-on-your-chest coffee."

As I walk into the kitchen, I see my grandma stuffing a turkey, and Drew, standing next to her, reading from the list. "Okay, now when you say 'cats,'" Drew asks her, "Is that referring only to the domestic pets, or all animals of the feline persuasion?"

Grandma laughs. "Honey, you can talk about whatever you want. I am just so happy to hear you and Charlie are back together."

"What are you babbling about?" I ask Drew as I putter over to the cupboard to grab a coffee mug that bids me to COMFORT THE DIS-TURBED. DISTURB THE COMFORTABLE.

"Remember how we told your grandma that we were secretly dating?" Drew asks, as I gently push him out of my way to get to the percolator.

"Yeah," I say crabbily as I pour my coffee. "Grandma, we lied to you about dating so you'd get off my back. I did have a boyfriend, but then we broke up, but I might have one again. He'll be joining us for dinner. I'll keep you posted."

Grandma and Drew both looked startled at my bluntness. "I was just awakened by a three-year-old jumping on my stomach, and I haven't had my coffee yet. I plan to be cranky for at least two cups."

My mother walks into her kitchen. "Mom, we already have a turkey, and it's in the oven."

"Your turkey is filled with chestnut stuffing. Your father wanted one with oyster stuffing," Grandma says. "I figure we'll each make a turkey, then guests will have a choice."

"Okay, Mom, in the first place, no one stuffs turkeys anymore, it can lead to botulism. The stuffing is being cooked on the side—"

"Feh," Grandma snorts contemptuously as she opens the refriger-ator. "Where's your butter?"

"On the side of the door in the butter dish," Mom says. "And in the second place, what the hell is wrong with chestnut stuffing?"

"This is a Christian house, Jacqueline. No swearing," Grandma says, pulling out a red square of Plugrá butter. "This is real butter. I need Oleo butter."

Mom inhales a quick half breath before steaming through her nostrils, "There is no such thing as Oleo *butter*. Just like there is no such thing as Velveeta *cheese,* or Cool Whip *cream.*"

"Jacquie, don't speak to your mother in that tone," Grandpa says as he reads the sports section at the kitchen counter.

"Well, how am I supposed to speak to her, Dad, as she stands in *my* kitchen insulting *my* cooking, and *my* food?"

"Well, that's a nice way to treat your mother, after all I've done to help you this week," Grandma guilt-trips.

"Mother, I already have a thirty-pound turkey in the oven. What on earth am I going to do with fifty pounds of turkey?"

"You could stuff it," my aunt Julia says bellicosely as she enters the kitchen.

Mom plasters a smile on her face. "Julia, darling. So kind of you to join us," she says as they give each other air kisses. "I must say, that face lift has settled in beautifully. It almost looks natural."

"Thank you, darling," Julia returns with equal affection. "I'll give you the name of my doctor. We sixty-something women need a bag of tricks to keep up our appearances."

I wince, and slip out of the room as I hear Mom sneer, "Julia, you know perfectly well, I'm fifty-five."

Knowing that my young aunt and uncle are in the living room, I slip upstairs into my old bedroom, climb into my old twin bed, put my coffee on my old nightstand, and hide under the sheets.

It's at that moment that I realize someone has had an accident.

"Ewwww!!!!" I shriek as I jump out of my bed and yank off the covers. "Damn it! Cindy!" I yell to my twenty-eight-year-old step-grandmother.

"Yes!" she says sweetly from the other room.

"Bodhi had an accident!"

"Oh dear," I hear her say loudly as she runs to my doorway, checks out the puddle in the middle of my old bed, then walks briskly downstairs. "Bodhi, are you still in your wet things?"

"Oh my God!" Mom yells. "My Ethan Allen sofa bed!"

Hmmm . . . on the plus side, maybe she'll have to get rid of it, and I can spend next Thanksgiving eve at home in my own bed.

Hope springs eternal.

The back of my pajamas now sopping wet with pee, I grab my overnight bag, pull out a jar of Laura Mercier Tarte au Citron Honey Bath, and yell down to my mother:

"Mom! Can I use your tub?!"

"Sure!" Mom yells back. "Just make sure the jets are back to where they are supposed to be!"

That sounds ominous. "What does that mean?!" I ask.

"It means Bodhi and Jasmine decided when they were in the bathtub last night to start firing the Jacuzzi jets at each other!" Mom yells back. "By the time they were done, it looked like Esther Williams should have emerged from the middle of my tub, surrounded by jets squirting every which way. By the way, your phone just beeped that you have a text."

I walk downstairs, grab my purse, and pull out my iPhone, which tells me I do indeed have a text: from Jordan.

> I called you at home, but you weren't there. Call me. I have news.
>
> xoxo
>
> J

"Call me. I have news." Five words that annoy me even more than, "It's not you, it's me."

I surprise myself by how quickly I delete his message.

. . .

Ten minutes later, I have put on a little soothing Sarah McLachlan on Mom's iPod speaker system, slipped out of my urine-soaked pajamas, and slipped into a heavenly scented bath.

Which, if anyone knows my life, is the cue for my phone to ring. Or, in this case, for someone to knock on the door.

"What?" I ask, angrily.

"Do you mind if I switch place cards with you?" Jamie asks through the door.

"As long as I'm next to Liam, I don't care what you do!" I yell back.

I hear Jamie's footsteps disappear. I close my eyes and immerse myself in the water.

Moments later, I hear someone pounding on the door.

I pop out of the water. "Yes?"

"Did you tell Jamie you'd sit at the kid's table?" my mother asks through the door.

"No!" I say.

Then I hear Jamie say to her, "I am twenty-five years old. There's no freakin' way I am sitting at the kid's table again."

"You can't just move your sister's name card to the kiddie table!" Mom chastises. "First of all, it's rude to second-guess your hostess by rearranging place cards . . ."

"You're not my hostess. You're my mom."

"And, secondly, I've put her between your aunt Ethel and your father's father. Do you really want that spot?"

"What?" I yell. "I'm not sitting next to great Aunt Ethel."

"It's either that," Mom threatens, "or I'm putting you at the table with the drunks."

"Yeah, that narrows it down," I hear Jamie mutter.

"Where did you put Liam?" I yell through the door.

"Do you want to see my chart?" Mom asks.

Before I can say, "Not really," Mom bursts through the door, carrying a medium piece of cardboard with two rectangles and a circle glued to it. "Here's my seating chart," she says, seating herself on the overstuffed white chair next to the bathtub (I always wondered why she put a chair there). "As you can see, I've tried to alternate seating between men and women, while also alternating the normals with the weirdos, and the drunks interspersed with both the potheads and the prescriptive drug addicts. The children's table is for anyone who plans to be sober."

"Fine," I say. "Put me at the children's table with Liam."

"But, darling, how will you get through the day without drinking?" Mom asks me in all sincerity.

"I just will," I say.

Mom looks confused. Jamie explains to her, "Charlie wants to seduce Liam tonight, and she needs all her faculties."

"Oh. Well, why didn't you say so," Mom says. "Godspeed. Nonetheless, I can't very well seat you next to your date. That's poor form."

"We can't bend the rules in the name of future grandchildren?" I ask.

On that note, Mom rips off the felt labeled with my name, and the one with Liam's name, switches us to the kid's table, and walks out.

Jamie turns to me. "Wait a minute. Did you just stick me next to aunt Ethel?"

"Oh it'll be fun," Mom says cheerfully from the other room. "She can tell you all about her bursitis."

"Wait! Mom!" Jamie yells as he walks out, and shuts the door behind him.

I turn on the Jacuzzi jets, and let the bubbles repopulate themselves.

There's another knock. "Yes?"

"I just had a thought," Dad says through the door. "You know what should be in your book of advice? Words that should never go together. Wine box, for example."

"Wine spigot," I continue.

"White Zinfandel," Dad finishes. "Speaking of which, I'm being sent back to the store for the second time this morning. Do you need anything?"

"I'm good," I say.

"Love you, Bear," Dad says.

I hear Dad walk away.

Thirty seconds later, there's another knock on the door. "What?" I yell.

Drew walks right in. "Am I considered a pothead or a drunk?"

Thirty-nine

You are beautiful.
Okay, so in your head, you just said to yourself, "No. I'm not." Didn't
  you?
You are beautiful.
Wait, no, shut up . . . . You are beautiful.
Now, how would your life be different if you actually believed me?

I recently wrote that to my great-granddaughter. It's a longer bit of advice than I usually write. But I don't know one woman who truly thinks she's beautiful. If you ask any of my female friends on any given day how they think they look, the best answer you'll get is, "Well, I'm okay." And I know some truly beautiful women.

I'll admit, there are a few women who actually do think they're pretty. As a matter of fact, they hide behind it. Because they don't think they're smart enough.

So, what would happen if we did think we were pretty? Or smart? What would we do if we thought we were good enough? If we didn't give ourselves a hundred reasons for why we're awful, all in a split second, all in our head?

I pondered this at 12:59 that afternoon. As I opened my eyes and mouth to finish putting on mascara in the mirror, I wondered how differently I would act around Liam if I couldn't give myself eighty-two reasons why he would laugh in my face if he knew how much I adored him.

I still can't help giving myself all the reasons.

But I decided to go for it anyway.

I hear my mother's doorbell ring, followed a few moments later by Alex and Sean screaming, "Liam's here!" I walk out of the bathroom and through the hallway to get a peek at him from the top of the stairs.

He is breathtaking.

Seriously, I realize I am holding my breath as I stare at him. He looks like a model in his dark blue suit. I watch as he effortlessly hands my mother a bottle of wine and some flowers, and compliments her on her home, then immediately begins listening to Sean's account of his recent run-in with a skunk, while letting Alex grab his arm and hang on him, and kisses Andy hello. It is all effortless, and beautiful, and . . .

Man. Breathtaking. That's what it is.

I walk downstairs, and into the mayhem.

Normally, if I were trying to seduce a man, I would have a different game plan. For clothes, I'd go with a cute little skirt, and some sparkly strappy heels, not the rather formal-looking long black skirt and shirt and modest black boots I currently wear. I would also probably try to hedge my bets by making sure it was dark out, that the target of my affections had been plied with booze, and that I had had a bit of liquid courage myself. And I would absolutely make certain that my entire family, on both sides, was nowhere near my zip code, much less in the same house, as my crush.

But I'm beautiful (sort of). I'm smart (most days). And I am confident (kinda).

Liam smiles warmly as he sees me. "Charlie, you look lovely," he says, leaning in to give me a kiss on the cheek.

"Thanks. You, too," I say quickly. Then I take his hand, and begin pulling him away from the crowd. "Can you come to the garage with me for a second? I need some help with something."

"Sure," he says, confused.

"Is that the boy?" Grandma asks scornfully, as I pull Liam through several rooms and dozens of family members to get to the garage.

"Rose, don't embarrass her," Mawv warns.

"So, is this the new jerk, or the old one?" Grandpa asks my mother as he lights up a Camel.

"The new one," Mom says, then catches herself. "I mean, he's not a jerk. He's just not the old one."

I choose to ignore them. I open the door to the garage, pull him in, and shut the door behind us. Then, before he can speak, I put my arms around his neck, and kiss him hard.

Fortunately, he kisses back. We quickly begin feeling each other up over our clothes, and kissing each other greedily.

Oh, my God! It worked! I always wondered what it would be like to kiss him, and now I know. And it's pretty good. I mean, I feel like I'm going to throw up from the nerves these past few minutes, but this feels good.

As I start to entertain the notion of hopping into my mother's Porsche, and making out for hours in the car like teenagers, I hear reality rear its ugly head.

Or, in my case, open the door.

Liam and I stop kissing, and turn to see my mother's Dad glaring at us.

"What are your intentions, boy?" he asks.

Before Liam can respond, Dad appears over Grandpa's shoulder, "I wouldn't recommend what I said to him thirty years ago."

The next six hours included the usual family fights. There was:

"And let's make a toast to the troops—"

"Who shouldn't be there!"

"Oh, it's Vietnam all over again. What happened to the list?"

Not to mention:

"Well, I'm a lady. So I won't say it, but I think Hillary Clinton is the *C* word."

"Hey, I voted for her. Let's not—"

"I'll say it. She's a crook."

And the perennial:

"Which brings us back to why Kermit the Frog is really Nirvana, and Fozzie Bear has a blocked Chi."

What? Not everyone hears that in their house?

Nonetheless, I was in Nirvana myself. Liam and I spent the day stealing glances, stealing kisses, laughing, and holding hands.

After we said our good-byes around eight o'clock that evening, Liam walked me to my car (at the end of Mom's driveway, next to Grandma and Grandpa's Winnebago), and gave me a kiss that knocked my socks off.

Or, at least it made me want to rip his socks off, along with all of his other clothes.

As we kiss, he says to me, "Your family's delightful."

"They're hideous," I say, beginning to nibble his ear. "Your place or mine?"

"Well, my bedroom has been defrosted."

I follow Liam back to his Victorian home. I park my car behind his. As I get out, he is already there, grabbing me, and lifting my shirt up slightly.

"Ah, your hands are cold!" I say, a little surprised.

"I know. I'm warming them up."

We're so desperate to be with each other that we make out for a few more minutes outside, despite the fortysomething-degree weather.

I'm practically climbing on him by the time we make it into his house, and onto his living-room couch.

Liam carries me to the couch and places me down before climbing on top. We fiercely make out, and begin the mating dance of clothes on, clothes off, when is the girl going to give in. (Although really I'm just being shy, because I already know I want to give in. I just don't want him to think less of me.)

And just as I unbutton his shirt, and pull it off his body, his cell phone rings.

Liam ignores it.

Fine by me. As we continue to kiss, I debate what to do next: allow him over the bra, beneath the shirt, or just let him take off my shirt. But how slutty is that an hour into the make-out session? Would it be . . . ?

And his cell phone rings again.

Liam stops kissing me. With a questioning look on his face, he pulls the cell phone from his pants pocket, and reads the caller ID.

His lips tighten up. "Well, *fuck* you, my dear," he says angrily to the phone before tossing it onto his floor.

Uh-oh.

I've never heard that tone of voice from him before. I've watched him fire a second assistant director for incompetence, get kicked out of his own home by his supporting actor, even get screamed at when my cousin Jenn was in labor. Throughout it all, the man stays absolutely, charmingly calm.

Which means I can guess who's on the phone. The ex.

As he stares down at the phone on the ground, fuming, I jokingly ask, "Is that an offer?"

Liam turns to me, confused. "What?"

"You said, 'Fuck you,'" I say awkwardly. "I was making a joke about . . ."

My question seems to shake the cobwebs from Liam's head. He

shakes his head a bit, then forces a smile. "Yes. As a matter of fact it is. Shall we head to the bedroom?"

Well, what girl doesn't feel a little shy at that moment. "Maybe . . ." I say coyly.

We neck all the way up the stairs. I sit on the bed, and he takes off my shirt in one quick, practiced move. As his hand moves over my bra, I debate when to let him remove that just as his home phone rings.

Liam stops mid kiss. Lifts his head ever so slightly, then turns to glare at the answering machine on his nightstand.

Of course, his machine goes off. We wait for the beep, and then, "Hey, it's me," a cheerful voice says into the machine. There's a long pause as the woman collects her thoughts. "I just wanted you to know that I had a great time seeing you in New York . . . and I really miss you. . . . And I know there's another girl now, maybe, and it's none of my business . . . But . . . I just, you know, miss you . . . sooo, call me back when you get this . . . anytime. Doesn't matter how late. . . . Okay, I love you. Bye."

Liam's entire body falls to the side of me. "Rrrrrrrrrrrrr . . . ," he growls.

And not in a good way.

You know, it's strange. I should be mad right about now. I mean, theoretically this should be, at the very least, the "heavy petting" night, if not the sex night. But I've been in Liam's position: I've been the moron torn between my new possible and my old standby. It's painful, it's awful, and you never know if you're doing the right thing.

I can't help myself. I sit up and ask him, "You really wanted to pick up, didn't you?"

Liam scratches his neck self-consciously. "I hate her, and I'm moving on. No."

His phone rings again. I wave. "Go. . . ."

After a moment of debate, Liam lunges for the phone. "This is Liam . . . ," he says quickly. Then, as the woman on the other line talks, his voice hardens. "No, dear. And I'm afraid I can't talk right at this . . ." He sighs heavily. "Of course she's with me!"

Uh-oh. I've been spotted.

"Well, sweetheart, *you* broke up with *me*," Liam says, an edge to his voice. "What was I supposed to do, hide in my house alone and knit afghans?"

He stands up and begins pacing around his room. "No . . . no! You're not allowed to be hurt. I'm the one who . . . oh, for God's sakes, quit crying!" I watch Liam turn into me before my eyes. As the woman talks on the other end, he begins slowly hitting his head against the wall. "Goddamn it!" he finally yells into the phone, scaring the crap out of me, and making me jump. "You want to have your cake and eat it, too! You either want to marry someone or you don't. Clearly you don't. Which is fine, but you need to let me get on with my life!"

I watch as Liam listens to the other woman defend herself. She talks for a while.

Finally he answers. "Sweetheart, I can't do this anymore. I love you, but I cannot have this kind of tension in my life. I need someone who's easy. And laid-back. And low maintenance. And you are not, nor will you ever be, any of those things."

Liam listens to her for another minute. "You know what? I've really got to go . . . . Yes, she's here, and I'm being a poor host. I want to be your friend, and maybe at some point I can, but not right now. Right now you need to call one of your girlfriends, and yell to them about what an asshole I am. Kelly, please . . . let . . . me . . . go."

Liam clicks the button on his phone, and puts it back in the charger.

I wait for him to talk. He doesn't. "You want to talk about it?" I ask anyway.

Liam turns to me. "Could you hand me that pillow please?"

"Sure," I say, giving him the king-size pillow on his bed.

"Thank you," he says.

Then he puts the pillow over his mouth, and screams a muffled, yet loud, scream.

He calmly hands it back to me. "Can I get you some wine?"

"Well, I . . ."

And he's already up and out his bedroom door.

I put my shirt back on, then follow him to the kitchen, where he grabs a bottle of red from a wine refrigerator. "Her name's Kelly," he tells me as he angrily yanks open a drawer to get a corkscrew. "She's a sports reporter for ESPN. Travels constantly. Between my traveling and her traveling, we just couldn't make it work."

"Wait. You don't mean Kelly Timbers, do you?"

He nods.

"You mean the one we saw on the TV that night at Score! Why didn't you tell me she was your ex-girlfriend?"

He begins twisting the corkscrew into the cork. "Well, at the time, I was trying to figure out how to get you into bed, and it seemed as though pointing out my ex-girlfriend on the telly might impede my goal," he answers, as though it's the most obvious reason in the world.

"Oh my God! She's beautiful!" I blurt out.

Liam glares at me.

I wince. "Sorry."

But then I can't help myself. "But, I mean, she's, like, stunningly beautiful. I always thought the only guy who would ever have a shot at being with her would either be an Abercrombie and Fitch model, or . . . well, you."

Yup, a man I'm trying to seduce has opened a bottle of wine, and I cannot help but espouse the virtues of another woman. I'm right on track for a healthy relationship.

"She broke up with me," Liam reminds me.

I think about that a moment. "No, she didn't," I let slip.

Liam's eyes widen. "I'm sorry," he says, almost sounding offended. "Were you there?"

"I didn't have to be. I'm a girl."

Then I enlighten Liam on a rule that I thought all men knew:

When women break up, more than half the time what we mean is, "I need this relationship to change." Or, "I need you to change." When men break up, what they mean is, "I want to break up."

Liam shakes his head as he takes two wineglasses out of a cupboard. "You sure have a lot of theories on dating,"

"What can I say, those who can, do . . . those who can't, teach," I joke.

He pours the wine. "I wonder if there are other things you could teach me?"

And before I can say anything else, he takes me by the waist, pulls me into him, and slides his tongue back into my mouth.

My God, he's hot. And he smells amazing, and his chest feels perfect, and I can almost put Kelly Timbers out of my head.

Almost.

I pull away from him, and turn my face to scrutinize him. "You're still in love with her, aren't you?"

Liam leans in to kiss me again. "Let's not talk about it. . . ."

Now I pull my whole body away from him. "I love you," I say quickly, and in a mild state of panic.

Well, that stops him cold. (Wanna freak a man out? Tell him you love him. Works almost every time.)

"I . . . love you, too?" he asks me back.

I nod. " 'Thank you' would have been rude, huh?"

Liam shrugs. "Well, yeah."

"I'll rephrase. I love you . . . as a friend. As my insanely hot friend who I'm really going to regret turning down. But I have to ask, why did she break up?"

Liam debates answering me. He shrugs. "I proposed."

I shake my head. "Was your proposal conditional in any way?"

Liam's jaw drops as though I've just sided with the enemy.

Which means "yes."

I rub his arm. "What happened?"

He shrugs. Answers in a very teenagery *I'm so over this lecture* kind of way. "She got a job offer in Connecticut, and wanted us to move to New York. I had just bought the house, and wanted to stay here. I proposed, she said yes, we looked for engagement rings, and then she burst into tears at Cartier, and said she needed to take the job in Connecticut. Then she broke up with me."

Liam leans into me, and begins kissing my neck.

Damn. It's like the neck is attached by some electric wire all the way down to my . . .

"Doesn't seem fair that you have to be the one to move," I say, as my knees practically lock from ecstasy.

"No, it doesn't," he says, right before beginning to lick my neck.

I take a deep breath that might resemble a moan. "Gold medals are a bitch to go after, aren't they?"

Liam stops mistaking me for a lollipop. He pulls back, and asks, "Why are you doing this?"

I sigh. "Because I could never be with a man who wanted to be with someone else."

His home phone rings again. We look at each other before I say, "If you propose to her right now, I guarantee she'll say 'yes.' And this time she'll mean it."

Overall, it was the most amicable breakup I've ever had. It took less than ten minutes, and he even told me he loved me.

So I guess the day wasn't a total loss.

Forty

Success always requires work—that's one of life's big shockers.

I jot down in my notepad as I wait at a red light on Sunset Boulevard.

I take a deep breath, and let out a heavy sigh.

On the one hand, I know I did the right thing. I had to encourage Liam to go be with the woman he loves. Otherwise, I would just be the placeholder girl that he dated while he pined for her for the next six months. And I really did like him as a friend.

So I made the right decision not to jeopardize my relationship with him.

Nonetheless, I feel like crap. I can't even cry, I'm so . . . resigned to the idea of never being part of a couple again for more than a few months at a time.

The light turns green, and I wonder what I can do to make myself feel better.

Fuck it. I pull my car over to the side of the road, open my glove compartment, and pull out my trusty pack of Marlboros. I rip open the cellophane tab, and light the cigarette so quickly, I don't even quite comprehend that I'm inhaling the first drag and making the conscious decision to smoke again.

The second puff is much more intentional. I open my window, in-hale deeply, hold my breath, then blow the smoke out through my nostrils and into the cold November air.

On the third drag, I hold the smoke in my lungs for so long, that I almost choke as I cough it out. After coughing several times, I stop puffing, and look at my half-smoked cigarette in disappointment.

Damn it. I had gone almost three months as a nonsmoker. And now my abstinence and self-discipline have disappeared in a puff of smoke.

If I quit now, I'd have to go back to it being Day One. I just don't think I have the strength for that.

I take another puff as I mentally flagellate myself. Why is this so fucking hard for me? And when is it going to get easier?

As I silently ask myself those questions about the cigarettes, I can't help but see how the same questions pertain to my relation-ships and breakups: Why are they so fucking hard? Am I making them hard? Is dating difficult for anyone but me?

I stare at my cigarette.

Debate.

I reluctantly stub out the cigarette in my ashtray. I suppose two breakups tonight won't kill me.

The road to recovery is a crooked one.

Okay, I messed up. And, yeah, quitting smoking is really hard for me. Maybe it's easier for other people, maybe not. Doesn't matter. Right now, I just have to be on Day One.

I pull away from the curb, and drive home.

As I head up into the Silverlake hills, and drive up my street, I see a small silver mustang parked out front. There's a man at my front door, leaving a bouquet of flowers on my doorstep.

I can't see his face. Although from the back, it looks like Jordan.

The man turns around to look at my car, and I see in the headlights, it is Jordan.

I pull into my driveway, and quickly get out. Jordan picks up the flowers, a dozen silver roses, and walks over to meet me.

"What are you doing here?" I ask, as I close my door and beep the alarm.

"You never answered my e-mail. I decided to drop by, and see if you wanted company."

He hands me the flowers. I sniff them. Ah, the smell of roses. There's no better scent in the world.

"I picked them out myself," he tells me. "And, I know how much you hate carnations, so there are none of those, and no baby's breath."

"They're beautiful," I say. "But where did you find roses in the middle of the night on Thanksgiving?"

"It's L.A. You can find anything here," he says awkwardly, putting his hands in his pockets, and looking at the ground.

This would be the perfect opportunity to invite him in to warm up. I don't. "So," I say. "What are you doing home?"

"Well, they had to do a location move over to the South of France. And, since most of the cast was American, we got the week off. I'm here until Saturday."

I nod. Decide not to say anything else. Jordan looks at the ground again, then looks up at me. "You were right about Stacey. She did hit on me."

I wait for more.

"I told her no, and she seemed to accept that. But, um, I still passed on the Germany job."

"So . . . does that mean you're home after Christmas?" I ask.

"Yeah, maybe," he says. "So what happened with that Liam guy?"

"Nothing," I say, shrugging. "Actually, turns out he's engaged."

"Oh," Jordan says, some hope coming back into his voice. "Hey, do you want to go grab a sandwich or a drink or something?"

I debate that. "Actually, I was thinking about making myself a hot chocolate. I have an early morning but, if you want, maybe you could join me for a quick cup."

Jordan smiles at me. "I'd like that."

So I made him cocoa, and we caught up on each other's lives. And I'll admit, I missed him. And I was tempted to ask him to stay the night. But, after about an hour I told him I was exhausted, and needed to go to bed.

We shared a good-bye kiss.

It was nice.

I asked him to call me when he gets back into town, but I'm not sure he will.

And I'm not sure if it matters.

I think I need a break.

I'm tired of defining my life by who I'm sleeping with. I'm tired of wondering if I'm good enough based on whether the men in my life think I'm good enough.

And I'm realizing:

You can't change the past. But you can say, "I'm going to live a happy life from now on, no matter what happened."

So I think I'm going to spend a little while being single. Not because I don't want to be in love with someone. But because I've decided—for now at least—that I need to love myself more. And part of loving myself is taking care of myself. Because here's what it comes down to:

If you were advising your great-granddaughter about the man you have a crush on at this moment—what would you tell her? Would you be protective, and tell her to kick this man to the curb because he's treating her so badly, or would you tell her to hold on to this man for dear life?

Now, why aren't you taking your own advice?

"The perfect love guide for every girl (and their granddaughters and grandnieces)."

—Cecilia Ahern, author of P.S. I LOVE YOU and ROSIE DUNNE

CHARLIZE "CHARLIE" EDWARDS leads a glamorous and successful life as the personal assistant to Drew Stanton, Hollywood's sexiest movie star. But she's also turning 30 and chronically single. Amidst the chaos of planning her sister's wedding Charlie develops a serious crush on Hollywood photographer Jordan—a man who might actually return her feelings.

"A hilarious cast of characters and the funniest, coolest heroine since Stephanie Plum...you will not be able to put this one down."
—MaryJanice Davidson, author of Undead and Unappreciated

KIM GRUENENFELDER

a total waste of makeup

a novel

"A hilarious cast of characters and the funniest, coolest heroine since Stephanie Plum...you will not be able to put this one down."

—MaryJanice Davidson, author of UNDEAD AND UNAPPRECIATED

St. Martin's Griffin